Dear Reader:

Glass Beach is a special story set in a place that is very dear to my heart.

In the 1830s, long before the American cowboy ever rode the range in our western territories, Californio *vacqueros* were sent to Hawai'i to teach Hawaiians to round up the wild cattle that gradually overran the islands after British captain George Vancouver introduced them in 1793.

Unable to pronounce their colorful tutors' names, the Hawaiians changed the word *Español* to *paniolo* and ever since, that word has become synonymous for cowboys all over Hawai'i.

Set on the island of Kaua'i in 1888, *Glass Beach* is the fictional story of a man with both honor and *aloha 'āina*, a deep abiding love of the land. Spence Laamea is a *paniolo*, and an illegitimate son suddenly named trustee of the ranch that his father bequeathed to a legitimate heir. What Spence never dreamed when he accepted the challenge was that he would be living in the same house with his father's beautiful young widow, Elizabeth Bennett. Nor did he ever dream that he would have to come face-to-face with the truth about his father.

And so the story begins . . .

To all of you, *mahalo nui loa*—thank you very, very much for your wonderful letters. I can be reached at P.O. Box 3533, Long Beach, California, 90803 or at my home page: www.nettrends.com/jillmarielandis

Aloha nui,

Jill Marie Landis

After All

The passionate and moving story of a dance hall girl trying to change her life in the town of Last Chance, Montana.

"Historical romance at its very best."

—*Publishers Weekly*

Until Tomorrow

A soldier returning from war shows a backwoods beauty that every dream is possible—even the dream of love . . .

"Landis does what she does best by creating characters of great dimension, compassion, and strength."

—*Publishers Weekly*

Past Promises

She was a brilliant paleontologist who came west in search of dinosaurs. But a rugged cowboy poet was determined to un-earth the beauty and passion behind her bookish spectacles . . .

"Warmth, charm and appeal . . . *Past Promises* is guaranteed to satisfy romance readers everywhere."

—Amanda Quick

Come Spring

WINNER OF THE "BEST ROMANCE NOVEL OF THE YEAR" AWARD

Snowbound in a mountain man's cabin, beautiful Annika learned that unexpected love can grow as surely as the seasons change . . .

"A beautiful love story."

—Julie Garwood

Jade

Her exotic beauty captured the heart of a rugged rancher. But could he forget the past—and love again?

"Guaranteed to enthrall . . . an unusual, fast-paced love story."
—*Romantic Times*

Rose

Across the golden frontier, her passionate heart dared to dream . . .

"A gentle romance that will warm your soul."
—*Heartland Critiques*

Wildflower

Amidst the untamed beauty of the Rocky Mountains, two daring hearts forged a perilous passion . . .

"A delight from start to finish!"
—*Rendezvous*

Sunflower

**WINNER OF THE ROMANCE WRITERS OF AMERICA'S
"GOLDEN MEDALLION FOR BEST HISTORICAL ROMANCE"**

Jill Marie Landis's stunning debut novel, this sweeping love story astonished critics, earning glowing reviews including a Five Star rating from Affaire de Coeur *. . .*

"A truly fabulous read! The story comes vibrantly alive, making you laugh and cry . . ."
—*Affaire de Coeur*

glass
B E A C H

Jill Marie Landis

JOVE BOOKS, NEW YORK

GLASS BEACH

A Jove Book / published by arrangement with
the author

PRINTING HISTORY
Jove edition / June 1998

All rights reserved.
Copyright © 1998 by Jill Marie Landis.
Author photo by Blaine Michioka.
This book may not be reproduced in whole
or in part, by mimeograph or any other means,
without permission. For information address:
The Berkley Publishing Group, a member of Penguin Putnam Inc.,
200 Madison Avenue, New York, New York 10016.

The Penguin Putnam Inc. World Wide Web site address is
http://www.penguinputnam.com

ISBN: 0-515-12285-8

A JOVE BOOK®
Jove Books are published by The Berkley Publishing Group,
a member of Penguin Putnam Inc.,
200 Madison Avenue, New York, New York 10016.
JOVE and the "J" design are trademarks belonging to
Jove Publications, Inc.

PRINTED IN THE UNITED STATES OF AMERICA

10 9 8 7 6 5 4 3 2 1

To all the people of Kaua'i, who have survived Hurricanes Iwa and Iniki and persevere because they love the land.

To Maile Kainoa Hermstad and her mom, Melanie.

To Bruce and Lin, Frank and Betty, Rex and Pam, Sue and Sam, Happy and Dick, Mel and Don, Pam and Mal, Dick and Dotti, Sharon and Tom, Stan, Sheba, Legs, Mary and Jimmy, all of the Anderson *ohana*, Hisashi, Fumi and Helen, Rhonda and Bill, Doug and Sharon, Deb and Fred, Robert (Lopaka) and Gail (Kaila) and Ryan (Drumoko), Barry, Hal, Scott and Laura, Roger, Hobie, Tyler, Michael, Pete, Steve and Kelly, Bunnie and George, Dennis and Judy, Murphy, Bill, Aimee and John, Ruby Jo, John and Robin, Steve, Diane and Jennifer and the eleven cats, Barbara and Steve, Lucy and the Gang at Kaua'i Vacation Rentals, North Shore General, Nancy, Marjorie, Carol and Nick, Kaden, Sully, and the Hanalei Hawaiian Civic Canoe Club.

To everyone at the Hanalei Post Office ... *Mahalo! Mahalo!*

To David, Shirlee and Mary at Borders, Lihue.

To Jenny and Rob Crawford, friends near and far.

Thanks to Donn ''Curly'' Carswell ... a great storyteller and historian.

To Jack Kettering (who actually took the time to read my books) and always loved to tease me about them. I miss him and hope he's reading over my shoulder right now. And, of course, to Karen, his angel lady.

glass
BEACH

Prologue

A YOUNG BLOND WOMAN with haunted blue eyes stood alone at the edge of the cliff, staring at the waves that battered the black rocks below with nightmarish force. Trade winds buffeted her from behind, coaxing her long fair hair free of the tight knot at the nape of her neck, teasing the hem of her worn and outmoded burgundy gown until it rose and tangled about her ankles and calves. Behind her, open pastureland rose gently, caressed the foothills that bordered lush green mountains etched with silver ribbons of falling water and crowns of mist.

Situated between the mountains and the sea, a rambling ranch house stood surrounded by lush tropical gardens. A whitewashed fence protected the profusion of blooms and greenery from the cattle scattered across the land. The house had been designed to face both the sea and the mountains. A wide, shaded veranda, called a lanai by the natives, wrapped all the way around the structure. Anyone inside

I

the house or on the lanai could see her, could watch what she was about to do.

If anyone was watching, she did not care.

Elizabeth Rodrick Bennett took a deep breath, inhaling the humid air tinged with the smell of salt and sea and the underlying musty scent that invariably comes from dampness lodged in shadowed corners. She captured a wayward strand of hair, tried to tuck it back into her chignon, but when the wind only loosed more, she let it go.

She had learned the hard way that one did not fight that which was stronger. She had learned to disappear behind doors and walls and prudent silence. To wait, to be patient, to bide her time.

Stacks of cobalt-blue-and-white Staffordshire were piled beside her in the grass. Depicting scenes that glorified America's independence, the pottery's artwork sang of heroes and battles, landscapes and architecture, all surrounded by flowers, ribbons, stars, banners. There were dinner plates, bread and butter plates, salad and dessert dishes, tea cups and saucers, covered serving bowls. A platter. Even a gravy boat. Enough pieces to serve twenty. In style.

When she had directed the young Mauna Noe foreman, Duke Makakani, to load all the blue-and-white pottery into a wagon and cart it out to the cliff, his dark Polynesian eyes had peered out from beneath the brim of his woven hat, shouting all that he did not say. Even as he carefully stacked the pieces on the grass with his square, work-calloused hands, even when he finished with a shrug and a smile, he lingered, waiting for her to change her mind and have him load it up again.

When she told him to go back to work, he did not comment on her odd behavior. How could he? With her husband dead, she was finally in charge—not only of Mauna Noe but, more important, of her own life.

Elation over her new freedom and independence rushed through her, stirred her heartbeat, almost, but not quite, coaxing a smile to her lips. She closed her eyes and tamped down the unfamiliar lightness in her soul, afraid she might never recover from such a heady surge of joy.

It was time to let her dreams soar, time to take them out of the darkness and give them new life.

The billowing white sails of a clipper ship on the far horizon caught her eye. Trapped between the white-capped azure sea and a pale-blue sky patched with scudding clouds, the freedom of the sailing vessel paralleled her new status. She watched the ship make progress, moving unimpeded under full sail. Soon she would be like that ship, sailing unfettered, able to carve out a place for herself here in the islands. A real home. A wonderful legacy for her precious child.

No more would she wear a mantle of shame. She would never have to depend on a man or be betrayed by one again. At long last sanity and a new beginning were within her grasp.

Right now, she would content herself with this symbolic task. Her hands itching to begin, she reached down and picked up a dinner plate, ran her fingertip around its decorative, scalloped edge. The heat of the sun, playing hide-and-seek behind drifting clouds, had seeped into the pottery until it was warm to the touch.

She gripped the edge of the plate and drew her arm across her midriff. With a swift outward arc and a flick of the wrist, she released the disk and watched it sail through the air and then plummet over the edge of the cliff.

The roar of the waves overwhelmed the sound of shattering Staffordshire, but the thrill that shivered through her was no less grand.

She grabbed another plate and then another, tossed them high and away, sent them sailing through the air to crash onto the rocks below. She began to move faster. Her body stretched and swayed with the rhythm of the task as she bent, straightened, and then hurled the fragile pieces into the sea.

The rapid pace kept her mind from wandering back to

the beginning, to the time and circumstances that had brought her here, to this island in the middle of the ocean. She refused to let herself dwell on the past. Not with the future unfurled so bright and promising at long last.

Another platter sailed over the cliff. Then a pitcher decorated with a scene commemorating the opening of the Grand Erie Canal. Then the domed lid of a vegetable dish. Finally the stacks dwindled to one last piece. Slowly, as carefully as if it were the greatest treasure on earth, Elizabeth lifted the broken teacup. She stared at the jagged ends that had once anchored a handle and noticed that her hand was trembling as she reached up and touched a pale scar that slashed through her left eyebrow.

She had not been married even a full day before she was treated to her first encounter with her husband's cruelty.

She shook off the lurking threat of all the dark memories closeted in the secret corners of her mind. How long would it be before the things of this place stopped reminding her of Franklin? How long before her breath stopped catching whenever she thought she heard the sound of his voice? The tread of his feet upon the wooden floors? How long would it be before she realized that Franklin Bennett was no longer a threat to her or her child?

Praise God, the man was dead. Dead and buried and finally burning in hell.

As she tightened her grip on the last piece of Staffordshire, Elizabeth searched the horizon. The ship had sailed out of sight. As she hurled the broken teacup over the cliff, saw it disappear forever, she vowed that from this day forward, she would never let lust lead her astray, nor would she find herself in such dire circumstances that she would be forced to surrender her independence to any man.

When her private celebration of freedom was over, she turned to go back to the house. Walking across the bluff, she realized she had expected a more buoyant sense of elation. But, for now, it was enough to know that she had destroyed something Franklin had valued so highly.

One

Mauna Noe
A few days later . . .

BENEATH THE WIDE ROOF of the lanai, Elizabeth sat in a
high-backed rocker, amid an eclectic gathering of wicker
furniture, watching the road. Milton Clifford, Franklin's
lawyer, had notified her that he hoped to arrive before one
o'clock to carry out the reading of her late husband's will.
The tall standing clock in the foyer had already chimed half
past. Over the years she had come to believe a clock was
a ridiculous thing to own on an island, where time was
better marked by the tides, the sunrise, sunset, and the
moon's many phases.

Anxious to have this last formality behind her, she tried
to follow her normal routine all morning, first reading to
Hadley, her daughter, then working in the garden. Finally,
after the midday meal, Elizabeth wandered out onto the
lanai to escape the close, still air inside and to wait.

She contemplated the lush garden surrounding the house,
a garden that she had created and nurtured with her own

hands and the help of an old Japanese *paniolo* named Toshi. The garden had become her place of refuge, a tranquil haven. There, in the fertile, moist earth, she had buried her hopes and dreams each time she turned her trowel. And then the unexpected had happened.

One evening during supper, without sign or warning, Franklin Bennett had collapsed and fallen facedown into a plateful of rice, sweet potatoes, and beef. Once again her life had taken an unforeseen turn. Fate had freed her to reclaim her buried dreams, to coax them into bloom.

As she tucked a strand of hair behind her ear, Elizabeth thought about all the things she planned to accomplish when Mauna Noe was legally hers. There was much to do and much to learn.

The house needed paint. The whitewashed fence was faded in some spots, peeling in others, and in need of repair. Cattle would be wandering into the garden if the gate were not rehung soon. She scanned the gathering of outbuildings and deserted workers' houses that lined the lane, an offshoot of the main road. An office and store were housed in one. There were a stable and the men's barracks. The tin roofs of one-room workers' houses blended into the backdrop of pastoral hillsides dotted with cattle.

Uilani, the housekeeper newly appointed by Elizabeth, was helping her sort through her duties as mistress of the vast holdings—duties her husband had forbidden her to carry out while he was alive. The responsibilities seemed endless, but independence, like everything else, came with a price.

Looking back toward the road, she spotted a lone rider crossing the open pasture. An imposing figure, the man sat tall and easy in the saddle.

Hidden in the deep recesses of the lanai, Elizabeth squinted out into the sunlight and watched as the magnificent black horse carried the rider closer. She knew at a glance that the man riding so swiftly and confidently across her land was not Franklin's lawyer, for it was his custom to arrive in a dilapidated, mud-spattered phaeton that had seen better days. She had met Milton Clifford when he came to the ranch to do Franklin's bidding. He was middle-aged and slight of build, a man who spent most of his waking hours at a desk. Not only was he stoop-shouldered and nearsighted, but from the infrequent occasions she had had to speak with him, she sensed he was too cowardly to stand up to Franklin.

The stranger on horseback looked like a *paniolo*. She hoped he had come looking for work and that he might agree to stay on until her finances were secured. But as he drew closer, her breath caught in her throat. From this distance, something about him—the way he sat his horse, the tilt of his head, was eerily reminiscent of her late husband.

She had watched Franklin on horseback countless times from behind the lace curtain at the window in her room upstairs. Whenever he was away from the house, she had vigilantly awaited his return so she would never be caught unaware. The very sight of her husband riding toward this house at the end of the day had always filled her with dread.

The similarity between the approaching stranger's erect posture and Franklin's was disconcerting, enough to send a shaft of fear stabbing through her.

As the rider progressed to within a few hundred yards of the fence surrounding the house, Elizabeth's heartbeat echoed the cadence of the horse's pounding hooves. Her thoughts flew to little Hadley, upstairs playing with Uilani's thirteen-year-old daughter, Maile.

Elizabeth stood up and walked to the edge of the lanai, gripped the railing, and waited with her heart in her throat as the rider drew closer. His wide-brimmed hat cast his features in shadow, but there was no concealing his broad shoulders, long legs, and strong bronze hands.

He was dressed in *paniolo* gear. A dried flower lei wreathed the crown of his hat. *Panini* leggings, leather gaiters, protected his white trousers from the thick, thorny brush and upland cactus. An open five-button linen vest topped a long-sleeved striped shirt. His feet were hidden behind leather taps, long, pointed flaps that covered his stirrups, but she knew his shoes would be caked with the iron-rich red earth of Kaua'i.

The closer he came, the more he reminded her of her husband—the way Franklin held his shoulders so rigid, always on the offensive, at attention, ready to command. This man was heavier than Franklin, even taller.

Franklin is dead. As she watched the stranger ride in, she had to keep reminding herself of that.

Squelching the urge to dart inside, to the safety of the house, she made herself recall the day she had watched, dry-eyed, as her husband's wooden coffin was lowered into the ground on a hillside not far from the house.

Franklin is dead.

Then how could it be that this distorted image of him was riding toward her?

She remained on the porch, a reluctant sentry, reasoning with herself, trying to reassure herself, trying not to be ridiculous. This unknown rider could not bode ill for her and Hadley.

But life had been disappointing her for more years than she liked to count. God had demanded a high price for her transgressions. So even as she tried to convince herself that nothing could stand in her way now, a shadow of dread hovered over her soul.

FOR A LIFETIME SPENCE Laamea had wondered about Mauna Noe, what this land might look like, how it smelled, how the air tasted. Two hours ago he had left the main road and ridden across miles of land without seeing any sign of human life, no *paniolo* on the hills, only lazy cattle and horses. From the top of the last rise, the ranch proper came into view, the stables, the corrals and bunkhouse. The workers' houses, remnants from plantation days, appeared to be deserted, but a vegetable garden flourished behind one of them and a fishnet was spread out on a small square of lawn.

As he drew close enough to see the two-story wood-frame main structure, he carefully studied the odd additions that protruded from each side like mismatched wings. He assessed them in the same way he had observed the rich grazing land and the green hills, the clear, cold streams that ran from the mountain peaks, as he rode across Mauna Noe. More than the *'āina*—the land—and the house, he wondered about Franklin Bennett.

Although he had never seen Bennett in the flesh, Spence had once owned a miniature portrait of him.

"Keep it," his mother, Penelope Laamea, had whispered to him as she pressed it into his hand the night she died. He was only seven at the time, so the power of the memory should have faded by now, but he still got chicken skin when he recalled the way her sad, dark eyes had glowed with a strange, faraway look, as if she truly could see what might one day come to pass. "Someday he will want you, Spencer. Someday Franklin will need you and call you to his side."

Spence had closely studied the portrait of the man who had fathered him and then walked out of his life, memorizing every detail, confused and fascinated by the pale *haole* face in the small oval frame, wondering how the man could be connected to him by blood when his entire *'ohana*, everyone around him, aunties, uncles, cousins—were all Hawaiian.

They called Spence *hapa haole*—half white—even though he took after his mother. He recognized Franklin Bennett's image in the arch of his brow, the slight narrowing of his nose, and his stance. *Haole* blood ran in his veins, even though his skin was tawny brown, and still darker where it had been exposed to the sun. Like his Hawaiian kin, his eyes were as dark as lava rock, his hair glossy black and wavy. He wore it long, past his shoulders, sometimes braided, most often tied at the nape of his neck.

When his mother died, neighbors put him on the steamer to O'ahu and shipped him, like excess baggage, over to his mother's family. Eventually he learned from his uncle the real reason his father had refused to acknowledge him. He was mixed breed, not white but half Hawaiian. Franklin's Southern background kept him from acknowledging Spence as his son.

But for years, deep down in his young heart, where secret hope hides from truth, Spence clung to the dream that somehow, someday, what his mother had predicted would come to pass, that Franklin Bennett would call him back to Kaua'i and grant him his name and birthright. He would finally hear his father call him son. One day he would become heir to Mauna Noe, one of the largest landholdings in the islands.

At fourteen, against his uncle's wishes, he left the Laamea house in Honolulu and went off to a ranch on the north shore of O'ahu to become a *paniolo*, stubbornly clinging to the notion that when his father finally recognized him, he wanted to be ready. He would not further shame the man he never knew but idolized. He would learn everything about ranching that there was to know.

Since that day he had worked from before sunup to well past sundown, spent many hard hours in the saddle driving other men's cattle for little more than room and board. Thinking back on his life now and the choices he had made long ago, he knew what a foolish child he had been to dream such dreams.

Years had gone by, and with every passing season as he waited for a summons that never came, Spence experienced a deeper sense of bitterness and betrayal. His mother had died of a broken heart rather than live without the only man she had ever loved. Over the years as he came to realize Franklin would never want him, he grew to hate the very idea of his *haole* father, the man his mother had loved more than life itself.

When Bennett's lawyer could not trace him on O'ahu, a

letter had come to him through his Uncle Robert, who was one of King Kalakaua's closest confidants.

Spence had held the summons in his hands, stared at the thin, wavering script, and felt nothing. Word of his father had sifted down to him over the years, bits and pieces of gossip and rumors that passed from Kaua'i to O'ahu, from the lips of sailors, to merchants on the wharf, on to someone who knew someone in the Laamea family. To Uncle Robert. To Spence.

Five years ago, they had heard his father finally got what he wanted, a *haole* heir.

It did not come as a shock, for long before that day Spence realized nothing could ever have made Franklin Bennett recognize him, for nothing would ever make him pure *haole*.

His heart had grown as hard as stone, so that the very name Franklin Bennett left nothing but a bitter taste in his mouth. Even now, as he shifted the reins to guide the big thoroughbred, Kāhili, toward the house, all Spence could muster were feelings of bitterness, of betrayal.

He was twenty-six years old. He was *keiki manuahi*, a bastard. He had squandered years that should have been filled only with carefree innocence, waiting to be recognized by a man who never even cared that he existed.

He had answered Milton Clifford with a curt note sent on the steamer. He informed the lawyer that he would attend the reading of the will. What he did not say in the note was that the greatest satisfaction he would ever know would come at the moment he stood in Franklin Bennett's home, looked the man's lawyer in the eye, and refused whatever paltry handout Bennett had bequeathed him.

SPENCE HAD ALMOST REACHED the fence that surrounded the house when he felt the twinge in his gut that always came from dwelling too long on the past, on things lost forever—a father's name, his mother's love, a lifetime with Kaala, his beautiful, doomed young bride who had taken her own life. Just then, a large, yellow-eyed owl, *pueo,* with streaked brown feathers and a flat face, soared overhead, then swooped low, diving toward him before it swung skyward and flew on.

He stared after the bird in awe, felt the hair stand up on the back of his neck. *Pueo* was his *'aumakua,* the god of his family, his ancestral protector. To be visited here, now, was surely an auspicious sign. Was it a warning? Or was good luck in the offing?

When he rode up to the gate, he noticed that it hung forlornly from one hinge. Spence grabbed the *maku'u,* the pommel of his saddle, and dismounted, then tied his horse to the picket fence. He nudged the gate open with the toe of his boot and stared up at the two-story frame house. Like the fence, the house was in need of repair.

It gave him a dark satisfaction to know that his father's home was not as perfect as he had always imagined. Franklin Bennett had let the place go to ruin. The shiplap wooden siding was bleached bare in spots turned ghostly gray. Dilapidated shutters hung unevenly outside some of the windows, while others were missing shutters entirely.

He walked up a wide path through a maze of low tropical foliage—*ti* with deep green and red leaves, *aloalo,* or hibiscus, heavy heliconia, red ginger, angel's-trumpets bent toward the ground. White plumeria with delicate yellow centers infused the air with a heady, pungent scent. Finally, he neared the lanai with its commanding view of the vegetation-covered knob of the ancient volcanic crater Kilauea. The open coastline fanned out beyond the crater.

It was a moment or two before he noticed a *haole* woman standing in the shadows. He knew there would surely be others at the reading of Franklin Bennett's will. Most certainly the man's widow would be present—but this woman was not dressed in the black garb of widows that *haole* liked to wear. She wore a faded blue dress banded by a worn collar and frayed cuffs. The gown was too big for her, the fabric too heavy for such a warm day. She looked uncomfortable.

She also looked too young to have been married to a fifty-five-year-old man. A tired wariness marred her delicate features and reflected itself in her eyes. Of medium height, she had golden hair and perfectly etched *haole* features set in moonlight-pale skin. She was altogether beautiful. Haunting.

She looked as fragile as a newly hatched bird.

Spence looked up into the perfect oval of her face and searched for some sign that she, like himself, might carry Franklin Bennett's blood in her veins, but in her features he recognized none of what his cloudy memory retained of his father's portrait.

A cloud drifted across the face of the sun. The trade winds blew half-heartedly. The barest hint of a breeze roused the fronds of the nearby pandanus trees from a quiescent lull. A stand of eucalyptus planted as a windbreak began to rustle, filling the air with a cloying scent.

The breeze lifted a lock of the young woman's hair and blew it across her face. He watched her reach up and draw a blond tendril behind her ear before she tilted her chin up, exposing the pale skin of her throat.

From her position at the top of the stairs the woman continued to watch him closely. She offered not a word in greeting but simply stared at him as if she were seeing a ghost.

Once again she reached up to smooth her fine, sun-gilded hair. Her hand trembled.

"Aloha." He nodded as he spoke the greeting. Allowing no flicker of the jumbled emotions he was feeling to cross his face, he met her intense stare, reminding himself that he had been invited. He had every right to be here.

"Aloha." Somehow she managed to reduce a word rich with many meanings to a salutation devoid of any emotion at all.

"May I help you?" She took one step away from the wall of the house.

"I'm Spencer Laamea. Milton Clifford wrote and asked that I attend the reading of Franklin Bennett's will."

He hadn't thought it possible, but she grew even more pale.

"The *will* . . ." she said softly, letting her words trail away as if she were contemplating the meaning of the word.

"This is Mauna Noe? The Bennett ranch?"

He knew damn well he was on the right piece of land. Spence watched her swallow, saw the pink tip of her tongue flick out between her lips. She was staring down at him through clear blue eyes edged with a hint of panic that she could not disguise, even as her gaze shifted away from him.

"Yes. This is Mauna Noe." She swallowed nervously again and scanned the horizon where the Pacific met the sky, then looked back at him. "How did you know Franklin?"

She made him uncomfortable.

Spence cleared his throat. "Isn't Mr. Clifford here yet?"

Her hand went to the high collar of her dress as if it were choking her.

"He's late. I wasn't aware that anyone else would be coming today. He didn't tell me." She appeared more and more distracted with each passing moment.

Somewhere in the house, upstairs perhaps, he heard a child's laughter.

He watched her lower her hand and then hide her fists in the folds of her skirt. Her full lips might have been set in a determined line, but she looked as though she was prepared to dash into the house if he took one step closer.

"Is Mrs. Bennett here, then?" He loathed the idea of finally meeting his father's widow face-to-face, but there was no getting around it. He would have to meet the woman sooner or later.

"I'm . . . Elizabeth Rodrick Bennett . . . Franklin's widow."

Spence could only stare as the realization of who she was sank in. This pitifully frail, absurdly young *haole* with skin the color of moonbeams had married his father. Had slept with him.

This woman had given Franklin Bennett a legitimate heir—a *white* legitimate heir.

Spence thought of the *pueo*, the owl that flew over him moments ago, and wondered if his *'aumakua* might not have been warning him to leave before it was too late.

Two

ELIZABETH TOOK AN INVOLUNTARY step backward. The moment she had introduced herself, the bronze-skinned stranger's full lips thinned into a hard line, his expression darkened with a flash of anger that reminded her of Franklin.

Struck silent as she stared down at the huge, scowling Hawaiian, Elizabeth thought her knees might buckle and she would tumble down the three wide steps to the ground and end up a puddle of nerves beside his muddy shoes. But, surprisingly, her legs held.

She fought to calm her racing heart by reminding herself that this man was *not* Franklin, that *no one* could touch her now.

Her heart continued to hammer out doubts. Who was he? What was he doing here? The fact that Milton Clifford had summoned him today could mean only one thing—this stranger was somehow connected to Mauna Noe, somehow involved with Franklin. An insidious suspicion—and fear of what he might say—kept her from asking him anything more.

Franklin had told her once that he had no living relatives. Any family ties in Georgia were severed when he left there just before the War Between the States. But, then, she would not have put it past Franklin to lie.

Looking away from him, staring up the road, she felt an intense wave of relief when she recognized Milton Clifford's covered buggy wheeling its way toward the house. The lawyer would be here in a few more minutes. The wait would be over.

She needed to retreat and pull herself together, to escape the chill in the visitor's eyes, to run from the loathing that she had somehow unwittingly aroused in him. She needed to focus on Hadley so that the anxiety this stranger had stirred up would quickly subside.

"If you'll please have a seat on the lanai, Mr. Laamea, I'll go in and ask Uilani to bring you something to drink."

Without waiting for his response, Elizabeth turned and rushed inside. She heard children's voices, laughter, teasing, an occasional squeal, drifting down the stairwell. She hurried through the dining room and out the back door, ran along the covered walkway that connected the kitchen to the main quarters.

Uilani was there, solid, steady, reigning over the huge cast-iron stove, bustling about the stifling room with confidence that bordered on arrogance. Until Franklin died, the two women had only shared stolen conversations. Elizabeth, confined to the house and garden, had most often seen the Hawaiian woman from afar. Like all the other hired workers, Uilani had been forbidden to speak to Elizabeth and Hadley. But the older woman had silently communicated that she was aware of what Elizabeth had had to endure.

Elizabeth's first act of rebellion had been to fire a stern, hateful *haole* woman named Mrs. Timmons, who had been Franklin's housekeeper since long before Elizabeth arrived. He had charged the woman to keep a close watch on his young wife whenever he was away from the house and to report any and all transgressions.

Mrs. Timmons followed his instructions with gusto. She was plump, her skin doughy pale and soft, her hair more salt than pepper. With a round face, a button nose, and a smile shaped like a little bow, Mrs. Timmons looked as harmless as penny candy.

She took it upon herself to make Elizabeth's life miserable.

A moment after Franklin collapsed, Elizabeth had stood in and calmly folded her napkin. Then she immediately turned to the hysterical, inconsolable Esther Timmons, told her to pack her bags and have Duke drive her down to Hanalei because she would not be needed at Mauna Noe any longer. Elizabeth wanted her gone before nightfall.

Then, shaken but determined, she had found Uilani and put her in charge of the cooking and the main house. Since Franklin's death, both of them were swimming in uncharted waters, but Uilani had taken to her additional tasks like a happy duck in a full pond.

Now, as Elizabeth stepped into the kitchen with the reading of the will and the stranger's arrival on her mind, she took a deep breath. "Uilani, an unexpected guest just rode in and Mr. Clifford is coming up the road. They'll both need something to drink."

Uilani dusted flour off her hands and then wiped them on the towel she had tied around her calico *holokū*, the Mother Hubbard–style garment adopted by Hawaiian women.

"Who da kine, da stranger?" Uilani's melodic pidgin English had taken some getting used to.

Elizabeth felt her stomach flutter. "A Mr. Laamea. I think he is Hawaiian. He said Mr. Clifford sent for him. Have you ever heard of him?"

Uilani's brow furrowed into deep lines. She shook her head. "I don't t'ink so. Mebbe not from Kaua'i?"

"I have no idea."

"How come you don't ask 'em?"

I was too afraid.

Elizabeth shook her head. "I just didn't."

"Anyt'ing else?" Uilani was watching her closely. The kitchen smelled of fresh-baked bread. A huge pot of beef stew, enough to feed all the *paniolo* at the end of the day, simmered on the stove beside what looked like a pot filled with a mountain of rice.

"Ask what the men will have to drink and make them comfortable in the dining room. I'm going up to see how Hadley and Maile are getting along."

DOWNSTAIRS, SPENCE LAAMEA DECLINED a glass of water and tried to refuse a chair at the long dining table, but Milton Clifford insisted. So there he sat, uncomfortable in the shabby yet formal surroundings, staring at the faded wallpaper, once a deep wine-red covered with golden oriental fans and turquoise peacocks. Heavy water-spotted drapes and threadbare indigo upholstery on the dining chairs further darkened the room. He would much rather have stood and leaned against the wall on the far side of the room. From there he could have watched the proceedings without being observed.

He wondered where the widow had disappeared to. The minute she told him who she was, she practically flew inside and vanished. He waited for her to return, but she had instead sent a housekeeper, a Hawaiian woman who did not hide her surprise when she found him lounging in one of the wide wicker chairs. The look she had given him along with the curt order to take off his muddy shoes made him feel as if he had been caught with his hand in the *poi* bowl.

He turned his attention to Milton Clifford, seated at the head of the table. The lawyer had spread out a sheaf of official-looking documents and now sat hunched over the pages, absently pulling at his lower lip with his thumb and forefinger. An empty water glass stood near his right hand. He was in late middle age, still possessed of a headful of white hair that appeared to defy combing. Fine hairs also sprouted from ears that were considerable in size and quite visible despite wispy muttonchop sideburns. Oblivious to the heat, he wore a dark wool suit and a smartly tied neckcloth. Small round spectacles with delicate wire frames balanced precariously on the tip of his nose.

Spence stared at the papers absorbing the other man's attention. They were covered with words written in a bold backhand. Spence wondered if they had been written by Franklin Bennett. It gave him an odd feeling to look at the will, as if his father lingered in the room.

Spence shifted on the hard chair. Cleared his throat. Stared out the window and wished Elizabeth Bennett would reappear and put an end to his waiting. Outside, Clifford had been polite but noncommittal, introducing himself with a handshake, thanking Spence for coming from O'ahu, chatting about the weather. If he knew Spence's connection to Bennett, he was too polite, or too wise, to let on.

Clifford looked up and caught him staring just as the arrival of Elizabeth Bennett drew their attention. As she entered the room quietly, Clifford leaped to his feet, pulled out the chair nearest his, and offered her a seat. They exchanged a brief greeting, and Elizabeth slipped into her place before she met Spence's eyes across the table.

She nodded slightly in acknowledgment.

Franklin's widow had combed her hair, but she was still wearing the same light-blue dress with frayed cuffs and water-stained hem. If she mourned his father at all, nothing about her dress or appearance attested to it, except perhaps the violet shadows beneath her eyes.

"I take it you have met Mr. Laamea?" Clifford asked her.

Spence found himself the object of her cool blue stare once more.

"I have," she replied softly. "He said you sent for him." Her statement was an unasked question, but her voice was warm and low, richer than Spence had imagined it would be. The sound of it seemed to reach across the room, stroke his ear. He found himself shifting uncomfortably on the chair.

Clifford adjusted his neckcloth as if it were suddenly too tight. "Yes, I did. Now that you are both present—"

The lawyer paused. A young Hawaiian girl, her hair plaited into two thick braids that trailed over a budding figure not quite hidden by her *holokū*, slipped into the room as silently as a drifting feather. She walked straight over to Elizabeth. The woman came half out of her seat, as if prepared to hurry from the room.

"Is Hadley all right?"

Spence couldn't help but note the fear threaded through her tone.

"Like go outside," the girl whispered back, casting a glance first at Clifford, then at Spence.

Spence watched the *haole* woman visibly calm. "Not without me. I will be finished here in a little while."

Dismissed, the girl slipped out of the room again. Through the open doors, Spence watched her lift her *holokū* and run up the staircase in the foyer.

"Now that we're all here," Clifford repeated, "I will proceed without any further ado."

Spence waited. Tense, silent.

Clifford took a deep breath and looked as if he were about to strangle. "Before I read the terms of Mr. Bennett's will, I'd like to say that he put much thought and time into these arrangements."

Spence couldn't help but notice that the lawyer did not, or could not, meet Elizabeth's unflinching gaze. He straightened on his own chair, his nerves suddenly taut, his heart pounding slow and heavy.

Unable to stop staring at his father's beautiful young widow, Spence watched her closely, memorized her every move. He could have sworn that a slight tremor shook her before she, too, pulled herself up and sat straight as a canoe paddle on the edge of the chair. He crossed his arms, determined not to let himself feel anything at all.

Milton Clifford adjusted his glasses on the tip of his nose and cleared his throat. "I'll read Franklin's words exactly as written by his own hand. 'First, to Hadley Elyson Bennett, I leave Mauna Noe, Mountain Mist Ranch.' "

Spence felt his gut tighten. Just as he had expected—Bennett had left the place to his legitimate offspring. He found himself unable to do more than stare across the table at the silent woman who had yet to show a flicker of emotion. Surely now she could relax, let the tension fall from her shoulders.

Clifford went on without pause. " 'The land shall be held in trust until Hadley Bennett reaches eighteen years of age. Until that time, Spencer Makamae Laamea will act as trustee of the land. He is to reside on the land, to develop and expand Mauna Noe, retaining fifty percent of all profits generated as long as he fulfills his obligations as said trustee.' "

If he had not been leaning against the table, Spence would have hit the floor. The man who had chosen not to recognize him in life had named him trustee over one of the largest non-Hawaiian holdings in the islands.

Spence looked directly at Elizabeth Bennett. She was staring at the lawyer as if he had sprouted horns. Her hands gripped the edge of the table so hard that her knuckles went white.

"What do you mean?" Her voice was filled with all of the anguish reflected in her eyes. "*What* does that mean?"

Clifford sighed. "It means that your late husband wants Mr. Laamea to live here, to oversee and manage the place until Hadley comes of age."

"But—why? Why him and not me? I'm Hadley's mother. I'm perfectly capable. How could Franklin do this?" She was visibly shaken, watching Spence with suspicion now, her expression one of incredulity, not to mention betrayal.

The lawyer pushed his spectacles up the bridge of his nose.

"Why don't I finish and then we can discuss all the terms?" Without waiting for a reply from either party, Clifford rushed on.

" 'All personal possessions, structures, and improvements on the land will be left in trust for Hadley Elyson Bennett, the above to be administered by Elizabeth Bennett. If Elizabeth Bennett should die, marry, or leave the ranch before Hadley reaches majority, the possessions, structures, and improvements will be transferred to Spencer Makamae Laamea, to be held in trust until Hadley Bennett reaches eighteen years of age.' "

"I don't understand." Elizabeth's hollow whisper cut Clifford off as effectively as a shout. She sat stock-still, her trembling hands clasped together in her lap, her pale skin stretched over delicate features reflected in the smooth tabletop.

"To simplify, Mrs. Bennett, Hadley will *eventually* inherit the ranch lock, stock, and barrel. Until then, *you* have been named trustee over everything on the land. Mr. Laamea here has been named trustee of the land itself, and he is to manage the business. You are both required to split any profits made during the thirteen years of his duties."

"But—"

"Please, Mrs. Bennett, there's a bit more. 'If in the event Hadley Bennett should not reside on the land or in the event of Hadley Bennett's death before reaching maturity, then full ownership and title of Mauna Noe, all personal possessions and improvements, structures, and properties will revert to Spencer Laamea, who shall become sole and rightful owner.' "

"This can't be true." Elizabeth concentrated only on Clifford, as if she couldn't bear even to look at Spence.

"I'm afraid it is," the lawyer said.

"But—"

"These are your husband's wishes." Milton Clifford was obviously very uncomfortable.

She glanced frantically around the room as if help might miraculously appear.

Clifford tried to calm her. "I'm sorry, Mrs. Bennett, but these documents are irrevocable." He slipped off his glasses and began to polish them nervously with the rumpled kerchief he had pulled out of his breast pocket.

"He left *this* man in charge?" Elizabeth's voice barely carried across the room. "But why?"

Milton Clifford's complexion slowly turned a mottled red and white. "I have no idea. Mr. Bennett didn't choose to confide his reasons to me. He did have me do extensive research into Mr. Laamea's qualifications, and when I discovered that he has worked in the ranching business on some of the major holdings on O'ahu, Mr. Bennett instructed me to contact Mr. Laamea through his family— when the need arose."

Elizabeth shook her head, her words coming slowly as she tried to fit the pieces of Franklin's grand scheme together. She looked at Spence.

"Who were you to my husband? Why has he put you in charge?"

"Neither of you knows who I really am, do you?" Spence spoke up, shocking them into silence. They turned and stared, obviously as surprised as they were confused by the turn of events.

There was a long pause into which Spence finally tossed another piece of the puzzle.

"I'm Franklin Bennett's bastard."

Elizabeth recoiled as if he had slapped her.

Spence smiled. "You heard right. Franklin's bastard. My mother was Hawaiian, good enough for him to keep as a mistress when he first came to the islands, good enough to woo away from her family and bring to Kaua'i, but when she became *hapai* with me, he refused to marry her. He never claimed me because she was not white."

They continued to stare, speechless, as if he were the devil himself, or Franklin, come back from the grave. "My mother stayed here on Kaua'i, lived on the other side of the island, waiting for him to change his mind, hoping he would come back to her. I was seven when she died. I was shipped to O'ahu and raised by my uncle and the rest of my *'ohana*."

"Oh, surely you can see how unfair this is!" The woman was appealing to Clifford now, not Spence. "Hadley is Franklin's rightful heir—"

Clifford interrupted. "Mrs. Bennett, Hadley is *still* the heir. Mr. Laamea has only been made trustee of the land until Hadley grows up."

Spence's voice rang loud and belligerent in the already tension-filled room. "Trustee? My *father* has made me nothing but an indentured servant to a little *haole*. Why should I stay and break my back for her child?" He lifted his chin in Elizabeth's direction.

Milton Clifford straightened the already perfectly aligned edges of the stack of papers in front of him. Then he looked at Spence and spoke very slowly, emphasizing one word at a time as if Spence had no command of the language.

"Because, Mr. Laamea, half the profits from this place for the next thirteen years—the time at which Hadley will turn eighteen—will be far more than you would ever see in a lifetime of work as a hired hand, or even as *luna*. Am I correct?"

"I still don't want it," he said. "Any of it."

"Are you mad?" Clifford asked in disbelief.

"He said he doesn't want anything to do with it," Elizabeth said, with more show of force than Spence would have suspected her capable of. "Let him go."

Clifford grabbed the pages again as if they were a lifeline to his dead employer. "There is *one* more contingency. I'm afraid Mr. Bennett foresaw something like this happening." He began to read again. " 'In the event that Mr. Laamea cannot be found, or if he refuses for any reason to accept the responsibility defined herewith, including residing permanently at Mauna Noe, full title of Mauna Noe will revert back to the kingdom of Hawai'i.' ''

He took off his glasses and pocketed them. Stared at Spencer. "In other words, King Kalakaua will own Mauna Noe if you, Mr. Laamea, refuse these terms today."

The lawyer looked directly at Elizabeth. "If Mr. Laamea refuses, then you and Hadley will have nothing, Mrs. Bennett. Nothing at all."

Spence was still on his feet, ready to walk out the door and not look back. He had lived half his life waiting for Bennett to acknowledge him. He had come here determined to walk away from anything his father offered, to spite the man. He would be damned if he was going to start feeling guilty just because some *haole* woman and her *keiki haole* were going to lose everything.

Spence picked up his hat and shoved it on his head. "Thanks, Mr. Clifford, but no thanks." He had not taken two steps when he heard Elizabeth Bennett's frantic cry.

"Wait!"

He paused, turned slowly, and stared at her, watching her wring her hands as a desperate expression flashed across her face. She was still seated, looking as small and fragile as a child, the dark circles beneath her eyes half-moon smudges of lavender.

"You can't just walk out like this," she cried.

"A minute ago you *wanted* me to leave."

Clifford intervened. "I think you should reconsider, Laamea. You're throwing away a potential fortune of your own."

"I'll have to work my ass off for them."

"You're a *paniolo*, a hired cowhand. You already work your . . . work hard for someone else with little compensation."

Clifford was right. Ranching was hard work and he had already spent twelve years of his life busting his *lemu* for someone else. He had no land of his own on O'ahu, no hope of ever having any. Why should he let his hatred of his father stand in his way?

He looked at the woman again. It was obvious she did not want him here. "Everything I do will have to be cleared through her," Spence reminded the lawyer. "What if she chooses not to cooperate?"

"It's up to the two of you to work things out."

Elizabeth shook her head, her frustration with him, with the situation, evident. "I don't want to answer to anyone. Not anymore. Besides, I don't even *know* this man. What assurance do I have that he won't harm Hadley just to have the ranch all to himself? You read the words of my husband's will yourself, Mr. Clifford. If Laamea decided to stay and Hadley were to . . . were to die . . . before she turned eighteen, then this man would inherit everything."

Spence felt the blood rush to his face. "I'm a bastard, Mrs. Bennett, not a murderer."

"You're Franklin's son, aren't you?" Her tone rang hollow, hopeless. "He's done this to punish me," Elizabeth whispered. "Even from the grave, he's still tormenting me."

She looked so betrayed, so bewildered, that Spence could not help but feel sorry for her. Why would his father have wanted to torment his own wife after he was gone?

"You know yourself that Hadley is very frail," the lawyer said, trying to appeal to Elizabeth again. "Franklin wanted to make certain that someone carrying his own blood inherited the ranch. That's why Mr. Laamea must choose today, here and now. Franklin had no faith in your ability to run this place, Mrs. Bennett. In fact, he told me he was afraid you would want to sell it to the first bidder and go back home to Maryland."

"He could not have been more mistaken." She was seething with anger. Two bright spots of color stained her cheeks.

"He had no assurance of that when he made out this will a few months after Hadley was born. If neither of his offspring was living on the land, he was determined it should be given back to the king. Why, I cannot say.''

She laughed. It was a bitter, broken-spirited sound. ''Because, Mr. Clifford, my husband hated me. Besides, you don't have to tell me how *obsessed* Franklin was with bloodlines. 'It's all a matter of blood,' he would say. It was his way of explaining away everything.''

Spence recognized those same words as Elizabeth mimicked a lazy Southern drawl. When he was a grown man, old enough to understand, his Uncle Robert had told him a story that his mother related about the day Franklin left her. Those were the very same words that Bennett was supposed to have said to Penelope when he walked out on her and left her *hāpai*, pregnant with his unborn child. *''I cannot marry you, Penelope. It's all a matter of blood.''*

Tainted blood was the reason Franklin had never claimed Spence as his own and he had never explained their relationship, not even to his lawyer as he drafted the will. Spence had simply been named overseer, number one *luna*, assigned the task of keeping this place on its feet—for Hadley Elyson Bennett.

In essence, his father had handed him his old dream with one hand and dangled it just out of reach with the other. He was to live and work on Mauna Noe, but it was too late to know his father, too late to be recognized as his son, for the old man had not even made mention of their relationship in the will.

Even if he saved a lifetime of *paniolo* wages, buying a ranch of his own would be impossible. If he accepted, more money than he had ever hoped of making would be his for the taking. All he had to do was put up with his father's widow and a little *haole* half-sibling he had yet to lay eyes on.

As he glanced over at Elizabeth, he discovered her watching him intently, her obvious suspicion mingled with anger, and he wondered why—for what twisted, absurd reason—his father had wanted all of them irrevocably tied to this place.

Spence sighed, wondering why life had never been easy. He had come here expecting to walk out on whatever his inheritance turned out to be and now suddenly found himself actually considering accepting. He tried to tell himself he would do it for a stake in the future, not merely to save the place for Franklin's widow and child.

"What monies come with the ranch itself?" He addressed Clifford, unable to look at the widow any longer. In order to accept the terms, to expand the ranch revenue, he had to have something to work with. The Lord knew he did not have more than fifty dollars to his name, not American, Chinese, Danish, Swedish, English, Mexican, or any other coin that was legal tender in the island realm of King David Kalakaua.

Clifford had the good grace to flush with embarrassment. He set his glasses back on his nose and hooked the stems around his ears. "This morning before I left Port Allen, I went over the accounts. Unfortunately, there is not much money available."

"How am I to make improvements without funds?"

"You *are* experienced at ranch work, are you not, Mr. Laamea?"

Spence nodded, felt the weight of Elizabeth's gaze on him, felt her measuring his worth. "Yes."

"Then I'm sure you will figure something out," Clifford said.

Elizabeth Bennett slammed her palms down on the table. "I won't stand for this, and I won't beg, either."

It was a moment before Spence realized that she was speaking to him. He looked directly into her eyes.

"You heard me. I won't stand for this."

Clifford extended his hand in a gesture of helplessness. "I'm sorry this is the way things worked out, Mrs. Bennett. I have been charged with administering the will to the letter. It will be recorded here and on Oʻahu."

"But, I have no money to fight this thing. I have no connections in O'ahu." She sounded desperate.

Spence remained poised in the doorway. He had more connections in Honolulu than he could count, including the king himself. He looked away, stared out the window for a moment, out across the rolling landscape to the crater and the sea. He did not owe this woman anything. He certainly did not owe his father the time of day, but his father was dead and the estate was on the brink of ruin.

It gave him a twisted sense of satisfaction to know that his father had been close to failure—just before it struck him that making a success of the place might be better revenge than walking away.

Franklin Bennett had not thought him good enough to claim because he was *hapa*, but if he took up this challenge, if he made something of this ranch, built it up and made it profitable, he could prove to the world that he was far more capable of running a vast estate than his father. Never in his life would he have another opportunity like this one. There were few Hawaiians left who ever would, either.

Laughter filtered down the stairs, the sound of light-hearted, carefree children. One of them was the child Franklin had wanted, the one he had cherished enough to hand everything over to. Spence looked around the dining room again. He had never had a home like this one. Never owned more than his clothes and his horse, never had any chance of owning more.

He had rehearsed this scene over and over in his mind, maybe a hundred times a day since Clifford's letter had arrived and it had been easy when he had not really expected his father to leave him more than a pittance.

He had spent his lifetime working on ranches with far less land than Mauna Noe, but he knew what it would take to pull a thriving cattle operation together. If the woman cooperated with him, and surely she would soon realize it was in her best interest to do so, he could succeed.

The bitterness which had simmered for years taunted him.

Walk out. Turn it down. Do it to spite the old man.

But the old man was dead. Franklin Bennett was beyond knowing or caring if Spence hurt him.

You will only be hurting yourself.

But not if he succeeded.

He would not let himself acknowledge the woman awaiting his decision. She looked furious and at the same time vulnerable. Whether she wanted to admit it or not, she needed him in order to hold on to this place.

Finally, after wrestling with his thoughts for a few more seconds, he faced the lawyer, not Elizabeth Bennett.

"I'll do it," he said. "I'll stay."

Three

ONE WEEK OF FREEDOM. One week, one delicious taste of independence before Franklin had reached out from the grave to slap her down. Not only had he usurped her power but he had sentenced her to thirteen years of living with her daughter's life in jeopardy.

She was not surprised when, immediately after the meeting, Milton Clifford quickly packed up his papers and left. The man could not get out fast enough, nor could he look her in the eye. Stunned by the complicated, inexplicable stipulations spelled out in Franklin's will, Elizabeth had walked out of the dining room without a word to the lawyer or to Franklin's bastard son.

As the late-afternoon sun slid down the sky, scattering shafts of sunlight and long shadows in through the open lanai doors, Elizabeth paced back and forth through the sunbeams. An essence of Franklin still lingered in the parlor, adding to her anger and disbelief. His collection of antique guns hung on the wall, hunting rifles mounted beside useless old pistols he'd brought with him from Georgia. Oil portraits of Bennett ancestors looked down on her, their expressions united in disapproval.

A dreadful collection of stuffed birds was displayed on side tables and shelves. Some of the fowl were so old that they appeared to be molting, while others still sported most of their plumage. Each had been mounted on a small wooden disk with a brass identification plate attached.

Wherever she looked, the expressionless, glassy-eyed stares of the hateful birds seemed to follow her. She knotted her hand into a fist and slammed it down hard on the padded back of a deep, overstuffed leather chair. Then she paced on, choking down her mounting panic and forcing herself to think.

There had to be a way to break the stipulations in Franklin's will. There simply had to be a way.

Walking over to the glass doors, she lifted her face to the breeze that swirled into the room. It cooled her heated skin but did little to comfort her soul.

Her uncle Joseph, if he were here now, would be telling her that this was another of God's ways of punishing her for her sins.

She had sinned—there was no denying that—but it was back when she had only just turned eighteen. Eighteen. Young, innocent, she thought love would provide her a way to escape her aunt and uncle's home.

How long would she have to pay for one youthful indiscretion? How long would she suffer for the death of innocence?

Elizabeth stared out at the frothy whitecaps dotting the Pacific and tried to assure herself that God wasn't punishing her. It was Franklin, not God, who had devised a way to keep her imprisoned with a stranger until Hadley came of age.

There *had* to be a way out. She would think of something. She had endured her marriage for Hadley, for her baby's right to this land, and she would endure this, Franklin's final insult, even though it meant dealing with his bastard son.

The Hawaiian wanted Mauna Noe all to himself. It was

the only explanation for the cold assessment she had seen in his eyes earlier, when she told him who she was. Now the only thing standing between Spencer Laamea and full ownership of the ranch was Hadley.

"I'm a bastard. Not a murderer."

The words slammed into her mind. Could she believe him? Or should she turn her back on Mauna Noe and the years she had suffered Franklin's abuse to save Hadley's inheritance and walk out? If she did they would both be penniless, fighting for their very survival.

This was her home. She refused to contemplate such an idea. Besides, no bastard was going to lay claim to Mauna Noe, not after she had spent years protecting Hadley from Franklin's unreasonable fits of rage, looking out for her child's safety and welfare since the day she knew she was going to be a mother. If she had to, she would guard Hadley every minute for the next thirteen years.

Her child was her life. Her reason for living. Her lifeline to sanity.

No matter how much she wanted to avoid seeing Spence Laamea, she had to deal with him, had to ignore the little ways in which he reminded her of Franklin and the anxiety that blossomed while she was in his presence.

An unsettling feeling crept over her, made the hair at the nape of her neck stand up. She turned around. Laamea was framed in the doorway, a small, water-stained traveling bag at his feet. He stood there watching her, his dark eyes assessing her from head to toe without any hint of embarrassment.

He appeared to be at ease, while her stomach churned. Unable to meet his eyes, she glanced at his hands. He had hooked a thumb in the front pocket of his pants as he leaned against the door frame. The other arm hung loose at his side, fist open, fingers relaxed. His straight black brows were drawn together in a scowl.

She clasped her hands together at her waist, lifted her

chin a notch, and met deep-set Polynesian eyes that stared back at her with startling candor.

"We need to talk," she told him, moving away from the windows, away from the light.

"You don't want me here."

"That is an understatement, Mr. Laamea, to say the least."

"My name is Spencer. I prefer Spence."

"You have no right to interfere in our lives." She was unable to hide her animosity. She felt as if someone else, some new Elizabeth, had taken over, given her the courage to argue with him.

"My father seemed to think otherwise."

"This whole arrangement is absurd, but then, knowing Franklin as I did, I shouldn't be surprised." She turned away from him, walked over to a side table, and found herself examining a stuffed barn swallow that had once skimmed over southern ponds and meadows. She felt just as trapped in time as the bird. Laamea shifted his stance, drawing her attention.

"None of this was my doing," he said, "and I don't like it any more than you do. I can't help but think that my father is laughing in his grave, but what I can't figure out is why he would do this to you and his son."

"His son?" She blinked, taken aback.

"Hadley? The heir?"

"Hadley is a girl. My daughter."

She could see that he was shocked, and it gave her a sense of satisfaction. "Along with the fact that she is *not* the son he wanted, she was sickly when she was born."

She had made certain that Franklin thought his child was more ill than was the case, although she had walked the floor for months praying that Hadley would finally thrive, praying that the searing bouts of asthma her daughter suffered would subside as she matured. But in no way did she want Spence Laamea to know that asthma still plagued her daughter.

"I am supposed to build this place up for a *girl*?"

"You are beginning to sound like your father," she mumbled.

"I never laid eyes on the man."

"Yet you came here today. You stayed. Why?" She knew he had not done it for her, or for Hadley.

"If I walked out on this chance, it would mean I had thrown away my only stake in the future. Besides, I suddenly realized my father was beyond caring if I dealt him an insult."

She began to pleat and unpleat tiny folds near the top of her blue skirt where it had once hugged her waistline. She had grown so thin over the past few years that the material hung loose on her body. Finally she looked up, met his eyes again.

"What do you know of Franklin?"

"Only what my mother chose to tell me: That she had loved him desperately. That their time together was short. He had just come here from the States and was trying to establish himself when he met her."

Elizabeth frowned. "I see." He might know nothing of Franklin's true nature, of how his cruelty escalated over the past few years. How much of Franklin's temperament had Spencer inherited? Would he believe what she could tell him about his father? Could she bear to tell him when doing so would only illuminate her own shame?

"Do you really think you're capable of running this place?" She knew she was treading dangerously close to quicksand, questioning his qualifications when she herself knew nothing about managing a ranch. But she was willing to learn.

"I've been a *paniolo* most of my life."

"A *paniolo*? Not a manager? Not a landowner? What do you know that I don't?"

"I know cattle. What about you?"

"I know that I will do whatever it takes to protect my daughter's interests."

"Then it appears you have no choice but to accept me as trustee. Otherwise you'll lose this place."

"One always has a choice, Mr. Laamea. Always. Though we may not like it."

"If I leave, your daughter loses everything," he reminded her.

"If you stay, what guarantee do I have that you won't try to harm Hadley?"

The minute the words were out, she knew she had made a terrible mistake. His entire posture changed. He came away from the door frame, whipcord-straight, shoulders rigid, hands fisted at his sides. He was as furious as if she had just prodded him with a hot iron. Dark anger hardened his mouth, drew his full lips into a taut line.

"That's the second time today you have questioned my honor."

She stood her ground, but beneath her skirt her knees were shaking. "You are Franklin's son."

HER ACCUSATIONS SENT SPENCE'S temper to the boiling point. He took a step in her direction, a swift move made without thinking. Elizabeth flinched, clutching her skirt, prepared to fly through the open lanai doors. When he witnessed her reaction, Spence felt his anger dissipate as quickly as it had been aroused.

She was looking at him as if who he really was did not matter. In her eyes, he would always be Franklin's bastard.

There was royal blood flowing in his veins, *ali'i* blood. His grandfather had been a *kahuna la'au lapa'au*, trained in herbal healing, descended from a long line of highborn Hawaiians, and his mother carried on that bloodline. Her only failing was falling in love with a man whose background and society forced him to let the color of her skin stand in the way of his ever marrying her.

Spence suddenly ached to be outdoors, away from this *haole* woman with haunted, distrustful eyes that accused him of things he had never done, would never think of doing. He needed to calm down, forget her insults, feel the air on his skin, the last warm rays of the setting sun on his face. He wanted to run his horse, Kāhili, along the foaming shoreline, to drink in the salt spray off the ocean, to listen to the sound of the pounding waves.

Twelve hours crossing the channel between Oʻahu and Kauaʻi by steamer and then the long ride across the rugged landscape had left him bone-tired, yet too wound up to give in to the fatigue. He rubbed his eyes, relished the idea of getting outside.

Unwilling to leave before things were settled, he forced himself to change the subject and ask about the portraits hanging around the room in hopes of giving Elizabeth time to collect herself.

"Who are all these men?" He nodded at the dour *haole* faces caged in gilded frames.

"Your father's ancestors. Some lived in England, some settled in Georgia—in America."

"I'm Hawaiian, Mrs. Bennett, not ignorant. I know where Georgia is."   .

He had no formal education, but his grandfather had taught him to chant his lineage back to the Creation. He could read and write and was educated in *na mea o' Ha-waiʻi*, the things of Hawaiʻi.

King Kalakaua, hearing of Spence's acquired knowledge through his uncle Robert Laamea, invited him into the Hale Naua or the Temple of Wisdom and Science. An elite group of men with Hawaiian blood had been brought together by Kalakaua, who was dedicated to promoting the revival of the ancient sciences and wisdom of Hawaiʻi so long out-lawed by the missionary factions.

Spence was more than Franklin's bastard, but he felt no satisfaction after putting Elizabeth Bennett in her place— not when she looked like a lost waif, adrift with nowhere to turn. She obviously wanted him out of the room as badly as he wanted to escape.

"Where should I put my things?" he asked her.

He saw her glance down at the bag at his feet and as realization dawned on her, her cheeks flushed with color.

"In the men's barracks," she told him flatly.

"No way in hell."

He had spent half his life in mildewed, leaking bunk-houses. If he was going to command any respect from the other men, if he was going to have the responsibilities of this place on his shoulders, he damn well wasn't going to sleep on a hard bunk.

"I'll not have you under the same roof with Hadley." Her voice shook with determination—or fear. It wasn't clear which.

"I'm not sleeping anyplace else." He reached for his bag and then started for the stairs.

"Stop!" she cried, arresting him in his tracks. She was frantic now, so much so that she forgot her fear, hurried to his side, and stood poised with one hand on the newel post as if she were ready to race upstairs ahead of him.

Standing so close, he realized she was more petite than he had noticed before. Her pale skin, her light hair and eyes, combined with her slight figure to make her seem ethereal, otherworldly, not a flesh-and-blood woman. He was close enough to feel the heat of her body, to hear her soft, quick intake of breath, to sniff the scent of white ginger that lingered about her.

"Franklin's old room is on this floor. Down the hall and to the right. You are never, ever to come upstairs to our quarters. I want you to stay *away* from my daughter."

He almost told her he fully intended to go anywhere he damn well pleased, but he was too tired to argue any longer.

She turned her back on him, put one foot on the bottom stair, a clear sign of dismissal. Then she turned around again. "Uilani will help you with anything you need. The linens have already been changed."

"That's not something I've ever worried about," he told her bluntly. "I'm used to sleeping without sheets at all, let alone clean ones. I'll eat dinner with the *paniolo*."

"Duke Makakani is *luna* here. I had planned to have him keep that position."

Remaining noncommittal, he replied, "I'll see how he and I get along before I decide."

"There are no other choices. He is the youngest, but he seems capable. Toshi is too old, and Melvin—well, Melvin is just Melvin. You come to me before you make any decisions concerning the stock or anything else of value."

"You don't have to remind me, Mrs. Bennett."

"Just don't forget." Her words were backed by false bravado. He could see her trembling, but before she continued up the stairs she paused to reiterate.

"And stay away from my daughter, Mr. Laamea. If you go near her, if I even suspect you of looking at her crosswise, I won't hesitate to kill you."

As he watched her march up the stairs, there was not a doubt in his mind that she meant every word.

STILL FURIOUS, ELIZABETH PAUSED outside Hadley's door to compose herself, wishing the whole day had been a bad dream.

There had been no surprise beneficiaries in attendance on the day her own father's will was read. Her aunt Sophie and uncle Joseph Rodrick, her father's older brother, had been at her side. The real shock came when they all learned that her supposedly well-fixed, fun-loving father had not a penny to his name. In life, Elyson Rodrick had kept her and her mother in grand style, showering them with the finest clothes, the most expensive horses, jewelry, a grand home staffed with servants. But his debts were monumental and there was no nest egg, no provision for any future that did not include him.

The day both her parents drowned in a sailing accident off the coast of Maryland, Elizabeth went from being a pampered, cherished fifteen-year-old to being an impoverished relation forced to depend on the kindness of her miserly aunt and uncle.

Former missionaries, the Rodricks possessed an abundance of religious fervor and a stubborn determination to force the same calling upon her. She rebelled and chose a path from which there was no turning back, a route littered with grief that had eventually led her here, to Mauna Noe.

She so wanted her life to be different now. She had thought that with Franklin gone, Hadley would be safe. Elizabeth sighed and opened the door. Expecting to find the girls reading or playing with dolls on the bed, her breath caught in her throat when she saw Hadley and Maile hanging out the open window, toys strewn about the floor and forgotten.

Afraid that she would startle them and send Hadley tumbling headlong out the window, Elizabeth picked her way across the room, through the mess, and grabbed the large bow in the sash on Hadley's pinafore.

"What in the world are you doing?" Elizabeth reeled her daughter in and stood her on her feet. Maile looked over her shoulder, smiling. The pretty young girl with mischievous dark eyes was kind to Hadley, but Elizabeth was not certain she was altogether dependable.

Before she could lecture the older girl on her responsibilities, Hadley explained.

"We had a good idea, Mama. We're lowering Alexander the Great to the ground so that next time I go outside with you I can get him. See?" Cheeks flushed, her long, curly blond hair dangling over one eye, Hadley pointed toward the window.

As her heart settled back into place, Elizabeth noticed that Maile held one end of a bedsheet in her hand.

"Go look, Mama." Hadley put her hand on Elizabeth's hip and gave her a nudge.

"Too short," Maile said, shaking her head. Elizabeth leaned over the sill and saw Hadley's favorite stuffed horse knotted into a corner of the sheet and hanging almost six feet above the ground, swaying back and forth, bumping head, then tail, against the side of the house.

"I told her to drop him, Mama, but Maile said he'd fall into the mud. But horses like mud, don't they? Papa's horses are always outside and they like it."

Maile laughed. "Dis *lio* not real."

"He is too, isn't he, Mama?" Hadley was affronted. "Alexander's alive. He's not dead, is he? If he was a dead horse we'd have to put him in a box in the ground, wouldn't we?"

Tears began to shimmer in the girl's sky-blue eyes, and her lower lip trembled. She put both hands to her temples, gasped raggedly, and ran to the bed, throwing herself on the mussed coverlet.

"Not Alexander! If Alexander is dead, too, I just can't *bear* it!" She lay there moaning and wailing, rolling from side to side.

"Pull Alexander up, Maile, and run along downstairs. I'm going to take Hadley out for a walk."

The girl reeled in the sheet and untied the horse, then made an attempt to refold the linen before she gave up and piled it on the end of the bed, well away from Hadley.

"Aloha," Maile whispered as she stood in the open doorway, watching Hadley's theatrics. "You like me come tomorrow?"

"You needn't whisper anymore, Maile. Mr. Bennett is gone."

Franklin had insisted that Hadley not be exposed to pidgin English and warned all the workers on the ranch that they were not to speak it in front of the child. No one had dared violate the rule while Franklin lived.

"Yes, please do." Elizabeth had to raise her voice to be heard over Hadley's wails. "I'll need your help every day from now on." Elizabeth closed the door behind Maile, walked over to the bed, and pulled her daughter into her arms.

She could feel Hadley's little bones beneath her skin and clothing. She was small for a five-year-old. "Too *damn*

small,'' Franklin said when he saw her for the first time.
''A runt.''

There was no denying that Hadley was fragile, one day
weakened by asthma, the next exhausted from the battle.
The child would go for weeks without an attack and then
suddenly, out of nowhere, the affliction would strike her
down.

Hadley tugged against her embrace, so Elizabeth let her
go but kept her close by straightening her pinafore and
running her hand over her sweaty hairline, brushing back
the damp curls. There were no tears on her face, which led
Elizabeth to suspect there had been more drama than anguish behind the scene she had just witnessed.

The idea of going for a walk did not cheer Hadley or
ease her melancholy. She leaned listlessly against Elizabeth,
staring out the window. When her daughter let go an
uneven little sigh, Elizabeth's heart quivered.

''I miss Papa,'' Hadley said forlornly. ''Don't you,
Mama?''

Like a toothache.

Elizabeth slipped her arm around Hadley's shoulders.
Drew her close.

''Yes,'' she said, forced to lie again, knowing she would
spend a lifetime perpetuating a lie for her daughter's sake.

She marveled at the depth of forgiving, unconditional
love of children. That Hadley could mourn a man who had
never given her a moment of his time, never communicated
with her, had amazed Elizabeth at first. Then she realized
that what Hadley really missed was a mythical father, one
Elizabeth had carefully fictionalized so that Hadley would
feel well loved by both her parents.

''Why did he have to die?'' There was a hitch in her
voice, and a little shudder shook her thin frame. They sat
side by side on the bed, staring out the open window at the
wide blue Pacific.

Elizabeth closed her eyes and rested her chin on top of
Hadley's head.

"Because the angels needed him, darling." Elizabeth felt weightless, adrift because she didn't know what else to say. Franklin had died of a stroke. It was his health and his failing business that forced him to find a wife with missionary connections, that drove him to father a child before it was too late.

"Are there horses in heaven?"

"Probably."

"What about *paniolo*?"

"Of course. They take care of the horses. And the cows." She knew Franklin was nowhere near heaven, but she was certain that some *paniolo* were there.

"What about fish? Are there fish in heaven?"

Elizabeth bit her cheeks, thankful that the subject of Franklin in heaven had easily been replaced by the ultimate fate of fish.

"Yes. Fish, too."

"What do they eat?" Hadley jumped off the bed and leaned on Elizabeth's lap.

Elizabeth frowned. What *would* fish eat in heaven?

"Let's go for a walk, shall we?" She needed to get out, to clear her head. Perhaps, she hoped, a walk along the bluff would help her sort out her tangled thoughts.

She might even come up with a menu for dearly departed fish.

Four

DUKE MAKAKANI SAT ON the low edge of the wooden lanai fronting the men's barracks, watching the setting sun singe the horizon with brilliant orange and deep purple. High overhead, the night sky was already hazy indigo, with big, thin layers of clouds that slithered across it like ghosts. Occasionally they dropped thin nets of gentle rain, sometimes they slipped by without a sprinkle. Stars twinkled between the clouds, lighting the way for more.

Sunset turning to dusk. His favorite time of day. A good time to watch the stars court the moon. Even in the waning light it was easy to smell the land and hear the sea, both as much a part of life on Kaua'i as breathing.

Ahiahi. Evening.

Duke held a coil of rawhide, a *kaula'ili*, fingering it absentmindedly while he watched the stars. Tomorrow he would replace his frayed old lariat with this new one that he had just finished braiding. It would not do for the *luna*, the one the others looked to for orders, to have a rope snap off the neck of a furious sharp-horned bull, endangering all of them.

45

Setting the rope aside, he stood, intent on heading over to the men's barracks, where he, Toshi, and Melvin ate the evening meal. His stomach was rumbling, his hunger piqued by the aroma of beef stew and onions. Nineteen and still a bachelor, he bunked with the others. As *luna*, he was entitled to one of the workers' houses now, but he had no need to move into one yet.

Lately, however, he had found himself looking forward to sharing his life with one particular *wahine*, to have her waiting for him when he rode in, tired and dusty, at the end of a long day. What would it be like to share his nights with a pretty little wife with dark, flashing eyes and a smile that lit up her face every time she saw him? What would it be like to put his arms around her and snuggle up close?

What would it be like to sleep without Toshi's snores echoing louder than a rumbling mill wheel and Melvin breaking wind under the covers all night long?

Chuckling to himself, Duke headed toward the opensided building filled with long tables and benches where Toshi and Melvin stood with plates in hand, waiting for Uilani to dish up beef stew, rice, and boiled cabbage. It wasn't until he had taken half a dozen steps that he noticed Spencer Laamea, Bennett's *keiki manuahi*, walking toward him.

Uilani had come running out to talk to Duke the minute he rode in, giving him the news about Laamea showing up from O'ahu—and being named in Bennett's will.

Just as Uilani had said, Laamea was *hapa haole*, broadshouldered like his father and maybe a little like Bennett across the brow, but nothing else about him reminded Duke of his former boss. He wondered if the man had inherited his father's temper.

Duke hoped Laamea would respect his expertise and stay the hell out of the way if he didn't know anything about ranching. Old man Bennett had insisted on running his own concerns, even though he could not get along with any of the hands or the neighboring ranchers. He had slowly run the place into the ground. But now that Bennett was gone, Mauna Noe might have a chance to recover.

Even the widow would agree. All the folks that lived and worked on the place knew that Elizabeth Bennett hated her husband—and with good reason. They had all been ordered to leave her alone, her and the little girl both. It was the way the old man wanted it, and no one ever crossed Franklin Bennett.

Laamea walked up to Duke and extended his hand, introduced himself, told Duke he was manager now. Then Laamea stood there as if Duke should know what to say next. Duke rocked back on his heels, shoved his hands in his pockets, and waited him out. It did not take long.

"I hear you're *luna*." In a tired motion, Laamea rubbed the back of his neck with an open hand and looked at the long table, the barracks. Duke felt the man's discomfort, could see it in his stance. "How long you get *luna* here?" Spencer wanted to know.

When his new boss easily slipped into pidgin, Duke finally relaxed.

"Since Bennett come *make*," Duke replied. Not much of a recommendation, a week, but he had been born on horseback and that had to count for something. Raised down in Hanalei Valley, Duke had never even been to the other side of the island, had never wanted to be anything but a *paniolo*. As a boy he begged to ride with the men, but they made him prove himself by digging guava, cutting suckers, stringing fences. Eventually he became a full-fledged *paniolo*.

When the time finally came that he was too old to work cattle, he would be content to end up like Toshi, a *papa aipa*, devoted to the land, assigned the easier tasks of checking paddocks, mending fences, counting stock, working in the gardens.

"I ride before sunset. Get one feel for the land," Laamea told him. Streaks of light bled from a lamp in the windows of the main house, shone through the tall torch ginger and shiny banana leaves. Night-blooming jasmine weighted the air with its heavy fragrance. Duke's stomach rumbled.

"Mrs. Bennett say t'ree men only work dis place." Spence sounded as if he couldn't believe it.

Duke confirmed it. "Plenty leave long time ago, when change from sugar to _pipi_. Get bad debt to the old man. Spend plenty money for whiskey, buy t'ings wit' high prices. Pretty soon, no get way to pay back. Break contract. Some run off, go other side Kaua'i. Some to other island. Honolulu."

Duke did not tell him that Bennett had them alter brands, that he stole cattle from the neighboring ranches. Ranchers in the area suspected, but no one ever had any proof. Bennett's men had to pledge their wages against items from the ranch store, goods so highly inflated in price that soon the workers were so deep in debt they might as well have been slave labor.

They lost most of the other _paniolo_, not to mention gardeners, fence men, dairymen, the blacksmith, because they hated Bennett. Some walked out on their contracts by using a silent form of blackmail, hoping he would not pursue them and risk their revealing his unscrupulous business tactics. Others paid Bennett off with horses, saddles, or other gear just to get out from under the debt and move their families off Mauna Noe.

"You know him well, the old man?"

Duke sensed Laamea's hesitancy and replied, "Much as anybody else 'round here."

Franklin Bennett was a man with plenty of enemies. A man who might even have been prayed to death. Duke had witnessed an _akua lele_, a fireball, the night before Bennett dropped dead. He had seen a bluish-white sphere suddenly appear, floating across the pasture. It flew over the big house and disappeared somewhere in the front yard. Everybody knew an _akua lele_ was an omen, a sign of impending death.

If Laamea wanted to know anything more about his father, Duke decided he would have to hear it from someone else. He did add, "I tell you straight, he care nut'ting for work. Lost plenty money. Pull up da sugar, try grow coffee." Duke laughed. "Den some sheep."

"I only going run cattle, build up stock. Work wit' you and the men. I not going lose money here," Spence vowed.

Duke shifted from foot to foot. Always a comforting sound during a lonely ride, the rowels on his spurs jingled in the darkness. Spencer Laamea seemed just as uncomfortable in his new role as Duke felt waiting for him to leave so he could go eat. He could hear Toshi and Melvin across the way, "talking story" around mouths full of food, trying to impress each other with tales of daring exploits that they told over and over again and never seemed to tire of hearing.

Finally Duke asked Laamea, "You like eat? Meet Toshi and Melvin?"

"Sure." Laamea shrugged. "Why not?"

Duke led the way. The talk died down. In the light that pushed out from under the overhang, Duke could see Laamea's striped shirt and creased white pants clearly. His shoes were scuffed, worn down at the heels, his leather gaiters scratched and trail-weary. A ragged-edged bandanna sagged loosely around his neck. His hat was water-stained, the lei around the crown dried and faded.

At least the new boss looked the part of a real *paniolo*.

"Take one plate," Duke said, suddenly aware of what Laamea must be feeling, wondering how he himself would act if suddenly thrust into the same situation.

Uilani had left the pots outside. Duke dished up his own heaping plate of food, piled on so much that he watched, helpless, as the stew gravy backed up and dribbled over the edge of the plate. Toshi and Melvin had started up again by the time Duke led Spence Laamea over to the table.

As they sat there, elbow to elbow, Duke was already feeling more at ease. As to what sort of man this *keiki manuahi* would turn out to be, it was too soon to tell.

• • •

ELIZABETH STOOD IN THE weak circle of light that shone through the open door of Uilani's one-room cottage, one hand clutching Hadley's, the other tight around a pillowcase stuffed with a change of clothing and nightgowns for them both, along with Alexander the Great. She felt foolish now that she was here, foolish and cowardly, but she was not going to have Hadley sleeping under the same roof as Spence Laamea.

"Mama? Can I go in and see Maile now?"

Hadley was looking up, her pale, oval face ghostly in the dim, wavering light. Outdoors she seemed smaller, more doll-like, as if the slightest breeze might blow her away.

"Of course, darling," Elizabeth told her. "Why don't you step up onto the porch?"

Elizabeth had never entered Uilani's house, but she had often wondered what the simple dwelling was like inside. Wondered what things Uilani treasured. From the porch she could see into the house. Woven mats covered the floor, calico *holokū* dresses hung on pegs on one wall. There was a long counter made of an old surfboard that held a washbasin and pitcher and a huge blue-green glass ball that had once floated a fishnet in Japanese waters.

Elizabeth saw Maile appear in the doorway. The girl alerted her mother, and Uilani came into view. Hadley, experiencing the joy of an unexpected adventure, sang out, "I'm here!" as if she was expected. "Mama and I came to see you. She said maybe we would sleep here, too."

Maile giggled. Uilani did not try to hide her astonishment. Elizabeth realized that the idea bordered on the absurd as she stepped up onto the small, lopsided porch and put her hands on Hadley's shoulders.

"Uilani, I know what an imposition this is, and you can certainly refuse, but I was hoping that you might let us stay with you tonight. Tomorrow I'll see about cleaning up one of the empty houses—"

"*E komo mai.*" Uilani stepped back, ushering them inside with a sweeping gesture, as if they were visiting royalty.

Remembering her manners, Hadley sat down on the porch, unlaced her shoes and left them by the door, while Elizabeth bent over to do the same.

Once she was inside, Elizabeth wished she had not acted on impulse. The place was no bigger than Hadley's small bedroom. Uilani and Maile slept on *lau hala* mats on the floor.

Maile had already taken Hadley's hand and was showing her a collection of shells in a tall glass jar on a table near the window. Hadley was seriously attentive, listening as Maile told her where she found each shell and about the creatures that once lived inside them.

Elizabeth took a deep breath and apologized again to Uilani. "I don't know how much you heard today when Mr. Clifford was here earlier—"

Guileless, Uilani admitted, "Plenty. I know Laamea come from Oʻahu. He going take care land. He Bennett's *keiki manuahi*—"

"Mr. Bennett's what?"

"*Keiki* dat come wid'out marry da kine, da muddah."

Elizabeth lowered her voice so the children would not hear.

"My husband put him in control of the ranch until Hadley comes of age. Franklin didn't think . . . he wasn't sure that Hadley would . . ." She glanced over at her daughter, unable to give voice to the terrible thought.

"Mebbe not so bad. Mebbe now you not worry. Be da kine fancy lady, go Hanalei. Make tea party. Get dress up." Uilani had her own ideas of how the mistress of a ranch should spend her time.

"I was looking forward to running this place. I wanted to make something of the ranch myself. Now that's all changed."

Uilani pursed her lips and shook her head. The motion

made her long black hair sway all the way down to her hips.

"No good you move outta your house. You da owner. You can stay, but no good you move outta da house."

Elizabeth did not know where else to turn. She hoped Uilani's roof did not leak and that one night in the musty little house would not bring on one of Hadley's asthma attacks.

"We'll try not to inconvenience you, Uilani. I can't move Hadley off the land or Mr. Laamea will gain title to it."

As if her words invoked his presence, she heard a heavy footfall on the wooden porch behind her. Elizabeth spun around. Spence stood outside, staring in as she had done earlier. He glanced down at the hastily stuffed pillowcase beside her on the floor. Hadley's nightgown, along with half of Alexander, had fallen out, giving away her plan. Laamea's gaze found Hadley next and lingered so long that Elizabeth was tempted to step into his line of vision.

Finally, he met her stare again. His expression was unreadable, but she knew she was in for another argument before he even uttered a word.

"What are you doing here?" He did not step up on the porch.

"We're staying the night with Uilani and her daughter."

"I want to talk to you alone."

"No."

"Look, Mrs. Bennett, I'm going over to that *kukui* tree to wait for you. We need to talk in private."

"Mr. Laamea—"

Hadley left Maile and ran to Elizabeth's side. "Who's is he, Mama?" Then, without waiting for a reply, the little girl called out to Spence, "Who are you, mister?"

Laamea said nothing. He simply stared at Hadley.

"This is Mr. Laamea, darling. He's . . . going to be living here at Mauna Noe." Elizabeth fought the urge to pull her daughter back and slam the door in his face.

"Why?" Hadley's tone was anything but warm.

"Because . . . your papa wanted him here," Elizabeth said.

"Are you a *paniolo*?" Hadley stepped out onto the porch before Elizabeth could stop her. "You *look* like a *paniolo*."

"Don't bother Mr. Laamea, Hadley. Come back inside and see what else Maile has to show you."

"*Are* you, mister?" Hadley folded her arms and didn't budge.

Spence shoved his hands into the pockets of his pants. "Yeah. I'm a *paniolo*."

"*My* papa was the *boss* of all the *paniolo*. He told them all what to do because he was a *very* important man."

Spence ignored her, spoke only to Elizabeth. "I'll wait by the tree." He walked away before she could refuse. Helpless, Elizabeth looked to Uilani for support.

"Betta go. Talk story wid him. Mebbe he not so bad. Plenty handsome, yeah?" The housekeeper strained to see Laamea in the dark shadows beneath the *kukui*.

Elizabeth put her hand to her forehead and sighed. Would this day *ever* end? Hadley and Maile were once more bent over the shell collection, Spence Laamea already forgotten as they started to sort shells by size and color.

"I'll be right back," Elizabeth told Uilani as she stepped outside. "Please don't let Hadley come out."

Still barefoot, she walked off the porch and started across the grass toward the huge *kukui* tree where Laamea waited. When her foot came down on one of the fallen *kukui* nuts, she winced, then quickly straightened, trying to hide her discomfort. Laamea came closer, until he seemed to loom over her, his features and expression eclipsed by darkness.

"What do you have to say to me?" she asked, although she knew what was coming.

"What in the hell are you doing here? Are you crazy?"

"That's none of your business." She kept more than an arm's length between them.

Spence sighed. "I'm making it my business. What's wrong with your daughter?"

"Nothing is wrong with her."

"She's bone-thin."

"She's always been small."

"Did you really plan on spending the night here?"

"I still do."

"Why?"

"I have my reasons." None of which she wanted to voice aloud. Not to him.

"Get your things and go back to the house."

"You have no right to order me around." Franklin had done enough of that to last her a lifetime. She had no intention of letting this man start.

"I have a right to do what's best for this ranch, and right now that means getting you back in the house. What kind of respect do you think I'm going to get around here if everybody thinks I threw you and the girl out of your home?"

"I personally don't care what anyone thinks of you." She could not see him clearly in the darkness, but she could feel his anger and frustration, was amazed that she was foolhardy enough to keep goading him, but she would not hold her tongue. Not anymore.

"You *should* care, Mrs. Bennett. You should care very much. How I get along with the *paniolo* will dictate how hard they want to work for me and that will affect profits. If you want your precious Hadley's inheritance to be worth anything at all, then you had damn well better care."

He surprised her by taking a step in her direction. Elizabeth lunged away so quickly that she forgot about the *kukui* nuts scattered over the grass and came down hard and uneven on one with her left foot. She slid, twisted her ankle, and began to fall.

Spence clamped his hand around her upper arm and tugged her to her feet. Still off-balance, she fell against him, hitting the hard wall of his chest, and sucked in her breath.

His hand went up. She shielded her face behind the crook of her arm. Her response was instinctive, uncalculated.

SHAKEN, SPENCE COULD HEAR Elizabeth fighting to control her ragged breathing. He righted her and set her away from him. Immediately she dropped her arm. The entire incident had happened so fast he wondered if he had imagined it.

For a brief time after Kaala died, he could barely keep his emotions in check. He became known for his temper. Quick to ignite, he was just as quick to cool off. He could still hold his own in a fight, but he had never hit a woman in his life. Nor would he.

Seeing Elizabeth's reaction to him, the way she had shielded herself from an expected physical blow, shook him deeply. Spence stepped away, giving her plenty of room. He could hear her straining for air, as if she'd just run up the bluff. Her hair was silvered with moonlight, her eyes were two wide, deep spots of color in a shockingly pale face.

"Go get your things," he said softly. "Bring the girl. I'll walk you both back to the house."

Her voice cracked on the word *No*.

"No, you won't get your things, or no, you won't walk back with me?"

A moment passed before she answered, as if she were weighing options she did not have.

"You really think I would harm her, don't you?"

"She's all that's standing between you and full ownership of Mauna Noe," she whispered.

"That and a rope. The last I heard, murder was against the law here in Hawai'i. Besides, what kind of man do you take me for?"

"You would be surprised what a man can get away with."

"What do you mean by that?"

He saw her close her eyes, press her lips together, and he knew he would get no answer.

"It's late, Mr. Laamea," she said with a ragged sigh. "It's been a very long, tiring day."

"Which is why you should go back to your house before it gets any later."

He could feel her hesitation, held his breath until she finally lifted the hem of her skirt and slowly picked her way through the nut-studded grass to the steps of Uilani's house. He waited there in the shadow of the *kukui,* praying she would reappear, wondering what the hell he was going to do if she refused, how far he should push her. Finally he saw the little girl silhouetted in the doorway, watched the child sit down on the lanai and begin to struggle with her shoes.

Elizabeth followed the little girl out and glanced in the direction of the tree. She waited, poised there, uncertain. Spence reached up and touched the brim of his hat with his thumb and forefinger, then turned away, knowing she did not want his escort back to the house.

He did not feel comfortable with the idea of going back there himself until they were settled in their rooms upstairs, so he headed back in the direction of the men's barracks. Would he ever feel at home with the *paniolo*? At supper, he had been awkward seated with the three Mauna Noe *paniolo*, not because they were strangers but because of the unspoken deference they already paid him as the new *luna hana,* head boss.

Besides the invisible barrier of his position here, he still sensed that no one was telling him the real truth about Franklin Bennett. What the men *did not* say, the subtle evasions whenever his father was mentioned, warned him that there was much he still did not know.

Elizabeth's reactions to him just now told him more than words could say. He had seen her dance on the brink of fear all day, watched her shudder whenever he raised his voice. When she hid her face in the crook of her arm—as she thought he would lash out and hit her—he knew for certain that she had suffered at the hands of a man.

And that man was his father.

Suddenly the trade wind came sweeping across the open plain, carrying with it the smell of rain. Loneliness sluiced through Spence as he walked past the corral toward the long, rough-sided building that housed the bachelors. As much as he had harbored childhood dreams of living here at Mauna Noe, he did not belong. Not in the bunkhouse. Certainly not in the main house with his father's widow either, but he'd be damned if he would let her win the first skirmish.

DISAPPOINTED THAT HER FIRST grand adventure was over before it started, Hadley whined and dragged her feet all the way back to the house. Trying to appease her, Elizabeth told four of her favorite fairy tales before she fell asleep. The night was hot and humid, the air buzzing with insect chatter. Certain that she had not heard Spence Laamea come in, and too hot to sleep, Elizabeth ventured downstairs to walk through the dark, quiet house, intent on going out to the lanai in hopes of a breath of cool night air.

It still felt odd, this moving about the entire house without fear of running into Franklin. For years the second story had been her and Hadley's domain.

She thought back to the time when she realized she was expecting a child. Desperate that nothing happen to the delicate new life budding inside her, she went to Franklin and bargained with him, humbled herself enough to get down on her knees and extract a promise that he would leave her alone for the sake of his unborn child.

She moved into the upstairs rooms, made them her own private retreat, tried to think of it as an oasis rather than a prison. Along with vases of flowers from her garden, she gathered all of the things she had brought with her from Baltimore, volumes of her favorite books, bits and pieces of unfinished needlework, a keepsake album from those sunshine years when her parents were still alive.

She kept to her rooms, afraid of running into her husband, never knowing what kind of mood he would be in. Sometimes he played the fine Southern gentleman, almost courtly. Then, as easily as the trade winds shifted, he would change, start bellowing because something in the house was not in its proper place, because something had been moved, or lost, or disturbed.

Mrs. Timmons would always appear on the run, her bright eyes snapping, her doll-like little mouth pursed. She would smooth his feathers, tell him in a soothing cadence that *she* would take care of everything, that *she* would put things to right for him. Her voice would calm him as she reminded him of some errand he needed to carry out, a new horse he wanted to ride, something she had read in the news. Eventually, she would change the course of his foul mood.

Once his attention had been diverted, once Franklin was on his way outside or settled into the overstuffed chair with a newspaper or a book, Mrs. Timmons would turn her stare on Elizabeth, a cold, superior look of disdain that said, "You see. I can control him, while you, who are his wife, cannot."

Now as Elizabeth walked down the stairs in the dark and let her hand slide over the satin wood of the *koa* handrail, she soaked up the blessed quiet, the solitude, and recalled how relieved she had been when Mrs. Timmons had left without argument, as if the woman had known the moment Franklin suffered his fatal stroke that her reign was over.

There was no longer any threat of running into Franklin or Mrs. Timmons, no worry of saying or doing the least little thing that might send him into a rage.

But now there was a new threat, a still undefined one. A glance down the hall told her that no light was shining beneath the door to Spencer's room. Elizabeth walked through the sitting room, through the open doors, to the lanai. Standing at the rail at the edge of the wide veranda, she stared out at the infinite stars that sprinkled the night sky. The familiar scent of her flowers perfumed the air with an exotic, cloying aroma. From the direction of the barracks, the haunting sound of guitars and ukuleles drifted on the breeze, faded, grew louder, then faded again, depending on the whim of the trades.

She closed her eyes, leaned against the rail, inhaled the pungent tropic scents and listened while in melodic, haunting tones, Melvin, Duke and Toshi sang Hawaiian songs. Although the words still sounded like mouthfuls of vowels to her, there was tremendous emotion in the harmonic blend of the men's voices.

She pictured them, the *paniolo* with their mud-stained shoes and boots and scuffed gaiters, cowhands who worked from before sunup to sunset for bed and board and a little cash. Men who were here not out of any loyalty to her dead husband but because they had no place else to go, no wives, no children.

What did they have to sing about? How could they laugh and talk and lift their voices in song after a long, hot day of work, knowing that tomorrow they would be right back in the saddle again, doing the same tasks over and over? How did they manage to summon joy when she could not?

She had grown hollow inside, like one of Maile's empty cowrie shells. It was time, she decided, that she change, or at least try to—if not for her own sanity, then for Hadley—to become more like the carefree, trusting young woman she had been before her life took so many dark turns. She had to reclaim some of the joy that once filled her heart.

A shooting star plummeted through the sky, fell so far that it seemed to disappear into the folds of the ink-black sea. Above her, hidden somewhere in the eaves of the house, a sticky-toed gecko chirruped. She found it appalling that the islanders did not object to sharing living quarters with the small brown lizards that had the run of the place. She remembered unpacking her things her first day here, her fear that geckoes might drop from the ceiling and land on her while she slept—but in only a few hours she had learned that she had far more to fear than falling geckoes.

The empty lanai was inviting, open to the night breeze and the sound of the music and the waves echoing with a constant, eternal heartbeat. She chose the battered wicker chaise, sat down and hid her bare feet beneath the trailing hem of her skirt. The sound of the waves reminded her of the fate of Franklin's Staffordshire dishes. She allowed herself a small sliver of a smile as she imagined the pottery lying in blue-and-white shards on the rocks, endlessly battered by the shore break. Being worn away bit, by bit, by bit.

SPENCE ENTERED THE DARK, silent house in his bare feet, listened to the soft hush of the heavy dining room curtains as the breeze brushed them against the window frames. There were no lamps lit in any of the rooms, but he easily found his way.

In the foyer he heard a soft, muffled cry that stopped him in his tracks, gave him chicken skin. He waited at the foot of the stairs, barely breathing, eyes straining to make out the furnishings draped in shadow. About to dismiss the thready whimper as a trick of his own imagination, he took another step in the direction of his room.

A shiver shot through him, rippled along his spine when he heard the sound again. His father controlled him from the grave. Was the man's spirit prowling the house?

It took a heart-stopping moment before Spence realized that the barely audible sound came from upstairs. He took the stairs two at a time, to the top of the landing, then stopped to get his bearings.

Along another hall that stretched the length of the house, four doors were situated, two on each side. Slowly, carefully, so as not to make a sound, Spence turned the knob closest to him. As the door swung inward, the night came alive with wheezing, now and then interrupted by a weak, mewling sound like the cry of a newborn kitten.

His eyes adjusted to the darkness, and soon he could see the outline of a small single bed against the wall between two long windows. The mound beneath the bedclothes was barely discernible. Hadley Elyson Bennett.

Curious, Spence crept forward until he was close enough to watch the child wrestle with her dreams. Hadley was lying on her back, arms spread wide like an angel's wings, both hands rested beside her head on her pillow, her fingers curled into fists. Each time she drew a breath, a shallow, ragged sound scraped the air.

My half sister.

Spence found it impossible to believe that anyone so small, so helpless, so very fair, could be related to him.

Had Franklin Bennett ever been proud of this sickly little girl? Proud the way a father should be? Had he carried Hadley on his shoulders? Laughed with her? Told her stories? Had he been the father that he had never been for Spence?

Had Bennett quieted Hadley's fears, answered her questions? Taught her to love this land, this *'āina*?

Hadley shifted once more, rolled over and murmured. The bedsheets rustled, twisted around her thin legs. A doll escaped the folds of the bed and fell to the floor, its china head knocking upon the wood. The child did not stir.

Spence braced his arm against the door frame and considered his towheaded half sister. No wonder Elizabeth Bennett had been desperate enough to want to move the girl out of the house, away from him. Her one claim to the ranch, her only link to Mauna Noe, was a child so very frail that her own father had doubted that she would survive, doubted it enough to make a bastard her trustee.

Spence stared down at the pale little girl who was the only obstacle between him and full ownership of Mauna Noe.

Five

ELIZABETH AWOKE WITH A start, sat straight up, and swung her feet off the chaise. Her heart pounded. Disoriented at first, she soon realized she must have fallen sound asleep on the lanai. The night had deepened.

She stood up and hurried through the parlor, past the stuffed birds with their blind glass eyes and the Bennett ancestors in their tarnished frames that hugged the walls of the room and watched her in silence. Not quite halfway across the parlor, she heard a slight creak in the floorboard overhead.

In the daylight when the birds outside were singing and the cattle bawling and Uilani's chickens running from the axe, she probably would not have heard the sound or paid it any mind, but now she froze, breathless, until it came again—the slight, heavy sigh of a wooden floor giving beneath a substantial weight.

Her throat constricted. She held her breath for a heartbeat and nearly choked on her terror.

Then she moved. She flew to the wall where Franklin's gun collection was mounted, pulled down an old wooden-handled pistol, and crept into the foyer and up the stairs.

She knew who was on the second floor as surely as she wished she had never laid eyes on Franklin Bennett or his bastard son. By the time she reached the top of the stairs, her heart was pounding so hard she almost tasted blood.

Her hand closed around the hilt of the pistol. The ancient split wood felt far from comforting against her palm as she entered the hall.

Even though it was dark, she saw him clearly, knew who it was standing in the doorway of Hadley's room, one arm braced against the frame, his forehead resting on his closed fist.

Driven by her need to protect Hadley, she felt all of her terror drop away. She raised the old pistol, pointed it squarely at the middle of Spence Laamea's back, below the place where his long black hair appeared as a stain on his shirt.

"Put your hands in the air very, very slowly." She steadied her voice, tried to sound fearless, even dangerous. Impossible with her knees knocking together.

Spence turned around.

"What are you doing up here?" She was frantic to see Hadley, to know that she was safe, but the man blocked her view.

"I heard something. A cry. Where were *you*?" Like her, he kept his voice low, barely above a whisper. He filled the doorway, towering head and shoulders over her, his hands raised beside his head. If he was afraid, he did not show it. She tried to see around him, to see if Hadley was all right.

"I fell asleep on the lanai." She owed him no explanation, hated the thread of apology in her tone.

She had fallen behind in her duty to her daughter, whose life was so fragile and so very dear. Since Hadley was born—God's precious gift, one Elizabeth thought she would never be worthy of again—Elizabeth had been vigilant in her protection of her. She would not fail her daughter now.

She walked toward Spence, the gun still aimed at his heart.

"What are you intending to do, blow a hole through me?" He shifted slightly.

"If I have to." They were so close she could see the shadowed contours of his face, but not the nuances of his expression. His voice sounded very calm, very matter-of-fact, for a man looking death in the eye.

"I told you I would kill you if you tried to harm my daughter. Step back out of the way." She waggled the gun back and forth.

When he complied, she walked past him into the room, hurried to her daughter's bedside, and listened to the tight but even cadence of her breathing. She reached down with her free hand, smoothed the curls off Hadley's forehead, adjusted the sheet around her shoulders.

When she turned around, her toe connected with something that skidded a few inches across the floor. She felt around until her fingers found the doll, then picked it up and laid it on the end of the bed, where Hadley would find it in the morning.

For half a second, she forgot about Spence lingering in the hallway, but her heart calmed somewhat, her fear ebbed slightly now that she knew Hadley was fine. She walked to the door, stepped out, and closed it silently but firmly behind her. Once more, the weapon was aimed at Spence.

"Go away," she demanded. "Go downstairs and leave us alone."

"Do you really think I came up here to hurt her?"

"I don't know what to think. Right now, all I know is that I don't like you."

"I feel the same about you."

"Fine. Then at least we don't have to live with false pretenses or feigned politeness," she told him.

"And I don't need to say please when I ask you to lower that pistol."

She glanced down at the weapon in her hands, not for long—only a split second—but time enough for him to grab the useless thing.

Elizabeth cried out. Not quite a scream, merely a yelp of surprise as he squeezed her wrist until she let go. When she lost possession, she began backing away.

He held the weapon up close to his face, inspecting it, though handicapped by the darkness. Then he laughed—a deep, melodic sound that should have been more menacing.

"You wouldn't have done much harm with this thing. It probably hasn't been fired in seventy-five years."

She refused to respond.

He shoved the pistol into his waistband while she waited, trying to make herself small.

"You get this off the wall downstairs?" He had not taken a single step in her direction.

She nodded, then realized he couldn't see her clearly in the dark and said, "Yes."

"I'll put it back in the morning on my way out."

Elizabeth was too shaken to make sense of his words. Something about putting the gun away.

"Good night," he said.

"What?" It was more of a croak than a word when she finally got it out.

"Good night," he said a little louder. "Next time you want to shoot someone, get a better gun."

With that, he turned and left her, his bare feet silent on the stairs.

Elizabeth sagged against the wall, limp as a dishrag. She rested her cheek against the cool surface and sighed with relief. When she was able to move, she steadied herself, ran her hand along the smooth plaster wall. *Good night.*

He had not threatened her or touched her except to take the gun away from her. When she thought back over the terrifying exchange, she realized he had not even raised his voice except to laugh. She went inside her room and closed the door. Leaning back against it, she whispered a silent prayer of thanks.

THE NEXT MORNING, SHE slipped on her faded blue gown again and went downstairs for breakfast with Hadley. The child finished eating long before Elizabeth was ready to leave her coffee and the quiet solitude, the view of the mountains and the sea, so she sent her to the parlor. Maile came in shortly afterward to play with her.

Elizabeth's contemplation was disturbed when Uilani entered the room.

"What is it, Uilani?" Elizabeth pushed the heavy coffee mug away and studied the woman's moon-shaped face, thinking of how they had spent years living within a few hundred yards of each other and yet had hardly exchanged a word until Franklin's death.

"Everyt'ing come good last night? T'ings all right in da house?" The woman glanced in the direction of Franklin's old room.

"Everything is fine," Elizabeth assured her, wishing it were so.

"You know you like stay wit' Maile and me, dat's all right, too. I owe plenty t'anks, *mahalo*, for long time ago, when you tell you husband you broke da chinee cup, not Maile. Dat day I know you one good kine *haole* lady. Feel bad for you, wit' bad husband. But now you get happy. Get one place live wit'out worry. Get one man do da kine work for you. Get happy now."

"*. . . long time ago, when you tell you husband you broke da chinee cup, not Maile . . .*"

Years slipped away as the memory suddenly surfaced. Elizabeth had just unpacked, left the bedroom to look for Franklin, walked through the house until she found herself out in the kitchen. There she discovered little Maile, no more than six at the time. The child was standing over the blue-and-white pieces of a broken teacup, her huge almond eyes flooded with tears and more streaming down her cheeks.

Uilani had hovered near the stove, unable to move or speak. She stood there with her hands clasped around a ladle, staring from Elizabeth to Maile and back.

Immediately, Elizabeth had dropped to one knee, picked up the cup and the broken handle, and then reached out to wipe a tear off Maile's cheek.

"Don't worry, honey," she told the girl. "It's just a cup. There's no need to cry."

She was trying to reassure Uilani that she was not upset when suddenly Esther Timmons, the housekeeper who had just welcomed Elizabeth to Mauna Noe, came upon the scene. The woman took one look at Elizabeth standing there with the broken cup in her hands, whipped around, and hurried from the room.

Elizabeth had barely gotten to her feet, the cup and broken handle still cradled in her hand, when Mrs. Timmons returned with Franklin in her wake.

The housekeeper's gaze darted back and forth as she took in the scene, her plump, liver-spotted hands folded atop one another. "You see? It's just as I said. She's broken a piece of the fine china," Mrs. Timmons said.

Elizabeth had arrived not an hour before, after a long, silent drive with Franklin from Hanalei Bay. She had been bursting with curiosity about the island, but after the simple ceremony beside the bay and Franklin's ensuing silence she had not felt like talking either.

Longing to make a new life for herself here, she had been brutally honest with him before their wedding ceremony. Laying her soul bare, she had taken him aside when she stepped off the inter-island steamer and admitted that she was not a virgin. Then, calmly confessing everything in a speech that she had so carefully rehearsed on the long voyage from Maryland, she told him the truth, that she had transgressed—only once—that in a moment of naïveté and abandon, she had been duped by a young sailor who had promised her marriage, drawn her into a two-night clan-destine affair, then sailed away on the morning tide.

She did not tell Franklin Bennett that she would have gone with the devil himself if he had promised to take her away from the confining, impoverished world of her aunt and uncle Rodrick. But she did quickly assure him that she had enough money to pay her way back to the States should he wish to decline his proposal.

Franklin immediately fell silent, weighing all she had said. She recalled watching a thin line of sweat bead his upper lip as she stood there in the relentless tropic sun beside the aquamarine waters of Hanalei Bay, waiting for him to say something, anything, in response.

He had surveyed the other passengers as they disem-barked, the *kānaka* swarming the dories unloading the long-awaited crates and barrels, the local businessmen there to collect their shipments. Then he carefully straightened his coat and adjusted the high, stiff collar. She had to strain to hear him over the low, rolling waves when he told her that he had brought her here to play the role of a rancher's wife, to bear him an heir.

Nothing more, nothing less. He had made it clear that he was shocked. She was only eighteen. He had expected her to come to him unsoiled, but he was not looking for love. He did not need her love, nor would he try to earn it. He only wanted respect, from her, from the community, which was why he had contacted a friend of her uncle, another former missionary, when he set about looking for a wife.

Her virginity was not the issue, he assured her, although she had no way of knowing at the time that he lied. He told her that all he wanted was an educated *haole* wife, with missionary connections. And an heir.

Much to her later satisfaction, having a *haole* wife hadn't helped him at all. The invitations, the business connections he had hoped to cultivate after their marriage, never panned out. It took more than a well-connected white wife to give Franklin Bennett the respect of the people he had offended.

And so their ride to Mauna Noe that day had been a silent one. There might not have been time or opportunity to learn the nuances of his tone, but there was no mistaking the harsh note of condemnation in his voice as he had stared at her and then at the broken teacup.

"What's going on here, Elizabeth?" Franklin had demanded.

She remembered following his gaze as it shot over to the quaking child, then to Uilani. The frigid look in Franklin's eyes chilled Elizabeth's heart. Little Maile shook so hard that Elizabeth feared she was going to swoon. Without thinking, Elizabeth quickly held out her hand, displaying the broken cup.

She even smiled. "It was just an accident."

Even now, years later, she could recall watching Franklin slowly reach out and lift the pieces carefully into his hands. With eyes downcast, his expression shuttered, he stared at the cup almost as if he were praying over it. Then very carefully and deliberately, her new husband had turned his gaze on her.

His face was florid with anger. The freckles on the back of his hands stood out against his sunbaked skin. To this day she could still recall the smell of his hair oil, the scent of bay rum. The deranged fury in his eyes.

"Just an *accident,* Elizabeth?" Smooth as honey, his tone held a very chilling threat. "There are no accidents."

Seeing the look in his eye, a look that bordered on madness, she knew she could not tell him the truth and cast blame on the little Hawaiian girl. That very morning she had spoken her vows, promised to love and to honor, to cherish and obey him—but as she looked at little Maile— Elizabeth knew she could do nothing under the circumstances but tell a white lie.

"I dropped it," she said, still smiling, still disbelieving the raw turbulence seething in his eyes. "I didn't mean to, I—"

She did not see his hand come up until it was too late.

But she certainly felt the force of it, the anger, the power and rage behind his swing. He hit her above the left eye, sent her reeling across the room, where she slammed into a worktable and crumpled to the ground. Blood flowed into her eye, dripped down onto the bodice of her new blue gown—her wedding gown, the one she had so carefully embellished with embroidery along the cuffs—until she saw him through a red haze.

"You bitch!" he cried out, towering over her, shaking with rage, the broken cup still clenched in his other fist.

"This was my mother's Staffordshire!" He shook the pieces at her. "How dare you put your hands on it? From now on, Mrs. Timmons and only Mrs. Timmons is to care for it. You don't belong anywhere near the kitchen."

Turning on his heel, he barked commands over his shoulder. "Get up. Get out of here and go to your room and clean yourself up. I don't want to hear that you were ever in here again."

Her aunt and uncle led a life of self-imposed discipline. They had been strict in their efforts to make up for what they saw as her frivolous, pampered upbringing. After she had humiliated herself with Johnny Huffington, the sailor, they went to desperate lengths to purge her of her shame.

But they had never, ever hit her.

No one had ever laid a hand on her in anger. Until that day, her wedding day.

Little Maile was nowhere to be seen when Elizabeth finally struggled to her feet. But Mrs. Timmons was there, watching her with her pouty little bow lips twisted into a smirk—watching, as she would delight in doing for the next seven years. Watching and waiting to report her every move to Franklin.

Later that afternoon Franklin called her into the parlor. Surrounded by the antiquities from his family estate in Georgia, he ignored the swollen cut above her eye and laid out his instructions for her routine at Mauna Noe. Because she had no moral fiber, she was to be watched day and night. She was not to talk to any of the help, only to Mrs. Timmons. She was never, under any circumstances, to associate with any of the Hawaiian laborers, not Uilani the cook, or the *paniolo*, should she ever cross paths with them. She was to stay within the confines of the house. When and if he felt he could trust her, she would be allowed in the garden. Except for one foiled attempt at escape before she conceived Hadley, she served her sentence for seven years. Seven years that, without her daughter by her side, would have been an eternity.

"You like one coffee?"

Elizabeth looked up, called back to the present by the sound of Uilani's gentle prodding, nourished by the kind understanding in the woman's eyes.

"I'm sorry, Uilani. I guess I was spinning cobwebs. Thank you so much for generously offering your home to us." Elizabeth was truly touched. "Hadley and I may still need your help."

"HELP WITH WHAT?" SPENCE stood in the door to the dining room, turning his hat around in his hand. The dried flower lei around the crown needed to be replaced, but Kaala had woven it for him, placed it there herself when they were first married, happy and innocent of what was to come. The lei was as dry as old bones now, and crumbling. He concentrated on the words Elizabeth had said to her cook and winked at Uilani. She laughed like a schoolgirl and batted her eyes at him before she left the room.

Elizabeth's cheeks blazed with color the minute she looked up at him. The rose tint highlighted her deep-blue eyes and gave her an alluring glow. The sight of her stirred him, and his immediate physical reaction to her surprised and irritated him more than he could say. He turned his irritation on her, the cause of his discomfort.

"Help with what?" he repeated.

She left his question unanswered and issued one of her own.

"Would it be too much to ask you not to sneak up on me like that?"

"It's impossible for a man my size to sneak anywhere, Mrs. Bennett." Uninvited, he reached for a chair, pulled it out, turned it around and straddled it.

"Why don't you call me Elizabeth? I prefer that to Mrs. Bennett."

He watched her carefully, his eyes searching her face until she was forced to look down at the table. Without wanting to, he noticed the way her lashes brushed her cheeks, the fact that her lower lip was fuller than the upper, the way her fingertips slid back and forth over the thick coffee mug before she wrapped them around the handle.

Reminding himself that this was his father's widow, he looked away. A bowl piled high with bananas, mangoes, and oranges sat in the middle of the table. He reached over the back of the chair and grabbed a banana, split the yellow skin, slowly peeled it, rotated the fruit, and started peeling another portion.

"I spent the morning over in the office going through the account books that Clifford left."

"And?"

"To be honest, *Elizabeth*, things are terrible. Franklin Bennett was in the wrong business." He gulped down two bites of banana, chewed, swallowed.

"Franklin came from a long line of landowners. He said he had a huge cotton plantation in Georgia." Elizabeth watched while he finished off the entire piece of fruit in no more than four bites.

"He died deep in debt. For one thing, he had to pay his workers here instead of relying on slave labor, as he had in the South. For another, Hawaii was settled by Yankees and they are much better at business. They don't keep extending loans to a man simply because of old family ties. Your husband managed to ignore the fact that he owned prime grazing land. He tried to raise sheep, which ruined a lot of pasture for a number of years, then he planted coffee and when that failed, cane sugar—all of that before he decided to concentrate on cattle.

"There are still outstanding bills for shipments of goods and staples. He died owing his creditors in Honolulu."

"Mr. Clifford didn't mention any creditors yesterday."

"If we can't pay them back, we'll have to declare insolvency, sell off everything that isn't nailed down."

"But that means we'll lose the place." She sounded as if she did not believe him.

"If we have to turn the ranch over to them, you and your girl will have to move and I'll lose my chance to make a profit here. How is it you've been here seven years and you had no idea things were so bad?"

He watched her shut down, watched the life go out of her eyes, and knew she would not come close to telling him the truth.

"How will we pay the bills without any cash?" Her perfect brow was marred by worry lines.

"I'd like to sell off some of the stock—"

"No."

"What in the hell do you mean, *no*?"

"No. If you sell off all the cattle, we'll have nothing left."

"I don't want to sell *all* the cattle. Duke says there are almost a hundred head more than we can handle right now. We can round some of them up, drive them down to Hanalei, and ship them to Honolulu. I'll use the profits to see about paying off the creditors."

She still had not said a thing. He had no choice but to sell off some of the cattle to save the damn place, and though it irked him to have to ask, he needed her permission.

"How long will it take you?" She set the coffee cup aside, leaned forward.

He shrugged, fixed on the frayed fancy stitching on the cuffs of her faded sleeves. "A couple of days. Then we'll have to move them down to Hanalei."

"If you are going to Hanalei, then I'm going with you."

He laughed aloud, looked her up and down. "*You're* going to help drive cattle down to Hanalei?"

"I am going, and so is Hadley. I see no reason we can't ride along in the buggy."

"Why don't you just go to town on your own some other time? Why add to my problems? The men have to concentrate on getting a herd of cattle down a switchback trail to the valley floor, not on a buggy that might slide down the face of the hill."

It was more than nine miles to Hanalei, a route that went down muddy trails and steep hills and deep ravines. Having her along would only complicate the situation.

"I don't consider it an outing, Mr. Laamea—"

"Spence."

She ignored him. "I'm going along to make certain you don't sell off Hadley's cattle and then abscond with the money."

He tossed the banana peel on the table, hard, then shoved off the back of the chair. Wood hit wood with a sharp crack. He did not bother to hide his anger when he picked up his hat and shoved it on. The damn woman set him off like a powder keg.

"You know, I took your insults yesterday, *Elizabeth*. Today I'm not in the mood."

She jumped up off her chair. His height made equality impossible, but she did not back down.

"I personally don't care what sort of mood you're in today or any day, for that matter. Those are *my* daughter's cattle. You need *my* permission to sell them, which I will give, as long as I am allowed to accompany you and the others down to Hanalei."

"You don't trust me." It was a statement, not a question. "Is that because I'm a bastard, or because I'm related to Franklin?"

"Because you're a *man*. That and the fact that you said yourself you've spent your life working for very little money and that you have barely a penny to your name. You agreed to the terms of the will so that you could gamble on making money before Hadley comes of age. What guarantee do I have that you won't decide to take what you can get now and disappear?''

''You have no guarantee whatsoever, Elizabeth. None at all.''

He fought for control because he could see that she was afraid of him—without reason—not because he had done anything to her but because he was Franklin's son.

''I think this discussion is over.'' Her words came on a squeak and a whisper.

It took every ounce of self-control that Spence could muster to keep from picking up one of the dining chairs and tossing it out the open window. *Hell,* he thought, *why waste a good chair?* He would get more satisfaction from picking up the damn *pa'akikī* woman and tossing *her* stubborn ass out the window.

''I don't plan to spend thirteen years of my life with you dogging my every step.''

Elizabeth Bennett confused him more than any woman he had ever known. Whenever he came face-to-face with her, either she looked like she wanted to jump out of her skin or she was goading him, accusing him of murder or thievery—or both.

''You'll just have to get used to it,'' she fired back. ''This whole situation wasn't my idea. It was your father's.''

''He was *no* father to me.''

''You're luckier than you think.''

She made a move to step around him, dismissing him as if he was not worth her time. Before he knew what he was doing, Spence reached out, grabbed her arm, and stopped her in her tracks. She spun around so fast that she dislodged some of the fine pins in her hair. A long, silken skein slid to her shoulder.

''Tell me what you meant by that remark.''

"Let me go."

It was the last thing he wanted to do, because he knew she would walk away before anything was settled, but her eyes accused him of things he would never do, so he quickly unclenched his fingers and let go.

Exactly as he expected, she spun around and hurried out of the room without a backward glance. Another hairpin hit the floor with a *ping*, and as she disappeared around the corner, he saw more of her hair collapse around her shoulders.

Six

Hanalei Valley

THE VALLEY LAY CRADLED beneath three densely timbered mountains and a perfect crescent-shaped bay, full as a calabash brimming with turquoise water. Waterfalls plunged from the peaks and ridges, tracing furrows down the mountain faces, tamed into winding streams before they reached the sea. Rice paddies flooded the bottomland of the valley floor, reflecting the sky on shimmering surfaces.

Here and there along the edges of the valley waterways, Hawaiians who had not moved onto plantations or died of *haole* diseases still dwelt in small family clusters. They clung to the old ways, the ancient ways that were slowly dying.

Terraced patches of taro—the starchy, life-sustaining crop Hawaiians called *kalo*—were bathed by the water diverted from the streams. Near the *pili* grass houses beside the waterways, horses stood belly-deep in grass, lazing away the day while their owners toiled in the watery fields.

Ana Pualoa waded into the knee-high, muddy water of

her uncle Raymond's taro patch and dreamed of another life. As the rich mud hidden beneath the opaque water squashed between her toes, she pictured a grand, white-washed, wood-frame house, a closet full of frilly, expensive gowns with ribbons and laces, draped chiffon, fitted waist-lines and bustle pads, the kind she made for the *haole* ladies of Hanalei.

She straightened and glanced across the rows of thin shoots standing in the terraced field of water, then lifted her head to catch the gently blowing trade wind. She watched her older brother, Chuckie, set the young shoots, slowly making his way toward her between the rows.

With the hem of her old shift tied up around her waist, her legs bare up to her thighs, she bent over and thrust another *huli*, a piece of *kalo* with leaf stems, into the mud. Her hand and forearm disappeared beneath the water to her elbow. Looking at her reflection, she sighed. There was no escape from the relentless sun that deepened the dusky hue of her skin, for her mother insisted she put in her time in Uncle Raymond's taro patch with the rest of her *'ohana*.

"Hooey! Ana!" Chuckie snuck up behind her, nearly scaring her out of her skin.

"What's the mattah, you, Chuckie?" She was so furious she slipped into the pidgin English she was trying to un-learn. "You trying make—" She paused, started over. "*Are* you trying *to* make me go crazy?"

"You dreamin' again or wot? Bettah you tend da *kalo*, not t'ink so much 'bout da kine *haole* t'ings. You crazy, girl. No *haole* man gonna look at you longer den dis." He held up his fingers, stained with rich brown mud, shoved them under her nose, and snapped them.

"Just wait, Chuckie, you'll see." She could not waste time arguing with him. Chuckie gave her almost as much trouble as his friend Duke Makakani, but thankfully Duke had not been around since he got work as a *paniolo* at Mauna Noe, up Waipake way.

When they were all three growing up, Chuckie and Duke

had thought they were so clever, ambushing her, pelting her with mud balls on the way to school, half drowning her in the bay during *hukilau*, hiding in the thick bushes and tripping her with vines. She spent more time chasing the two of them down the beach road than doing anything else during the long, lazy days of their childhood.

Now that she had turned eighteen, she was far too old for such nonsense, and thankful that Duke was no longer around to interfere in her life. If she was lucky, she had seen the last of him and had only to suffer Chuckie and dream about finding a rich, handsome husband.

"Hey, Ana, you deaf?"

"I hear, Chuckie, but I *not* going speak wit' you." She stuck her nose in the air and turned her back on him. Her haughty manner slipped when she had to reach into the filthy burlap sack slung over her shoulder for another young plant.

Chuckie laughed and poked her with a muddy finger.

"Get outta here, Chuckie. Get back over dere." She nodded in the opposite direction.

"You not like me bodda you, eh? You like spend time t'inking 'bout get marry."

"Get away, Chuckie, before I tell Uncle Raymond you boddering me."

"You fancy kine *haole* talk slip away fas'."

Ana straightened, shifted the bag on her shoulder, and waded between the rows to the edge of the patch. She climbed out onto the grassy, two-foot walkway between the fields and marched over to Uncle Raymond, who stood in the shade of the small wooden shed beside his grass house.

Uncle Raymond, his wife, and their brood of four-going-on-five all lived in the grass house together.

"Uncle, I have to go to work."

"You working," he reminded her. "For me."

"Mrs. Randolph say could I come early today. She get some mending for me an' she want be fit for one new dress."

His straight, dark brows jammed together at a point above the bridge of his nose. "You like making da kine clothes for one *haole* lady bettah den dis kine clean work?" Then he threw back his head and laughed, one of his favorite pastimes.

Ana couldn't help but smile. Men who laughed a lot always made her feel like the sun had just come out from behind the clouds.

"Sorry to tell you, Uncle, but I like making dresses for *haole* ladies plenty more den planting *kalo,* picking *kalo,* bagging *kalo.* I like it plenty more den anyt'ing to do with *kalo.* Any*thing,* I mean." She crossed her fingers behind her back, hoping he would let her go early.

"Den you betta go on."

She stood on tiptoe. Uncle Raymond lowered his face within reach of her lips, and she gave him a quick peck, first on one cheek and then the other.

"Aloha, Uncle. See you tomorrow."

Ana was careful not to lose her balance on the narrow two-foot-wide mounds. One misstep and she would fall into the murky, shallow water, and then her bath in the stream would take longer than usual. She tried to look her best whenever she called on Mrs. Randolph, the *haole* lady who had taken her under her wing at the request of the local schoolteacher. Ana's teacher told Mrs. Randolph that she saw something in Ana—"An intelligence and determination that should be encouraged," she said.

Mrs. Randolph offered to teach her to sew in exchange for Ana's working a few hours in the afternoon at her bed-and-board. It took some effort on the part of both ladies to get her mother to agree. Mrs. Randolph told her she had "natural ability" when it came to mending and taught her to make dress patterns and sew garments by hand, two skills that she worked hard to master.

Ana liked working for Marion Randolph, better than the first *haole* her teacher sent her to. That *wahine* was always telling her, "Comport yourself with dignity—as a young

lady ought—and do not behave like some indolent heathen." Becoming an indolent heathen was apparently the
worst of all sins, although she never found a commandment
against it in her Bible. Ana always tried to show up at Mrs.
Randolph's "spit-and-polish perfect," as the landlady liked
to say, not so much to please her employer but because she
could not risk looking her worst when there was every
chance that a wealthy prospective bridegroom might be in
residence at the bed-and-board.

Less than an hour after she left the *kalo* patch, Ana stood
on the lanai outside Mrs. Randolph's, tugging at the bodice
of her candy-striped navy-and-white *holokū* and adjusting
the long, flounced hem over her bare feet until her toes
hardly showed even when she took a deep breath. She knew
without anyone having to tell her that she looked like perfection in the new dress.

Ana was proud of the height she inherited from her Hawaiian parents, proud of her straight back and long limbs.
It did not hurt to have ample breasts, either. She saw the
way men watched her when she was out walking on the
beach or down the road with her sewing basket swinging
in one hand. She secretly liked the feeling of superiority
and command it gave her whenever she tested her flirting
skills on the sailors from the inter-island steamer. They fell
all over themselves trying to impress her—not that she
would ever consent to settling down with a sailor. She was
after a much bigger catch.

As she knocked on the door and called out to Mrs. Randolph, Ana was convinced that one day, if she held tight
to her dream, if she continued to study and emulate the
ways of her mentors, if she plied her dressmaking trade in
the homes of enough plantation wives, met enough of their
bachelor relations and sons—then surely in the not-too-
distant future she would find herself mistress of the grand
home she had always wanted.

Sooner rather than later, her taro-patch days would be
over.

• • • •

DUKE SAT IN THE saddle, rocking to the gentle, familiar sway of the horse beneath him as he headed toward the corral, where close to thirty head of cattle waited to be driven down to Hanalei. The sky was clear and blue, the trades blowing softly. Here and there, clouds brushed the mountaintop and then moved on.

From the corral he could see the back of the ranch house. Word around the barracks was that Elizabeth Bennett insisted on traveling to Hanalei with them. Duke was as curious as Toshi and Melvin to see what was going to happen next.

Franklin Bennett's old black covered buggy was drawn up to the back of the house, empty and awaiting occupants. Melvin had oiled the wheels and greased the axle, but there was no denying that the old thing had seen better days. No matter the condition of the rig, Duke could not really blame Elizabeth Bennett for wanting to go with them to the valley. According to Toshi, who had been working at Mauna Noe longer than anyone, she had not been off the ranch the entire time she had lived here—except once. And without going into detail, Toshi told them that Bennett had dragged her back home in the middle of the night.

Duke looked over the milling, bawling cattle. The *pipi* sensed something was about to happen, and even he had to admit that since Laamea's arrival there had been an element of raw tension in the air.

He looked toward the house again and saw Elizabeth Bennett step out the back door. Her little girl clutched her hand, excitement written all over her face. The poor little *keiki* had legs as skinny as a hen's and skin as pale as a hulled *kukui* nut. Uilani followed them out of the back door, and as she moved to the edge of the lanai, the breeze billowed her *holokū* around her. She looked like a calico cloud holding a picnic basket.

Bennett's widow's mouth was set in a firm, determined line. She had on a dull, wine-colored dress and a curious little hat trimmed with pale ribbons. It offered no protection from the sun, so in Duke's mind the hat was good for nothing but worry.

He watched her pause at the top of the steps, saw her glance over at the buggy and then look around, uncertain. Laamea appeared almost instantaneously, riding up from the stable side of the house on Kāhili, the big black horse that he brought with him from Oʻahu.

Duke shifted in the saddle, determined not to miss anything, especially when things were just getting good. Uilani had told him that whenever the widow and Laamea were together, they argued like two cats in a sack.

Forgetting about the bawling cattle secure in the corral behind him, Duke concentrated on the scene on the lanai. Elizabeth Bennett's feelings were clear. She looked tense and distracted the minute Spence rode into view.

Laamea waited on horseback while she gathered up her skirt and marched down the stairs with the girl in tow. She paused momentarily beside the buggy and lifted the *keiki* inside, then with a flash of white petticoat and a brief show of ankles, she climbed aboard unaided and took up the reins.

Although the man offered her no help, Laamea did not ride off until the widow had the rig moving slowly away from the house. Duke saw the little girl's pale hand extend beyond the edge of the buggy top as she waved good-bye to Uilani.

Duke signaled Melvin and Toshi into position. As soon as Laamea whistled, he opened the gate and started the cattle moving down the road. Just the two other *paniolo*—one of them as old as dust—Laamea and himself, were going to drive the cattle to Hanalei. Spence had said that he hoped some of the men on the smaller ranches along the way might lend a hand—even though he couldn't afford to pay them.

Spence Laamea had plenty to worry about. Enough to make his head hurt, Duke thought. He would never forget the look on Laamea's face on the afternoon when he noticed that some of the cattle they found up in the hills were tagged with blatantly altered brands. Laamea had demanded to know who the rightful owners were, then told Toshi and Melvin to round up all the stolen cattle and return them. Duke and the others were amazed, but also silently pleased to finally be working for a man of honor.

Laamea might not be able to pay them anything yet, but after what he had done with the stolen cattle, they were certain that as soon as the ranch made any money they would get their wages. His act of goodwill toward the neighbors would go a long way toward helping to establish his name and his credit.

As the *pipi* ran out of the pen and the men closed in around them, whistling and shouting, " *'Ai lepo! 'Ai lepo!* Eat dirt!'' Duke thought back to his own childhood, his free and easy life growing up in the valley. Fishing, riding bareback, swimming, riding the waves—his youth had been full of sunlight and laughter.

And Ana Pualoa.

If he lived to be a hundred, he knew he would carry the memory of the way she looked as a child in his heart forever. They had grown up together, raised in grass houses on the same *kuleana*. Her brother was his closest friend. He could not exactly remember when he knew for certain that he and Ana were meant to be together, probably the first time he ever laid eyes on her. It was something he had always known, something written on his soul before he was even born.

Ana Pualoa with her long brown legs, laughing dark eyes, and flashing smile had captivated him the first time she smiled at him. Of course, he was only a little boy then, so he could not possibly have let her know how he really felt. Instead, he did what any boy would do—he made her life miserable. Kept her thinking about him.

One thing he did know for sure, Ana could be as *pa'akikī* as a cross-eyed mule. When she finally came to the conclusion that she loved him, she would have to think it was all her own idea.

Since he had left the valley, he had been over to Anahola, to Kilauea, too, but he had not been back to Hanalei for two years. He had wanted to give Ana time to grow up—not to mention time to miss him desperately. Just thinking about seeing her again after all this time gave him chicken skin.

For now he tried to put Ana out of his mind. He had plenty to worry about on the trek to the valley—stubborn *pipi*, a sudden downpour, shark attacks on the cattle as they swam out to the freighter in the bay tomorrow.

There was plenty to worry about today, but one thing he did not have the slightest fear of was that Ana would no longer be his. They were meant to be together.

Princeville Ranch, above Hanalei Valley

THE HILLSIDE WAS AWASH in mud and leaves as rain clouds crept down the face of the mountains and drenched the valley below. Exhausted, her hands aching and knotted around the wet leather reins, Elizabeth fought the urge to put her head down and sob. Hadley was perched beside her on the edge of the cracked leather seat, her initial excitement faded, staring wide-eyed and silent over the edge of the precipice before them.

Elizabeth had lost track of time since Spence Laamea had ridden up beside the buggy and gazed down at her with an arrogant look that shouted, "I told you so."

Her hat was nothing more than a sodden ball of felt. The water-stained ribbon met its fate almost as soon as the rain began, pelting them and blowing in under the buggy's hood. Her hair was as big a disaster as her hat. It straggled, dripping and forlorn, around her shoulders. Her clothes were wet. She felt chilled despite the heat, and she was worried to death about Hadley.

The very worst thing of all was that in her deepest heart of hearts, she had decided Spence had been right all along. She had had absolutely no business insisting that they come along. She had risked Hadley's health in the bargain. As it was, the child was wet, hungry, and tired—and they still had to negotiate the steep, muddy switchback road down into the valley.

The same path that Spence, Duke, and the others had disappeared down more than an hour ago with the cattle.

When the wind blew in the right direction, she thought she could still hear the animals bawling, but then the sound would be drowned out by the rain spattering against the top of the buggy, the leaves rustling on the trees, and the roar of the surf somewhere in the distance.

"Mama, are we almost there?"

Elizabeth sighed and wiped her face with her hands, then put on a smile before she looked over at Hadley. The child had discarded the blanket that Elizabeth had made her put over her lap, insisting it was too hot and itchy. But each time the rain intensified, Elizabeth watched Hadley shiver and grew more terrified that she would catch a cold.

"I'm certain that Mr. Laamea will be back in just a few minutes to lead us down." She was certain of no such thing and she knew she was not fooling Hadley either.

"You said that a long time ago." Hadley's whine ended with a cough.

Elizabeth did not like the thready sound of her voice or the slight wheezing. Reaching over, she brushed Hadley's damp and matted curls.

"He can't be much longer now." Could he? She never imagined she would find herself wishing to lay eyes on the man. Right now she would give anything in her power to have him appear over the edge of the hill.

"Is there any more chicken?"

"No, dear." She should have listened to Uilani and carried more food. The men ate like horses, and the basket that she thought bottomless had been empty after the noon break.

"I'm hungry," Hadley whined.

"You're tired. Why don't you lie down on the seat and try to nap?"

"No. I'm not sleepy. I'm *starving*, Mama." She flung herself against the seat, and when Elizabeth did not respond immediately, she started to cough. "I'm *dying* over here!"

"Hadley, I want you to lie down and relax. Do you remember the story about the boy who cried wolf?"

"No!" Hadley's wheezing intensified.

Elizabeth put her arm around Hadley's shoulders and was pulling her near when she caught sight of Spence's hat, then his broad shoulders, as he topped the hill. Rain dripped from the hat brim and sluiced down his yellow slicker.

"We made it down without any trouble, but it was rough. The side of the hill is slick as glass and thick with mud. Tide is high, and the river is running too fast to take the cattle across. I think maybe you should turn back. If you don't want to go all the way back to the ranch, maybe they will put you and the girl up at Princeville." He glanced over his shoulder at the outbuildings of the ranch on the hilltop.

"I want to go on."

"Then give me the girl and I'll take her down on my horse—"

"No! I don't wanna go with *him*," Hadley shouted, leaning back into the corner of the buggy seat.

"I will absolutely not give her over to you." Elizabeth wondered how Spence had the nerve to expect her to relinquish her daughter into his care.

His reaction was immediate. His eyes blazed, his brows dove to meet each other. His mouth hardened. He glanced over at her daughter, and she knew it was only the child's presence that kept him from cursing her on the spot.

"As it is, we're going to have to tie lines to the buggy in case it starts to slide. I don't want to worry about both of you."

Elizabeth was plagued with doubt, but she simply could not let him take Hadley down the hill.

He looked at Hadley the moment the girl started coughing and wheezing again. Elizabeth tightened her arm around her daughter's shoulders. Spence's expression darkened. She let go of Hadley and picked up the reins.

"Have it your way, Mrs. Bennett."

SPENCE TOLD HIMSELF TO calm down, that the damn fool woman was no kin to him, that he didn't care if she broke her damn fool neck on the way down the hill. If she had been anyone else he would have lambasted her for her stupidity and muleheadedness. But she wasn't anyone else—she was his father's widow.

She was a woman without enough honor to leave an outright cattle thief, a man whose underhanded business dealings had nearly bankrupted him. A man Spence suspected of beating her. Maybe in *her* mind she deserved whatever she got, but he couldn't understand why she was so hell-bent on taking the girl with her.

"Duke!" Spence shouted over the downpour, calling out to the young *paniolo*, who was already halfway back up the hill. "Yell down to Melvin. Tell him to bring plenty of line. She's coming down."

Duke did not appear the least bit surprised.

When he had the men in position and two heavy lines tied to the buggy, Spence rode up beside the rig. Elizabeth was clutching the reins, staring down into the valley. The mountains were completely hidden in thick gray-white clouds that trailed almost to the valley floor. Her skin was paler than usual, her eyes bright blue and wide with fear she was fighting hard not to show. The child was seated well back on the seat, clutching the dinner basket, her shoulders hunched forward. Her feet dangled far above the floorboards.

"You can still change your mind, you know. Once we start down there is nowhere to turn around."

Elizabeth shook her head, stiffly, as if movement was an effort. "We'll be fine."

"What if you're not?" Not wanting the girl to hear, Spence barely spoke above the sound of the rain.

Elizabeth whipped around to face him. Her cheeks were tinted with spots of high color. The fabric of her burgundy gown was soaked and clinging to her breasts, pressed over her thighs.

"We'll be just fine," she insisted. She looked away and shifted the reins, holding them so tight that the translucent skin across her knuckles looked as if it might tear.

He planted his forearm on his thigh and leaned down toward her. "Why are you doing this?"

She turned toward him again, a challenge burning bright in her eyes. "Do you think I like this? Do you think I want to be here? Those are my daughter's cattle down there, Mr. Laamea. I have looked out for her welfare since the day she was born and I don't intend to let a little mud stop me now."

"There's more than a little mud waiting for you over that hill."

"I've faced worse."

"Bugs in the flower garden?" He stared at her faded gown. "No money for new dresses? I'm sure you had more problems than you could count, living up there in that big house at Mauna Noe."

A lost expression darkened her blue eyes. She looked away quickly, stared out across the valley as if she were peering through the mist, seeing another place and time.

"Yes, that's it, Mr. Laamea. My biggest problem in life before you arrived was that I had no money for new dresses." Then she turned back and hit him with a clear, straightforward stare. "Now, may we please go?"

He took off his hat and whacked it on his thigh, sending a spray of droplets into the air.

"Just remember this was your idea, not mine."

HALFWAY DOWN THE HILL Elizabeth knew she should have listened to him. She and Hadley bounced unmercifully each time the wheels of the buggy moved forward more than an inch. The mare fought the trappings every step of the way, slipping and sliding, losing her footing more often than not. Elizabeth was aware of Spence riding as close beside the wagon as he could manage on the narrow road. Behind them, the *paniolo* on their well-trained cow ponies struggled to keep the lines taut.

With each lunge of the buggy, Hadley let out a shriek. Elizabeth's palms were raw from fighting the reins. Once they were over the crest of the hill and on the way down the incline, she realized that her efforts were useless. The mare's instinct for self-preservation had taken over, and the animal fought the trail herself.

Elizabeth spotted the cattle below, milling off to the side of the road, churning up a quagmire of mud along the riverbank. The water was a deep, muddy green-brown. Pieces of wood, limbs of trees, reeds, and bamboo whirled by in the current as the water made its way to the bay.

The entire valley floor was a patchwork of flooded fields. Staring through the curtain of rain, Elizabeth saw nothing but mud, water, and gray, gray sky. She felt as if she were descending into purgatory.

"Mama, I want to get out!" Hadley grabbed her arm and started crying in earnest when they hit an exposed rock in the middle of the road.

As she turned to call out to Spence, everything seemed to happen at once. Hadley chose that moment to stand up on the floorboard of the buggy and demand to be taken back up the hill. The mare tripped and went down on her forelegs. The buggy lurched and threatened to vault end over end. Then the axle broke with an audible groan and a sharp pop. The vehicle started to tip. Elizabeth made a grab for Hadley and shoved her to the floor before she found herself flung headlong over the side of the wagon.

The last thing she remembered was the gritty taste of mud, a sharp blow to the ribs, and the sound of Hadley screaming.

SPENCE SAW THE GIRL first. She had landed frighteningly close to the jagged furrow gouged out by the plummeting carriage. Hadley Elyson Bennett had escaped death by a hairsbreadth, but there was no denying that she was alive. She was squawking for her mother like a baby mynah bird. Kneeling in the middle of the road, Hadley alternately sobbed and wheezed, staring at the crumpled carriage, her eyes huge blue saucers—the only color on her mud-caked face.

"Duke! Melvin! Get hold of the lines. I don't want to risk it tumbling over Elizabeth." *If it already hasn't*, Spence thought. His heart was pounding, his mouth had gone dry.

"Duke!" he yelled again. "Get the girl." Then he dismounted, dropped the reins, and left Kāhili where he was rather than have the horse lose his footing and career into the already distressed buggy. He began slipping and sliding toward the crumpled burgundy stain on the side of the hill.

Elizabeth lay with one side of her face pressed into the mud, her arms flung out beside her. Her silly hat was missing. Her hair was plastered to her cheek, covering her face. He could not tell if she was breathing, and he was afraid to find out.

I should have stopped her. I should have insisted.

He had let his temper win, and now, because of it, Elizabeth Bennett might be dead.

Spence reached out, noticed his own hand shaking as he touched her shoulder. She did not move, so he gently brushed the hair back off her face and cupped her chin in his hand.

He leaned close and whispered, "Elizabeth?"

God, just let her open her eyes.

Her eyes did not open. Her lashes never fluttered, but in another second he heard her sigh, saw her struggle to push herself up out of the mud.

"Hadley?" she whispered. "My daughter . . . ?"

Spence glanced back over his shoulder to be certain before he answered.

"She's fine. Duke has her."

"Is she . . . alive? Is . . . she all right? I have to see her."

"She's all right. She's crying." Spence answered without hesitation, and that seemed to calm her. Her terror was palpable. Again she struggled to rise. Spence forced her to lie down and then quickly felt along her rib cage, moved his palms to her waist, listened for a cry of pain.

He had thought she looked like a frail bird when he first saw her. Now he knew for certain that she was little more than skin and bones beneath the ruined gown.

"Stop that. Stop touching me." She shoved at his hands, streaking them with the mud from her own. He ignored her, turned her over, and continued his cursory examination.

"Nothing seems to be broken."

"That's because nothing *is* broken." She shrugged him off and sat up, tried to push herself out of the mud and only succeeded in sinking both her hands deep into the gook.

"The least you could do is help me," she cried in frustration.

"A minute ago you told me not to touch you." He easily pulled her out of the mud.

"Would you mind not yelling?" Elizabeth struggled to climb up the trail toward Duke, who was still in the saddle, holding Hadley across his lap. The child was hunched over, her shoulders narrowed. It looked as though she was fighting to breathe.

Elizabeth's clothes were soaked and heavy with mud.

The ooze sucked at her shoes, tried to hold her captive. Every step was an effort.

Spence stood with his hands fisted at his waist and watched for all of two minutes before he let out a curse and stepped up behind her. He swung her up into his arms.

She whipped around to face him, reached out and grabbed the shoulder of his slicker.

"What are you doing?" She fought to get out of his arms, surprised him with her strength.

"What do you think I'm doing? You want to get to the girl or do you want to knock us both down?"

She quieted immediately, managing to hold herself rigid and as far away from his chest as she could.

Her obvious repulsion made him pull her closer.

Duke started down, his horse carefully working its way to them until Elizabeth was close enough to reach up for Hadley and take the girl's hand. Spence felt awkward watching the exchange.

The child was clearly agitated and wheezing. She reached out to her mother. In Hadley's eyes was a silent plea for Elizabeth to take her into her arms.

Spence looked down at Elizabeth. Tears slipped down her cheeks, streaked her muddy face. She stroked the girl's face with her open palm. Spence gently lowered her to the ground, holding her until he was certain she was steady on her feet before he stepped back. Then he reached up, took Hadley from Duke, and handed her to Elizabeth, trying not to think about the cattle milling around on the riverbank, the drizzle, the fact that they had to get the broken-down buggy, the woman, and the child down the hill and across the river.

"Hadley, Mama's here. You're all right, dear." She spoke to the girl in low, soothing tones. "That silly old buggy just decided to hurry, that's all." The slight laugh she added sounded too strained to fool even the child.

She was shaking like a leaf, but her attempt to make light of the near tragedy helped calm the girl. Hadley's breathing slowed, the wheezing lessened almost imperceptibly. She even gave Elizabeth a weak smile. Standing there in the rain, watching Elizabeth hold the little girl in her arms, Spence knew why his father had doubted Hadley would live very long. The child reminded Spence of a fragile glass lamp globe, and the thought made him jumpy.

"We need to get off this hill." Afraid that Elizabeth might slip, Spence took Hadley back from her.

She looked at her daughter lying in his arms, then up into Spence's eyes. It was the first time she had ever looked at him with anything other than suspicion and animosity.

"What should we do now?"

He knew what it cost her to ask. It had been unwise of her to come today, and the price she had almost paid was very dear. It surprised him to note his temper had dissolved. He had no desire to throw the accident up in her face. All he wanted to do was get everyone down the hill without further mishap.

"I'm going to let Duke take the girl. You're going with me. Stay right here and don't move."

He handed Hadley to Duke and started after Kāhili.

"Are we gonna fall again? My *papa* would never have let me tip over in a buggy. I don't want to do this if we are going to fall." Hadley's fear stopped him in his tracks.

"No, baby," Elizabeth said, trying to reassure her.

But Hadley was looking directly at him, not at her mother. He stared at the little *haole* girl, searching for the slightest similarity, something of Bennett that they might share. There was none. Her liquid blue eyes were exactly like her mother's. She was small-boned, delicate, spoiled.

He could feel Elizabeth fretting beside him.

"You're not going to fall again," he told the girl, hoping to God it was true. Then he looked at Elizabeth and said, "This time I'm in charge."

"THIS TIME I'M IN charge."

Before Spence put her up on Kāhili, Elizabeth had expected an I-told-you-so, at the very least. She could tell he was angry by the rigid set of his shoulders and the way he avoided her eyes as he put his hands on her waist to lift her up onto the horse. Very, very angry. Not only was the buggy irreparable, but they had lost valuable time.

No one had to tell her it was all her fault.

What worried her was the way he nursed his anger in silence. He was Franklin's son, which made her wonder if and when his temper would surface, and then because he was *not* Franklin, she wondered if he could forgive and forget.

Can I ever forgive myself? Her own pigheadedness had almost gotten Hadley killed. In one second, all she had endured to ensure her future, the years she had suffered Franklin's abuse and insults, might have come to naught. Worse than that, the unthinkable might have happened—she might have lost her precious little girl.

It had taken all the stubborn determination she could muster to hang on to her sanity and a scrap of pride while Franklin was alive, but maybe, she decided, it was time to let go of some of the iron will forged during those lost years and begin listening to sound advice.

But can I ever trust this man?

He was holding her too tight. She looked down at his arm around her waist. He was holding her too close for propriety or for her own peace of mind, but she was too exhausted to care. She gave in and leaned against him. In no time at all she was lulled into a calm she had not known for a long time, a calm that she tried to attribute to the even pace of the big horse and the man's warmth.

Her eyes kept closing. She was wet and tired and hungry. Her only halfway decent dress was filthy, she had lost her hat, and her hair was glued to her neck. All she wanted was to get comfortable, share the man's warmth and close her eyes, but that would mean further giving in to her weakness, and to him.

Duke rode close beside them, holding the sleeping child

in his arms as if he were used to carrying such a burden around with him all day long. The young Hawaiian seemed to know that she did not want Hadley out of her sight, and she would be forever grateful for his understanding. Riding in silence most of the way, they followed the road through the wide, mist-shrouded valley.

"Where are we going?" she roused herself enough to ask.

For a moment she thought that Spence had not heard, but then he said, "Duke told me there is a bed-and-board down by the beach."

"I can't go to a hotel looking like this—" She reached up and touched her hair. Her fingers came away filthy with mud, but she knew there was no alternative. She must get Hadley out of the rain and get both of them cleaned up. It would be hard enough to meet someone if she were looking her best, but right now she would rather crawl under a rock. A trunkful of butterflies had taken up residence in her mid-section.

She had not mingled in polite society for years, but now she was about to do so—covered in mud and escorted by her husband's illegitimate son.

Seven

ANA ABSENTLY GLANCED OUT the window as she passed through the sitting room at Marion Randolph's bed-and-board. At first she thought the two riders she saw outside were apparitions, so ghostly did they appear when viewed through the delicate lace curtain and the gently falling rain. As they drew closer to the house, she knew they were real. She recognized one of them.

Duke Makakani was back.

She ran across the parlor and flung open the front door. Mist sifted in on the trades, featherlight, a cool, moist caress. She stood sheltered on the lanai as the two *paniolo* rode closer with a woman and a girl.

Duke Makakani still had the devil's own sparkle in his eyes. He had filled out. The planes of his face looked harder, stronger, more manly. She watched him smile in recognition and knew she was in for a heavy bit of teasing. He was even more handsome than she recalled, his smile wide and natural.

But no matter how handsome, he was still just Duke, Chuckie's best friend. Folks knew *paniolo* did not make much money and her mind was already made up—she wanted to marry a rich man—*haole* or Hawaiian, it didn't matter.

"What you doing here?" she called out as Duke and his companion—*hapa haole* by the looks of him—pulled rein at the hitching post.

Duke dismounted so smoothly that he did not even awaken the sleeping child in his arms. The man with him, a few years older and even taller than Duke, said something to the bedraggled *haole wahine* riding with him. The *hapa* dismounted first, then reached for the woman. Ana saw her hesitate before she let the *paniolo* put his hands on her and lower her to the ground.

"What are you doing here?" Duke asked Ana as he stepped onto the lanai.

"Where you get that *kaikamāhine*?" The little girl's clothing was so muddy, her face and hair so filthy, that Ana could not tell if she was Hawaiian or *haole*. Surely she wasn't Duke's.

"Somebody give to me. I come see if you like be one muddah." When he laughed at her shocked expression, Ana pursed her lips and rolled her eyes. Duke might look different, but he had not changed at all. She doubted he ever would. She had told Chuckie once that she thought God made Duke just to drive her crazy.

By now the other *paniolo* and the woman had reached the lanai. With her limp, stringy hair she looked like a wet cat that somebody had tried to drown as she stood fussing over the girl, who had awakened and was now standing on the lanai. The stern *hapa* man was studying the front of the boardinghouse with a preoccupied frown.

Duke took Ana by the arm and led her a few feet away. "These folks need stay here tonight." Duke nodded toward the woman and child. "Mrs. Bennett."

Ana was about to go inside and find Mrs. Randolph, but at Duke's words it dawned on her that the wet-as-a-cat woman was none other than the widow of *Franklin* Bennett. Everyone on the north end of the island had heard rumors about Franklin Bennett and what went on at Mauna Noe. She took another look at the widow.

"Hey—Ana." Duke waved his hand in front of her face. "Get Mrs. Randolph."

"*She* owns Mauna Noe now?" Envy snaked through Ana. She decided on the spot that she would make a far more impressive mistress of the huge cattle ranch than this woman would.

"Sort of, I t'ink. She get share wit' him." Duke nodded in the direction of the other *paniolo*. "He's Bennett's *keiki manuahi*, Spencer Laamea."

Ana gave the other man a long second look. He was as wet as the others, not as muddy. His eyes looked tired, but he was still handsome. He might be *hapa*—and a bastard— but he was "sort of" owner of Mauna Noe.

That was all she needed to hear.

"No need make eyes like *pipi* at him. He get plenty worry wit'out you make more," Duke warned.

She had always hated the way Duke seemed able to read her mind.

"I make cow eyes at anybody I want," Ana whispered to him. Spencer Laamea was beginning to look impatient. Forgetting Duke, she stepped up to the *hapa* and gave him her warmest, her most sincere smile. The same one she had practiced for hours. "I go get Mrs. Randolph for you."

Before she went inside, she ran her hand down her long hair, thankful that she had washed and rubbed it until it shone. She smiled brightly and boldly into Laamea's eyes. Then holding her head high and moving as regally as she imagined Queen Kapiolani might, she tried to glide, not walk, into the house. She could feel her hair swaying nicely around her hips with every step.

Ana could not resist a sly glance over her shoulder to see if Spencer Laamea was watching.

He wasn't. He was looking down at the muddy *haole* lady beside him.

• • •

MARION RANDOLPH, THE PROPRIETRESS of the bayside bed-and-board, came bustling into the sitting room. Elizabeth felt like a wet mud hen with her equally wet chick as she stood clutching Hadley's hand, trying not to drip on a colorful floral-print carpet runner.

Marion was thin, wiry, and in constant motion. The home she opened to visitors was decorated with an eclectic array of furnishings. Native-woven *lau hala* mats and shining wooden calabashes were displayed amid a gathering of rococo chairs. A Boston rocker sat invitingly near a window, and beside it an open scrapbook graced a marble-topped table. Lace curtains softened the room. A lamp with a pitted silver base and a glass shade adorned with painted roses lit a dark corner.

"Oh, my." Mrs. Randolph quickly took in Elizabeth's sorry state after introducing herself and Ana, who had gone to fetch her. "What in the world happened to you, ducks?"

There was no getting around the truth.

"We tried to come down the road in a buggy, but it was too slippery. We tipped over." Elizabeth expected censure, but instead Marion started clucking over them. She put her hand on Hadley's shoulder and, unmindful of the mud, led them straight through the sitting room to the kitchen.

"Follow me," she trilled. "Heaven knows, I like nothing better than a challenge. You poor dears. We'll have you right again in no time at all."

"I'm afraid we didn't bring a change of clothes," Elizabeth admitted softly. "I didn't think—"

"Oh, posh! I have plenty of things lying around here. Bound to find something to fit you and even the girl. Ana, put some more water on to boil. We're going to need a lot of it. Then run upstairs and dig through that old trunk of clothes and see if there is anything in there suitable for these ladies." She put her hand beneath Hadley's chin, turned her face up to inspect it closely. "What's your name, dear?"

"Hadley Elyson Bennett. My papa was Franklin Bennett and I live at Mauna Noe."

Elizabeth was pleased that despite Hadley's sheltered existence, she wasn't the least bit shy or standoffish.

"My condolences on your husband's death, Mrs. Bennett," Marion Randolph said, as she dove into a huge pantry and began tugging a large wooden washtub out by its rope handles.

Elizabeth tried to help, but the woman brushed her off. "I'm from New Zealand, Mrs. Bennett. We women take pride in doing heavy work. Keeps one fit, you know."

From the looks of Marion's slim build, Elizabeth did not doubt it. The heavy tub thudded and bumped across the floor until it was placed just so. The room was overly warm from the stove, the air close and humid, but having been chilled to the bone earlier, Elizabeth did not mind the heat. Hadley had slumped down on a chair, resting her head against the table.

While her hostess bustled back and forth, testing the boiling water, setting out cold beef, tomatoes, and bread, and seeming to be everywhere at once, Elizabeth stayed out of the way and wondered how much she would have to pay for bed and board.

"Your husband's death was very sudden. I guess that was a blessing, wasn't it, Mrs. Bennett?" Marion Randolph peered at her over the top of her slim rectangular eyeglasses.

"Please, call me Elizabeth," she said, shifting uncomfortably. "Yes, it was."

While the Hawaiian girl, Ana, came into the room carrying a mound of clothing in her arms, Marion took a huge kettle of steaming water, held it over the tub, and added it to rainwater that she had carried in from the tank outside the back door.

"Esther Timmons stayed here after she left your place." Mrs. Randolph hefted another bucket, dumped rainwater into the tub, and stood back. "Looks like enough for the little girl. Get yourself out of those clothes,'' she told Hadley, who slowly roused herself and obeyed without question.

Elizabeth helped her unbutton her dress, wondering what Esther Timmons might have said. She did not have to wonder long.

''She claims you fired her.'' Marion had her back to the room as she added more wood to the stove.

Elizabeth stiffened. She would make no excuses for herself. ''I did.''

Marion closed the oven door, straightened, and turned around.

''Good on you, then. That old biddy was a hateful thing. Stayed here three days waiting for the steamer and by the end of the first hour I was fed up with her. I don't know why you didn't let her go sooner.'' Marion's openly conspiratorial attitude was heartening. ''Years ago it was rumored she had set her cap for Franklin Bennett. I'm sure when he sent for you it must have upset her.''

She had set her cap for Franklin . . .

The simple statement ignited blinding insight. No wonder Esther Timmons had been so vindictive, so spiteful toward her. And no wonder she left without argument after Franklin died. If she had cared for him, her reason for staying on was gone.

Elizabeth kept her own counsel as she helped Hadley into the tub. Naked, her daughter looked even smaller and more frail.

Marion sat down at the table with a cup of tea while Elizabeth knelt on the floor beside the tub and bathed Hadley with a soft cloth and a bar of scented soap.

''I remember the day you arrived on Kaua'i,'' Marion said, smiling down at Elizabeth. ''You looked like you wouldn't last out the week. The long voyage certainly had not agreed with you.''

Elizabeth soaped the cloth and slid it across Hadley's bare shoulders and back without comment. It was not the voyage that had not agreed with her. She had been very weak when she left Maryland, barely recovered from a brush with death. The train trip across country and the voyage from San Francisco had not been easy. Only her stubborn will to survive and the chance to begin again kept her going.

"I'm sorry I don't remember meeting you," Elizabeth apologized. Everything had been so new—so exotic, and so different from Maryland. Franklin standing there, stern and commanding in a white suit and straw hat, looking far older than she had imagined. The minister waiting nearby to perform the ceremony.

"I was down at the landing, waiting for a shipment from Honolulu—some fabric, bottles of wine, a few other trinkets—and there you were. The whole valley knew, of course, that Franklin Bennett had sent away for a wife. He had let it be known that she was from missionary people. That his bride-to-be was from one of the eastern states."

Elizabeth colored and hid her burning cheeks as she reached down into the water and pulled up Hadley's foot to wash between her toes. The child was still listless, idly running the water through her hands, watching it trickle between her fingers. Thankfully, the wheezing had subsided.

Marion Randolph talked a steady stream, asking no questions. Elizabeth found that she liked the woman, appreciated her constant banter, for it gave her time to adjust to having the companionship of someone other than Uilani.

Marion's hired girl, Ana, seemed preoccupied and hardly spoke a word until she asked to be excused. When Marion agreed, the girl bid them good-bye and hurried away. Elizabeth thought that Maile would one day grow up to be as beautiful as Ana Pualoa.

"She's a natural seamstress," Marion told Elizabeth as she poured herself another cup of strong black tea and added a dash of fresh cream. "Lives on her family's land, the *kuleana* up the road."

"There you go, Hadley," Elizabeth said, helping her stand up in the now tepid water. "All done."

Marion handed her a towel, which she wrapped around Hadley before lifting her out of the tub.

"You're lucky that Franklin owned the rights to Mauna Noe."

When Elizabeth looked quickly over at her, Marion added, "Oh, it's no secret, ducks, that the old man left the place in trust for the girl with you and his son."

"How do you know that?" The will had been read only a little over two weeks ago. Elizabeth knelt where she was on the damp wooden floor beside the washtub as she dried Hadley's hair. The girl had all but disappeared within the huge towel.

"The coconut wireless is faster than a telegraph." Marion laughed. "Your housekeeper no doubt told a fish peddler or a passing *paniolo*, who carried the news to the next holding, where—while talking story to a plantation worker—someone might have passed the news on to the ferryboat pilot and then on to Hanalei town. This is an island, remember. It doesn't take all that long for news to spread. Especially when there isn't usually much of anything happening. Everyday occurrences become big news."

Marion began shuffling through the pile of clothes. "These were my daughter's things. Pamela went off to school on the mainland two years ago. I'm sure something here will fit Hadley."

"How long have you been widowed?" Elizabeth asked.

Marion paused and straightened up. "Why, I'm not a widow. It's no secret that I was never married. I came here years ago, already had Pamela." She lowered her voice to a whisper so Hadley could not hear. "You see, I was not married when I found myself in the family way, but I refused to give up my child. I came to Hawai'i to start a new life, but I was not about to hide my past. I think when you hide a secret like that, someone is bound to find out about it, and then the whole package blows up in your face. It's better to have it all out in the open.''

Elizabeth thought of her own life as a deep, dark armoire stuffed full of secrets. Lately she had been feeling that they were about to tumble out all over the place.

She admired Marion Randolph for doing what she had once wished she had the strength to do herself. She often thought that if she had stayed in the States, perhaps moved to another city, she could have raised her child alone.

But she had been young and frightened, with no way to support herself or the babe. And had she chosen that path, she would not have Hadley now.

''Do you own this place, Marion?'' Elizabeth was intrigued by this independent woman, the likes of which she had never met.

''My family was well-off and gave me plenty of money to leave New Zealand. They were more than happy to send me off to start over as far away from them as possible. I came here, bought this place. I've been here ever since, added on guest rooms over the years. I miss my Pamela, though. She doesn't get much chance to write, what with her studies and all.''

Elizabeth watched while Marion selected some items and then decided they needed to be aired and freshened up.

''You don't mind wearing the towel a bit longer, do you, ducks?'' She tweaked Hadley's ear gently. ''I'll just pop these out to the lanai for a breather. They smell a bit musty from the trunk.''

Elizabeth's anxiety had built to the point that it could not be denied. ''Mrs. Randolph—''

''Marion, dear.''

''Marion.'' Elizabeth cleared her throat and began again. ''Marion, I don't know what you charge your guests, but—''

''Don't worry, Elizabeth. I'm used to taking chickens in payment whenever I help someone out around here. Chickens, bananas, coconuts—all work as well as currency.''

''I intend to pay, it's just that Mr. Laamea, Spencer . . .

Franklin's—'' It was all so very embarrassing. ''You see, we came to town to sell off some cattle, and by tomorrow we should have funds—''

''Stop.'' Marion held up her hand. ''I don't talk money in the kitchen or in front of children. Two very strict rules here. Don't worry your pretty head over it.''

''I can't accept your charity, Mrs. Randolph.''

''Marion.''

''Marion. I don't want to inconvenience you, either.''

''You'll pay me when you get the money, won't you, dear?''

''Of course.''

''Then, please, let me take that little girl up to bed before she falls asleep right here in the middle of the kitchen. After the tub is refilled, you can take a bath and relax.''

WITH THE DAWN, THE valley that Elizabeth had seen first as a gray miasma became paradise. She awoke to sunshine streaking across her pillow, a gentle, joyful call to start the day. Hadley, still asleep and curled up beside her, had passed a quiet night after they had both been cosseted and coddled by Marion Randolph.

Having lived on Kaua'i for nearly twenty years, the woman peppered her speech with Hawaiian words and phrases. A steady stream of Hawaiian neighbors came and went, from fishermen to farmers and their wives. They stopped by over the course of the evening just to ''talk story'' with Marion and her guests. Despite her past, it seemed that Mrs. Randolph was well loved and respected— at least by the Hawaiian community.

Anxious to find Spence this morning, Elizabeth woke Hadley. She was relieved to see that the child showed no lingering sign of yesterday's trauma other than insisting on relating the entire episode of the buggy crashing downhill— in glorious detail and pantomime—to a rapt audience of Mrs. Randolph and two botanists from New York who were traveling the islands to study the native flora.

It amazed Elizabeth that Hadley felt perfectly comfortable holding court. Thankfully, the audience was far too polite to ask what in the world Elizabeth had been thinking when she brought her daughter down the trail in the rain.

Wearing a borrowed yellow muslin dress that was a bit snug in the bodice, Elizabeth excused herself and Hadley after a delicious breakfast of apple sausage and fried taro and went to find Spence and the others. Before he left her yesterday afternoon, he had said they would be loading the cattle aboard the ship this morning if weather and surf permitted.

As she walked along the bay hand in hand with Hadley, she could not help but marvel at the grandeur of the three mountains that seemed to rise out of nowhere behind Hanalei.

Purple mist hid in the creases and folds of the mountains' upper reaches as cloud shadows played tag over their faces. Far up the valley a rainbow shimmered and then faded into sunshine. On the bay, the steamer *Kilauea* and other smaller craft bobbed at anchor. Birdsong filled the air.

The hypnotic lull of the sea caressing the shore echoed in Elizabeth's heart as they strolled through the soft sand. For the first time in many, many years, she felt something gentle stirring inside her and knew a sense of peace that she had not thought to experience again.

At the end of the beach near the river's mouth, she spotted Spence on horseback beside an empty cattle pen. Her newfound tranquillity evaporated as quickly as the morning's first rainbow. He stood out from the others, more commanding, the obvious leader of the group. Toshi and Melvin, along with a few other Hawaiian riders she did not recognize, were mounted on cow ponies, each holding a long braided lariat tied around a struggling cow. They dragged the animal through the surf line, headed toward a dory manned by three more workers. Four head of cattle had already been hauled out to sea and were secured around the neck, hanging on opposite sides of the smaller boat.

They bawled in terror, their eyes wide and rolling, their heads tied above the water.

Spence shouted commands in Hawaiian and pidgin while the men whistled and hollered at the terrified cow.

"Mama, lookit!" Hadley let go of her hand and started running down the beach.

"Hadley, don't run!"

At the sound of her voice, Spence looked down the strand but offered no greeting. When Hadley continued running down the beach toward the men, Elizabeth gathered up the skirt of her borrowed dress and ran after her. The little girl moved with a speed that surprised her. Finally, Elizabeth, with her carefully combed hair falling around her shoulders, breathlessly caught up with her daughter and planted a hand on her shoulder.

"Hadley, did you hear me calling you?"

Hadley turned to her mother, her bright eyes guileless. "I just wanted to see the cow swim, Mama."

Swimming, terrified cows were the last thing Elizabeth wanted to see up close. One longboat had already pulled up beside the ship. Above it, a furiously bawling cow in a sling was being hoisted out of the water. Deckhands waited aboard ship to grab the lines.

With scarecrow-thin shoulders and a shirt so big on him that it billowed in the breeze, Toshi looked older and more frail than any of the other *paniolo*, but he and his horse were both in the water, swimming beside the last reluctant cow as it was dragged to the dory. Melvin was on the shoreline, holding the other end of the line taut, laughing. Duke was in the longboat directing the men aboard the steamer.

Elizabeth tried to contain Hadley, who was watching the unfolding drama and inching closer to the tide line. The cattle bawled in a chorus of anguish and panic, while the men called out to one another in words she did not understand, but the meanings were clear.

"Do not think you are allowed to get your feet wet, Hadley Bennett," she warned, raising her voice in order to make herself heard. Hadley took a step closer to the water, nudging her foot toward the foam.

"Aw, Mama."

"We were wet enough yesterday to last a month of Sundays. Don't forget, you are wearing borrowed clothes."

"They itch, too."

Elizabeth started with surprise when Spence spoke from directly behind her, where he stood holding the reins to his horse.

"She's probably hot in that wool," he said.

Hadley turned on him immediately. "I am *not* hot. You don't know anything about it."

Elizabeth was appalled. "Hadley Bennett, apologize to Mr. Laamea at once."

"I don't like him, Mama. He thinks he's the boss of the *paniolo* now, but he's not, is he? My papa was the real boss of them."

Elizabeth's heart went out to Hadley, but she refused to let her get away with rudeness. "Mr. Laamea is helping us because Papa is no longer here. You will apologize, Hadley, and from now on mind your manners."

Hadley hung her head and dug the toe of her shoe in the sand. "I'm sorry," she mumbled.

"That's not quite good enough." Elizabeth glanced at Spence. He was concentrating on the men in the bay, not Hadley.

The girl looked up at Spence. "I'm sorry," she yelled.

Elizabeth felt Spence staring. "I'm sure Mr. Laamea heard you that time."

"Why does she remind me so much of you?" he asked.

Elizabeth saw that Spence was actually smiling. She stood there in awe. When he was not scowling, he was one of the most handsome men she had ever seen. It was the first time he had looked at her with something other than annoyance in his eyes, and she momentarily forgot the circumstances of their meeting and the animosity between them.

For an instant she found herself wishing that they were merely two people alone on a beach on a jewel of a day, a handsome young man with a winning smile and a young woman who longed to be carefree and happy and . . .

The elusive, seductive daydream was shattered when she realized that it was exactly that kind of romantic thinking that had gotten her into trouble with Johnny Huffington. She had learned the hard way that there had to be more to a relationship than daydreams and lust for a handsome man with a ready smile.

Down the beach, the encouraging shouts of the men suddenly turned into cries of distress. Without a word, Spence jumped into the saddle and raced Kāhili toward the ruckus. The horse's hooves threw sand and water as Spence rode directly to the guide ropes. He urged Kāhili into the foaming water and spurred him on, heading straight for Toshi.

The older *paniolo* had somehow slipped off his horse and become entangled in the lines. He was caught, thrashing around with the heavy cow beside him in the water. His shouts had turned to high-pitched, panicked cries. Duke was screaming curses and orders from the longboat. Elizabeth's heart leaped to her throat when she realized that her foreman was yelling about blood and she recognized the word *mano*—shark.

The sounds of Toshi's odd combination of Japanese and Hawaiian screams and the sight of Spence flinging off his hat and leaping out of the saddle made Elizabeth want to grab Hadley and run, but she was too mesmerized by the unfolding drama to move.

Duke stood in the longboat, his hand shielding his eyes from the water's glare as he watched for any sign of shark. The men aboard the steamer leaned over the side, shouting encouragement to Spence as he dove after Toshi, who had disappeared from sight.

"I think I should go swimming, too," Hadley announced.

Elizabeth had all but forgotten that Hadley was still beside her.

"You will *not* go swimming." Without taking her eyes off Spence or her hand off Hadley's arm, she tried to soften the reactionary harshness of her tone. "You don't know how to swim."

"I'll bet I could swim if I had a horse to ride in water. Does it hurt the cows to ride in the swing? Do people ever ride in the swing?"

Elizabeth concentrated on the surface of the water where Spence had disappeared a moment before. She might not like being forced to deal with the man, but she certainly did not wish him dead.

"How come everybody's so mad?"

"They aren't mad." *Where is Spence? Why doesn't he surface?*

"They're all yelling, Mama."

"That doesn't mean they're mad." *How could someone stay under this long and survive?*

"When Papa yelled he was mad. Very mad. Remember, Mama, how Papa would yell and yell and you told me that when I heard him yelling I should stay in my room?"

Elizabeth finally dared to breathe again when Spence broke the surface of the shimmering water at last. His shirt was plastered to his skin, the muscles in his shoulders bunched as he pulled Toshi, head and shoulders, out of the water. A jagged cut across Toshi's forehead streaked his face red on one side.

"Mama, look! Mr. Laamea just caught Mr. Toshi like a fish." A moment later Hadley whispered, "Mr. Toshi's bleeding."

"I'm sure he'll be fine," Elizabeth said, hoping it was true.

Caught up in the moment, she grabbed Hadley by the hand and walking as quickly as she could, hurried toward the empty cattle pen and the other *paniolo*, who were milling around.

When Elizabeth realized Spence was dragging the wounded man through the water, trailing him like bait in his wake, she offered up a silent prayer for their safety. But as Spence cut through the water with sure, strong strokes, she slowly relaxed. One of the Hanalei men urged his horse out into the shallows and reached for Toshi. He carried him to the beach, dismounted, and laid him on the sand.

Without his burden, six long strokes brought Spence to the shore. His hair had come loose. When he finally reached the shore and stood up, it rippled in dark, thick waves around his shoulders. As he emerged from the water with his striped shirt plastered to his skin, his soaking-wet pants and knee-high gaiters, he was a striking combination of two worlds, two cultures.

Elizabeth watched him go down on one knee in the sand. He turned Toshi's head and with gently probing fingers inspected the wound, a gash along the hairline.

"Go get my saddlebags." Spence looked up at her expectantly.

"Me?" She looked down at Hadley, leaning against her thigh, her usually smooth brow marred with concern for the old *paniolo*.

"The girl will be all right," Spence told her, indicating Hadley with a nod. "I'll keep an eye on her."

"There are sharks—"

He shook his head impatiently. "Not here on the beach. I'll watch her. Go."

Toshi moaned. Elizabeth looked around. The other men were all busy trying to untangle the cow and quickly load the other animals aboard the ship. There was no one else to do Spence's bidding.

"Hadley, dear—" She was about to issue her own warning to the girl when Spence whipped around and looked at Hadley.

"Stand right there and don't you so much as wriggle," he ordered.

The girl instantly stiffened straight as the ironwood pines near the shoreline, but she did not budge. "You are *not* my papa."

Elizabeth gathered up her skirts and ran over to Spence's horse. The muscles in her legs screamed as the heels of her shoes sank into the soft sand. Finally she reached the big animal and slowed to approach it gingerly. Her father gave her her first pony when she was six, but up close, because of his size, *Kāhili* was almost as intimidating as Spence. She took a deep breath, then reached up and untied the saddlebags. The horse's withers quivered just before he swished his tail. Laamea's leather saddlebags were well worn, with a beautiful pattern of leaves, stars, and crescents stamped around the edges, like a flower *lei*.

She hurried back. Hadley had not moved. She was watching Spence closely, fascinated.

Toshi was conscious but dazed. Spence had him sitting up and had stripped off his own shirt to hold it against the old man's wound. Elizabeth decided that in his half-naked state, Spence was more intimidating than ever. His skin was smooth and dark, stretched over well-defined chest and shoulder muscles. When he looked up and caught her staring at him, she felt the blood rush to her cheeks. She thrust out the saddlebags.

''Hold this,'' he directed, urging her to take hold of the makeshift bandage.

The only way she could help was to kneel in the sand beside him. Their hands met as their fingers came together on the bandage. Spence glanced over at her, their gazes touched, then he quickly looked away. Elizabeth tried to focus her attention on Toshi, on the bloody shirt, on anything but Spence Laamea's exposed pectorals.

Aunt Sophie would have fainted dead away.

Beside her, Spence opened a saddlebag. Elizabeth watched as he sifted through an assortment of small bundles tightly wrapped in *tapa* cloth. He opened one of them and carefully sifted out what appeared to be ash. He closed his eyes for a moment.

She could feel him drawing inward, shutting out everyone on the beach, the men and animals creating a commotion behind them. He opened his eyes, put the ash on his fingertips, and rubbed it into Toshi's wound. Rewrapping the bundle, Spence quickly put it back in the saddlebag and untied another. Like the first, it also contained ashes. These he rubbed atop the others, mixing them.

"What are you doing?" Hadley wanted to know.

Spence, concentrating on Toshi, let the question go unanswered. Finally he looked up at Hadley, who was standing so close to him that she was practically leaning against his shoulder.

"I put a mixture of ashes of *'awapuhi* and small-leaf bamboo on his cut."

"Why?" The child persisted.

"It will make him better."

"How do *you* know?"

"My grandfather was a *kahuna,* that's a very wise man, like a doctor. He called his work *la'au lapa'au.* He cured people by using things he found growing on the land. He taught me how to gather and use healing plants when I was a boy."

"When you were little like me?" Hadley piped up.

Spence did not look at her. "Yeah. When I was little like you."

Suddenly Elizabeth could not concentrate. Her ears were ringing. The world around her began to shrink into a long, thin tunnel. Uncle Joseph's face swam before her eyes, and his voice came back to her over the sound of the surf and the bawling cattle, as if she had just heard it yesterday. She wanted to run but could not move. She saw him reach out to her, offer her a cup of steaming herbal tea. She tried to turn away from his arthritic, misshapen joints, the yellowed fingernails on his pale, tapered hands.

"Drink this, Elizabeth. It will take away the morning sickness. After today you won't be bothered with the illness anymore."

"What is it, Uncle?"

Her aunt Sophie's voice intruded, harsh, more cunning

*than she had ever realized. "It's nothing but a bit of herbal
tea, child. Something to settle your stomach. Drink it."*

Their strict principle and unbending wills had been impressed upon her since the day they became her guardians.
After her affair with Johnny Huffington, she had become
an embarrassment, a sin-tainted pariah living under their
roof.

*"Drink this," her uncle said again. "You'll feel better
in no time at all."*

She trusted Uncle Joseph with the same innocent trust
that had gotten her with child. She reached for the cup of
herbal tea. Uncle Joseph left an entire pot of it beside her
bed, and as he directed, she sipped it until it was gone.

A few horrific, agonizing hours later, so was her unborn
child.

"Elizabeth?"

Alarmed when the color drained from her face, Spence
took her by the shoulders. "Elizabeth, are you all right?"

She inhaled with a startled gasp as if surfacing from deep
water. She blinked a few times and looked around, disoriented.

"I don't need two of you passed out on the sand," he
told her.

The concern in his voice belied his frown. She was surprised to discover that his hands had such a gentle, caring
touch.

"I'm fine, I was just . . ." She couldn't tell him she had
just relived one of the most terrible events of her past, one
that had set her life on a downward spiral. "It must be the
sun."

Spence heard the evasion. Passing clouds fanned out to
obscure the sun. The trade winds bathed them with a re-
freshing breeze that lifted her sunlight-blond hair and set it
teasing about her pale throat. The heat was certainly not
the reason for her distress, nor was it the reason he felt hot.
He let go of her, turned his attention to the old *paniolo*.

"Toshi will be all right." He tried to forget the feel of her beneath his hands. "The cut has stopped bleeding."

HE USES HERBS TO cure.

Elizabeth watched Spence help Toshi to his feet. Hadley stayed close beside him. Moved by a need to protect, Elizabeth quickly stepped over and reached for Hadley's hand.

Shaken more by the flash of memory than the events of the morning, she watched Spence help Toshi over to the shade beneath a *kamani* tree.

"Mama, you're squeezing my hand too hard." Hadley squirmed and tried to withdraw.

"I'm sorry," she said, releasing her just enough to appease, too afraid to let go entirely. In the blink of an eye, Spence Laamea had just introduced another threat into their lives.

Elizabeth had lost her innocence, her trust, her unborn child another lifetime ago in Baltimore. She knew better than most that herbs could kill as well as cure.

And Spence Laamea had the knowledge to use them.

Eight

AT LEAST THE GRASSY lawn beside the bed-and-board was cool and shaded. Ana had spent half the morning sitting there, watching the beach road and waiting for a chance to talk to the handsome *hapa* who, according to Duke, had "sort of" inherited Mauna Noe.

She had not seen Spencer since yesterday when he left the *haole* and her girl with Mrs. Randolph and rode off with Duke to get Chuckie and some of the other men to help bring cattle across the river.

Yesterday Duke told her that Spence Laamea planned to leave town as soon as the cattle were loaded on the steamer. She had to see Laamea one more time, long enough to make one good impression before he got away.

Ana reached up, smoothed her long hair, and concentrated on staying cool. Her striped *holokū* was still clean and barely wrinkled. The plumeria blossoms pinned above her ear gave off a heady, pleasing scent that swirled around her each time the trade winds tickled them. That morning she practiced smiling so much at her reflection in the water of the shimmering *kalo* patch that her cheeks ached.

There was no way Spencer Laamea could resist her charm.

Ana kept her gaze on the road and her sights aimed high. She had never seen the ranch at Mauna Noe—had never been out of the valley—but it was not hard to imagine a house twice the size of the bed-and-board. It was no trick to picture herself as the mistress of such a grand place, either. She imagined opening the front door, welcoming the neighbors in. Of course all the local ladies would come to tea. She would plan gala picnics, outings, and excursions to the beach, just the way Mrs. Randolph did for her visitors.

In the evenings, when they were home, she and Spencer would sit on the lanai and make plans. They would leave Duke in charge while they took grand voyages, sailing away to every part of the world for a year and a day, coming back to Mauna Noe whenever Spencer needed to sell off more cattle to make more money. Money that he would use to buy her beautiful clothes and jewels and fine horses.

Ana sighed. Her dream was so wonderful it made her heart hurt, not to mention the satisfaction it gave her to imagine leaving Duke behind, slaving away on her behalf.

"What you doing, Ana?"

She nearly jumped out of her skin when the sound of Duke's voice shattered her pleasant fantasy. She stood up, shook out her dress, and glared at him.

"Go 'way, Duke. I mean it. You going ruin everything."

"Why you hiding like a *mo'o* in the grass waiting for one big juicy bug?"

"I not hiding." Where did he come from? Calling her a lizard. Setting her teeth on edge.

She wanted to grab her hair and shout in frustration when she saw Spencer Laamea finally coming up the beach road leading a fine gray mare behind him.

"Leave me alone, Duke. Get away. Go boddah somebody else." She waved her hands as if she were trying to shoo away a fly.

Spencer had almost reached the house. Ana took a deep breath and brushed a blade of grass off her skirt.

Duke followed the direction of her gaze, and a slow, very irritating, very knowing smile spread across his face.

"So," he said.

"So what, Duke?"

"So no use you t'rowing yourself at Laamea. He get more trouble den can handle. No need you make more."

"I not planning make *pilikia* for him. I planning make him happy." She looked down her nose at Duke. "*Very* happy."

He had the nerve to laugh in her face.

Ana turned her back and marched away, trying to calm down before she reached the rich *hapa haole* rancher. He dismounted just as she came around the side of the house.

"Aloha!" she gaily called out, hurrying across the yard to the hitching posts. "You going home soon?"

She knew that he was leaving as soon as he collected the widow and her daughter. She had heard as much and more while she helped Mrs. Randolph iron the *haole* woman's shoddy gown and the little girl's clothes this morning. She had been at work on them when Elizabeth Bennett and her daughter returned to the house with one of the Mauna Noe *paniolo* who had cut his head on a cow.

While Mrs. Reynolds bandaged up the old cowhand and then conversed with the Bennett woman over tea, Ana had listened intently, hanging on the widow's every perfectly spoken word.

"No, Hadley and I will not be staying another night. Yes, I would appreciate some food to take along on the journey. Mr. Laamea will settle the account as soon as he comes back to get us."

Now Spence was here, and all Ana could do was stand staring up at him. For the life of her she could not think of one thing to say—so she chose the thing foremost on her mind.

"You need one wife."

"What did you say?" He looked down at her as if she were nothing more than a pesky mosquito.

"Wife." She remembered to smile directly into his eyes. "You need wife. Sunday the minister say a man need get good wife, she help fight temptation of the fleshes."

She had his complete attention now. Her confidence mounted. Now she was getting somewhere.

"The temptation of the fleshes?" He could not take his eyes off her.

Ana was more than pleased. He seemed *very* interested, not to mention the fact that he was staring at her as if he had never seen anyone like her before—which was exactly what she wanted him to think. She would have to be extraordinary to catch a rich *hapa haole* rancher like him.

She tossed her long hair. "You don't want suffer sins of fleshes by get tempted, do you? Not very good t'ing at all. I t'ink one good wife keep dem from coming tempted."

"Keep *what* from getting tempted?"

"The fleshes."

He made a choking sound. Scanned the yard, then stared at the bed-and-board so hard that Ana looked over her shoulder to see what he was interested in.

The *haole* woman was standing there, framed in the doorway. She had changed out of Mrs. Randolph's borrowed dress and was once again wearing the terrible one she had showed up in. Her skin was pale like a fish belly, but Spencer was staring at her anyway.

"Are you supposed to be out alone?" He spoke to Ana without even looking away from the Bennett woman.

"I work for Mrs. Randolph. Not all the time. I come and go."

"I see." He tied the reins to the hitching post and started to walk away.

Ana remembered her dream, her big ranch house, voyaging around the world like King Kalakaua, the priceless jewelry.

"Wait!" she cried out and grabbed his arm before the dream ebbed away.

He stopped dead in his tracks and turned around.

"So? You like take me back wit' you to Mauna Noe?"

Spence shook his head. His eyes cut over to the front door and back to her again. "You know what? I get plenty trouble already."

DUKE WAITED UNTIL SPENCE walked away and Ana stood forlorn at the hitching post before he left the shadows of the house and joined her.

"So, you try catch one *beeg* fish, eh? Looks like you get one hole in net, Ana."

"Shut up, Duke." She did not take her eyes off the other man until he disappeared inside the house.

"Maybe you bettah run back to the *kalo* patch, not get mixed up with *hapa* an' *haole* around here. You not going end up with anybody but me."

She whirled around so fast that her long, shining black hair flared like a cape. "You *pupule*, Duke. Crazy. You been in da sun too long. You the last man I t'ink of marry." She laughed, but there was a nervous sound to it. "Why you talk like dat, anyhow?"

He shrugged. He knew she did not stand a chance with Spence Laamea. She was meant to be his since forever, but she was hardheaded and he did not want to see her get hurt.

To his way of thinking, he had to put a stop to the nonsense right away.

"You never going marry Laamea. You gonna marry me," he told her.

She folded her arms beneath her breasts. He caught himself staring down at the bodice of her dress, remembering her swimming naked in the pool beneath Kalihiwai Falls. They had been older than children but not yet adults the last time they swam together in the pool beneath the chilly waterfall. He felt himself quicken just thinking about the way she had looked, her satin skin shimmering with beads of water and her black hair slick and damp, shining almost blue in the sunlight. A rainbow had appeared on the mist kicked up by churning froth. She had laughed, tried to dive through it.

Ana was and always would be his.

Seeing what a beauty she had become, Duke suddenly realized he could not risk waiting very long for her to come to her senses. He glanced over his shoulder at the house. There was no one in sight. He reached for her before she could protest, grabbed her shoulders, and pulled her close against him.

"What you do—?" Her question became a muffled squeal when he covered her mouth with his and began kissing her. She squirmed, balled her hands into fists, and beat them against his chest. When that did not work, she started kicking him in the shins with her bare feet.

She was not strong enough to hurt him. He traced his tougue against her lips until she opened for him. Her mouth, soft and warm, tasted like the sweetest *liliko'i*, the passion fruit. Finally, after he had kissed her long and thoroughly, after she had settled into the rhythm and pulse of his exploration and seemed to be enjoying herself and kissing him back, Duke abruptly let her go.

"See? You and me. That's the way it going be, Ana."

She blinked in surprise. Then she pulled back her arm and let fly with an uppercut to the jaw.

As the sunlight burst and faded and he began to see stars whirling in his vision, he wished he had not been the one who taught her to fight.

INSIDE THE BED-AND-BOARD, Elizabeth stood back as Spence crossed Marion Randolph's crowded sitting room.

"I hope you haven't been waiting long," she said, taking a step back. She had a habit of standing more than an arm's length away from anyone.

"I just got here," he told her.

She had seen him out front, talking to Marion's hired

girl. They made a striking Hawaiian couple, standing there against the backdrop of Hanalei Bay, so much so that Elizabeth found herself wondering for the first time if there was a woman in his life, if he had left someone behind on O'ahu.

She had felt comfortable again, dressed in her freshly laundered gown rather than the restrictive one Marion had loaned her—until she saw the beautiful Hawaiian talking to Spence. Compared to the lovely young girl, she felt like a wilted *hau* blossom beside an orchid.

Spence looked out of place and uncomfortable in the room full of artfully arranged clutter. He asked after Toshi. She told him the *paniolo* was much better, occupying his time talking to Marion's Japanese cook.

She waited for him to say something else, but he fell silent. Strained seconds ticked by. Finally she asked, "How much money did we get for the cattle?"

"Money?"

"From the sale." When he looked like he had no idea what she was talking about, Elizabeth's mantle of calm began to unravel.

"No cash exchanged hands yet. I thought you realized that would be the case."

"How am I supposed to pay Marion?" She began to flush. How was she going to settle the account with Marion Randolph, who had done so much for her and Hadley—the laundry, the meals, warm baths, a bed for the night. Camaraderie without questions.

"You'll have to ask her to take credit."

She pointed in the direction of the river. "You just loaded our cattle onto a boat that already left the bay and you don't have a dollar to show for it?"

"Why don't we sit down, Elizabeth?"

She started to sit, caught herself, and stiffened. "I will *not* sit."

"Then excuse me if I do. I was up before dawn fighting those animals and I'm tired." He sat in the Boston rocker, stretched his long legs out and crossed them at the ankles. His bare toes and ankles were as brown as his sun-stained face. He had put on a clean shirt, although it was wrinkled and, like his pants, slightly damp and watermarked.

He actually did look exhausted when he leaned his head against the back of the rocker and closed his eyes. If he was trying to get her to feel sorry for him, his plan would not work. Every man she had ever trusted had either let her down, duped her, or abused her. She was not about to be deceived again.

She let him take the cattle off Mauna Noe, sure that he was only doing what had to be done. Now a portion of the stock was gone, and he claimed there was no cash to show for it. Not only was she filled with regret, but she felt an increasing panic.

"If you twist that piece of skirt any harder it's going to split in two. That cloth doesn't look like it can take much more."

She had not even realized she was clutching her skirt in her hands. She let go and the heavy material dropped back into place. Then she found he was watching her.

"What about the money?"

"You sure you don't want to sit down?"

She shook her head.

Spence shrugged. "I have never seen a more *pa'akikī* woman in my life. You have a head like a rock."

To prove him wrong, she sat down on a chair across the room.

"Well?" She crossed her arms, waiting for an explanation.

He sighed, stretched his arms out in front of him, then let his hands drop to his thighs. "Plantation owners and ranchers deal through agents in Honolulu. The agent sells the cattle and makes a commission off the sale." He was speaking slowly, explaining it all as if she were Hadley. "Franklin dealt with a firm named Jensen and Carlisle. Its agents extended Mauna Noe credit—loans for supplies and

equipment secured against the deed. They will sell the cattle
in Honolulu. I directed them to send us a bank draft for
any monies left from the sale—after they have deducted
their commission, shipping costs, a payment against what
is still owed them. And the cost of a Durham bull.''

''*A new bull?*''

''You don't need to shout, Elizabeth.''

''I'm not shouting.''

He did not argue. He simply leaned his head back, closed
his eyes again, and smiled, further infuriating her.

''You made that decision without even consulting me.''

''I didn't know you had expertise in stud bulls.'' He
looked her up and down. She wanted to pull one of the
drapes over her head. ''If I had, I certainly would have
discussed it with you.''

''You are insufferable.''

''And you have no choice but to put up with me.''

''I'd thank you not to keep reminding me.''

She didn't want to show Spence Laamea any sign of
weakness, but she was very, very tired of fighting an uphill
battle just for a little peace in her life.

Spence sat with his head back, eyes closed. The rocker
creaked against the floor, a slow, steady sound that matched
her heartbeat. Neither of them broke the silence. Elizabeth
folded her hands on her lap and stared out the window,
through the delicate lace curtains. Outside, the sound of
rustling palm fronds sang a duet with the shuffling banana
leaves.

They might have been a couple of long standing, without
a need for words during moments of quiet contemplation.
Elizabeth turned away from the view outside and studied
Spence.

He was asleep, his head rolled to one side. His full lips
were no longer set in the firm line that was slowly becoming so familiar. In sleep he became vulnerable. Younger.
Nonthreatening.

Elizabeth could not bring herself to look away. For the

first time since he had walked up to the lanai at Mauna Noe as a complete stranger, she saw him not as Franklin's bastard son but simply as a man.

Had he loved? Did he love someone now? If so, where was she? Certainly he had no commitments, no ties, or he would not have been able to stay without making arrangements on Oʻahu. If Spence had been conceived when Franklin arrived in Hawaiʻi, then he was around twenty-six years old. Her own age.

Over the past two days he had surprised her. He proved able to take command. Even Duke deferred to him. When Toshi was injured, Spence had not panicked. He did not let danger to himself stand in the way when he dove into the bay after the other man. His size and strength still frightened her—so did his knowledge of herbal medicines—but as yet he had given her no real reason to fear him. What terrors she faced came from her fears for Hadley, from her own mind. From her memories.

As she sat there staring at him—his hands, his bare toes, the hollow at the base of his throat that showed where his shirt collar gaped open—she used her eyes the way a blind man might use his hands, exploring him, reading him.

What kind of woman would he love?

Unbidden, unexpected, she felt something stir inside her, feelings she had not known in a decade. Something tempting and at the same time very, very dangerous awakened.

Suddenly, as if he felt her eyes on him, as if the dangerous trail of her thoughts and her riot of forbidden emotions had awakened him, Spence opened his eyes. Their gazes met and locked across the room. Not long—no longer than the flash of a whitecap on the crest of a wave—and yet the exchange was so intimate in its awesome silence and great depth that it left Elizabeth breathless and shaken.

"Well, I see you two found each other." Marion fluttered into the room.

Spence shifted in the chair, uncomfortable and disoriented. He made himself focus on Marion Randolph, on anything but the illicit, inexplicable thoughts he had just entertained about his father's widow. In a matter of seconds he had drifted into a deep sleep, lost himself in flashes of the ocean, the cattle, blood and mud, only to awaken and fall into Elizabeth's deep-blue eyes.

Since the day he had realized that Franklin Bennett was not ever going to come and claim him, Spence had never lied to himself again. He was not about to start now either, so he faced the truth of what had just happened. For that split second between full consciousness and sleep, when he opened his eyes and looked into Elizabeth's, as he hovered there on the edge of his dreams, his body had reacted, tightened, ached. And he knew.

He wanted her. His father's wife. A *haole* woman.

Even now that he was fully awake, fully aware of the world they inhabited with its layers and layers of taboos, the idea was still more seductive than it was abhorrent.

Marion Reynolds was going on and on about the way she polished old wood with alcohol, muriatic acid, linseed oil, and lemon. "But," she was saying, "lemons are hard to come by when there is too much rain. And isn't there *always* too much rain in Hanalei?"

Sunshine outside the window belied her words.

Spence looked over at Elizabeth again. She was watching Marion with an intent expression, but he sensed that she was not listening. As if she felt his eyes on her, she shifted her gaze momentarily, flicked it over to him, caught him watching. She looked away.

"Marion—" Elizabeth fidgeted once again with her skirt. Anything but look at him. "Mr. Laamea just informed me that we don't . . . that I can't . . ."

"Pay." Marion swiftly ended her misery.

Elizabeth nodded, her eyes too bright.

Spence stood up. "The agency will be sending us funds within the next few weeks. If you could extend credit for last night?"

"I have dealt with plantation owners and ranchers long

enough to know how things work around here. Besides, this is an island.'' She smiled at each of them. "I do know where you live.''

It wasn't until Marion laughed heartily at her own joke that Spence saw Elizabeth relax. She should have known how money was managed, how the agency system worked, but he was beginning to think that Franklin had kept her in a cocoon.

Spence started for the door. The room felt too small, too crowded to hold him. He was in his element outside, on horseback, or in the sea. He wanted out.

"Where's the girl?" He looked to Elizabeth, wondering if he could ever bring himself to call Franklin's other child by her name.

"Upstairs. Resting under protest. She was coughing a little so I made her quiet down.''

He could help the girl. He knew what was wrong with her, knew she had asthma. *Hano.* For some reason, Elizabeth pretended it was not so.

"She can ride back with Duke. I bought you a mare,'' he told her.

"You bought me a horse?"

"I didn't think you would want to walk back to Mauna Noe.''

Elizabeth gave him a tight smile. "I would like to talk to you outside. Will you please excuse us, Marion?''

"I'll go tell Hadley that you're ready to leave,'' Marion volunteered, hurrying out of the room.

Elizabeth led the way to the lanai, pausing just outside the door while Spence closed it gently behind him. She whirled on him before the latch finished clicking into place.

"Before you say one single word, think long and hard,'' he told her. "I'm not in the mood to listen to your harping.''

"*Harping?* I am *not* harping. Not only did you buy a . . . a bull, but a horse, too? We have to ask Marion for *credit* and you announce that you bought a *horse*?"

Horses were plentiful on Kauai. Chuckie had sold the mare to Spence for next to nothing. He paid cash, out of his own small stash of funds, planning to add the expense to the ranch accounts when they were solvent. But he was not going to make explanations to her on demand. If he started now it would never end.

"Elizabeth, this is never going to work if you fight me every step of the way."

"You should have consulted me before you ordered a new bull or bought that horse. You should have *explained* that there would be no money exchanged until after the sale in Honolulu."

"You should have stayed at the ranch," he fired back.

"I wanted to look out for Hadley's interests."

"By dragging her along in that broken-down buggy? Insisting on driving down the hill? Risking her neck?"

As soon as the words were spoken, he wanted to call them back. But it was too late. Her eyes already reflected her guilt.

It's better this way, he thought. Better to keep the animosity between them alive than to build a bridge that would lead to heartache. Better to live behind invisible walls as tall and strong as the lava rock foundations of the ancient *heiau*, Hawaiian temples, built centuries ago. Fortifications so sound that they still stood.

"I'll get Hadley ready," she said softly, not looking at him again.

"Fine. I'll get the others and meet you out front."

"Fine."

ELIZABETH WENT BACK INSIDE before he was off the lanai. She got as far as a low *koa* wood bench placed just inside the door before she sat down heavily, feeling shame to her marrow.

Outside she had experienced a sudden burst of clarity. She was no longer afraid that Spence Laamea would hit her. He did not have to. He fought with words, not blows, but they fell just as hard.

Mauna Noe

NIGHT INTENSIFIED ELIZABETH'S ANXIETY—gave it depth and breadth and a life of its own. Darkness nourished her fears until they grew into a nameless, faceless monster that fed upon past, present, and future nightmares.

She awoke in the middle of the night, her nightgown bunched around her thighs, her skin damp with perspiration. The trades had stopped. The air lay humid and as still as death over the land. Every worry surfaced in the dark as she lay staring up at the mosquito netting suspended from the ceiling.

She and Spence had not exchanged more than two words on the way back to Mauna Noe. He had ignored everyone. Duke carried Hadley. Toshi complained of a headache. Melvin stared at the horizon, lost in his own thoughts. Bedraggled and tired after the afternoon ride through the heat, they parted company without a word.

Now, lying in bed, she was plagued by doubts and questions.

Franklin had been living deep in debt, and she never even knew. How much longer would they have been able to go on had he lived? What would she and Spence do now if they could not borrow on his agency account? Would Franklin have given up the land? Would she soon have to?

The very idea made her sick.

While Franklin had forced her to live in isolation, her world had been crumbling. She had watched, unaware, unable to question him as one by one the *paniolo* had taken their families off the land and moved on, as one by one the workers' houses became vacant. As Franklin's little kingdom fell apart.

What could I have done?
Nothing.

What if the agent could not sell the cattle for enough money to cover everything? When could she pay Duke and Melvin, Toshi, Uilani, provide them with supplies or hire more hands?

How long would Laamea stay on if he could not get the place on its feet? If they made no money, the only way he could prosper was if Hadley were to die before she was eighteen and he inherited everything. After that, it would be too late. The land would belong to the Hawaiian monarchy again.

Elizabeth sat bolt upright, pressed her hands to her temples, and took a deep breath. She drew up her knees, locked her arms around them, and rocked slowly back and forth. A gathering of her favorite things filled the room, among them a white orchid that was blooming. The long stalk was an elegant, simple strand dotted with silken blossoms, chalk-white in the moonlight that poured through the window.

Without warning the stillness of the night was shattered by a sound that always filled her with dread. Suddenly all her dark thoughts about the ranch, the agency debt, Spence Laamea—all of it vanished. She threw back the twisted sheet and raced into Hadley's room.

The child's labored breathing echoed on the close night air. She found her daughter hunched over, a tiny ball in the middle of the bed shrouded by mosquito netting. Elizabeth's hands fumbled with the glass chimney atop the hurricane lamp. She reached for the matches on the high shelf near the table and prayed that the moisture in the air had not dampened the sulfur tips.

"Mama's here, Hadley. You'll be all right."

She spoke in as calm a tone as she could muster, fighting to calm her shaking hands so she could strike the match. After four frustrating attempts, the match finally sparked, then flared to life.

She almost cried out, so great was her relief. Cupping the flame, she lit the lamp, shook the match out, and then replaced the chimney. Every movement seemed to take hours. After setting the wick, she hurried to Hadley's bedside.

Her daughter's eyes were wide and wild as she sucked air in and then labored to expel it. Her shoulders were bowed inward as if she had shrunk inside herself. Elizabeth began to massage her back in slow, steady circles.

"Hadley? Hadley, listen to Mama. You have to breathe slowly. Remember what the doctor told you? Don't try to gulp air. Breathe in and out . . . slowly." *How could she breathe out slowly when she could barely breathe at all?*

Hadley struggled to exhale. The sound coming from her throat was raspy and ragged, worse than Elizabeth had ever heard it. She put her hand to Hadley's forehead, forced her to sit up. There was a slight bluish tinge around her baby's mouth.

The nearest doctor was miles away.

Oh, God. Oh, God, help me!

She bit her lip to keep from crying out. She had known that this day of retribution would come—the day when she would have to atone for her sin. God was taking her precious daughter to make her pay for the unborn child she had been unable to protect.

It wasn't my fault. It wasn't my doing. Uncle Joseph made the tea. Uncle Joseph and Aunt Sophie wanted the child dead.

Forgive me. Don't take her. Don't take Hadley.

She prayed frantically, silently, grabbed her girl up in her arms, held her, petted her, rocked her. She would breathe for her if she could, there was nothing she wouldn't do to save her daughter.

Terror gripped Elizabeth's heart in tight bands. One of the men would have to ride for the doctor, but she did not want to let go of Hadley long enough to run to the window and cry for help.

Two years ago, during just such a spell, Franklin had cursed a blue streak but nevertheless sent one of the men racing for help. By the time the doctor arrived, Hadley's attack had eased on its own. The doctor informed her, well out of Franklin's hearing, that there was nothing he could do that she had not already done—that she would just have to wait for the attacks to subside.

At the sound of bare feet slapping against the stairs she remembered with a wave of relief that they were not alone in the house.

"Mama," Hadley wheezed, clutching her hand. Frantic. She pleaded with her eyes, begged Elizabeth to do something. To save her.

Elizabeth felt her own tears, wet and hot. No consolation as they burned their way down her cheeks. When she looked up, Spence was standing in the open doorway. The lamplight gilded his bronze skin. His hair was loose, huge and wild, shimmering around his head in midnight waves. A stark white piece of fabric tied low on his hips covered him from waist to mid thigh. His leather saddlebags dangled from his right hand.

SPENCE STARED AT ELIZABETH as he crossed the room. Every mother's greatest fear ravaged her face. Her eyes, like those of the child in her arms, were wide blue pools of terror. Silver tears glistened on her cheeks. Her voluminous white lawn nightgown pooled around her.

He knew she was not thinking of anything but her child when she reached out to him, held out her hand crying, "I don't know what to do."

Spence went directly to her, took her hand, and squeezed it, saying without words, I am here. He went down on one knee beside the bed.

She let go of his hand, adjusted Hadley's weight, hiccupped down a sob. "I heard her and ran right in. I don't know how long she's been like this."

"May I?" He looked to her for permission before he

touched the girl. He half expected her to refuse.

When she nodded slowly, he knew it was because she had no choice.

Spence reached down, laid his hand on Hadley's chest, and closed his eyes. He was not a *kahuna la'au lapa'au* like his grandfather, nor even a trained apprentice. He knew he had to tread carefully here. All he knew he had learned when his grandfather had taken him along to gather healing plants—at the beach, up the valleys, high in the mountains.

His grandfather told Spence that he had been gifted with a natural talent for diagnosis and collecting, but that his *mana*, his power from the divine, would take him down another life path.

To try and treat the girl using the ancient way meant that he first had to appeal to the gods of his ancestors for help. Hunkered down beside the bed, he placed one hand lightly on Hadley's chest, closed his eyes, and whispered in Hawaiian, appealing to Ku, Kane, Kanaloa, and Lono—the *akua,* the old gods.

Elizabeth sat behind her daughter, propping her up, watching Spence intently as he drew within himself. Was he offering prayers in Hawaiian? She did not know, nor did she care, as long as it helped Hadley. Aunt Sophie and Uncle Joseph would have been horrified at such an appeal to pagan gods. His words had a cadence, soft and low and very soothing. She closed her eyes and offered a prayer of her own.

"Don't take her, Lord. You have my other child."

When she opened her eyes again, there was Uilani standing in the doorway, wringing her hands, watching Spence with a sort of reverence mingled with awe. Since Franklin's death Uilani had refused to come to the house late at night.

His prayer ended. He looked over at Uilani. "I'll need boiling water, a mortar and pestle. Some towels or maybe a sheet."

Uilani rushed off to do his bidding.

"She has asthma," Elizabeth said.

"*Hano* is the Hawaiian word for it."

"Franklin hated these bouts. He never came near Hadley when she had an attack. He hated weakness in any form." Elizabeth remembered Franklin hovering in the doorway, lingering in the hall, cursing. The memory was so clear that she could feel him out there now. Thankfully Franklin had found Hadley's illness so repulsive that he rarely touched the child. He feared that threatening her or physically harming her would bring on an attack, so he dealt with her by distancing himself.

He never directed his anger at Hadley—only his neglect.

Elizabeth looked down at Spence's hand, so strong, so large. It covered Hadley's chest. Spence gently massaged Hadley's shoulders and throat. He ran his hands down the girl's arms to her wrists.

"Keep rubbing her back," Spence told Elizabeth. His voice, so deep and low, had a calming effect on her as well as Hadley.

When Uilani came back with a wooden bowl of steaming water and a sheet folded over her arm, Spence took them from her and set them on the floor beside his knee. It wasn't until that moment that Elizabeth noticed a tattoo—hundreds of small, closely aligned black triangles that started at his waist just above his hip and disappeared beneath the fabric. Appearing again below the hem, the tattoo continued down the outside of his thigh to his knee.

He reached for the saddlebag on the floor beside him. When he opened it and began to sort through the bundles, Elizabeth felt a wave of apprehension.

"What are you doing?"

"Looking for eucalyptus bark."

"You will *not* give her anything."

"I'm going to put some bark in steaming water for her to inhale." He turned to the housekeeper. "Close the windows, Uilani."

Again, the woman did not hesitate. She closed the windows and left the room. Spence untied a bundle, carefully unrolling the papery cloth and exposing the eucalyptus bark. Elizabeth recognized the pungent odor.

He crumbled the dry bark into the water, lifted the bowl, and swirled it. Elizabeth inhaled deeply. Her eyes began to water.

"Hold this." He handed her the bowl. Then he took the sheet and draped Hadley's head and shoulders and the bowl in Elizabeth's hands.

Elizabeth's heart sank as she looked down at the shrouded, wheezing lump in the bed.

"Mama?" Hadley gasped, tears in her voice.

Elizabeth rubbed Hadley's back, her heart breaking. So young, so young to have to suffer this way. To be so very afraid. "It's all right, baby. Don't worry."

"Mama . . . wh—where . . . is . . . Papa?" Hadley wheezed harder.

"Hadley." Spence's voice was firm but not harsh. The child stopped crying aloud. "This is your tent. Don't be scared. Just sit and breathe the steam. Can you feel it? You should be breathing easier already."

The room was stifling with the windows closed. The labored wheezing continued, but Hadley was no longer crying for Elizabeth or for her papa.

Spence used the respite to search through his bag again until he found a few precious silvery leaves of the *'āhinahina*. Anticipating his next request, Uilani stepped forward. Elizabeth had not even heard the woman reenter the room. The housekeeper handed Spence a stone mortar and a small pestle. He sprinkled the leaves in the bottom of the stone bowl and began to crush them.

"These are *'āhinahina* leaves, from high on the island of Maui. I will make a tea—"

"No!" Elizabeth cut him off before he could finish. Spence looked up in question. A second before he spoke she had been more than willing to trust him.

"Elizabeth, I'm trying to help—"

She shook her head. "No. No tea. She is *not* drinking or eating anything out of that bag."

"But—"

"No." Her eyes were cold, determined.

Spence continued pulverizing the leaves. Hadley's breathing had eased somewhat, but to ensure a restful night, he wanted the girl to ingest the '*āhinahina* tea.

"I need a little more water, Uilani. A cup. Teapot," he said.

"*Did you hear me?*" Elizabeth's voice was reed thin, strangled with fear—or anger—he could not tell which.

Their conversation was hushed and hurried.

"I'm trying to save your girl, Elizabeth."

"Are you?" she whispered. "*Are you?*"

He lowered the mortar and pestle to the edge of the bed. Closed his eyes, shook his head. Then he looked up at her again, willing her to listen.

"Who stole your trust, Elizabeth?"

"Too many to name," she whispered. *Too many to speak of.*

The leaves had been reduced to minuscule bits and pieces. He held the bowl, listened to Hadley's labored breathing. Elizabeth was staring at the tented sheet.

Spence reached up, gently put his hand on her shoulder. She looked down into his eyes.

"Trust me," he said.

I want to. God how she wished she could, but even considering it terrified her. She had trusted before. Put her destiny in the hands of men. Each and every time she had been betrayed.

Her father had died in a senseless tragedy, taken her mother and their love for her, left her with nothing.

Johnny Huffington had taken her virginity, her honor, sailed out of her life, and left her pregnant.

Her aunt and uncle had taken the joy from her life, driven her to try to escape them, and then caused her to abort her unborn child.

Franklin had taken what was left of her trust when he offered her a chance to start over, then turned his fury and his fists on her.

I want to trust. But how could she?

Beneath the sheet, her fingers tightened on the wooden calabash. Hot water splashed over the edge, seared her skin.

Spence squeezed her shoulder, trying to communicate the urgency of the situation as he whispered, "Elizabeth, I can save your daughter's life if you let me."

Nine

A SHUDDER RIPPED THROUGH her. She closed her eyes. If he was lying in order to get his hands on Mauna Noe, she would lose more than the land. She would lose her precious daughter, her reason for living. The decision was hers alone. She had made some horrendous choices in her life, and now God was forcing her to choose again.

There was no one she could turn to, no one she could trust.

Uilani handed Spence the teapot and as he sprinkled the leaves inside, the housekeeper laid her hand on Elizabeth's shoulder. Elizabeth looked up into the woman's sympathetic eyes, the eyes of another mother. Uilani nodded twice. "Let 'em."

Hadley's wheezing had grown harsh, desperate. Spence pulled back the sheet, set the bowl of steaming eucalyptus on the floor. Elizabeth covered her mouth with her hand, swallowed a sob. Her daughter's lips were blue.

"Help her," Elizabeth cried.

Hadley should not have to suffer for what she had done. No just God would let her.

"Help her, please," she begged him.

The dread in Elizabeth's eyes gave Spence cause to hesitate for a split second. Her intense fear made him doubt himself. If the *'āhinahina* failed to help, if the girl died, Elizabeth would blame him for killing Hadley for the land. There were no guarantees.

Without a moment to spare, Spence reached for the girl, gently took her head in his hands, tilted her face up. He smoothed his hands over her cheeks.

"Hold her head up," he instructed Elizabeth, whispering now.

She was afraid her hands would fail her. She cradled Hadley's head and shoulders while Spence poured a thimbleful of tea into a glass. In the wavering lamplight, the liquid was colorless, odorless. He quickly blew on it before he held it to Hadley's lips.

"Drink," he urged as he put the glass against her lower lip and slowly tipped it up until the herbal brew trickled into her mouth.

The little girl arched, sputtered as if she were drowning.

Elizabeth cried out. Uilani stepped forward and helped Elizabeth hold the child down. Spence tried again, tilted the glass. This time he saw her work her throat to swallow.

Tears were streaming down Elizabeth's face, coursing hot and unstoppable, dripping onto the bodice of her nightgown. Catching her bottom lip beneath her teeth was the only thing that kept her from sobbing aloud. Spence poured more liquid over the edge of the glass and between Hadley's lips.

Hadley shuddered and then ever so slightly, her ragged breathing began to ease. Spence gave her another sip of the herbal tea. This time she seemed to sense that the brew was helping, and she accepted it. The tightness in her throat diminished, and very soon she was able to expel air with less of a struggle.

Elizabeth felt the knot around her heart loosen a bit. She bent, kissed Hadley's sweaty face, brushed her fair hair back. Elizabeth's hands were trembling like those of a palsied old woman. Finally she looked at Spence again.

He was intent upon Hadley, watching her slightest reaction until she was breathing easier.

Not until after he was certain that the attack was subsiding did Spence lean back on his heels. He offered up a silent prayer of thanks, touched the child's throat and upper chest. Then he looked at Elizabeth.

Her face, which had been so ravaged with fear, was now awash in relief. Her attention no longer focused on the girl, she was looking at him intently. Her fair hair was sticking to her forehead, her neck. The scooped neckline of her nightgown had slipped so low that he could see her breasts. He quickly shifted his gaze, looked into her eyes, could almost read the thousand thoughts running through her mind. She started to speak, struggled for words, and lapsed into silence.

He did not want her thanks. He wanted her trust.

Now that the crisis was past, now that his heart was no longer pounding with his own fears and doubts—now that he was calm and the room was still and Hadley's breathing was settling into a more even cadence—now just looking at Elizabeth, he was moved deeply, as a man is moved by a woman. He found himself wanting her, yet despising himself for his weakness—especially here and now—when his only concern should have been the child.

Elizabeth tried to find her voice, tried to think of a way to tell him how she felt, of her gratitude. Like a mute, she simply sat there while her hands caressed her daughter's face. Uilani waited silently beside her, a solid, calming presence.

Elizabeth opened her mouth to speak, but nothing came out. No word of thanks, nothing but a swift, soft intake of breath, an odd, gulping sob. Spence filled the awkward void.

"I will carry her to your room. You will sleep better with her close by." He reached out for Hadley, waited for

Elizabeth to let him take the child from her arms. "Bring the tea," he told her when she did.

As she followed Spence down the moonlit hallway, relief came over her in giddy waves. Her past and the present had collided in Hadley's room tonight, and she had been forced to look deep into that past and weigh it against the present. Forced to let go of her fear, she made a choice—thankfully, the right one—and the heavy burden around her heart lightened.

Now she walked barefoot down the stretch of hallway with the teapot and the small glass in her hand, following the huge man with her child cradled in his arms, and every detail became exaggerated. The sway of his shadow-black hair against his shoulders, the moon-stained slash of the ghostly white fabric bound around his hips and thighs. When they passed by an open window, the jagged-edged pattern of his pagan tattoo was illuminated.

Spence walked into Elizabeth's room, went straight to the bed, and laid the girl against the pillows. He gently straightened Hadley's arms and legs and then pulled the sheet up to her chest before he drew the edges of the mosquito netting together.

Elizabeth hovered behind him. He turned and found her closer than he expected, backlit by the milky whiteness of moonlight, the filmy gown more revealing than modest. Her hair was like a fall of moonbeams over her shoulders. He could hear her unsteady breathing.

"She will sleep a while." Spence reached for the teapot. Their hands touched, fingers brushed and danced away. He braced himself so he would not spill the tea and fought to ignore his body's immediate reaction.

My father's widow. The reminder did little to cool his blood. In a perverse way it only stirred him more.

She stood as silent as the ghostly apparition she appeared to be.

"Give her more tea when she wakes up. She should have some at least five times a day for a while," he said softly.

"Thank you. I don't know what I would have done with-out . . . without your help." She left it there, her thanks. An unwanted offering hanging between them.

The sound of her voice and her scent eddied around Spence like temperate waters, rolled over him like a gentle summer swell, luring him, urging him to forget all that she was, all that she had been to his father. To forget she was *haole*.

A chill rippled through him, as if Franklin Bennett's ghost had stepped into the room, haunting the deep shad-ows in the corners, where moonlight did not reach. He shiv-ered again, felt as if his father had run cold, lifeless fingers down his spine.

"Good night, Elizabeth." He forced himself to concen-trate on what he had accomplished this night, rather than on her scent, her voice, her nearness. He had saved her daughter. Maybe now she would not fight him at every turn. Maybe now he had earned her trust.

To get to the door he was forced to pass close beside her. The hem of her voluminous gown teased the outside of his leg as he brushed by. The whisper-soft touch set more tingling than the tattooed skin along his thigh. As he left the room and made his way back along the hall and then down the stairs, he tried to convince himself that the twisted knot in his gut was only a leftover reaction to the earlier crisis.

But in his heart and soul, he knew it came from need.

ELIZABETH LAY AWAKE LONG into the night, listening to the breath wheeze out of Hadley's throat, waking her just enough to give her more tea every hour, thinking about what happened—and what might have happened had Spence not been there.

Holding Hadley's little hand in hers, examining the per-fect fingers, the ivory nails, she thought about the man downstairs, a man of mixed blood and many contradictions. By day he dressed the part of a cowhand, in shirt and pants and worn leather shoes. Gaiters laced up to his knees. A panama hat. By night he wore a native wrap, pagan and wild, his flesh barely covered, decorated with primitive artwork. He radiated mystery and mysticism.

Even though the urgency had passed and Hadley was out of danger, Elizabeth chastised herself. What kind of a mother was she, obsessed with Spence, unable to stop thinking of him, of his near-nakedness, of the tattoo that snaked down his body?

Something deep and dangerous was stirring inside her again, just as it had in Marion Randolph's sitting room. A restlessness she could not deny, a hunger. Today she had felt the awakening of desire, and to her consternation, that desire had been fueled by Spence Laamea. Still too aroused to sleep, she found her imagination running wild. What would it be like to touch that dark, tattooed skin? To feel his flesh pressed against hers?

She had known two kinds of lovemaking in her life— one frantic, fumbling, and furtive; the other harsh, cruel, and vindictive. What kind of lover was Spence Laamea?

She closed her eyes, blocked out the moonlight, tried to extinguish the forbidden thoughts. She forced herself to keep her eyes closed. She tried breathing deep, even breaths. She let go of Hadley's hand and fought to ignore the tingling ache at the juncture between her thighs.

Her mind drifted. Her consciousness remained alert to Hadley's every breath even as she slipped through the curtain of sleep and imagined herself on the lanai as Spence came riding toward her, his hair wild and free, a length of fabric tied around his hips. The horse thundered closer, hooves churning above the ground until the animal shimmered and evaporated as suddenly as a rainbow. Then Spence was riding the crest of a wave. He came toward her through the crystal froth of foam, reached out his hand.

"Come with me, Elizabeth. Trust me."

Her blood pounded in her ears. Unable to resist, she walked toward him, gliding effortlessly into his arms. He wrapped his strong brown arms around her, held her in his embrace. She heard the beat of his pagan heart, felt it drumming through her, heating her blood, driving her over the edge. She felt his touch, his hand covered her, stroked the mound between her thighs. She gasped, frantically moved her hips, brought her body up to meet his, and looked into his eyes. Those dark, exotic eyes were filled with unbridled longing. She lifted her mouth, offering it to him, starved for the taste of him.

He closed his eyes as he lowered his head, then just before their lips met, he opened his eyes again. They had faded to green—green eyes filled with loathing, not longing. Franklin's green eyes. *Franklin.*

The dream had become a nightmare. The terrible image startled her awake. She sat straight up in bed, fully expecting Franklin to be there, standing over the bed, looking at her with the same revulsion as in the dream. Trembling like a leaf, she glanced over at Hadley, thankful that her erratic movements had not disturbed her child.

Elizabeth crossed her arms over her breasts. The sensitive bud between her legs pulsed, echoed her need. Nothing had changed. Not even motherhood had changed her. After all these years she was still the wanton her aunt and uncle had chastised and punished. Still the fallen woman Franklin had abhorred.

"Are you laughing, Franklin?" She turned toward the darkest corner of her room and whispered, "Did you plan this? Did you force Spence and me together, knowing something like this might happen? Are you laughing at me from hell?"

From the corner of the room there came only silence.

The trades started again, teasing the curtains at her windows. She heard rain sweeping across the land, first in the palms and the *hau* bush in the ravine, then louder on the slick banana leaves near the back of the house, and finally on the roof.

Elizabeth covered her face with her hands. How could she face Spence tomorrow, the next day, or the next? Would he see remnants of the secret lust in her eyes?

Memory of the dream threatened to lead her senses astray. She reeled them back in. Tomorrow, when she saw Spence again, she would thank him for saving Hadley. Then she would tell him that from now on, she would trust his decisions regarding the ranch. She owed him that much.

She would be cool, collected. She would comport herself with dignity when she saw him and lock away the feelings he had unwittingly awakened. She was the one who had no moral fortitude, not him. Spencer Laamea deserved her thanks and her trust.

But how was she to trust herself?

WHEN THE DAWN CAME shining through Elizabeth's window the next morning she was already wide awake, listening to the raucous mynah birds running across the rooftop, celebrating the new day. The sunlight melted away some of the fears of the night, dissolving the ghosts but not the erotic images of Spence Laamea.

Elizabeth rose and dressed as Hadley slept on, her breathing easier after a night of the *'āhinahina* tea. As much as she hoped Spence was already up and out, she knew she could not put off seeing him sooner or later, not with the man living under her roof.

He was in the kitchen with Uilani, one hip leaning against the sideboard, a mug of hot coffee in his hand. He was dressed in his *paniolo* garb, everything but muddy shoes and gaiters, which he always left on the back lanai. Gone was the exotic island warrior of last night. His hair was tamed into a long, thick braid, the pagan tattoo hidden beneath his trousers. Elizabeth wondered if it had all been a dream—until her heart skipped a beat and her skin went hot, then clammy.

The two of them stopped talking when Elizabeth entered the kitchen. Uilani smiled her way. Spence took a sip of coffee and watched her over the rim of the mug.

"Good morning," she said, hoping her agitation did not show in her demeanor or her voice.

Spence nodded. Uilani, frying taro at the stove, replied, *"Aloha kakahiaka."* Good morning.

Skittish as a drop of water in a hot frying pan, Elizabeth wished she had waited upstairs until Spence left. She poured herself a mug of coffee, wondering what to say to him, where and how to begin.

"Hadley bettah?" Uilani slipped hot gray-purple slices of fried taro onto a platter and set it in the warming oven.

"Oh, yes," Elizabeth replied, thankful for an opening. "She's sleeping soundly. Her breathing is almost normal." She could not keep from looking at Spence.

He was watching her intently. She nearly lost her grip on the mug of hot coffee. Tightening her grasp, she turned back to the housekeeper.

"Thank you for last night, Uilani. How did you know we needed help?"

"I not sleep. See the light. T'ink maybe I bettah come see."

"Thank goodness you did." Elizabeth looked at Spence, took a deep breath, and set her coffee mug on the table. "May I speak to you in the parlor?"

Elizabeth paused just inside the parlor, where the doors and windows were already wide open. Outside, light rain fell from a passing cloud even though the sun shone brightly. The liquid sunshine created a rainbow that bridged the ravine in the distance.

She felt Spence move up beside her. He stared out at the rainbow. As she struggled for a way to express her thanks, they watched the rainbow shimmer until it began to fade. As the rain moved out over the ocean, it left behind diamond droplets of moisture that shimmied down the leaves, bejeweled the thick grass.

"Uilani tells me she feels Bennett's ghost here at night. Do you?"

"Sometimes I fancy I do," she confessed.

"Are you afraid?"

"Of Franklin's ghost?" She shook her head. There was nothing the man's ghost could do to harm her that he had not already done. "There are worse things to fear." She met his intense gaze. "Do *you* believe in ghosts?"

Deep within her, Elizabeth knew what his answer would be. The man she saw last night, the pagan warrior who had come to her aid and then haunted her dreams, would surely believe in spirits and other ancient mystical beings.

"Before the missionaries, all Hawaiians believed in ghosts, *lapu*. Many still do. That part of our lives, our culture, is too deeply instilled in legend and song to ignore. *Mana*, the life force, lives everywhere in nature—in the animals, trees, fruit, stones, mountains, the sea and all its creatures. I cannot deny the beliefs of my Hawaiian ancestors."

Despite the heat of the day, Elizabeth felt a chill pass through her. She rubbed her arms. It did not take a lifelong belief in ghosts to feel Franklin's presence still haunting this place.

"I want to thank you for what you did last night," she said, unwilling to dwell on Franklin or his ghost. "I owe you not only my thanks but an apology for my attitude."

She felt his burning gaze. He was looking deep into her eyes as if he were trying to read what was really hidden behind her words—

I thank you. I will trust you.

I dreamed of you last night.

Embarrassed, she quickly dropped her gaze, afraid if she held his long enough he would divine the illicit, unbidden thoughts racing through her mind.

"It would help if you would say something," she whispered.

"I don't want your apologies, Elizabeth, or even your thanks. I did what I had to do. I tried to help your daughter and I succeeded. I told you what I wanted last night. I want your trust. I want us to be able to work together."

"I put my faith in you last night," she reminded him, "when I entrusted you with my daughter's life. Anything beyond that pales by comparison, doesn't it? If we have to give up this place to Franklin's creditors, we all lose. From now on, do whatever you think best. All I ask is that you consult me."

She had thought it would disturb her more, acquiescing to his expertise, but she felt as if a heavy weight had just slipped off her shoulders. She looked out at her garden, longing to immerse herself in it as she had not done since Franklin died.

"We are going to mend fences today, replace the *kiawe* wood that has rotted. While we're out we'll check the stock."

She nodded, uncomfortable, wishing she knew more about what needed to be done. She looked up quickly and caught him staring at her bodice. Her body reacted immediately, her nipples tightened. His gaze lifted, his eyes locked with hers for an instant, the longest of her life. Then he nodded in farewell and walked out.

DUKE PULLED REIN NEAR the edge of the cliff and let his horse graze while he watched the ocean. Today was Kāloa Pau—a good day of the month to fish the reef. Maybe he could convince Laamea to let him quit early, to hunt shellfish and gather *limu*.

Fishing and picking seaweed might take his mind off of a certain *wahine* in Hanalei. He reached up and rubbed the still tender spot on his jaw where Ana had hit him.

What a woman. Nothing like her. Last night he had dreamed of making love to her, figured it had to be the full moon and the scent of the white ginger blooming beneath his window that fueled his desire.

She had grown up faster than he expected, blossomed into a beautiful young woman while he was away. One thing was for sure—he would have to move quickly now.

Her loveliness would not have gone unnoticed in the valley.

He had one plenty big decision to make in the next couple of days—to stay on at Mauna Noe or tell Elizabeth Bennett and Laamea that he was leaving and then move back to Hanalei. He wanted to keep an eye on Ana until she realized she was going to be his wife.

He smiled, thinking that as long as he steered clear of her right fist, things would work out.

"Something out there makes you happy?" Laamea drew his horse close to Duke's.

"Good *limu* picking, I t'ink." They slipped into an easy discussion in pidgin on fishing.

Laamea was staring down at the cove below them, at the rocks and the cove with its shimmering reef and black lava rocks exposed by the low tide. "What's all that blue down there?"

"Dishes," Duke replied.

"Dishes?" Laamea urged his mount closer to the edge of the bluff. "What kine dishes? What you talking about?"

Duke loved nothing better than a good story. "Jus' after Bennett come *make,* Mrs. Bennett have me put 'um all in da wagon, drive 'um out here an' pile 'um up."

"All the dishes?"

"Fancy ones only. So I load 'um up. Bring 'um out. Leave 'um wit' her. Plates, da kine cups, everyt'ing." He shook his head. It was still hard to believe. "She tell me go, so I drive little way away. T'ink maybe she change mind. But she broke 'em all."

"Broke all the good dishes?" Laamea squinted against the sunlight on the water, trying to make out glistening blue and white shards that littered the rocks.

"Yeah. All of 'em. I t'ink den she *pupule.*"

"Crazy, all right. I wonder why?"

Duke shrugged. "Who knows. I never know what *haole* t'inking anyway." He glanced over at Laamea, suddenly remembering the man was *hapa.* "Sorry."

Spence shrugged. "No worry. Me either. I never been around them much."

Duke laughed. The more he got to know the man, the more he liked Laamea. The least he could do was give him a couple more full days of work before he quit to go keep an eye on Ana.

ELIZABETH WAS IN THE garden planting *ti* cuttings when she noticed a wagon coming up over the swell in the road. She put down her trowel and stood up, brushed her hair back off her face. She waited until the wagon passed the turn off the main road and started toward the house. Curious, she wondered who the caller was. When the rig pulled closer, she saw that the driver was a woman. A rush of delight hit her when she thought it was Marion Randolph. Her new acquaintance would be the first social caller she had ever entertained.

With her next breath, she recognized the ramrod-straight posture, the jaunty stylish hat tilted just so, the starched white blouse with pleated puffed sleeves. It was definitely not Marion Reynolds, but Alberta Baxter.

The Baxter holding bordered Mauna Noe. It was the closest *haole* ranch, much smaller but, according to Franklin, very productive. Alberta's husband, Emory Baxter, was an astute businessman, born on Oʻahu, a descendant of missionaries who came in the first wave to convert the islanders. Baxter was one of the men with whom Franklin had hoped their marriage would help cement relations.

His plan had failed miserably.

Elizabeth had not laid eyes on Alberta since one fateful night shortly after she arrived at Mauna Noe, and she could not fathom what Alberta was doing here now. She tried to brush the dirt off the poorly mended yellow calico dress that she saved for garden work. The skirt was hopelessly stained with dirt and sap. Leaving a bucketful of red *ti* cuttings behind, she hurried up the steps, hoping Alberta had not caught sight of her.

She hid on the lanai and took frantic seconds to remove her shoes, a few more to run inside and call out to Uilani to make tea. Next she hurried upstairs, where Hadley was playing quietly in her room with Maile. Elizabeth ducked in, saw that Maile had artfully arranged all of Hadley's toys around her on the bed. The girls had not noticed her, so she ducked back out and went into her own room to change.

The water in the pitcher on her dresser had been warmed by the sunlight streaming in the side window. She poured some into the washbasin and then dampened a towel. After washing her hands she sponged off her face and neck, then brushed her hair away from her face.

Racing to the tall standing closet on the far side of the room, she flung it open and rifled through her pitifully wanting collection of gowns. Hanging forlornly alone was the faded burgundy, the blue gown with embroidery on the cuffs, and an emerald velvet that she had worn only once, because it was unsuited to the weather. In better condition than her other things, it was the only one worthy to receive callers.

Quickly she changed out of the calico and donned the emerald velvet. By the time she struggled with the buttons, perspiration was trickling along her temples. As she stood before the mirror and toweled off her face, she stared at her image, trying to remember the naive girl who had last worn the green velvet. Her hair was pulled back severely into a long, thick braid. She was much thinner than when the dress had been fashioned for her. It hung from her shoulders, barely touched her anywhere. She was dwarfed by the yards of velvet.

I look like a hedge. She glanced back at the closet.

Better a hedge than a rag picker.

The muffled sound of voices drifted up from downstairs. She recognized Uilani's, pictured her housekeeper at the door, ushering Alberta Baxter in. Elizabeth took a deep breath, straightened her sleeves, ran her hands over her hair, and left the room.

Uilani informed her when she reached the foyer that Alberta Baxter was waiting in the parlor.

"Do you have any more of those cookies you made for Hadley yesterday?" Elizabeth asked.

"I get. No worry. You go. Make a tea party like da kine lady." Uilani bustled away, all smiles, as her bright-orange calico *mu'umu'u* billowed around her.

Elizabeth knew she would never be the proper mistress that Uilani expected her to be. Before her courage failed her, she left the foyer and went into the parlor. Alberta Baxter appeared to be nearly forty, although the sun might have added years to her fair skin. Seated in Franklin's favorite deep-cushioned leather chair, she had her hands poised daintily atop each other in her lap. Her knees were pressed together. She was craning her neck, staring back at a stuffed frigate bird perched on a marble-topped table beside her chair.

"Aloha, Mrs. Baxter," Elizabeth said from the doorway.

Alberta looked up, startled. "Good morning, Mrs. Bennett." She echoed Elizabeth's cool formality. "I hope I'm not interrupting anything, calling without warning like this?"

She looked past Elizabeth, into the hallway, bobbing her head on her long, thin neck like a chicken crossing unfamiliar territory, her curiosity as transparent as glass.

"Not at all." Elizabeth kept her voice low, trying to hide her agitation. She was already stifling in the velvet gown. "Uilani is fixing some tea."

"How nice," the woman said absently, trying to scoot forward in the chair but finding herself mired in the broken-down cushion.

Elizabeth chose a firmer seat and sat head and shoulders above Alberta Baxter. She tried to smile, but it felt more like a grimace because it was devoid of feeling. She offered no polite conversation, simply let Alberta squirm in the chair until she finally stopped.

"I came to offer our condolences on your late husband's

death. It came as quite a shock to Emory and I when we heard from Milton Clifford that Franklin had passed on,'' Alberta said.

"Thank you," Elizabeth nodded, adding nothing, wondering why Alberta had chosen to call today.

"It must have been quite traumatic for you, dear." The woman leaned forward from the waist and sank another inch into the chair cushion.

"It was very sudden." Elizabeth almost expelled a sigh of relief when Uilani entered with a tray of tea and cookies.

She wanted to jump up and hug her housekeeper when she saw the extra care she had taken, lining the cookie plate with a banana leaf, placing a bougainvillea blossom on each carefully folded linen napkin. Uilani set the tray on a low table. Elizabeth leaned forward to serve, felt perspiration trickling down between her breasts.

"Thank you, Uilani." She hoped her smile communicated her appreciation. She poured a cup of tea for Alberta.

"Are you planning to run this place alone?" Alberta was forced to plant her feet wide and grip the arms of the chair in order to pull herself up and out so that she could balance herself on the edge and take the cup and saucer Elizabeth held out to her.

"I was looking forward to it." Elizabeth remembered Marion's coconut wireless and suspected that Alberta had already heard about Spencer Laamea's arrival but was playing coy. She decided to let the woman fish for information.

"But now you won't have to?" Alberta pursed her lips near the edge of the cup and blew on the steam rising off the amber liquid.

"No." *I lost my independence before I had a chance to assert it.* Elizabeth offered Alberta a cookie and then chose one for herself. She took a bite and hoped it wouldn't stick in her throat. As she stared at the woman sitting across from her, well heeled and polished in her starched white shirtwaist and navy skirt, she wondered how Alberta even had the nerve to darken her door.

"Milton Clifford mentioned that some relation of Franklin's has come to take over." Alberta left the rest for Elizabeth to explain.

Watching Alberta uncomfortably fixed on the edge of the chair trying to balance a teacup and saucer with a cookie hanging precariously close to its edge, Elizabeth decided to tip her own hand.

"Actually, Franklin's will appointed myself and a . . . very close relation . . . as trustees for Hadley. The details are all very complicated, so I won't bore you with them."

"A cousin?" Alberta's eyes grew wide. She looked about to burst with curiosity.

At least Clifford had made an attempt at discretion. Alberta Baxter wanted to know the details so badly that she had come herself to ferret them out. Elizabeth waited until Alberta held her cup to her lips and took a sip.

"Actually, Spencer is not Franklin's cousin. As it turns out, my new partner is Franklin's son by a Hawaiian woman he knew when he first came to the islands."

Elizabeth watched in satisfaction and hid her smile against the rim of her own teacup as Alberta Baxter made a choking sound and tea spewed down the front of her perfect white blouse.

SPENCE WAS ON HIS way to the barn when he noticed the wagon outside the garden gate. He signaled Duke to go on without him, tied Kāhili to the hitching rail beside the wagon, and headed for the house. He sidestepped a garden trowel and a bucket of abandoned *ti* cuttings near the stepping-stone pathway. When he sat down on the top step to unlace his shoes, the sound of Elizabeth's voice drifted out of the parlor windows.

"My new partner is Franklin's son by a Hawaiian woman he knew when he first came to the islands."

Spence did not recognize her tone. She sounded cool, calculating, and determined, as if weighing every word for its impact before she uttered it.

"Really?" a strange female voice replied. "I was not aware that Franklin ever had another wife."

"Franklin never married the Hawaiian woman," Elizabeth said.

The Hawaiian woman. A picture of his beautiful, gentle mother immediately came to Spence's mind. It hurt to hear her so easily dismissed.

"They lived in *sin*?" The unseen caller gasped.

He felt his temper flare. His mother's only sin was that she fell in love with the wrong man.

"Some might call it that." Elizabeth's voice had a distant quality to it. Spence knew without seeing her that she had taken on the thoughtful, far-off look that came over her so often.

"This man can't be very old," the woman said, prompting Elizabeth.

"I suppose he's around my own age," Elizabeth replied offhandedly. Then in an aside she added, "He lives here in the house with us."

Spence supposed the busybody was salivating by now. China rattled. He pictured Elizabeth drinking tea as he leaned back, propping his elbows on the edge of the step. The sun was high, the lanai bathed in shade. He glanced toward the open doors, continued to listen to the conversation inside.

"Oh, my. What about Hadley? Does this mean she'll have to share ownership of Mauna Noe with Franklin's . . . well, with his . . . *bastard*? And what of you, my dear? What will people think when they find out you and this man are living under the same roof?"

China rattled again. Elizabeth must have stood, for when she spoke, the sound was closer to the window.

"I really don't see what concern that is of yours, Alberta. In fact, I can hardly believe you even had the audacity to come here today after the way you treated me seven years ago."

Alberta's gasp was audible even to Spence. He had

sparred with Elizabeth and had seen her angry, but he'd never heard her speak with such venom. He got to his feet, determined to see who this caller was and find out why Elizabeth held such animosity toward her.

Spence set his shoes down beside the door without a sound and entered the foyer. The breeze cutting through the open hallway had lifted a tasseled table runner on a half table in the entry, folded the cloth back over an etched glass bowl. Absently, he turned it back into place as he listened to the ongoing exchange. Elizabeth could not fault him for spying. He stood in full view of the door where either woman could have seen him if she had looked his way.

"Surely you must know that my hands were tied," Alberta told Elizabeth.

Elizabeth had moved so she could look out at her garden. She sounded as if she were reciting a tale about someone else.

"Franklin set out to punish me on the very day of our wedding. Not an hour after I arrived here, he hit me so hard he tore open the skin above my eye. Nothing I said or did pleased him. Finally, on the sixth day, I had had enough. I thought if I did not get away from here that one night he would surely kill me."

In the foyer, Spence's blood ran cold. He had to remind himself to breathe. Elizabeth was talking about Franklin Bennett, his father, painting a terrible portrait with words. It was an image that Spence's own mother had never even hinted at. His fingers tightened on a tassel on the table runner, remembering the scar that cut through Elizabeth's delicate right eyebrow.

"Elizabeth, my husband agreed that—"

Elizabeth cut the woman off as if she had not even spoken.

"Franklin beat me until I could not see out of one eye, and then he dumped me in my room. I waited for him to go to sleep, then I crept out of the house with nothing but the clothes on my back. I bridled a horse in the barn, rode bareback through the night.''

She turned around, looking Alberta in the eye. Lost in the telling, she still had not noticed Spence in the hall.

''I had no idea where I was or where I was headed until I saw the light in your window. Thinking I was safe at last, I broke down sobbing, tears and blood running down my face as I rode up to your house. I'll never forget your expression when you opened the door and saw me standing there.''

Spence closed his eyes. She had stood up to him from the first, been irritating as hell, but there was nothing in him that would let him strike a woman. How could his father have? What kind of animal had spawned him?

He had to strain to hear Elizabeth now. Her voice had faded, but not her determination to finish.

''All I wanted was for you to give me shelter, to take me in until I could contact my aunt and uncle and beg for passage home. Do you remember what you told me, Alberta?'' She did not wait for a reply. ''You said that I was married now, that a woman's duty dictated she obey her husband, not shame him. Your own dear Emory was irate . . . but at *me*. He was preparing to bring me back here when Franklin came charging down the lane. He had beat his horse into quite a lather tracking me down. When he hauled me off, screaming, begging you to help me, you and Emory said nothing, Alberta. Nothing at all.''

''Franklin was your husband.''

''Franklin was either insane or an *animal*. Or both.'' Elizabeth ground out the words. ''You sent me back to him without a second thought. You never once came to call to see how I was getting along. For all you knew, he might have killed me that night when he brought me home.''

Spence took an involuntary step toward the parlor door, but Elizabeth held her own.

''Do you think I could ever forget that? How could you have the audacity to show up here today and tell me how sorry you are that Franklin's gone? How *dare* you snoop into my life and business affairs? If I want to live under the same roof with *fifty* men, *haole* or Hawaiian, I don't see how that is any of your concern—or anyone else's—for that matter.''

''Well, I *never*. I don't intend to sit here and be insulted any longer.'' Alberta set her cup and saucer down with a crash, reached for the arms of the brown leather chair and pushed herself out of it. She was visibly shaken, her face drained of color.

Spence wished he could see Elizabeth clearly, but with the long, open windows behind her, her expression was in shadow. He refused to let her face this woman alone any longer.

He drew Alberta's attention the minute he stepped over the threshold into the parlor. Up close, he studied the lines around the woman's mouth, the pinched lips and the narrow, faded hazel eyes. Beneath her beribboned hat, her hair showed streaks of gray at the temples.

Alberta did not bother to hide her shock when she saw him, nor did she bother to be discreet. She stared at him with open curiosity and disgust.

Elizabeth was as white as a sheet. Her hair was damp around her face.

''I'm Spence Laamea,'' he said, with as much false cordiality as he could muster. ''I take it Elizabeth has told you all about me, Mrs.—?''

''B-Baxter,'' the woman stammered. ''Alberta Baxter.''

''I couldn't help but hear some of Elizabeth's story,'' he said, easily moving past Alberta, crossing the room until he stood close to Elizabeth. She stiffened, but not so the other woman might notice. ''Given the circumstances, I think it would be best if you left now,'' Spence advised Alberta.

Their caller looked from one to the other, then turned on her heel and fled the room.

Spence watched her departure through the lanai window.

Just outside the door the woman grabbed her shoes and without bothering to put them on, hugged them to her chest and raced down the stairs. She ran through the garden to her wagon, tossed her shoes in, and scrambled up into the seat. Lifting the reins, she tugged her horse's head until it turned the wagon back toward Anahola. With a lurch, the wagon wheels rolled.

Elizabeth put the length of the room between them. She did not say a word, but worried the velvet fabric of her skirt, then clasped and unclasped her slender fingers.

"Was it all true?" Spence prayed it was not, but he knew she was telling the truth.

"Yes."

"All of it?"

"All of it."

When she hung her head in shame, he walked up to her, put his hand beneath her chin, forced her to look up.

"No shame, Elizabeth. Never be ashamed," he whispered for her ears alone. "He made you suffer enough. Don't punish yourself."

ELIZABETH FELT HER LOWER lip tremble and she cursed the sign of weakness. His kindness was melting her faster than the heavy velvet dress. It had been so very, very long since anyone had stood up for her. Never had she suspected that when she found an ally again it would be this man.

"Why don't you go take off that dress before you pass out? You look like you're about to faint."

She tried to smile and failed miserably. Reminding Alberta Baxter of the horror of the night she had escaped had only magnified the incident, bringing it all back with horrifying clarity.

A few minutes ago she felt very alone. Now Spence stood before her. It was tempting to imagine falling into his arms, letting herself break down and cry—but it was a temptation she could never, ever give in to. She pulled herself together enough to wonder what brought him in so early.

"Were you looking for me when you came in?"

"I saw the wagon and came to see who was here. I really think you should go change. Your face is red. I've seen big men felled by the heat."

Elizabeth wiped her brow with the back of her sleeve. She felt sweat snaking down her back.

"You need help getting up the stairs?"

She shook her head. "I can manage, thank you."

"We need to talk," he said.

She shook her head, unwilling to relive her humiliation, knowing he must have many questions. "I . . . Not now, please."

"No. Not now. Now you change. We'll talk later."

SPENCE WATCHED HER WALK away, the heavy velvet dwarfing her, dragging her down. He tried to imagine her petite frame sustaining his father's abuse. Obviously the man had not beaten her about the face very often—except for the scar in her eyebrow, her fine features were still unmarred. Still lovely.

Questions were branded on his mind. He could not let the sun go down without getting some straight answers. After Elizabeth disappeared up the stairs, Spence went in search of Uilani.

Ten

SPENCE CLOSETED HIMSELF IN his father's office, a cramped space in a small building behind the main house. Most of the structure was devoted to a store where the *paniolo* and their families could buy goods on credit against their wages, though the accounts showed that the store had not been open for more than two years. The space was full of leftover supplies, cobwebs, mildew, and gecko droppings. The office had not fared much better. There was only a big desk and an old safe in one corner. The safe was empty, the door standing wide open. A cane spider had taken up residence inside.

Spence had not gleaned any personal information about Franklin Bennett from the things the old man had left behind in the office. The sturdy *koa* desk built four decades ago by Hawaiian boys at a missionary school nearly filled the cramped space. When he arrived, Spence found nothing of value in or on the desk—no letters, no lists, no notes. Neatly stacked in the top drawer was a pile of contracts made between his father and the Jensen and Carlisle Agency in Honolulu, copies identical to those Milton Clifford had left for him to peruse along with the ranch accounts.

Except for the papers, it was almost as if his father had no past, no future, not even a present when he died.

Who were you, old man? What were you thinking when you beat your wife? Why did you set things up so that we'd be trapped here together?

Spence looked up and saw Uilani crossing the yard with Duke. His *luna* had just said something to make the woman laugh uproariously, reminding Spence of how long it had been since he had felt like laughing himself. Thinking about all he had heard earlier from Elizabeth's own lips made him wonder when was the last time she had laughed.

Uilani came in first and sat down on a stool in front of the desk, leaving Duke standing near the open window. Spence nodded to both of them. Uilani's smile had faded; her dark eyes were serious as she watched him.

"Time I get supper," she said.

"I have questions I want to ask about my father. Both of you been here since before he died, both of you worked closest to the house, to Elizabeth." Spence turned to Uilani first. "A few minutes ago, I heard Elizabeth tell a visitor that Bennett used to beat her."

Uilani appeared uncomfortable. She fanned her vibrant orange calico skirt up and down and frowned in thought.

"I not work alla time in da house until da old man, he die and 'Lizbet tell the *haole* housekeeper to get out." She shrugged and smiled. "Dat housekeeper, she one bad *wahine*. Alla time keep eye on 'Lizbet for him when da ol' man not heah. Only place she can go is garden. Alla time she take da girl, too."

"Did Elizabeth ever see anyone but Franklin and that other housekeeper?"

Uilani shook her head. "Nobody. No lady frien's, and she never leave. No new dress ever. No pretty t'ings. Only place she go, garden."

"Did you ever see him hit her?"

Uilani sobered, nodded. "First day she come. Den, she get *hāpai* and he stop. One day, I cook. Hear her tell him if he hit her again, he never see da *kaikāmahine*, da girl, dat she take Hadley far away. After that, he pretty much leave her alone."

"Once she was with child he never hit her again?"

"Not like b'fore. Not so Hadley see. Still come plenty mad. Still yell alla time. Everyday he come worse until he die. I t'ink mebbe head explode, yeah."

Spence sighed. Proud, independent Elizabeth had lived the life of a prisoner, but at least Bennett had stopped beating her after she became *hāpai*, pregnant.

At the window, Duke had slipped down into a crouch and leaned against the wall, listening intently.

Uilani put her hands behind her back, planted them on her hips, and stretched. Her elbows poked out like meaty wings.

Spence turned to the *luna*. "What about you, Duke? What do you know about my father and Elizabeth?"

Duke shrugged. He never cared for getting in the middle of family business. He had heard the old man yelling at Elizabeth plenty over the last two years, but then, the old man yelled at everyone. He never saw much of Elizabeth himself, she was either working in the garden or walking along the bluff with the girl. She was never without the child. He and the others were warned to keep their distance, and none of them was fool enough to cross Bennett, even to say hello to her.

He told Spence Laamea as much and then fell silent again.

Spence felt sick at his stomach but had to ask, "Did he ever beat the little girl?" He could not imagine Elizabeth allowing it. Even after so brief a time, he knew she would die defending the child.

Both Duke and Uilani shook their heads. Spence found that to be some consolation, but it would never be enough to clear his father's slate.

"Uilani, you can go on back to the house. I know Toshi and Melvin won't appreciate me keeping you from putting supper together. *Mahalo* for your *kōkua*. Duke, I'd like you to stay a minute."

AS UILANI SAID GOOD-BYE and left, Duke wondered if Laamea wanted to see him alone because he was going to let him go. If so, it would save him the trouble of having to quit, since he was determined to go back to Hanalei and Ana anyway.

He looked up and caught Laamea looking damned uncomfortable. Probably trying to work up the nerve to tell him to pack up and leave. Duke let the man dangle a bit.

"You from Hanalei, yeah?" Laamea asked.

"Born and raised in da middle of one *kalo* patch."

"You know of a dressmaker down there? Somebody who can come live here for a while, mebbe sew up some new clothes for Mrs. Bennett?"

Duke was hard-pressed not to laugh out loud when it turned out Laamea was asking for his help. He stood up, shook out his long legs. A minute ago he thought he was going to get fired and now Laamea asks if he knows of a seamstress in Hanalei.

"Dat Hawaiian *wahine* works for Mrs. Randolph make plenty good dresses."

Spence leaned back in his chair and stacked his hands behind his head. "After we finish the fencing, I'd like you to ride down to Hanalei and see if she'll come stay up here for a while. She can have one of the empty houses. Take Kāhili with you. Stop off at the plantation at Kilauea. When we drove the cattle past there, the manager mentioned that he would like to buy Kāhili if I ever wanted to sell.

"Use the money to buy dress material in town if you can get it or from the plantation store at Kilauea. Get whatever the seamstress thinks she will need to make some clothes for Elizabeth and the girl. If you need to ask for credit, tell them they'll be dealing with Mauna Noe's new boss, that I stand behind my word.''

Across the room, Duke shoved on his hat and lingered in the doorway, eager to leave. He hoped that replacing all the bad fence would not take much longer than a week or a week and a half at the most. Soon enough he would be in Hanalei, calling on Ana. He figured it would not take longer than a week to get her to move to Mauna Noe, especially since she had set her sights on his boss.

Lucky for me, Duke thought, *that Spence Laamea has so many worries he did not even act like he remembered Ana Pualoa*. From the way his boss had looked when he asked about Elizabeth Bennett and the old man, Duke did not think Laamea would notice Ana—no matter what kind of a scheme she might hatch.

ELIZABETH LAY ON HER back in the grass on the cliff above the cove, arms wide, eyes closed. Beside her, Hadley lay spread-eagle, too, chattering like a mynah bird.

''How come the sky is blue during the day, Mama, and then black at night? If the sun lights it in the day then the moon lights it at night, then why isn't it dark blue instead of black? Do you think the clouds go all the way around the world and then come back? Or after it rains are they all empty and gone forever? What do you think, Mama?''

''I don't know, honey. What do you think?'' As Hadley began to expound on her own thoughts about the color of the sky and the journey of the clouds, Elizabeth relaxed and let the warmth of the sunbaked earth soak into her. It had been days since she had confronted Alberta Baxter and with every passing one she felt her spirits lighten a bit.

Spence's words—''No shame. No shame, Elizabeth''— had played themselves over and over in her mind. *No shame*. She had felt ashamed of herself for so many things for so long that she was afraid she might not know how to live without it, or what other feeling might fill the void.

Even though she had not consciously been avoiding him,

she had seen little of Spence over the past few days. He rose early, ate his meals with the *paniolo*, and came in long after she and Hadley had retired. But some nights as she lay in bed on the verge of sleep, she would hear him come in downstairs, hear his footsteps in the hall below, and then the door to his room would close. On those evenings, her pulse would race, her face would flush, and sleep would evade her, dancing like a teasing child on the edge of her consciousness.

With Spence in charge of the ranch work, she had time to concentrate on putting in a vegetable garden, and she had enlisted Maile's help. The girl was proving to have a green thumb and a natural affinity for plants. Now neat rows of rich turned earth filled with vegetable seedlings bordered Elizabeth's tropical flower garden. Every day she and Maile hoed weeds and kept unwanted seeds from taking root amid the string beans, cabbages, carrots, tomatoes, celery, and corn.

"Mama, can we go down to the beach?"

A shadow fell across Elizabeth's eyes. She opened them and found herself staring at the tip of Hadley's nose. The girl had rolled over and was leaning across her, hovering just inches from Elizabeth's face. Since her daughter's last terrible asthma attack, Elizabeth had been giving her the *'āhinahina* tea Spence had prescribed, and Hadley was thriving. She had even gained weight.

Hadley was frowning down at Elizabeth, her forehead furrowed, her little mouth set in a serious line. Elizabeth thanked God that her daughter had inherited nothing of Franklin's looks or personality. Hadley asked for so very little that Elizabeth decided she should take the time to play with her.

"Yes. We will go to the beach," she said. Hadley let out a squeal, stood up and began to twirl around the hillside with her arms sticking straight out.

Seeing her daughter so happy, Elizabeth did not even try to hold back a rusty laugh. She pushed herself to a sitting position, brushed the grass off her hands, and stood up. She had taken time to mend a torn shoulder on the yellow calico dress she wore, but closing the long tear had required many stitches. The result of her handiwork resembled a long, jagged scar across the seam. Still, the yellow cheered her, and as isolated as they were, the mended and stained gown was still fine for garden work and walking along the beach.

"Hold my hand," she said. Hadley reached for her and held on tight as they made their way down the narrow trail that disappeared over the edge of the bluff and ran alongside the ravine. A waterfall, no more than a small trickle when the weather was clear, dropped over a tumbled span of black rocks. *'Awapuhi* ginger and *ti* grew wild along the trail. The tangy scent of fallen, rotting guava permeated the warm, close air beneath the bluff. A hundred shades of green tinted the hillside.

When they reached the beach, Hadley started to run toward the water's edge, but her shoes quickly sank in the deep, coarse sand. She stopped dead in her tracks.

"Can I take off my shoes, Mama? Pleeeese?"

Elizabeth's first inclination was to tell her no, but the morning was perfect, the surf breaking on the outer reef. The water was almost still, clear and smooth as glass. It looked as inviting to her as it did Hadley. She thought of Marion Randolph and knew what her answer would have been.

"Not only can you take off your shoes, Hadley, but you can put your feet in the water. And"—she leaned close and whispered in the child's ear—"I'm even going to take off *my* shoes and stockings and go wading with you."

Once again Hadley squealed with the delight of childhood—the magical time when joy and excitement come from all the little things in life. It took so very, very little to make Hadley happy. In the short time since Franklin's death, the girl had begun to blossom as her world opened up to her. She had been to Hanalei. She was spending more time with Maile and Uilani, getting to know Toshi when the old *paniolo* helped with heavy work in the garden.

Elizabeth wished her own horizons were expanding as quickly. She was determined to put the past behind her, to try not to worry about the present—the ranch debts, the future of Mauna Noe. Spence Laamea's unwanted effect on her.

The wonderful morning gave her reason enough to celebrate life, to embrace innocent joy and let herself drink in the sun and the sea and revel in the fact that she and Hadley were alive in this tropical paradise that she wanted so very desperately to call home forever.

SPENCE HAD JUST REINED in atop the bluff, pausing to stare out at the endless blue Pacific water and to wipe the sweat from his brow with his shirtsleeve, when a flash of yellow caught his eye. He walked his mount close to the edge of the cliff and watched in amazement when he recognized Elizabeth and Hadley frolicking in the foam at the water's edge. From high above the beach, they looked like two children, Elizabeth in her old yellow gown the color of a faded *hau* blossom, and Hadley stripped down to her sleeveless white petticoat.

Spence caught himself smiling at their antics, chuckled when he saw Elizabeth run backward, trip, and land on her bottom in two feet of water. Her skirt billowed up around her thighs, giving him more than a glimpse of her shapely calves and knees. His hand tightened on the reins when she drew her skirt higher, exposing her thighs. He told himself to ride on, to head up toward the high pasture where Duke and the others were working, but some force stronger than his will compelled him to ride down the beach path.

He tied the horse in an umbrella of shade at the bottom of the hill, sat down on a rock, stripped off his boots and gaiters, rolled up his pants, and jogged across the beach toward Elizabeth and the girl. Hadley was singing at the top of her lungs, waving both arms over her head, taunting the waves. She spun around in the midst of her dance and saw him. She froze, her eyes wide, her mouth open. Her nonsense song died. Elizabeth was still sitting at the water's edge, her back to him, leaning on her elbows. The tide swirled in over her legs and sucked back out, leaving her feet and ankles covered with sand.

Hadley continued to watch Spence close the distance between them. For days he had wondered if the little girl had ever seen her father hit Elizabeth—the question was driving him crazy. Hadley ran over to where her mother sat watching the water, scanning the horizon beyond the reef.

''That *man* is here, Mama.''

Spence watched Elizabeth's head whip around. She quickly struggled against the weight of her sopping-wet skirt to drag herself to her feet. Her thin yellow gown clung to her, outlining her figure from the waist down, and the delicate lace pattern along the hem of her petticoat showed through the fabric. Nothing about her attractive legs was left to the imagination.

As he drew near, he saw her catch her breath, raise her chin a notch. Her breasts rose when she drew her shoulders back, and he knew she had no notion of how provocative she looked standing there in the wet dress. Sunbeams danced in her hair.

Spence tried to deny what seeing her was doing to him, but the longer he looked at her, the more he was helpless to leave. How could he not admire this lovely, deceptively frail woman whose inner strength had sustained her through Franklin Bennett's wrath and allowed her to survive for her child?

Over the past few days Spence had avoided her, given her time to recover from the scene with Alberta Baxter, given himself time to digest all he had learned. Questions still remained unanswered, and they haunted him. Why had she come here in the first place? What had brought her to Kauai, into his father's life? What had made her desperate enough to stay?

Hadley was running toward him. When the girl reached

his side, Spence noted that the dark circles beneath her eyes had faded. Her cheeks were glowing with color, and she had even begun to fill out a little. The '*āhinahina* tea was working.

"What are *you* doing here?" Hadley demanded.

Elizabeth put her hand protectively on the girl's shoulder. "Hadley, don't be rude to Mr. Laamea," she said.

"But what's he doing here, Mama?"

"He just came to talk," Elizabeth said softly. She glanced up at Spence, who confirmed her hasty explanation with a nod.

Hadley eyed him suspiciously and sidled up closer to her mother. "Mama said I couldn't go way out there," she pointed behind her, off toward the horizon, "but I been in up to my waist."

Spence felt awkward as he always did around this child, his half sister.

"Your mama's right. It's not a good idea to go out there until you can swim," he told her.

"My papa was the *best* swimmer of all. Better than you." Hadley craned her neck to look up at Spence. Her expression dared him to deny Franklin's prowess in the water. When Spence failed to comment at all, Hadley shot off toward the shoreline and began to walk down the beach.

Elizabeth watched Spence, her wet hem gathered in her hands, the ends of her blond hair trailing in damp clumps over her shoulders. She could feel her heart hammering in her ears.

"Is everything all right up at the house?" she asked, wondering what he was doing here, why he had sought her out.

"All quiet. Maile is weeding. Uilani was cleaning a couple of chickens for dinner."

"I should get back to help Maile," Elizabeth said, wringing out her skirt, suddenly guilty as she pictured the young girl toiling in the hot sun.

Content for the moment, Hadley played alone in the shallows, throwing handfuls of water into the air. Elizabeth called out a warning for her not to go in any further and then turned her attention to Spence. She had known this day was coming, that he would want further explanations.

The sun had already begun to dry her gown. The skirt felt lighter when she let it drop around her ankles. She moved out of the froth at the tide line, shielded her eyes with her hand, and looked up the side of the cliff that walled in the cove. Bare, gnarled roots of pandanus and pine stood out like exposed veins against the cliff face. She marveled at the plants' tenacity to survive on the rock wall.

"I really should be getting back." Making a halfhearted attempt to avoid the inevitable, Elizabeth reached up and tucked her hair behind her ear.

"First we need to talk. Come." He started toward a *kamani* tree not far away.

"But Hadley—"

"We'll be close enough."

She thought of the day Spence had pulled Toshi free of the tangled ropes in Hanalei Bay. He was a strong, capable swimmer. He had already saved Hadley's life once.

They walked in silence toward the natural canopy of the spreading tree with its flat, shiny round leaves. Elizabeth sat on one of the huge, twisted roots that hung over the sand below it, where she could see Hadley at play. Spence preferred to stand, leaning one shoulder against the thick trunk. All around them, leaves almost the size of saucers lay piled one atop the other. The ground was littered with emerald-green and dried brown pods, as well as shoots from seeds already sprouted in the loose sandy soil.

Spence hated to question her. He felt like a prowler compelled to sift through the secrets of a past she had locked up tight and stowed away, but the questions were gnawing at his soul. He had to know.

"Why did you come here, Elizabeth? How did you meet my father?"

She folded her hands atop the damp skirt. The breeze whipped a strand of hair across her lips.

"Why is this so important to you?" she asked.

"I never knew my father, and what I did know of him doesn't fit with what I have learned since I came here. I'm only trying to piece the truth together."

Elizabeth stared down at the sand, dug her toes into it, buried and unburied them as she spoke. "Franklin wrote to a friend of his who was a member of the same missionary society as my aunt and uncle. Uncle Joseph Rodrick was my father's older brother. He and his wife, Sophie, took me in when I was sixteen, after both my parents died in a boating accident.

"Franklin wrote to this acquaintance who was once stationed here in the islands and told him that he was getting on in years and had decided it was time he had a wife and an heir. He was looking for a union with someone who had close missionary connections. He thought it would help his business standing in the islands."

Spence shifted his arm on the tree and looked down at the crown of her head, watched her reach for a seed pod and rub the shining surface of the bright-green skin between her thumb and forefinger. He waited until she went on.

"Because of an . . . indiscretion on my part, I had brought shame into my uncle's home. So when Franklin's letter was passed on to my aunt and uncle, they decided it would be best if I accepted his offer. Moving halfway around the world would give me an opportunity to start over."

Spence was still wondering just how terrible her indiscretion might have been when she said, "I never laid eyes on your father until the day I sailed into Hanalei. All I knew of him was what he had written to my uncle—that he was in his fifties, he was a rancher with a large holding, and he intended to be a good husband despite the difference in our years.

"Franklin was waiting on the beach when the dory from

the steamer came ashore. He had already made all of the arrangements. We were to marry right there at the river mouth beside the bay, and then he would bring me directly to Mauna Noe.''

It gave Spence an unsettling feeling to hear that Elizabeth had come to his father as a mail-order bride intent on putting the past behind her and starting over. She had never even met Franklin Bennett, never been courted or wooed by the man.

''I made a fatal mistake that day.'' Her voice dropped so low that Spence could barely hear her above the waves spilling over the exposed reef at low tide, lapping against the shore. ''I did not want to start a marriage based on a lie, so I told your father what I had done.''

Elizabeth took a deep breath. Not since the day of her marriage had she ever repeated the story aloud. Never once had she thought she would be telling it to this man—but he was Franklin's son. He deserved to know the truth about what kind of man his father had been.

She was tempted to look at Spence, but not yet. She was not ready to see any censure in his eyes.

No shame, he had said. But where would he draw the line? What did he hold to be shameful?

No shame. Not anymore.

She had survived Franklin and the past, and so she decided to draw strength from that. She continued, ''I told him that I had fallen in love with a young man named Johnny, who had turned out to be a scoundrel. Johnny promised marriage, and because I was looking for a way out of my situation I convinced myself I was in love with him. I agreed to sneak away, to spend two nights with him at a waterside inn. I awoke alone on the morning of the third day, waited and waited, and then searched the waterfront. Finally I met someone who knew him. Johnny had sailed out of my life on the morning tide.

''My aunt and uncle had been searching frantically for me and had enlisted help. Because I had nowhere else to go, I returned to them. They had no pity, no sympathy, of course, but they did not throw me out, even though I had shamed them. They set out to make me see the error of my ways.''

''Were you *hāpai* when you got here? Pregnant? Is Hadley Franklin's child?'' Spence concentrated on the little girl skipping through the shallows. If Elizabeth had been *hāpai* when she arrived, it would have been enough to set his father's wrath against her.

''Blood is everything, Penelope.'' Would Franklin have accepted Elizabeth's bastard? Had he claimed the girl simply because she was *haole*? Had Elizabeth told him the entire truth?

Elizabeth denied it with her very next words.

''Hadley *is* Franklin's daughter. He made certain of that. After I told him of my affair, he told me it did not matter, that he was only looking for a wife with missionary connections, that he wanted an heir. But after he brought me to Mauna Noe, he refused to consummate our marriage for weeks, just to make certain I was not with child.''

She had been humiliated when Franklin forced her to show him the evidence of her first menstrual flow after her arrival. Esther Timmons was to see that she never left the house those first few months—Franklin did not trust her with so many men around.

''Once a slut, always a slut'' was the topic of one of his favorite lectures.

Finally she looked at Spence, reminded of the erotic dreams she had had of late, and she was certain that Franklin might have been right about her lack of virtue.

Spence had not yet commented on all she had said. Instead, he watched Hadley at play. He was so quiet that Elizabeth had a brief moment of hope, but then he spoke and she knew he had heard every sordid word.

''So he waited to bed you until he was certain you were not *hāpai*?''

''Yes.''

''But he did not hold back his fists.'' Spence tried to put himself in his father's place, tried to imagine that much outrage and frustration, but he knew in his heart that nothing would have compelled him to strike this woman, or any woman. He would have put her back on the boat and sent her home to Maryland first.

''No. No, he didn't hold back.'' She thought it would hurt more, this slow process of opening, one by one, all the rusty locks on the door to her memory. But with each lock that snapped, she felt light flood in and warm her soul.

She had unburdened her darkest secrets to this man, secrets that no one else in the world knew. As she talked about Franklin and all that had happened, she kept asking herself why she should open up to Spence Laamea at all.

But then she looked down the beach at Hadley, remembered that he had given her back her daughter one terrible night a few weeks past. Because of that, he deserved the truth about his father.

Spence marveled at her inner strength. He knew the rest from what he had already pieced together from Uilani and Duke's information. Once Elizabeth had become *hāpai*, she had somehow used her condition to negotiate a truce. But before that, she had not been able to avoid Franklin's mad rages.

''Why did you stay?'' he wanted to know.

''After the night I ran to the Baxters' and they refused to help me, I lost all hope of escaping the island. I knew that once Hadley was born, I could never leave her behind. Franklin was so disappointed in her that he lost interest in me and thankfully, shortly after Hadley was born, he lost his ability to . . . to . . . father a child. One night he tried, but failed to . . . to . . .''

''I understand—no need to say it,'' Spence told her.

''Anyway, his impotency made him furious. He went wild that night, beat me senseless, blamed me. The next day I told him that if he ever hurt me again, or if he ever dared touch Hadley, I would make certain that he would never see her again, that I would escape somehow and take her away.''

Spence knew Franklin could have just as easily killed her and raised Hadley alone. How had she managed to survive?

''Weren't you afraid?''

''With every breath. Hadley's frailty was my only protection, and I made it seem far worse than it was most of the time. I told him she was sick even when she was not. Franklin was convinced that she would not live very long. I promised him that I would fight to keep her alive, that if he left us alone I would never tell her what an animal he was. I promised him that Hadley would grow up thinking her father was all a father should be.''

''Did he . . . love the girl?'' It was the last piece of the puzzle. Spence had to know.

''He barely tolerated her when she was healthy. About the only contact she had with him was when she was allowed to curtsy and tell him good night—like a trained pet or a little mechanical doll. Luckily, Hadley's asthma put him off. Franklin was afraid to go near her. He hated weakness of any kind.'' She turned to look at Spence, to admire his bold, handsome features, his broad *paniolo* tan face, his steady hands.

''I know, Spence, that had he ever known you, Franklin would have admired your strength. I think if he could have overlooked your Hawaiian blood, he would have been so proud.''

Years ago her words would have meant the world to him. Today, they were not worth the sand under his bare feet.

As they watched Hadley climb around the rocks at the far end of the cove, glimpsing flashes of her white petticoat against the coal-black lava rock, Spence felt as if his own world had just shifted out of balance, that if he were to look around he would find that everything in it—the mountains, the ocean, the sky—had just changed.

Everything he had ever believed about his father was a

lie. All of it. Franklin Bennett had lived a life without honor. Spence was truly thankful that he had never even laid eyes on the man.

Even more disturbing was the knowledge that his own reason for hating Elizabeth on sight had been founded on the misconception that his father had loved her, had treasured her and her child.

The truth was that Franklin Bennett had never loved Elizabeth. The old man had never even laid eyes on her, or she him, until the day they were wed.

Elizabeth had never been precious in Bennett's eyes, and her daughter's only saving grace was that she was white, legitimate, and carried Bennett's blood. Elizabeth and Hadley had been pawns, nothing more than possessions that Bennett kept under lock and key.

Spence thought of the animosity he had felt toward her and the deep-seated hatred that he could not disguise the day he came to Mauna Noe. No wonder she had been so threatened by him. No wonder she had not wanted him in her home and had argued with him at every turn.

If he had not helped Hadley through the asthma attack, if he had not happened along and heard what she had said to Alberta Baxter, he would still be living under a misconception and she would still be barely civil to him.

Elizabeth had loved her child and Mauna Noe enough to endure and hold on, but she had never loved Franklin Bennett. Spence did not know which would eventually have a more profound impact on his life—the knowledge that his father had been an unscrupulous blackguard or the realization that Elizabeth had never loved the man.

Hadley came trudging up the beach, worn down by play and sunshine. When she reached them, she walked around Spence and over to Elizabeth, where she leaned against her mother's knee and looked up into her face.

Then Hadley looked directly at Spence. She straightened her shoulders exactly as Elizabeth did when she confronted him and frowned, trying her hardest to look intimidating.

Spence had to stifle a smile. The girl looked like a wet duckling, her sopping-wet petticoat clinging to her spare frame.

"Are you feeling sad, Mama?"

"No, honey." Once the words were out, Elizabeth realized she was not merely placating Hadley. For the first time in a long, long while she really did not feel sad. Telling Spence about her past, putting her life with Franklin into words and letting them go had lightened the burden. It had been far more of a struggle to hold the past behind locked doors.

"Look." Hadley opened her hand and showed Elizabeth a triangular fragment of white pottery that lay in the center of her palm. The edges were already worn a bit smooth. Elizabeth turned it over to reveal a border of blue and white flowers on the other side. She set it back on the girl's hand.

Hadley stared at Spence again. "My papa was taller than you. He could ride fast as the wind and he worked all day long with the *paniolo*. He never had time to sit around and talk to Mama. He was always busy." She worried the piece of china between her fingers.

Spence watched Elizabeth's reaction as Hadley defended her father's memory. She sat without any show of emotion, and then she said, "Hadley, why don't you walk over to the rocks and toss the piece of pottery back?"

Hadley left to do her bidding without argument.

"Why did you do it?" Spence asked.

Elizabeth turned toward Spence, her eyes wide and serious. "What do you mean?" she asked.

"Why did you break the china?" Spence rubbed his toe against the root of the tree.

"Because it made me feel better." There was the slightest hint of a twinkle in her eyes.

"Do you always do whatever makes you feel better?"

"Not necessarily. But in this case, yes."

"You kept your promise. She believes Bennett could walk on water."

Elizabeth focused on the surf. "The man was Hadley's father. What should I have told her? That her father refused to spend time with her because she was weak and sickly? Should I have told her that he had not one shred of honor or decency? That he was a monster? Hadley was never going to know a father's love or know what having a decent father was like, so I created the illusion of one for her."

She turned to him and spoke with such frankness, with such intensity and love for her daughter. Spence knew that if she ever looked at him with half as much love in her eyes, he would do anything, go anywhere, give up everything for her.

"I love my daughter more than anything in this world. She is all I have. I wanted her to be happy, that's all. I wanted her to think that her father loved her, so I made excuses for Franklin's outbursts and his neglect."

"Did he ever hit you in front of her?"

She shook her head. "No. He was careful never to hit me in front of anyone—except once, in the kitchen, the day I first came here. Uilani saw it."

Spence admired her calm. She seemed so detached, so removed from the memory of what must have been a horrific situation. She had lived a lie for her child, kept the truth from her, hiding the abuse she suffered, always walking a thin line between Hadley and Franklin.

A sudden intense and terrible question began to gnaw at his gut. Had Franklin treated his own mother the same way? Had he beat her, too? Had Penelope done the same thing and lied to him about Franklin, painting a word picture of a man who never existed? Had Penelope Laamea shielded him from the truth the way Elizabeth protected Hadley?

His mother convinced him that Franklin was a good man who would surely come back to her one day and claim him. Would she have done that if she thought Franklin might beat him? Had she known the truth—that Franklin would never claim him? Was she like Elizabeth, creating a dream father for him?

"Are you all right?" Elizabeth leaned over, reaching out, about to touch him, afraid of the terrible expression of confusion on his face. She could see that his thoughts had traveled to another place and time. What must he be feeling now that he had heard the truth?

Spence could not answer her, for he did not know whether he was all right or not. He could not breathe. He could not even think. Down the beach, Hadley was trudging back and forth. Her early exuberance gone, the girl looked tired, ready to get out of the hot sun but not about to give up the freedom and the joy of the beach.

Spence looked away from the girl and locked onto Elizabeth's concerned gaze, a lifeline to the present. Even with her hair still damp and clinging to her neck and shoulders, in a mended gown that did not fit her well, she was so very, very lovely. So very real—not a figment of his imagination or his past. She was vibrant and alive. Not a memory like his poor, doomed first wife, Kaala. He reached out, expecting her to flinch. She did not move. With the tip of his finger, he touched the scar that cut through her otherwise perfect eyebrow.

"He did this?"

Elizabeth could not speak, so she merely nodded. There was a sure, quiet strength about Spence Laamea that made him unlike anyone else she had ever known. His voice was low and deep but touched with a melodic cadence that hinted at a mixture of English and Hawaiian. She felt herself melting toward him until they were so close that she perceived the warmth radiating off him, drawing her near, like a magnet.

I can't.

She tried to break the spell. He was the man who haunted her waking hours and came to her in her dreams.

It's impossible.

He was handsome, he was exotic. He was part Hawaiian, and she was *haole*. He was forbidden, and yet she wanted him in ways she had never dreamed of wanting a man.

Not him. Not ever.

Something elemental and primitive inside her responded to Spence and kept on responding to him—something she could not deny or ignore. She closed her eyes and tried to break the spell.

Despite the shade of the *kamani,* despite the trade winds that brought relief from the intensity of the sun, she felt hot all over. Anxious. Excited. Wanton.

She snapped her eyes closed. Fought the pull.

Spence was inexorably drawn to her by something significantly greater than either of them. Whatever it was, he knew Elizabeth felt it too—he saw the startled amazement in her eyes just before she shut them—as if that could stop what was happening, as if closing her eyes might help her deny fate.

I can't. It is impossible. Not her. Not with my father's wife, my half sister's mother.

His father had never loved Elizabeth, nor she him. Truth be told, his father had probably never loved another living soul in his life.

Before he knew what he was doing, Spence leaned down, touched his lips to hers, understanding on a visceral level that he could not go another heartbeat without sampling her, without sharing some level of intimacy.

Their lips met in a whisper-soft touch. It should have been enough, should have set off a warning in both of them, but if and when the warning came, they both ignored it.

Elizabeth felt his tongue trace the seam of her lips, as gentle as the slide of a raindrop down the length of a leaf. She shivered.

Spence marveled at the softness of her mouth, the tangy scent of mango that lingered at the corners of her lips.

Time and place and the strictures of society's rules fell away like broken shackles. Spence slipped his arms around her. Elizabeth leaned into him. It had been so long since she had been touched with tenderness, held as if she were someone precious, someone to be treasured. The kiss deepened, no longer a taste, a touch, but so much more.

"*Mama!* You let go of my mama!" Hadley's frantic shout had the effect of a lightning bolt.

Elizabeth put her hands on Spence's shirtfront and pushed. Spence pulled away from her, straightened his hat, and frowned at the child standing with her hands on her hips glaring up at him. Hadley's cheeks were bright with anger and sunburn. The color intensified the blue of her eyes. She looked like a miniature version of Elizabeth with her tangled blond locks and fretful expression.

"Don't you *ever* touch my mama." The little girl's voice had climbed to a high-pitched squeak. She was shaking with rage.

Spence pictured himself in this situation, more than six feet tall, nearly two hundred pounds, and any other time he would have seen it as comical, but not here and now, not with this woman and this child. He looked at Elizabeth and found her staring at her daughter as if she were just coming out of a trance.

At a complete loss for words himself, Spence sat on the *kamani* root, dazed, wondering what had happened to his common sense, wondering what had possessed him to kiss Elizabeth.

"Mama, *why* was he kissing you?"

Elizabeth made a small, choking sound. "I . . . he . . ."

Spence tried to rescue her. "I was trying to help her, the way I helped you the other night. She had something in her eye," he said lamely.

Hadley took a step closer to her mother. This time the accusation was put directly to Elizabeth. "But you had your lips smashed together," she said mournfully.

Elizabeth had regained a semblance of control. She pulled herself together and refused to lie to her daughter, who had seen them with her own eyes. "You're right. We did. Mr. Laamea was just . . . telling me something and . . ."

Spence tried again. "And it made your mother sad . . . so . . ."

"So . . . he gave me a little kiss, that's all. To make me feel better," Elizabeth finished, with a sigh of relief.

She looked at Spence, who appeared as uncomfortable and bewildered as she felt.

What had just passed between them was unthinkable. Shocking. For Hadley to have witnessed her transgression made it even worse.

"It won't ever happen again." Elizabeth spoke more to Spence than to Hadley. She meant every word as she stood up, shook sand out of her partially dried skirt, and held out her hand to the child. Hadley looked as if she was too angry to touch her, but after hesitating for a second, she shot Spence a parting glare and then took Elizabeth's hand.

They left him sitting there alone and walked down the beach, hand in hand, without looking back.

Eleven

AN ALLEY CAT HAD more moral fortitude.

With every step up the hillside from the cove, Elizabeth inwardly fumed and fussed over what she had just done. Head down, arms and legs pumping up the steep trail, she refused to turn around and look back at the beach, afraid that Spence was watching.

How she ever could have let him kiss her was beyond her imagining. What had she been thinking? Certainly not about the scandal that would have ensued if someone like Alberta Baxter had happened upon the scene.

Beside her, Hadley trudged along, grumbling continuously about being hot, tired, hungry, and itchy.

"Mama, I can't stand it," she whined. Her voice, an octave higher than normal, grated sharply on Elizabeth's already frazzled nerves.

"You're just feeling itchy from the saltwater. As soon as we get to the house you can take a bath." She reached for Hadley's hand, trying not to vent her impatience on her daughter.

"But I'm itchy *now*!" Hadley finally balked, went limp,

and hung from Elizabeth's hand for a second before she let go and plunked herself down in the middle of the path. Unfortunately, the mosquitoes were thickest in the ravine, and they began to attack. Elizabeth took a swat at a very determined pest when it landed on her collarbone.

"Hadley, stand up and stop whining." She tugged once on the girl's hand and then let go, turned around, and headed up the trail, praying that Hadley would follow.

As she continued on for a few yards, she wondered what she was going to do. She could not lock herself away and avoid Spence Laamea forever. It had been hard enough skirting him for just the past week. Now she could not even trust herself to be alone with him.

Abruptly she halted in the middle of the path and turned around to watch Hadley. The child was lying on her back, her arms folded over her chest.

"I'm *dying* back here, Mama, and you don't care!"

Hadley had never been so stubborn and willful, at least not while Franklin was alive. Elizabeth reminded herself to be patient. Not only was Hadley having a hard time adjusting to the death of the perfect father, the father she herself had created, but she was probably tired as well.

Sighing, wishing she had stayed in the garden all morning, Elizabeth walked back down the trail. When she reached Hadley, she went down on one knee, brushed her daughter's matted hair off her sweaty forehead, and then cupped her chin in her hands, forcing her to look up.

"I think Uilani has some *haupia* in the kitchen. How would you like some?" Tempting her with the promise of the slick coconut pudding, Elizabeth then kissed the tip of her nose. Although her daughter still tried to look upset, Elizabeth could tell she was wavering.

"Can I have two bowls?" Hadley sniffed.

"If you get up right now and start walking. The sooner we get back, the sooner you'll get to bathe and wash the salt off."

Hadley sighed, a long, audible sigh. "All right, then,"

she conceded, allowing Elizabeth to pull her to her feet. As they started up the trail together, Elizabeth found herself lost in thought.

"Secrets always come back to haunt you."

Marion was right.

Hadley's steps began to falter again, so Elizabeth shortened her stride. She tried to call Johnny Huffington's face to mind, but she could hardly remember what he looked like. She found that most disconcerting, considering that once she had willingly given him everything she possessed—her heart, her virginity, her good name.

To think she had just let herself be swept away again by Spence's soul-searing eyes and warm voice—

"Mama!"

"What?" Once more Elizabeth felt the pull on her hand.

"I simply cannot make it back," Hadley moaned, covering her eyes with her arm.

"Keep walking." Elizabeth slowed her steps yet again, tempted to sit down in the path and start whining herself.

"Mama?"

"What, honey?" She swatted a bug away.

"Why were you kissing Mr. Laamea?"

He was kissing me.

Elizabeth always took pride in Hadley's excellent memory, in the way she could recite pages verbatim from her storybooks after only one or two readings. But at that moment Elizabeth saw that memory as a curse. Hadley would never forget the incident at the beach, nor would she let Elizabeth forget it.

"Mr. Laamea and I are . . . friends, Hadley. We are trying to work together to keep this ranch going." It was a faulty excuse but one she hoped the child might accept.

"If you are working together, does that mean you'll have to kiss him a lot?"

"Definitely not. That was the last time I'll ever have to kiss him." *Have* to kiss him? *I practically initiated it.*

Finally they came up over the rise. She could see the

house with its wide, welcoming lanai, its long windows that faced the sea and the grand mountains in the distance.

As always, an overwhelming sense of homecoming and possessiveness came over her. She loved the odd yet imposing wooden structure set on the gentle swell of land. In the garden, Maile was a blur of purple calico. In the house, Uilani had started the midday meal and the aroma of browning onions floated in the air. Elizabeth's mouth watered.

Despite Franklin and all that had come to pass, she still loved this place. Slowly, over the years, the house itself had comforted her, embraced her. Hadley had been born in the room upstairs.

Before the reading of the will and all its complications, before Spence Laamea had ridden over the horizon, she so wanted to make this place hers and Hadley's, to make happy memories here.

Elizabeth paused to let Hadley catch her breath and continued to contemplate the house. Everything appeared so normal, yet in the blink of an eye, in the instant it took for Spence Laamea to kiss her, it had all changed. From now on, she would have to guard not only Hadley's future but her own traitorous body as well.

AS ANA STOOD FIDGETING with her sewing basket, then her hair, then the ruffled hem of her best *holokū*, she kept sneaking glances at Duke, who was wrapping her bundle of clothes and rolling a woven sleeping mat in a piece of oilskin. He flipped the rawhide strips and tied them around her things. They were nearly ready to leave.

She like the way the red fabric of her gown set off her dark coloring to perfection and had angled for a compliment when Duke first arrived, but naturally he was stingy with kind words to her. Duke would be the last one to tell her how wonderful she looked, so Ana gave up.

"Why you taking so long?" She had been urging him

to hurry since he had arrived at her mother's door an hour ago to relay Spence Laamea's request.

"No need hurry. We still gotta stop at Kilauea and get the stuff for make dresses, you know."

Ana sighed and watched him tug on his saddle cinch. "Spencer Laamea is waiting. Bettah we don't take too long." Thinking of the rich and handsome owner of Mauna Noe, Ana preened until Duke paused with his hand on a rawhide tie to watch her. She could tell it was beginning to irk him that she had spoken of nothing but Spence Laamea since Duke arrived.

"Laamea is waiting for you to come to Mauna Noe so you can make clothes for da *haole* lady. That's all."

Undaunted, she handed him her sewing basket, lifted the long hem of her gown in one hand, and grabbed the saddle pommel with the other. He gave her a shove up as she seated herself astride and squirmed around, adjusting her skirt—but not before she let him catch a glimpse of her bare feet, ankles, and calves.

Life on horseback was second nature to everyone on Kauai, and like the other *keiki*, Ana had been riding since she could walk. Duke did not have to concern himself with watching her every step of the way back to Mauna Noe, yet she felt his eyes on her as he followed her up the steep, slippery road to Princeville.

Once they reached the top and the land opened up along the bluff, they rode side by side. Ana caught herself glancing over at him more often than not, mostly with great irritation whenever she realized she was thinking about how handsome he was and about the way he had kissed her the last time they were together.

The memory had haunted her for weeks, had come to her when she least expected it. Late at night, while she lay sleeping on the *lau hala* mat on the floor of the little *pili* grass house with the rest of her family, she would recall the way his lips tasted, the way his mouth felt against hers. And then, in the darkness, she would feel the same sweet, desperate ache in her breasts, the same stirring need his kiss had evoked.

Worse yet, though she could still recall the taste and pleasure of the only kiss Duke had ever stolen from her, she could hardly even remember what Spence Laamea looked like. Now, as she struggled to picture the rancher, she caught herself sneaking glances at Duke and wondering if Laamea was anywhere near as handsome.

Not that it mattered in the least, she quickly reminded herself. Duke had nothing she wanted. What she had set her mind and her heart on was living in the grand house at Mauna Noe, a house that surely had real doors and lots of glass windows. She thought of the trips abroad and the jewels. Only Spence Laamea could give her those things.

Until Duke rode up to the house today she had almost despaired of ever seeing Spencer Laamea again, let alone of putting her scheme of winning his heart into action. Then, just like the sudden appearance of a rainbow during a trade wind shower, Duke had appeared. He was all smiles, teasing Chuckie, kissing her mother, telling them that she was to move to Mauna Noe to work as a seamstress.

Her mother had argued that Uncle Raymond needed her in the taro patch—until Ana grabbed her cousin Ruthie by the ear, dragged the girl over to her mother, and said, "Ruthie does not'ing all day but swim, fish, play. Time for her to quit making lazy and get to work with Uncle Raymond."

Her mother had studied Ruthie carefully and then laughed. "I t'ink maybe you right, Ana. Ruthie coming big enough to work, after all. You go Mauna Noe. Make fine dresses, make fine name for yourself."

"What you so happy about?" Duke asked, calling her back.

The breeze whipped the tall grass around them. Over time it had insistently forced the pandanus on the open hillside to grow at an angle away from the sea.

"I just knew Spencer Laamea gonna change his mind,

want me come to Mauna Noe," she said. Her glorious
dream was on the verge of becoming reality. Ana studied
the rolling hills and the wide, deep ravines. Fields of sugarcane were dispersed amid the open pastureland.

When Duke did not respond, she stole a sideways glance
at him. Beneath the brim of his woven hat, adorned with a
wreath of fern, his brow was knit in a tight frown.

She wondered what had brought the rain clouds to his
face. "What's wrong with you, Duke?"

"Laamea never change his mind and ask for you."

"Then what I doing riding to Mauna Noe?"

"He say, Duke, go to Hanalei, bring back da kine seamstress. Just so happens, I know you. Dat's all."

"So . . . Spence nevah sent for *me*?"

Duke adjusted the reins. Shook his head no.

"He even know *I* the one coming?"

The irritating man shook his head no again.

Ana pursed her lips. So, Spencer had not sent for her,
not exactly. He needed a seamstress—any seamstress. A
wave of disappointment washed over her, but being resil-
ient, she told herself not to worry over such a small setback.
She was going to be living on the same ranch with the man
day in and day out. Night in and night out. Surely there
was no way he could resist her charm.

"Now you smiling again. How come?" Duke slowed his
horse until they were riding almost thigh to thigh.

"I got no worry. No *pilikia*."

Duke let the irritating conversation drop and rode on in
preoccupied silence, hoping he had not made a mistake.
Ana had talked of nothing but Laamea since they left the
valley. The man might not have taken notice of her in Hanalei, but once she was living on the ranch, things might
shift like the wind and take a direction Duke did not want
to think about.

He felt a quick, fiery jolt of longing. She was more beautiful than a perfect sunset over calm water. He could almost
taste her lips—ripe and tempting as a succulent mango. Her

eyes flashed and snapped, filled with wonder as she admired the landscape. Her enticing round bottom was at home in the saddle, her shoulders straight and proud, breasts high and shapely. They bounced temptingly as she rode easily along. He tried to imagine what it would be like to undress her slowly, to savor the sight of her, to run his hands over her sleek brown body and feel the long, silky length of her black hair sway in an ebony cascade around him.

Lost in the sensual daydream, Duke was unprepared when his horse faltered. He nearly went sailing over the roan's head. Ana looked back at him, her smile flashing, her laughter as gay as the sound of the *'elepaio*, the fly-catcher.

"You better be careful, Duke," she called back. "You break you leg, then I be only one working at Mauna Noe and you be looking for one job." With a rich, lilting laugh, she kicked her horse into a run and raced on ahead of him toward Kilauea plantation. It was not bad, he mused, being left behind, not when he could admire the way the trade wind breeze lifted the hem of her red dress, exposing her shapely brown legs up to her thighs.

ELIZABETH STOOD ON A four-legged stool beside a wall of shelves in the ranch store across the wall from the office. After commandeering an apron, rags, and a broom from Uilani, she was armed for work, ready to sort and clean and organize while Hadley and Maile sketched pictures of the stuffed birds in the parlor. Despite the hour she had already spent working, she had made no discernible headway at all.

The high shelves beyond her reach were still coated with dust and gecko droppings. Cockroaches had taken up residence in every darkened nook and cranny. Whenever she moved a box, a tin, or a gunnysack, a host of the shiny black creatures came running out. Each and every time they surprised her, she squealed and almost lost her balance on the stool.

The newer bags of rice, flour, and potatoes that Uilani used were closest to the door, none of them infested with bugs or coated with grime yet. But a few steps beyond the door chaos reigned, with an assortment of cloth sacks of rusty nails, bolts of woven *palaka* plaid fabric in navy and white, a few bottles of liniment, kerosene, old tins of canned staples.

If Franklin had been able to keep workers on the place and keep the ranch running smoothly, this room would still be a bustling hub of activity, where the *paniolo* could buy supplies on credit against their earnings. Wives of men with families would come to get necessities they could not grow on the land or catch in the ocean.

Someday, she vowed, someday when Mauna Noe was out of debt and back in full operation, the store would once again see much use, but until that day, she was determined that the place be restored to some semblance of cleanliness and order.

Elizabeth was on tiptoe, stretching to slap a dust rag back into the corner of a shelf above her head, when she heard Uilani's unhurried gait on the lanai. She blew a strand of hair out of her eyes and stepped off the stool as Uilani walked up to the open door.

"You bettah come see dis," the housekeeper said without preamble. She tipped her head in the direction of the workers' houses.

Elizabeth put down the dust rag and wiped her hands on the front of her apron. "Is something wrong?"

"Some *wahine* moving into one empty house. Nevah seen her before. Looks like *pilikia* to me. You know her? How come she here?"

"A *wahine*?" Elizabeth frowned. "A *woman* is moving into one of the abandoned houses? I haven't heard anything about that."

She did not have to guess who *would* know. She wondered why Spence had not bothered to tell her—unless he wanted to keep it from her until the woman was settled in. She felt an immediate flare of anger and something more, a tension that almost hurt.

She refused to admit that she might be the least bit jealous—because of the complications.

Without taking time to remove her apron, Elizabeth crossed the room. Uilani followed close on her heels. They went around the lanai, down the steps, and along the lane lined with coffee trees, the remnants of Franklin's failed attempt at a productive crop. It was a short walk to the row of identical houses, so her curiosity would soon be satisfied. Once they passed Uilani's own house, Elizabeth caught a flash of red behind one of the windows two houses away.

She picked up her pace, Uilani's heavy gait pounding down the lane behind her. Just as Elizabeth reached the bottom step at the edge of the covered porch, the lovely Hawaiian girl she had seen at Marion Randolph's bed-and-board appeared in the doorway. Outfitted in a brilliant red dress that highlighted her dusky skin and glowing Polynesian eyes, the girl watched her closely with a haughty air of disdain and pride.

Refusing to be intimidated, Elizabeth met the girl's cool, assessing stare and caught herself reaching up to touch her hair.

"I'm sorry," Elizabeth said, "I know I met you in Hanalei, but I do not recall your name."

The girl's chin went up a notch. "Ana. Ana Pualoa."

Since Ana offered no other explanation for her sudden appearance, Elizabeth had no alternative but to ask, "What are you doing here, Ana? Have you come to visit Duke?"

Surely that's it, Elizabeth thought, relaxing somewhat. It would be unseemly of Ana to move into Duke's house, so the girl was taking up temporary residence in a vacant one.

"Mr. Spencer Laamea sent for me." The girl slowly swung her head to one side, executing an obviously practiced move that caused her long hair to slide across her shoulders.

"Mr. Laamea." Elizabeth's newfound calm evaporated. She did not know what to say. "Mr. Laamea—"

"—sent for me," Ana reiterated. "Duke went Hanalei, get me."

A slow, simmering burn began to numb Elizabeth's reactions. She stood there staring at the girl, wishing herself someplace else. Spence Laamea would not dare set up a mistress on the ranch, but she could think of no other reason why he would send Duke to Hanalei for the lovely young girl.

Could he have already slept with her the night they stayed over in the valley? Had he already tasted her charm, lusted for her, and simply could not live without her any longer? Had they known each other before he came to Kauai? Elizabeth watched Ana Pualoa waiting for her to leave as if she were nothing more than a mildly annoying interruption in a busy day.

"He told you to move in here?" Elizabeth wanted to be certain that she had heard right before she confronted Spence.

"Who?" The girl slid her fingers through her long hair. A hint of a smile teased the corners of her lips.

"Mr. Laamea. Did *he* tell you to move into this house?"

"Duke say Spencer tol' him tell me move in here."

"I see." Elizabeth remembered Uilani was still standing at her shoulder when the woman whispered, *"Pilikia."*

The girl was trouble, all right. Elizabeth refused to embarrass herself by asking exactly *why* Spence Laamea had summoned her. Instead she said, "I'm going to speak to Mr. Laamea about this, since he failed to tell me you would be arriving today."

Without waiting for a reply, Elizabeth turned around and started back toward the house. When they reached the lanai again, she told Uilani, "I'll be in the storeroom finishing up. If Spence comes in, tell him I want to see him, please."

Uilani walked away grumbling under her breath.

Elizabeth thought chances were slim that she would see Spence very soon. Since the day on the beach, he had given her a very wide berth, something for which she had been grateful—until now.

When he arrived within the hour, he caught her off guard, on her hands and knees wiping down a back wall of the store before she moved a barrel of pickled beef back into place.

Spence walked inside, took a cursory look around, and then stood speechless at the sight of Elizabeth on the floor with her shapely bottom waving in the air.

Finally, he managed, "Did you want to see me?"

Elizabeth whirled around, dropped the rag, and wiped her hands on the apron before she got to her feet. Avoiding him, it seemed, was not the answer—not when seeing him again sent such an intense jolt through her. She cursed her unfettered reaction, cursed the way her heart jumped and her palms went all hot and itchy. All she could think of was the way she felt before he had kissed her on the beach, the way he tasted when he did, the scent of salt and sea, and the savory sweetness of the gentle glide of his tongue across her mouth.

"Elizabeth?"

She shook off the wayward, immoral thoughts and struggled to remember why he was there. Then with trepidation she remembered—the girl in the red dress, Ana, with her haughty, bewitching eyes.

"Ana Pualoa has just moved into one of the empty workers' houses. She claims you sent for her." She waited for him to explain, to deny it, to temper the girl's curt explanation.

"I did."

His open admission stopped her cold. "Why?"

"She didn't tell you?" Even in the dim light that fought its way through windows streaked and clouded with grime, Spence could see the bright flags of color on her cheeks.

"No, she didn't."

"She's a seamstress. I sent Duke to bring her here so she could make you some new clothes." He watched her hand go to the neck of her gown and flutter there like a bird before she moved it to touch her hair. She brushed a long lock away from her dirt-smudged face. At the last second he stopped himself from stepping forward, from reaching out and brushing away a cobweb marring one of her smooth cheeks.

"Dresses?" she whispered. *New dresses?* She looked down at her faded, poorly mended yellow gown, then at the mess around her. The floor where she had just knelt was still damp with the outline of her knees, and so was her soiled skirt.

It was true that her gowns were worn. She had not had anything new since Maryland, but there was much dirty work to do now that she had taken charge of the house and the running of it and no real occasions in her life that would warrant new gowns—at least not yet. Besides, there was no money for new dresses, certainly not since Spence had bought a bull and a horse, definitely not after what she still owed Marion Randolph for a night's room and board and what they still owed Jensen and Carlisle. There was not a dime extra with which to pay for a new wardrobe.

She wondered if Spence had lost his mind—until she remembered how beautiful Ana was, how young.

Hiring her a seamstress was a very convenient way for a man to explain moving a beautiful young woman onto the place. Elizabeth looked up at him and felt her anger resurge.

"Surely you can think of a more plausible explanation." She wanted to force him to admit the truth, even though she was terrified to hear it.

"What do you mean by that?" He crossed his arms over his chest.

"For one thing, I can't afford new dresses."

He looked uncomfortable. "The draft from the agency will be here any day."

"We have no guarantee how much we will get."

"Those were prime cattle that we shipped. We'll get paid well."

"And then you propose to squander the money on your little *seamstress* under the pretense of having gowns made for me?"

"She's not my 'little' anything," he shot back. Her eyes were clear, dark blue, wide and doubtful. Suddenly he wondered if he had gone *pupule*. If he was not crazy, he hoped he was mistaken about what he thought he saw in her eyes.

"You're not *jealous*?"

She looked away quickly, fingered a tin of beets. "Don't be insulting. Jealous of what?"

Once he had put a name to her feelings, Elizabeth realized with chagrin that he was much too close to the truth. What bothered her even more was that she was afraid he might very well be right.

"She's not *my* little seamstress, for one thing. She's yours. I would think you would be happy to have something other than those rags you wear, if not for your own pride, then for Hadley. You are mistress of Mauna Noe now. Once in a while you should dress the part."

Elizabeth looked around the room, then down at the rag she'd been using. His thoughts obviously ran along the same lines as Uilani's. "For whom?" she wondered aloud. "The geckoes? The cockroaches?"

"For yourself. For the girl. Soon we'll need supplies. You'll have to go to Hanalei again. And what about callers? If anyone comes by, will you wear that green velvet gown and melt yourself again? Or are you keeping it in case it snows?"

"How dare you!"

"Look, my father might not have cared about what you wore, but I would think you would not want to disgrace this place by looking like a rag doll."

At that, he thought that she might be too furious even to speak, but then she surprised him. "Does Ana Pualoa accept credit for her services, like everyone else on this island?"

"I'm going to leave now, Elizabeth, before I say or do something I'll regret."

"Do that, please. I refuse to have Hadley exposed to anything indecent."

"You let her grow up with a man who was a cheat and a liar, a man who couldn't curb his temper or bring himself to love an imperfect daughter—and you say you don't want her exposed to anything *indecent*?"

Elizabeth closed her eyes against his quick verbal assault. The accusation cut her to the quick because it was justified. The truth hurt like the very devil, who was still tempting her with Spence even now as they stood arguing. She sucked in her breath and fought back the same needful feelings that had driven her to kiss him on the beach. Her fertile imagination replaced her attraction to him with images of the beautiful Ana occupying his arms, savoring his kisses.

"I don't care what you do with Ana Pualoa," she lied. "All I'm asking is that you carry on your little indiscretions outside my house so my daughter is not aware of them."

It was bad enough that Hadley had already seen her and Spence kissing on the beach. She did not want her to see anything worse.

"Is that all you wanted?" He tried to keep emotion out of his tone, keeping his voice low, even.

Shaken but resolved, Elizabeth nodded. "Yes. That's all."

Without a word of apology, without making any excuses or further explanations about Ana Pualoa, Spence started to leave. Then he surprised her by stopping abruptly in the open doorway.

"You'll never see me as anything more than Franklin's bastard, will you, Elizabeth? I hope to God you will never be this hard on Hadley when she grows up."

Before she could respond, before she could deny his words or even sort out what he had said, he was gone.

Elizabeth stood there, staring out the open door at the corral in the distance where Melvin was breaking in a new cow pony. Beyond the churned-up red dirt in the stable area, the open rolling pasture lifted to meet the base of the mountains. White clouds hovered over the highest peaks.

She had thought that keeping her distance from Spence all week would temper her attraction to him. She had thought that not seeing him would help cool her lust. Instead, face-to-face, she felt that deep, forbidden yearning emerge again. It started small, from where it lay curled up like a seed inside her, a seed that needed only a glimpse of him to start it growing, feeding off of her weaknesses, her years of intense loneliness, the faded memories of the love she thought she felt for Johnny and what she had so longed to find before she married Franklin.

Dear God, why not any other man? Why couldn't someone else stir the embers of the fire she had thought was extinguished so long ago? Why not someone safe, someone who would not turn her life upside down? Why this exotic, forbidden Hawaiian?

Why did it have to be Franklin's son?

She fought back the tears as long as she could, until they welled up in her throat and stung her eyes and she thought she would surely choke on them. Then Elizabeth walked to the door, closed it, leaned back and buried her face in her hands. Alone in the shadowy storeroom, she wept as she had not allowed herself to do for a very long time.

Twelve

ELIZABETH CAREFULLY UNWRAPPED THE moist burlap bundled around a clump of 'awapuhi roots. Cupping the root ball in her hands, she held up the wild ginger plant and inspected it for bugs before she leaned forward on her knees to set it into the hole she had prepared. Two days past, Toshi had come riding up to the back door with the bundle tied to his saddle. He told her he had collected it from the dense forest beside a stream not far away.

"Bring you plant for da garden," he explained, then he proceeded to tell her how Hawaiians used the bulbous ruby blossom filled with slimy juice for soap. Proudly grinning a holey smile, the old *paniolo* had snapped off a bloom and crushed it in his workworn, weathered fingers until the juice flowed. When he wet it, the sap foamed.

She thanked him profusely, deeply moved. She had been reduced to paying him nothing but room and board, but he thought enough of her gardening skills to bring the offering. Elizabeth now pushed the earth back into the hole, covering the roots, leaving the pointed shoots of new growth peeping out of the soil. As she lightly pressed the rich soil into place, she heard the soft chime of spurs. Her breath caught in her throat. She kept her eyes lowered.

She had been avoiding Spence Laamea for three days. Not only that, but when Ana Pualoa had come to the house, ostensibly to take her measurements for a new gown, Elizabeth had told the girl there would be no new dresses.

She took a deep breath, admonishing herself to be calm, and finally she looked down the garden path.

Relief and a surprising wave of disappointment went through her when she saw that it was Duke Makakani, not Spence, making his way through the maze of slick green leaves and rainbow-hued plants. His dark brows were knit in a frown. His broad Hawaiian features were shadowed by his large hat, but the serious, almost pensive look on his face was hard to miss.

Elizabeth leaned back on her heels and dusted her hands off against each other. Duke took off his hat when he reached her, held it by the brim and turned it nervously. She had the sinking feeling he was going to tell her he was quitting.

"What is it, Duke?" Elizabeth tried to smile, her courage wavering. If Duke left, Spence would have only two *paniolo* left, old Toshi and Melvin.

He shifted from foot to foot, ducked his head, rolled his hat brim and then straightened it, acting more nervous than she felt. Finally, he looked up at the hills, then back at her.

"Ana tell me you don't let her sew new dress," he blurted. "She feels plenty *kaumaha*. T"ink mebbe she gonna lose her job and Spence gonna send her back down to Hanalei."

Elizabeth sighed. It seemed the tempting Ana had acquired more than one champion here on Mauna Noe.

"I'm sorry she's worried, Duke, but I have no way to pay her for her time or her materials. If I did, I would rather pay the money to you and the other men before I ordered new gowns. You've worked without pay long enough, and if we keep running up debt, we'll never get clear."

He slicked his tongue across his lips, looked toward the barn. When he met her eyes again, he was still frowning.

"I get one house, plenty food, fish. Lotsa beef. What more I need right now? Besides, Spence get plenty money pay her."

Elizabeth stiffened. Had the draft come in? Had someone brought the packet of mail to the ranch and delivered it to Spence, not to her? She felt her hackles rise.

Duke said, "He get good money for da kine horse, you know. Money for cloth and t'read, everyt'ing Ana pick out for you at Kilauea."

"What horse?"

"Kāhili."

The image of Spence riding up to the ranch house that first day on the high-spirited Arabian mix flashed through her mind.

"Spence sold Kāhili?"

She saw Duke nod and felt her insides lurch.

"He sold 'em to da manager at Kilauea. Send him wid me when I go down Hanalei get one seamstress fo' him."

"*You* chose Ana?"

A glowing smile lit his face and he shook his head. "Mo' bettah have her here den Hanalei."

"More better for you?"

"Plenty." Duke's dark eyes shone as he looked down the road toward the camp houses.

So that's the way of it, she thought. Duke and Ana. Not Spence and Ana.

Spence, it seemed, had sold his prized stallion to buy fabric in order for her to have new gowns. *Why?* A knot thickened in her throat. She blinked away the sting at the back of her eyes. She had accused him of bringing a mistress onto the ranch, when in reality he had sacrificed the one thing of value that he owned—for her.

"Where is Spence?"

"In the barn."

Her cheeks burned with embarrassment when she

thought of the way she had so coolly dismissed Ana the day before.

"Would you please tell Ana I'll look forward to a fitting this afternoon?"

Duke smiled. "Sure."

"Thank you—"

Before she could finish, Hadley came running across the lanai, jumped off the bottom step, and zigzagged down the path toward them. Duke put on his hat and tugged the brim in a quick good-bye salute before he sidestepped Hadley.

"Mama—" Winded, Hadley put her hands on her knees as she stopped to catch her breath. She was breathing much easier since she had been drinking the herbal tea that Spence had prescribed.

"Please try to remember not to overexert yourself, Hadley," Elizabeth admonished. "You would breathe easier if you walk."

"That's . . . no fun. Besides," she said, taking another gulp of air, "Maile wants to know if . . . if we can go on a picnic. Just her and me."

"If you'll wait until tomorrow, I'll take you both to a picnic on the beach."

"But we want to go today."

Elizabeth turned back to her work, patted the ground around the new *'awapuhi* and then poured a bucket of water onto the loose soil. Hadley continued to plead her case as the water bubbled up and settled the dirt around the ginger.

Elizabeth began to stack her garden implements inside the bucket and leaned forward to grab a small, sharp scythe she used for weeding.

"I promise, we'll go tomorrow, but this afternoon I have something— Ow!" She pulled back and stared down at her palm, where a crimson stain began to flower along a deep slice.

As blood began to flow down Elizabeth's hand toward her wrist, Hadley leaned over her to see what had happened.

She quickly straightened, spun around, and went running toward the house.

"Hadley? I'm all right—" Elizabeth called after her as she disappeared inside. Quickly, one-handed, she untied the threadbare apron she saved for garden work and wrapped it around her hand. Blood soaked into the cloth quickly at first, but when she tightened the cloth, the spread slowed.

Carefully this time, she picked up the scythe, then the trowel, and tossed them into the bucket. She stood up and started down the path until she noticed that one of her tallest *ti* plants was top-heavy and precariously close to breaking off. Hadley had not returned and the bleeding beneath the bandage seemed to have slowed considerably, so she stopped to snip off the top of the *ti*, planning to put it in a vase where it could take root.

She called out for Hadley again, but there was no answer. No doubt she was already inside, pestering Uilani to make a picnic.

SPENCE LET GO OF a cow pony's hind leg and straightened with a sharp hoof pick in his hand. Melvin doubled as blacksmith, but there was no way one man could care for the twenty head of horses on the ranch. Even though his father had had no talent for business, Spence had to admit the man had been adept at picking and breeding good horse stock. Run-of-the-mill horses were plentiful on Kauai and could be had for as little as ten dollars, but the Mauna Noe stock rivaled the king's own stables. Had he not sold Kā-hili, he would have had a chance to strengthen the animals' bloodlines even more.

He was contemplating bartering a stud fee with the manager at Kilauea when Elizabeth's girl came running into the cool, shaded interior of the barn. Hadley was wheezing, not as hard as she did during an attack, but struggling for breath. Just outside the barn door, Melvin began beating a glowing hot horseshoe into shape on the anvil.

"I'm sorry, I'm sorry—" Hadley gasped.

Spence set the hoof pick on a shelf behind him and went down on one knee. Shock hit him in the gut when Hadley threw her arms around his neck and sobbed, "I'm sorry I been bad to you. You gotta get the medicine leaves for Mama. She's hurt bad. She's bleeding."

Before Spence could even ask what the girl was talking about, Hadley pulled back, turned a tearstained face up to him, and pleaded, "You can't let her die."

"What happened?" Alarmed, Spence pulled the child's arms away from his neck to break her stranglehold. Hadley wiped her eyes on the sleeve of her dress.

"Mama cut her hand. I don't want her to die. You have to get the leaves, you have to help her the way you helped me—and Toshi when he was bleeding. I'm sorry I was mean to you, Mr. Laamea. Really, really sorry. Please say you will help Mama."

Spence was on his feet, ready to go to Elizabeth. "She cut her hand? How?"

"In the garden, with that little crooked thing. She said 'Ow' and then she held up her hand and it was cut. She's still in the garden."

Spence's heartbeat settled back into place. "Show me where she cut it."

Hadley held out her hand and drew a line down the middle of her palm with her forefinger. "Like that," she said, forcing back a sob. "She needs the medicine leaves. We have to get them."

"She sent you to tell me that?"

The girl stared up into his eyes and then slowly nodded.

Hadley had not moved away from him but stood close to his leg, staring up at him without so much as blinking. Spence felt uncomfortable under the little girl's close perusal.

"I left my saddlebag at the *koa* shack up on the ridge. I'll go get it and come right back." Spence started across the barn toward the tack hanging on the wall.

"I'm s'posed to go, too." Hadley dogged his heels all the way.

"You sure?" Spence stopped and shook his head. He couldn't imagine Elizabeth turning the girl over to his care.

"Sure I'm sure. We gotta hurry, though."

"I'll saddle up and we'll go by the house and see about your mother."

"No. We have to hurry, because she needs the leaves." Hadley's shoes pummeled the ground as she danced from foot to foot.

Maybe Elizabeth was trying to make amends for the argument over Ana, he decided. Taking a halter off the wall, he pulled a saddle off a fence rail and headed for the gentle mare he had chosen for Elizabeth. He made quick work of saddling the animal.

The short ride to the *koa* shack would give him time to get to know this little half sister of his. Once more, he looked down at Hadley. The tears had stopped, the slight wheezing diminished, but the girl was still looking up at him, watching him hopefully.

"You ever been on a horse before?"

Hadley's eyes bugged. She nodded her head.

"You scared?"

"No." The child's gaze roamed up and then down the horse's long legs. The huge animal towered over her.

"You sure?" Spence thought she looked scared enough to wet her drawers.

Hadley nodded yes. Spence led the gray mare out into the sunlight. The girl followed, silent for the first time. Spence glanced over at the house, hoping that Elizabeth had turned her daughter over to his care as a sign of trust.

"Let's go." Spence reached down for the child, who weighed no more than a feather, swung her up, and plopped her in the front of his saddle.

Hadley grabbed handfuls of mane and held on tight as Spence mounted behind her. Once he was settled and had the reins in hand, Hadley looked back at him, her excitement unable to wipe out all the fear in her eyes.

"Don't let me fall," Hadley whispered.

Spence hesitated. He cleared his throat. Finally, as he kicked the mare and took off toward the hills, he slipped his arm around the little girl's waist and said, "Hang on, Hadley. I won't let you fall."

ELIZABETH SET THE BUCKET down, pulled off her shoes and stockings, and went into the kitchen. She walked over to the washtub full of suds, unwrapped her hand, and plunged it into the tepid water.

Uilani was at a table cutting up sweet potatoes. She went to Elizabeth as soon as she spied the bloody rag.

"What happen?"

"I cut my hand on the scythe. It's nothing, not very deep at all. Where are Hadley and Maile?" Elizabeth pulled her hand out of the water, checked the smooth sides of her cut, and pressed the edges together with her other hand.

"Hadley?" Uilani immediately looked worried. She glanced toward the window. "Maile go home. I t'ink Hadley wit' you." She turned around, frown lines creasing her forehead like winter storm waves on the horizon.

Water droplets ran down Elizabeth's arm, dripped from her elbow as she took off through the kitchen, along the lanai, and charged into the dining room.

"Hadley?" She ran to the bottom of the stairs. With every step she tried to convince herself that Hadley was safe, that there was no longer any threat to her. "Hadley? Come down here right now."

She waited for Hadley to call down, but the only sound she heard was the frantic beat of her own heart as it thundered in her ears.

"Hadley Elyson Bennett! Answer me."

Nothing.

She hiked up her skirt and ran up the steps, flung open the door to her daughter's room, dashed in and out, then into her own room. The trades slammed the door behind her, and the hollow echo rang in the hall with finality.

Blood was oozing from her cut again as Elizabeth flew down the stairs. Uilani was waiting at the bottom.

"Not there?"

"No, she's not. The last time I saw her was in the garden when I cut my hand." Elizabeth tried to remember what Hadley had said. "Are you sure the children didn't go on a picnic?"

"Sure. Maile go home, den going pick *'opihi*." The cone-shaped limpets that grew on the rocks were a favorite treat.

"Hadley said something about the beach, but I told her she was not allowed. Maybe Maile took Hadley with her." Elizabeth headed for the door.

"She know better than to take Hadley wit'out tell me first."

Elizabeth wanted to think that was true, but Maile was only thirteen—

"Besides, I see Maile go. She go all by herself."

Nearly frantic, Elizabeth implored, "Then where is Hadley?"

THE *KOA* SHACK ON the ridge was drafty and falling down, made of single-wall construction, thrown up years ago as a place for the *paniolo* to take refuge from wind and rain. Spence rode up to the shack and reined in.

"Hold on," he told Hadley, who had traveled in silence all the way from the house. "I'm going in to get my saddle-bags with the leaves in them." Dismounting, he paused to look back. Hadley was still clinging to the mare's mane for dear life. She was not going anywhere.

Spence ducked into the shack, grabbed the saddlebags off the bed, and opened them to be certain that all his bundles of cuttings were inside. He had been sleeping in the *koa* structure to avoid running into Elizabeth in the house. He could no longer trust himself to spend his nights under the same roof.

Spence hurried back outside and started to mount up again.

"Why did you kiss my mama?"

Spence missed the stirrup.

"Why did I kiss your mama?" He didn't know what to say. He finally got seated. They rode along in silence as he tried to find an answer, but he was hard-pressed for one, since he did not know how to explain it to himself.

Because she let me.

Because I had to.

Because I wanted her.

"Didn't you ask her?" Spence tried to shift the question back to Hadley.

"Yes."

"What did she say?"

"Remember? She said she was feeling sad and you were making her feel better."

"Don't you believe her?"

"If she was sad, it was about Papa, wasn't it?"

"You could say that."

"I get real sad about Papa, too."

Spence found it a pity that Hadley missed a man who didn't deserve one moment of her grief or the shedding of a single tear.

"Because you miss him," he said.

"I just want my papa to come back." Carried on the wind, the girl's softly whispered, heartfelt words were barely audible, but they reached Spence somewhere deep inside all the same.

From the vantage point on the gently sloping hillside, Spence looked out over Mauna Noe land to the sea. He remembered all the long, frustrating years he had waited in vain, hoping and dreaming that Franklin Bennett would come back and acknowledge him.

"If your papa could come back, I'm sure he would," he told her.

"But he's dead."

"That he is."

"They buried him in a big box and put it in the ground."
It wasn't so much a statement as a clarification Hadley
made for herself.

"That's what happens when people die."

"He can't ever come back."

"His spirit is not really in there." Spence hoped he was
not going to confuse her. He wondered what, if anything,
Elizabeth had ever told Hadley about death? He knew it
would take longer than the ride back to explain how the
Hawaiians believed that in death a man slips from the physical into the spirit world.

"He's not really dead?"

"His body is in the ground, but his spirit—" Spence
paused. Bennett's spirit was certainly still lingering here,
still controlling them through the tenets of his will. "His
spirit is here, even though you can't see it. He will always
be with you." He did not know if she was grasping any
part of what he said. "You know what a spirit is?"

Hadley turned around as far as she dared and looked up
at Spence through a blond curl over her eye. "Like a ghost?
Maile told me about ghosts. I don't think I like them."

"Your father's spirit won't hurt you."

"Can I talk to him?"

Spence would like to give the old man a piece of his
mind himself. "Sure."

The child rode along in silence, but Spence could almost
hear the wheels of her little mind turning. They had yet to
come in view of the main house or any of the outbuildings.
Spence shifted the reins, let the mare pick her way over the
rocky ground.

"You know," he began, thinking of Elizabeth again,
"your mother is very young. Someday she will marry
someone else."

Someone haole.

Someone acceptable for a white woman.

"Will I have to have a new papa then?"

"Anyone your mother marries will only be your stepfather. Your real father will always be Franklin Bennett."

Thanks to Elizabeth, Bennett would no doubt keep Hadley's loyalty and admiration, even though the man did not deserve one ounce of it.

ANA WATCHED ELIZABETH BENNETT step out of Uilani's empty *hale* and stand on the lanai. The *haole* woman looked up and down the dirt road. She had been calling Maile's name along with her daughter's. She looked like she could not decide whether to head down to the beach or go back to the house.

Before Elizabeth Bennett looked up again, Ana stepped out of the little wooden house she had chosen and started down the road to look for Duke. The Bennett woman ran down the steps and met her in the center of the rutted lane.

"Have you seen Hadley? My little girl?"

The *haole* woman certainly was a fright with her windblown, tangled hair. The skirt of her poorly mended yellow dress was filthy. She always looked like she had been rolling in the garden. Perspiration streaked her temples.

Winning Spence Laamea's heart would be no challenge if the only competition she had was Elizabeth Bennett. But as it was, Ana hardly ever got to see him. The man had a bad habit of disappearing whenever she was around.

"Ana, have you seen Hadley?" The Bennett woman asked again.

"Spencer rode off wit' her, little while ago."

"Spence? Which way did they go?"

When Ana pointed toward the mountains, the *haole* became even more distraught. For the life of her, Ana would never understand *haole* folks. She hoped Spence Laamea's being *hapa* wouldn't make him *hapa pupule*, half crazy.

An idea came to her when she saw how upset the widow was that Spencer had taken off with her daughter.

"Little girl look like she been cryin'. Spence holding her on da horse. The girl look plenty scart." Anything she could do to drive a wedge between the two of them could only help her own cause.

Elizabeth Bennett grew considerably paler. For a moment, Ana thought she was going to grab hold of her for support. Then suddenly, without another word, the woman turned around and started running for the barn.

Ana watched her go, unable to stop the smile playing at the corners of her mouth, wishing she could be there when Elizabeth Bennett caught up with Spencer.

She gazed up at the clear sky above her and practiced swinging the voluminous skirt of her favorite *holokū* in one hand while she continued her stroll down the road toward the corral where Duke was breaking horses.

ELIZABETH URGED HERSELF TO stay calm, to think logically, not to jump to conclusions—but all she could dwell on was Hadley, of how young and defenseless she was.

What if Spence had saved Hadley's life just to get her to let down her guard? What if everything he had said and done up to now was all a hoax? She was a terrible judge of character. Her brief affair with Johnny Huffington and her marriage to Franklin Bennett had proved that.

She found Melvin sweating over an anvil and a portable forge just outside the barn door. Every ring of the hammer against the hot iron seared her heart. It seemed to scream, "Hadley, Hadley, Hadley."

"Melvin!" she shouted over the noise, but the huge Hawaiian continued to shape the glowing horseshoe. He plunged it into a bucket of water beside him and then looked over at her as the iron hissed and sent out a plume of steam.

"Melvin, did you see Spencer and Hadley?"

For a moment he looked perplexed, as if he had no idea what she had just said. Finally, agonizing moments later, he nodded.

"Dey left."

She took a deep breath. "Where did they go?"

He shrugged. "Rode away."

"What did Spence say? Did he say anything to you? About where they were going or why?"

"Nut'ing."

"Saddle me a horse, please. Now."

He moved so slowly that she nearly came out of her skin as she followed him from the anvil into the barn, wishing she could invest him with her will to hurry, actually thinking about shoving him from behind to make him walk faster.

Finally he had a gelding saddled and ready for her to ride. Ignoring the pain in her hand, Elizabeth gathered up her skirt, took the reins, kicked the horse into a run, and burst from the shadowy interior of the stable into the sunlight.

Thirteen

SPENCE SAW HER BEFORE Elizabeth saw him. She was as graceful and competent as if she had been born in a saddle. On horseback there was nothing unsure or tentative about her. His admiration for her skill heightened as she leaned over the horse's neck and urged it over a fallen tree trunk, taking the jump with ease.

Her hair flew out behind her, loose and free. Riding astride, she had hiked her dress around her knees, and every so often the yellow material fluttered up. Her skin flashed ivory in the sunlight. His gut twisted. His hands ached to touch her.

He wished to God he had never kissed her.

"Mama!" Hadley shouted.

Spence raised his hand and waved again. Hadley mimicked him, but when Elizabeth failed to respond, Spence realized she could not distinguish them from the thick stand of *koa* trees.

"She must be coming to find us," Hadley told him.

Spence looked down at the top of the little girl's head. Accustomed to the horse now, the child was bouncing up and down and waving to her mother. The sound of her voice carried to Elizabeth, and she suddenly looked up, searching for them.

Spence caught his breath. His hands tightened reflexively on the reins when he saw her horse stumble and nearly throw her headlong onto the rough, rocky ground. Her narrow escape forced her to take more care, but she continued to scan the hillside, searching for them, as she rode on.

Spence whistled, a loud, shrill sound that made Hadley clamp her hands over her ears, and Elizabeth finally slowed her lathered horse. The gelding still wanted to run. Spence watched her fight the animal as it danced sideways. Then Elizabeth raised one hand to shade her eyes. He waved again, as did Hadley, and finally she saw them.

Spence tightened his arm around Hadley and rode to meet Elizabeth. It was not until they were a few yards apart that he read the frantic expression on her face.

"What are you doing with my daughter?"

Before Spence could answer, Hadley shouted, "Don't worry, Mama, we got the leaves!"

Elizabeth rode closer, eyes only for her child. Spence could almost feel the anxiety in her gaze as it roamed over the girl, scanning her from head to toe, inspecting every inch. Once Elizabeth was satisfied Hadley was all right, she retreated into icy composure and turned a cool, level stare on him. The gelding remained restless beneath her.

"Well?" She arched the scarred golden brow.

Spence looked at her right hand, noted the ragged, torn piece of towel tied around it.

"Hadley came running into the barn, said you sent her to get me so that I could dress your cut. She was upset."

"I did no such thing."

"But you *did* cut your hand," Spence said.

"Yes, but I did not send her to get you. I would never—" She stopped abruptly. He finished for her.

"—trust me enough to send her to me alone."

She did not acknowledge his statement. She did not have to. Spence watched the color rush back into her face.

"Hadley, did you tell Mr. Laamea I sent you to get him?"

Spence felt the girl slump back against him and then make a slight shrug.

"Hadley—" Elizabeth would not let up.

"Yes?" It was barely a whisper.

"Did you lie to Mr. Laamea?"

"But you were bleeding, Mama. I didn't want you to die like Papa." There was a hitch in the child's voice.

Spence immediately put a stop to the questioning. "She was plenty upset. I took her with me to the old *koa* shack on the mountain to get my saddlebags." The words came easily to Spence, even though, for the life of him, he had no idea why he felt compelled to defend himself.

"*Koa* shack?"

"Up the side of the mountain. I've been staying up there." It was all he would say, the only excuse he would make. He could not tell her he had vacated her house because since the day he touched her hair, the day he kissed her, he could not trust himself to sleep under the same roof with her.

HADLEY IS SAFE.

For the moment that was all that mattered. Elizabeth felt her heart slowly shudder back into place, and she tried to manage the horse beneath her as she listened to Spence make excuses for Hadley's behavior.

Her little girl had never lied to her before, and the fact that she had lied to Spence—even though she had done it to help—left a band of sadness around Elizabeth's heart. It was a small thing, the white lie, but a step toward the loss of innocence.

When she had finally seen Spence and Hadley on the hillside, she was arrested by the sight of the man and her daughter together. Spence was, after all, Hadley's half brother. It was something she had put in the back of her mind. Didn't they have a right to know one another, to forge some kind of a bond?

Hadley made no move to leave him. In fact, she looked very comfortable sitting there with Spence, who kept one arm wrapped securely around her waist.

The look on his face was anything but complacent, though.

"No matter what I do, you'll always jump to the wrong conclusion about me, won't you, Elizabeth?" There was a cold, even chill in his tone. Elizabeth knew he had every reason to be angry with her.

"I'm sorry—" She truly was, but Hadley cut her off before she could finish.

"Mr. Laamea told me Papa was still here," the girl said.

"What?" She looked at Spence again. "Why in the world would you—?"

"She had a lot of questions."

Spence kept his warm, dark gaze steadily locked with hers, willing her to listen. "She was talking about the burial. Big questions for a little girl. All I said was that her father's body was in the grave, but his spirit wasn't. I don't know what your beliefs are, Elizabeth, but she needed some sort of explanation."

"He said I could talk to Papa anytime I wanted," Hadley chimed in. "But Papa's not a scary ghost."

Spence clarified.

She watched the man fighting a smile. She could see that Spence and Hadley had formed a bond on their ride up the mountain. He had answered Hadley's questions more satisfactorily than she had.

Because of Aunt Sophie and Uncle Joseph, because of their unwavering religious fervor and its negative effects on her own life, Elizabeth had long ago decided to let Hadley choose what she wanted to believe in when she became old enough to do so. But her little girl had needed explanations for life's mysteries now—she needed to understand her father's sudden passing.

Spence Laamea—not Elizabeth—had been the one to provide those explanations. Elizabeth felt as if she had failed her daughter when she needed her most.

"We should get back and see about that cut," Spence said. "Duke needs help with the horses."

Until now Elizabeth had all but forgotten about the cut on her hand, just as she had forgotten what Duke had told her earlier—that he, not Spence, had chosen Ana Pualoa to be her seamstress. Elizabeth looked at Hadley, seated so confidently and securely in front of Spence, and she sighed.

"Do you want to ride back with me, Hadley?" Her hand was throbbing, the gelding eager to run again. She was almost relieved when her daughter shook her head.

"No. I wanna stay with Mr. Laamea." Hadley gazed up over her shoulder at Spence with nothing less than hero worship in her eyes.

Elizabeth wished for an instant that her own life could be as simple, that she could let her guard down and crawl into Spence's embrace. She wanted to experience again what she had felt when he kissed her beneath the *kamani* tree, to give in to her need rather than suffer this continual ache whenever she saw him, this deep longing for more.

But did she love him? Could she have fallen in love in a few weeks or was her need for him only sparked by lust? Was she acting out of need and longing to escape her predicament, the way she had in Maryland when she met Johnny?

She looked up at Spence and found him watching her closely with unfathomable eyes. She could only hope that her own thoughts were as easily camouflaged. Their gazes locked and held—one, two, three long seconds.

Spence was the first to turn away. Heading his horse in the direction of the ranch house, he rode off with her daughter tucked safe and secure in front of him.

• • •

ANA HOOKED HER BARE foot on the lowest fence rail, leaned her elbows over the top, and watched Duke swing his leg over the back of a wild-eyed young mare and jump to the ground. He dusted off his thighs, retied one of his gaiter lacings, and then straightened and came toward her, head up, smiling the wide, open smile she had known her whole life.

It irritated her every time Duke smiled and her heart jumped a beat the way it did now. She found herself wishing it was Spencer Laamea, not Duke, who made her feel as happy as when she was dancing the *hula* or when she stood on a hilltop at night, watching falling stars. As he walked toward her with a slow, easy gait, she wished that Duke, not Spence Laamea, was part owner of Mauna Noe. She wished he had land and money and lived in the big white house down the lane.

"What you doing here?"

He was still smiling, so she knew he wasn't irritated by her sudden appearance.

"I come see what Mrs. Bennett say. You talk wit' her yet?"

"Yeah. She like you go dis aftahnoon, start make dress."

"Yeah?" She grasped the top rail. Finally she would have a chance to see the inside of the rambling ranch house and to put herself in Spencer's path.

Duke nodded and smiled again. Ana cursed her fickle heart when it skipped another beat.

"So, t'ings going good for me, yeah?" Ana thought he looked too sure of himself, too certain that she might just fall into his arms again soon. It would not do for him to think that she had given up catching Spencer Laamea's eye.

"What t'ings?" he asked.

She tipped her head, made certain he saw her smiling a dreamy, faraway smile. Then she began to twirl the end of a lock of her hair.

"Mrs. Bennett ride away, mad wit' Spencer 'cause he

go off wit' da little girl. She one mad *haole*, I tell you straight." She ran her splayed fingers through her hair, swept it off the side of her face and tucked it behind her ear, then checked the other side, made certain her hairpins were still holding a white gardenia in place. Duke's smile quickly faded. His face puckered up in a tight frown.

She almost laughed. "It going be *so* easy for me to get Spence attention now. Working in da house, sewing da dresses alla time. He going to fall for me, I make sure."

When Duke's frown suddenly evaporated as fast as a noonday rain cloud and when he stood there, watching her with that crooked smile again, Ana began to get uneasy.

"What you looking at?" she demanded.

"You. You are one crazy *wahine*."

"I mebbe one crazy *wahine*, but I going live in a real house wit' real windows from now on."

"You like you place you get now?" When one of the horses sauntered up to him and nudged him on the shoulder, Duke reached behind him and absently began scratching its smooth, velvety skin.

Ana was not about to admit to him that she loved the little house. She was beginning to like it more than anything she had ever had in her life, and she had to keep reminding herself it was only temporary. Everything about the little box *hale* was perfect, from the glass windows to the wooden floor to the fact that it was up off the ground and did not leak.

No, she wasn't about to let him know she just might be content in a house that size, especially when she still had her eye on Mauna Noe's ranch house.

She shrugged. "It's all right. Small, though."

"Small? Who you kidding, Ana? That little house bigger den one you whole family get in Hanalei."

She sighed. Most of the time Duke Makakani was the most taxing man alive. He was no longer looking at her but staring at a point over her shoulder, so she turned around to see what had captured his attention.

"Looks like Laamea not make Mrs. Bennett so mad aftah all," Duke said with a chuckle. "Lookin' plenty all right to me."

Ana glared at the trio riding in. Duke was right. Elizabeth Bennett and Spencer appeared to be treating each other more than friendly. Spence still had the girl on his horse and was listening intently to something the woman was saying.

"Maybe you better go t'row yourself down in front of Spence's horse. Maybe if he trip over you, you get him pay attention."

Tickled by his own joke, Duke threw back his head and laughed so hard that Ana felt like reaching over the fence rail and landing another right hook to his jaw. Then she remembered that Spencer was close enough to see and decided it might not be a good idea.

"When you gonna see it, Ana?" Duke said as she hopped down off the fence and smoothed the evenly gathered yoke of the *holokū* she had made herself.

"See what, Dukie?" She used the childhood nickname that always used to make him see red. This time, though, he only laughed.

"Dat you wasting time chasing Laamea. You and me, Ana, we gonna be married."

She could not believe the nerve of the man. Ana looked over at the huge ranch house with so many windows she got a headache trying to count them and then at the lanai where she imagined sitting in a rocking chair with Spencer, watching the sunset, their steamer trunks all packed for the next voyage.

"Oh, I don't t'ink so, Dukie. You and me? Married? Not for one minute." She hopped off the fence rail and turned her back on him.

Duke watched Ana walk away, her hips swaying provocatively, her flashing eyes dancing as she headed toward Spence, Elizabeth, and Hadley. Any fool with eyes in her head could see that Laamea was attracted to the widow and she to him. Any fool but his Ana.

He hoped that when she realized Laamea wasn't going to take her bait she didn't wind up too heartbroken. Then again, if she did, he would certainly welcome the chance to help her get over it.

SPENCE DISMOUNTED, REACHED FOR Hadley, lifted her out of the saddle, and stood her on the ground. He expected the child to run to Elizabeth, who was already leading her horse over to Melvin, but Hadley was still standing beside him, practically clinging to his side, like an *'opihi* to a rock.

Spence ostensibly tried to ignore her, but he took care to keep an eye on her when he started toward the barn. Before he had taken two steps, Ana Pualoa came rushing up and stepped right in his path.

"Aloha!" she greeted him with a big smile.

Spence was beginning to wonder if Ana had some sort of affliction, the way she was always swinging her head around, tossing her hair over her shoulder.

"Aloha," he replied. He had respected Duke's choice, hoping that Ana would prove to be a deft seamstress, but she seemed a bit *pupule* to him. Spence wondered what conclusions Elizabeth would jump to when she saw him talking with Ana.

The girl did not appear to be going anywhere anytime soon, so he asked, "You doing all right?"

She nodded, tossed her head again. "I like the house just fine. Dis aftahnoon I going start fit one dress for Mrs. Bennett."

"Good." Spence nodded. Waited for her to move. Elizabeth was looking his way now, closely watching the exchange, which she could not hear. Then she called out to Hadley to go inside with her. Spence felt a tug on his hand and looked down at the child.

"Aren't you going to go in and fix Mama's cut?" Hadley's brows were pulled tight together. Her bottom lip in a pout. He could feel her squeezing his hand.

Spence nodded to Ana. "If you need anything, let Uilani or Duke know." He did not know how to get Hadley to let go.

He was forced to step around Ana to get to the barn. Hadley was still clinging. Elizabeth stood near the open stable with a pensive expression on her face as he walked up to her.

"Does your hand hurt?" Spence handed the reins to Melvin. Hadley finally let go of his hand so he could untie his saddlebags.

Elizabeth looked down at her bandaged hand, then back up at him. He expected her to stubbornly deny her pain if she had any.

"It's throbbing a bit," she admitted with a slight shrug.

"Don't worry, Mama. The leaves will make it feel better, just like they did my cough," Hadley assured her.

They all walked up to the back of the house together, the three of them, Hadley sandwiched between Elizabeth and Spence.

Like 'ohana, Spence thought. *Family.* But the child and the woman were not his family. If not for the will and his father's machinations, he would not even be here. He would have lived his life on O'ahu and never laid eyes on them.

No, not family. Not *'ohana.*

They went directly to the kitchen, where Uilani poured them tall glasses of juice and then brought a wooden calabash of water and clean rags to the table near the window so that Spence could dress Elizabeth's wound.

Before he began, Uilani came back with a packet in her hands.

"*Paniolo* from Anahola way bring dis up from Hanalei," she said.

Elizabeth reached out for the mail packet and thanked Uilani, then looked at Spence.

He watched her hesitate before she set the packet down.

"Do you think the credit voucher might be in it?" She was staring at the packet as if it were lethal. He hoped for her sake, for all of them, that the sale of the cattle had brought excellent returns. She had laid her injured hand, palm up, on the table. The raw wound sliced all the way across her hand.

"Would you like me to open it"—he indicated the packet with a nod— "or do this first?"

"Open it," she said softly.

Hadley was seated across the table from them. Although she was silent, her eyes missed nothing. "What is it?"

"The mail," her mother said.

Spence pulled the string that bound two letters, one fairly thick, one thin. He shuffled them and recognized the seals on both. Once was from Jensen and Carlisle, and one was from Robert Laamea, his uncle.

He set his uncle's letter aside without explanation.

"This is from Jensen and Carlisle." He unfolded the papers and glanced through them, then looked at Elizabeth, his expression unchanged.

"Well?" She scooted to the edge of her chair.

Spence could not hold back a smile any longer. "There is enough credit in the account to keep us going for six months."

She reached for the page. "Really? Let me see."

He handed over the drafts from the agency. She scanned the letter and documents and then read them again.

"Thank heavens." She sighed, relieved. "There's even enough to pay the men and Uilani."

"Plenty to cover the cost of the new bull and your mare," he added. "Maybe enough to hire more men in a few weeks."

She nodded in agreement. "It would be better to wait, I suppose." Then she looked up, startled.

He knew what she was thinking.

"Did we just agree on something?" Spence pulled his saddlebags closer and started laying out his herb packets, afraid to look at her, afraid that what he was feeling might be written on his face.

Choosing ashes of *'ahu'awa* and powdered leaves of the *lama* tree, he mixed them together.

"I think we did," she said, a trace of amazement in her voice.

When he looked up again, he caught her smiling, but it faded as quickly as a shadow after a cloud passes by. For an instant, though, her blue eyes had sparkled and years had slipped from her face.

Her smile might be gone, but it would be a long time before he forgot it. A glowing blush still tinted her cheeks. Spence concentrated on her cut, almost afraid to touch her hand. Afraid he might not be able to hide his feelings— feelings that confused even as they tempted.

"Uilani can dress this if you need to get back outside," she said softly, giving him a way out.

"No." Spence reached for her hand, gently cupped it in his, and brought it toward him. She moved with it, leaned across the wooden surface of the table. His thoughts ran out of control. He imagined tugging her into his embrace, clearing the table with a sweep of his arm, kissing her, pressing her back onto the hard wooden surface. Touching her, raising her skirt. Sliding her beneath him. Sliding into her.

"Does it hurt, Mama?"

Spence jerked, said, "I'm sorry," when Elizabeth winced.

He had forgotten Hadley. She was watching them intently, head and shoulders above the table, her eyes focused on the cut. Tearstains still streaked her cheeks. Her curly mop of hair was matted and tangled.

"It doesn't hurt, honey," Elizabeth assured her.

"Mr. Laamea will fix it." Hadley sounded as if she was reassuring herself more than her mother.

"I'm certain he will." Elizabeth looked over her shoulder and found Uilani right there, watching and listening, ready to help.

"Uilani, could you please take Hadley upstairs and wash her face and help her change clothes? By the time you come back down, we'll probably be through here."

At least she hoped Spence would be through quickly. He was still holding her hand, gently swabbing the wound, so gently that she did not even have call to wince. His hands were warm and sure, offering comfort and healing, not hurt. Uilani left the room with Hadley in tow, and Elizabeth found herself wanting to close her eyes and let the odd sensations quivering through her compound and spread.

Instead, she tried to fight them, kept her gaze locked on Spence's ministrations and focused on his movements, not on what his strong, sensual touch was doing to her insides.

Once he finished washing her cut, he smeared it with the ashes and pulverized leaves and bound it with a clean strip of cloth. Finally, he let go. The connection between them was broken.

A sigh escaped her. She met his eyes. He was watching her closely, so intimately that she wondered if he knew what she was thinking.

"Thank you," she said, hoping her voice would not betray her. Then, before she could say or do anything that might give him an indication that her emotions were running riot, she made an excuse to leave. "I need to go upstairs and clean up before Ana comes in. I've decided to let her fit me for a new gown. Since you went to the trouble to . . . to send for a seamstress. Duke told me that you sold your horse to the manager at Kilauea to pay for the fabrics."

"No need to look so embarrassed, Elizabeth."

"I accused you of something sordid and you were blameless."

He began packing up his bundles, carefully dusting fine grains of ash into his hand to clear the tabletop.

"I'm apologizing, Spence," she whispered.

"Accepted." He had not counted on Duke's telling her the way things were, had not wanted her to know about what he had done, for the dresses were a needed gift. But he was glad things were out in the open.

He pushed back his chair, stood and shouldered his saddlebags, anxious to be far away from her, out in the open where he could rein in his emotions. He had no business thinking about her, about what he wanted to do with her or the ways in which he wanted to touch her.

"If that cut starts to hurt, I can give you something for the pain."

"No."

Spence heard the same immediate, frightened response to his offer that she had given on the night Hadley was so gravely ill. There was something in her past that made her wary of his potions and cures, something she had not told him.

"I'll be going, then." There was nothing left for him to do but go back to work, even though he was tempted to use any valid excuse to linger.

Elizabeth saw him poised to leave, wished there was some way she could ask him to stay but deep inside she knew that fostering any kind of relationship other than a business one would be dangerous to both of them. As he turned to go, she looked down at the tabletop.

Then suddenly she said, "Wait, Spence."

Spence had just reached the threshold. He halted. Turned around. She held out her hand. "You forgot your letter."

Fourteen

Honolulu, September 1888

Dear Spencer,

  I hope this letter finds you well. Although my selfish sadness was great when you wrote to say you had decided to stay on at Mauna Noe, I can understand your reasons for doing so and only hope that guarding over Bennett's land for his daughter will be enough to sustain your happiness for many years. Know that whatever decision you make in the future, I stand behind you. Know also that Kalakaua asks about you often and that he is still ready to bestow upon you—whenever you choose to accept it— the honor of becoming a Privy Councillor of State, Knight's Companion of the Royal Order of the Crown of Hawai'i.

Spence lowered the letter and let his mind wander as he continued to contemplate the carefully penned script. He could hear his uncle's voice in his words, could almost see

229

his expression—calm, serene, disappointed. Robert Laamea would never force him into anything, not even if he thought Spence was making the wrong decision. Spence had learned that long ago when he chose to become a *paniolo* instead of apprenticing himself to his grandfather to become a *kahuna lau'au lapa'au*, a traditional herbalist.

Robert had warned him against going to Kaua'i permanently, tried to convince him that his place was on O'ahu, where his uncle was a privy councillor to the king, but when Spence had said he wanted to leave, Robert harbored no animosity.

A year ago, the king had been reduced to nothing more than a figurehead by the Hawaiian League, a *hui*, a group of *haoles* who organized to secure government reform and stop Kalakaua's lavish spending. The Hawaiian League drafted a new constitution and forced the king to sign it by threatening to attack him and declare a republic. He was reduced to the right to reign but not to rule.

Picturing his uncle seated at the secretary desk in his sprawling home in Honolulu, Spence lifted the page and began to read again.

Our King is unhappy, Spencer. There is much disagreement within his cabinet. The members vote often against His Majesty's wishes, so much so that he avoids meeting with them. Kalakaua travels often to the Big Island, hoping to establish agricultural ventures there. Recently he decided to visit Kaua'i, speaking often of his trip to Hanalei in '74 when all the people turned out to greet and support him.

He sends his greetings and notice that he will sail to Kaua'i to visit you on the fifteenth of this month—not as reigning monarch traveling with pomp and circumstance but as my friend and companion.

His Majesty will be arriving without fanfare and will only allow himself a few hours with you at the most as he travels around the island for the day on horseback. I have tried to convince him that Mauna Noe would extend him hospitality for as long as he was content to stay, but he said he dare not leave Honolulu for long, not with the threat of losing what little power he has left hanging over him.

And so, Spencer, I will be arriving with our King to see for myself that you are well and satisfied with your new position as trustee of Franklin Bennett's daughter's land.

Aloha nui. Until we meet again, I remain your uncle,
Robert Laamea

''What do you mean, the *king* is coming to visit? Ouch!'' Spence watched Elizabeth flinch, but her gaze never wavered. She was poised in the center of the parlor with Ana kneeling behind her, pinning a length of plaid fabric atop the dress she already had on.

''Sorry,'' Ana mumbled around the pins in her mouth.

Elizabeth rubbed the spot on her hip where Ana had used her for a pincushion and repeated her request that he explain.

Spence took off his hat and tossed it onto the deep leather chair behind him.

''The letter I received from Honolulu was from my uncle Lopaka, Robert Laamea. He's one of the king's most trusted friends. Kalakaua has decided to get away from everything that's going on in Honolulu and come to Kaua'i. He hasn't been here in quite some time.''

''The *king* of Hawai'i is coming *here*?'' As Elizabeth inspected the parlor with a critical eye, the shabbiness of the furnishings, the worn, threadbare carpets, the faded wallcoverings—all of it seemed to deteriorate before her very eyes. Even the stuffed birds looked bald.

''He'll only be here for a few hours on the afternoon of the fifteenth,'' Spence said, noting her frantic expression.

''The fifteenth of *this* month? Ouch!'' Elizabeth jumped again.

''So sorry,'' Ana mumbled.

''I think we should stop for today, Ana,'' Elizabeth told her, afraid that if she did not call a halt to the oddest fitting she had ever endured she might bleed to death before it was over.

When Elizabeth looked down at the young seamstress, Ana was peering around the back of her skirt, trying to smile at Spence despite the picket fence of pins protruding between her lips. Elizabeth warned herself to ignore the hungry look in the girl's eyes.

While Elizabeth waited for Ana to unfasten the length of cloth, she turned and found Spence surveying the room. He stopped when he spotted Hadley's bare toes sticking out from beneath the covered table in the corner.

''What's she doing?'' He tipped his head in the little girl's direction, almost afraid to ask.

Elizabeth rolled her eyes. ''She's Sleeping Beauty.''

''Aha.'' He nodded. ''Who is Sleeping Beauty?''

''A princess in a fairy tale. I'll explain some other time, perhaps when I don't have a king to worry about.''

Suddenly from beneath the tablecloth came a very loud response. ''I know why the king's coming!''

Elizabeth stifled a smile and a sigh. ''Why is that, dear?''

''He's coming to try the slipper on me.''

''That's Cinderella, not Sleeping Beauty.''

Spence wanted to know, ''Who's Cinderella?''

Hadley shouted back, ''Me. Because I just woke up and changed my name.''

''Never mind,'' Elizabeth told him, almost freed from the yards of cloth Ana had pinned and wrapped around her like a cocoon. Elizabeth wondered if Marion Randolph had been serious when she expressed confidence in Ana's abilities.

Hadley called out loud and clear again, ''Cinderella was

a poor, downtrodden girl who had to do all the dirty work and put things to rights, Mr. Laamea.''

Spence closed his eyes and shook his head.

"Which is exactly what I'll have to do by next week," Elizabeth said, looking around again and wondering how she could somehow transform the parlor and dining room into a place worthy of a royal visit. "I'll need help," she murmured. "Advice—"

"The king will only be here a few hours at the most," Spence repeated, watching in amazement as Elizabeth worked herself into a state, becoming more animated than he had ever seen her. She went on as if he hadn't opened his mouth, took a step toward the open doors to the lanai but was yanked back by Ana tugging on the fabric still pinned to her skirt.

Elizabeth chewed on her thumbnail. "There'll be food to prepare. What does a king eat? I'm sure he is used to the finest foods.''

"He'll be pleased with whatever we give him, the simpler the better. He's not traveling with an entourage, he just wants to get away from O'ahu, see the countryside. I think he's looking for any show of support. All we have to do is entertain him for a while and then he and my uncle will move on to the next stop.''

"Your uncle?"

"He'll be with Kalakaua.''

"Your *uncle*—"

"Is one of his closest confidants.''

"Why didn't you ever mention your connection to the king before?''

"Would it have made any difference, Elizabeth?''

She knew that if Spence had been the king himself the day she found out he was Franklin's son, she would have treated him exactly the same way. "I know nothing of Hawaiian politics and next to nothing about Kalakaua.''

"It's not a pretty story, especially the last few years, not for the Hawaiian people, anyway. Kalakaua wanted to give the Hawaiians a monarchy they could be proud of. He borrowed a fortune from Spreckles, the sugar king, and became so indebted that he was forced to give up more and more power in return.''

"I'll need help," Elizabeth mumbled to herself, only half listening to him.

"Uilani—"

"Will have her hands full cooking," she fired back.

"What about Ana?" Spence asked.

"Yes?" Ana slipped a straight pin loose and smiled up at Spence.

"I was talking to Elizabeth," Spence told her.

"How come you say my name?" Ana sniffed.

"I was just asking Elizabeth if you could help her prepare for the king's visit." He looked around for his hat as Ana stood and began to bundle up the material and her sewing basket.

"The king is bringing a slipper for *me*!" Hadley shouted. "I'm going to squeeze my foot into it even if it's too big." Now even her toes had disappeared beneath the tablecloth.

Spence thought that if he did not escape the three females and get back to the things he knew—men, horses, and cattle—he was going to lose what was left of his mind.

"Why would she think Kalakaua was going to bring her a shoe?" he asked Elizabeth.

"So I can go live in his castle—why else?" Still under the table, Hadley spoke up for herself.

There was a thump and then the table started to list precariously to one side, so much so that the stuffed owl atop it began to tilt. Spence made a quick lunge and righted the table and the owl.

"The slipper is part of the story." Elizabeth was beside him now, bending over, raising the cloth to peer under the table.

"Come out *now*, Hadley."

"I'm Cinderella," her daughter reminded her.

"*Now*, please, Hadley."

"Oh, Mama." Hadley crawled out backward on her hands and knees. Undaunted, she jumped up and grinned at Spence. "Aloha, Mr. Laamea."

He shifted uncomfortably. "Aloha, Hadley."

"I was going to let you kiss me like you kissed Mama so I would wake up, but I'm not Sleeping Beauty anymore, so you don't have to now." By the look on her angelic face he could tell that *she* knew exactly what she was talking about even if he did not.

Elizabeth gasped when Hadley mentioned the kiss.

Spence's own discomfort fueled his urge to leave. Ana, holding her basket and a mound of plaid fabric, stood by in shock and disbelief. Her gaze darted from Spence to Elizabeth and back.

Elizabeth was the first to move, muttering something about having to hurry to get a message to Marion Randolph.

"Women," Spence grumbled as he reached for his hat. For the life of him, he could not figure out why an informal visit from Kalakaua would rattle them so.

RAIN ROLLED OFF THE roof in waves, ran in translucent cords from the eaves to create a shimmering silver curtain that enclosed the wide, comfortable lanai like streaming liquid glass. Elizabeth stood in the shadows, enchanted by the flickering torchlight, listening to the singing ukuleles and guitars, marveling at the way Mauna Noe had come to life with the arrival of King David Kalakaua.

He had appeared late on the afternoon of the fifteenth as scheduled, greeted by gray skies, with no fewer than eight men who had accompanied him from Honolulu on his impromptu, unannounced journey around Kaua'i. He was fifty-two but looked younger, of strong, Hawaiian build with sad eyes, regal bearing, and a legendary capacity for champagne.

Both Uilani and Spence had convinced Elizabeth that dinner should be served outside so that everyone could be accommodated, but because of the heavy rain, the meal had been spread out on the lanai floor, on *lau hala* mats. Uilani shooed Elizabeth out of the kitchen and cooked for days—traditional island favorites that she was certain the king would relish.

Elizabeth had engineered simple refurbishment in the house, polished furniture, and directed Ana in the mending of draperies and the making of cushions and pillows. She even stood still long enough for another torturous fitting. Hadley squirmed, wriggled, and pretended to wheeze through a fitting herself, and by the day of the king's arrival, both of them had new gowns to wear—odd combinations of western and island fashion.

Marion Randolph enthusiastically accepted her invitation and arrived a day early to help Elizabeth gather and arrange the huge bouquets of *ti* leaves and heliconia, bird-of-paradise, and ginger, which decorated the lanai as well as the parlor, dining room, and foyer. The king brought *'ilima* leis—traditional slender, soft, orange-yellow strands—from O'ahu to Spencer and Elizabeth. Spence surprised Elizabeth by having woven long, open-ended *maile* and *mokihana* leis, a tradition of Kaua'i, for the king, his uncle, and one for her.

As she sat beside Marion and Hadley in the lengthening shadows of the wide veranda, charmed by the music and the voices blended in song, Elizabeth watched Spence, who was seated on one side of Kalakaua, his uncle Robert on the other side.

With the arrival of Kalakaua, she was treated to a side of Spence that she had never suspected he possessed. Relaxed and composed, he exuded dignity and decorum, even as he laughed and conversed with the king and his uncle. There was a lighthearted side to him that he had never shown, at least not around her.

Even now, he was laughing with the king over something his uncle had said. His head was thrown back, his eyes shining, and his laugh had a deep, resonant sound of joy that carried across the lanai and wrapped itself around her heart.

"He is quite a man," Marion leaned over and whispered in her ear. "I don't blame you for looking at him like he's a great big helping of coconut pudding. Have you slept with him yet?"

"Of course not!"

Elizabeth was shocked, not as much by her friend's bluntness as by the fact that Marion had caught her staring at Spence. Worse yet, she had somehow divined her thoughts. Elizabeth was thankful that twilight hid her raging embarrassment.

Was it so apparent, then, this obsession of hers with Spencer Laamea? Could *everyone* see it? She scrutinized each and every face on the lanai, let her gaze linger on each one. Until she looked at Robert Laamea, Spence's uncle, she thought that no one was paying her any mind.

It appeared that Robert, like Marion, was watching her closely. When she looked his way their gazes locked and somehow, without changing his expression in the least, he easily communicated his disapproval.

"No need to worry, ducks," Marion told her. "Your secret is safe with me. I'm assuming Spence doesn't have the least idea what you're feeling, does he?"

Elizabeth answered with a slight shake of her head. "I hope not," she whispered. If Spence knew or even suspected that she harbored such intense feelings, what would he do?

Probably leave the island on the next steamer, she decided.

Finally, she collected herself enough to look Marion in the eye, half expecting to see censure even though her friend's tone had held a note of teasing. What she saw on the other woman's face was understanding and warmth, a shared concern that one found only in the closest of friends.

The expression fostered Elizabeth's need to confide in Marion in a way she never had anyone else.

"I feel like such a fool," she whispered. "Not to mention a wanton trollop."

Marion dipped her fingers into a small wooden bowl of pinkish, sticky *poi*, brought them to her mouth, plunged the gooey mass inside, then smacked her lips as she licked her fingers clean, and finally shrugged. "Why?"

"*Why?*" Elizabeth was thankful that her hushed whisper would not carry over the sound of the rain. "Because it's improper. It's . . . immoral. It's perverted and depraved to lust after any man, let alone my . . . my stepson." A shiver that she wished had been fueled by disgust shot through her. "Isn't it?"

The singing had stopped and while the men debated loudly over which song should be performed next, Marion leaned closer and whispered, "You are a widow. Spence Laamea is *not* now and never was your stepson. He's not a child. He is as old as you are and not related to you by even one drop of blood. You're young and healthy, Elizabeth. Why should you be immune to his charm? My God, the man is a walking Polynesian Adonis. If I were a little younger, I might set my cap for him myself."

Elizabeth looked at Marion again to see if she was jesting, but Marion was absorbed, staring across the lanai at Spence. There was definitely a gleam in her eye.

Elizabeth lowered her whisper even more and leaned closer, "He is *hapa*, Marion."

"What does *that* have to do with the price of *taro*?" Marion shot back.

"A *haole* woman and a Hawaiian man? I know that *haole* men marry Hawaiian women all the time, but . . ."

"The shoe doesn't *ever* fit on the other foot, does it, ducks? That's the way of it only because *men* make the rules." She licked down another helping of *poi* before she went on. "I've always contended that rules are meant to be broken. You don't think I've lived a celibate life down in Hanalei all these years, do you? I've had more than a few lovers since I came to the islands—and more than a few of them were not *haole*.''

Elizabeth caught herself gaping and quickly snapped her mouth shut.

''Does my lack of moral fiber disgust you?'' Marion did not seem concerned in the least whether it did or not. She seemed to be asking merely out of curiosity.

What surprised Elizabeth most was that she was perfectly honest when she replied, ''No. Not really.'' Looking at Spence again, she understood completely.

''One just has to be circumspect about these things. If you do not flaunt your relationship, if you do not do anything to call attention to it, people will give you a certain amount of latitude.'' Marion paused while Uilani leaned close enough to pass a tray of *limu*. Then she went on.

''Life is too short, time moves too fast not to grasp what you want with both hands, Elizabeth. You have done your penance here at Mauna Noe, and even from the little I know of Franklin, I suspect you have endured more than a woman should have to endure. If loving Spence Laamea is what brings you happiness, then by all means, love him with everything you have for as long as you can so that you never look back in regret.''

Across the lanai, Spence was singing harmony in a duet with King Kalakaua. Their voices blended clear and true in a sound rich with life. There was a touch of sadness in every note, a finality, as if once the voices were stilled, not only would the song end but so would proud, ancient lineages and a way of life.

Spence had finished his meal and leaned back casually, half reclining on one elbow, hatless, shoeless, comfortable with the others and with himself. Suddenly their eyes met across the lanai and held. Elizabeth felt her breath catch in her throat, felt as if he were singing only to her.

Her hand went to the high collar banded about her throat, her fingers slipped beneath the fabric. Seeking some relief but finding none, she held the plaid material away from her fevered skin. It was impossible to look away from Spence, to break the hold his dark eyes had on hers. The grayness of the day had ebbed away with the sunlight, the lanai was now bathed in *kukui* torchlight that flickered and played across his strong *hapa haole* features, highlighting his lips and eyes, his thick, wavy hair.

Not until the last notes of the song were smothered by the sound of the rain was she finally able to break his stare. She looked down at the uneaten food on her plate. The appetite she had ignored all day vanished.

"Mama, can I go and sit by Spence and the king?" Hadley tugged on her sleeve, calling Elizabeth back to the moment, forcing her to think of something other than the ache of longing inside her. It did not go without her notice that her daughter had finally referred to Spence by his given name and not as Mr. Laamea.

"No, darling. Spence is busy talking to the king and his uncle right now. Besides, it looks like Ana is going to dance. You see? She's getting up and moving over beside Melvin and his guitar."

Hadley fell silent, suddenly engrossed in watching Ana Pualoa. The girl wore a thick *haku* lei around her head. More flower leis bedecked her green *mu'umu'u*. She looked radiant, young and lovely.

"Have you ever seen the hula, Hadley?" Marion spoke to the child, then to Elizabeth. "Have you?"

Elizabeth shook her head no.

"I can guarantee you'll never see anything like it. Ana is wonderful, too. She moves with the grace of a palm frond waving in the breeze."

"I didn't know you could wax so eloquent, Marion." Elizabeth laughed.

"Ana is very inspirational. In fact," her friend nodded in Spence's direction, "if I don't miss my guess, you had better hope that your Mr. Laamea isn't inspired by her himself. I know Ana—and I know that look on her face."

Elizabeth knew exactly what Marion meant without asking. Ana had begun to sway to the music of the ukuleles and Melvin's guitar, lifting her hips and bending her knees with openly sensual, provocative movements. All of the girl's attention was focused on Spencer. Everyone noticed and no one, including Spence, seemed to mind. The men were all bewitched by Ana's talent and grace.

A slight motion near the far corner of the lanai caught Elizabeth's eye. Duke was there, standing against the railing. The young man's eyes never left Ana, his feelings for the girl were written clearly on his face.

"Like I said, ducks," Marion reminded Elizabeth, "don't wait too long. Make your own rules, build yourself your own little kingdom up here at Mauna Noe, and don't look back. Don't ever look back."

Fifteen

"MAKE YOUR OWN RULES, build yourself your own little kingdom up here at Mauna Noe, and don't look back."

Marion's advice obsessed Elizabeth. When Hadley fell asleep in her arms, she slipped away from her guests, thankful for an excuse to leave and no longer be forced to watch Ana dance as if she were performing for Spence alone.

She looked down at her beautiful, peacefully sleeping little girl, ran a hand over Hadley's curls, then leaned down and kissed her on the cheek.

"Sleep tight, little one," she whispered, marveling at the way her daughter's perfect lashes shone golden in the lamplight. Elizabeth traced the tip of her finger over Hadley's fine brows down to the tip of her button nose, then sat back and stretched.

The scent of Manila cigars drifted up from downstairs, where the music and singing had dwindled to a lone guitar tuned slack-key and the talk had turned to the price of *pipi*, imported Arabians, treaties and councils, *haole* organizers, and legislature. The men's voices were deep and often boisterous, peppered with laughter, quick to flare with opinion and just as quick to die down to low murmurs.

Elizabeth rose, turned out the lamp, and closed the door silently as she left Hadley's room. Lost in thought, she tried to imagine how Spence would react if she gave in to her feelings for him. Would she be able to live with the repercussions if she did? Would it be fair to Hadley?

She did not notice Robert Laamea waiting for her in the foyer until he stepped out of the shadows into a ring of lamplight.

Elizabeth gasped.

"I'm sorry. I didn't mean to startle you." He spoke without a trace of pidgin English. His diction was smooth and cultured. He was taller than most *haole* men, broad-shouldered. Spence took after Robert Laamea far more than after Franklin, she noticed. In the soft yellow glow of the lamplight, except for his uncle's thick moustache, Spence could easily have been mistaken for Robert.

"I wasn't expecting anyone to be in here," she said, folding her hands together. Uilani's and Marion's voices carried through the open windows as they worked together in the small kitchen directly outside.

"The king is enjoying himself," Robert told her.

"I'm glad. It is an honor to have him visit Mauna Noe." The rain had let up somewhat, and patches of stars had begun to shine in the fabric of the night sky. She extended an invitation for them to stay.

"I'm certain we can find a place for everyone to bed down if His Majesty would like to wait out the rain and continue the journey to Hanalei tomorrow."

He shook his head. "This is Kaua'i, Mrs. Bennett. It could rain for a week. The king plans to be on the steamer tomorrow."

He looked so much like Spence that she was disarmed and felt at ease with him almost immediately, so she was taken aback when he said, "I see in your smile the reason Spencer did not come home."

"What do you mean?"

"Spencer came here only because he grew up obsessed with the notion that Franklin Bennett would one day acknowledge him. That obsession became loathing, but still it nagged at him. He felt compelled to attend the reading of the will even though, just weeks before, Kalakaua had asked him to join his innermost circle. Spencer gave up that privilege when he chose to stay here."

"I didn't know."

"How did you convince him to stay, Mrs. Bennett? Did you have to do any more than look at him with that startled blue-eyed gaze, or did you appeal to him with your look of helpless vulnerability?"

His smooth transition to chilly condemnation and the accusation that she had somehow used feminine wiles to keep Spence here shocked her speechless—but not for long.

"He stayed for the money he stands to make once he has Mauna Noe running profitably again," she told him bluntly.

"Spencer never cared for money in his life. If he had, he would not have become a *paniolo* against my wishes." He clasped his hands behind his back, walked over to the window at the far end of the foyer, and stared out into the dark drizzle.

"He stayed because of you, Mrs. Bennett. I saw the way my nephew was looking at you earlier."

"What are you talking about?" She felt a slow heat creep into her face.

"I am alluding to something that should not—cannot—be, Mrs. Bennett. Spencer is falling in love with you."

"No." The denial escaped her on a hush of breath. No. The man was wrong, he had to be wrong, for if there was the remotest chance that Spence *did* harbor any feelings for her, she knew it would be so easy to give in to her own desire.

"You will *both* be ruined by this thing, Mrs. Bennett."

"There is nothing—"

"Then tell me you don't care for him."

"I—"

"You can't, can you?"

Was she so very transparent that both Marion and Robert Laamea had discovered the secret she thought she had hidden so well?

"Send him home to O'ahu," Robert Laamea told her.

"I can't," she whispered.

"If you care for him at all, you will stop this before it is too late." His ebony eyes bored into hers. "Unless it already is."

She shook her head in denial. "No. *No*. You're wrong. Spence does not even care for me." She closed her eyes. "Most of the time we are arguing—"

"Then it should be easy to send him away."

"If he leaves before Hadley is eighteen, title to the land reverts back to the king. I have little funds, nothing with which to buy more land. My daughter will lose her inheritance, her home."

Hearing the truth spoken aloud gave her the courage to stand her ground. She refused to let this man intimidate her or make her feel sordid, not when she was far too likely to do that on her own. She was guilty only of lusting after Spencer, nothing more.

"I *never* seduced your nephew into staying here at Mauna Noe, sir," she argued. "He stands to make quite a bit of money over the next few years if he stays. I will not be insulted in my own home, nor do I wish to make a scene, but I will if you do not stop accusing me of something I have not done."

He bowed slowly from the waist in a courtly manner. When he straightened and took a step toward her, she could see a deep sadness in his eyes.

"You have just shown me what Spencer sees in you, Mrs. Bennett. I was wrong. It's not the cloak of vulnerability you wear so well, it's your stubborn determination that fires his blood." He ran a hand over his silky black moustache. "This can never ever be more than a love affair between you. You know that, don't you? Even if you should find someone willing to marry you to Spencer, the *haole* community will censure you both. Mauna Noe stands to be completely ruined.''

She looked over her shoulder, afraid that someone might come upon them and hear every word.

"I refuse to discuss this any further," she said.

Outside on the lanai someone called for another toast. The odor of cigars had grown heavy and cloying, the tone of the voices more argumentative. The excitement and joy of the evening were gone. Elizabeth wanted to go upstairs and closet herself in her room, to forget that tonight she had been forced to look deep into her heart and soul.

"Think about what I've said, Mrs. Bennett. I foresee nothing but heartache for both of you. I care too much for Spencer to see him ruined."

She turned away from him without a good-bye, intent upon the task of organizing the cleanup. She had not gone two steps toward the lanai when Spence came through the door.

Elizabeth stopped in her tracks. Robert Laamea had not yet had a chance to leave. He was still there, standing near the window, watching them both.

"Uncle," Spence said, smiling in greeting before he looked at Elizabeth. "The rain has let up for a time. Kalakaua is ready to leave."

"Fine. I'll go make certain no one needs anything else." Aware of Robert's intense scrutiny, she was anxious to leave, afraid her feelings might give her away.

Spence watched Elizabeth until she was gone. Then he joined his uncle at the far end of the foyer. When they were alone together, they slipped into Hawaiian.

"The king still wants you with him, Spencer."

Spence looked out the doors, stared into the night. Men and shadows were moving back and forth on the lanai, making preparations to leave. As much as he admired David Kalakaua, he was glad he would not be riding with him, glad he did not have to answer to anyone other than himself.

"I cannot leave yet," he told his uncle.

"Because of the widow."

Spence turned back. "If I leave, she will lose this place."

"That is why you stay? The only reason?"

"Yes." He could not tell his uncle that the thought of leaving Elizabeth would tear at his heart. He could not say that Elizabeth was to him what mist is to the mountaintop, that being near her quenched his soul's thirst in a way nothing had in years. Not since Kaala. He crossed his arms, leaned against the wall, and tried to appear at ease.

"If I leave, the land reverts to Kalakaua. No doubt he would sell it to the highest bidder, trade it for a horse, or whatever latest fancy strikes him."

"If our king did not like to spend money on appearances he would still be a king in more than name only."

"True."

"Kalakaua would give the land to you, if you asked."

Spence straightened. "What do you mean?"

"If you left here, broke the will, and the title reverted to the king, I'm certain he would grant it to you outright if you joined the Privy Council. Then you could do with Mauna Noe as you pleased. You could even give it back to Mrs. Bennett."

Spence unbuttoned his shirt collar and ran his hand around his neck. If he held title to Mauna Noe outright, he could turn the deed over to Elizabeth and ride out of her life.

She could easily find someone else to manage the place, someone of her own choosing, not Franklin's. She could get on with her life. If he left here, it would not matter where he went or what he did. He might just as well be part of Kalakaua's inner circle.

The trade winds came alive again, prompting the last of the clouds to move on. The lace curtains at the window billowed like sails. Spence moved toward the window to catch the breeze. He could see the mountains—dark, hulking silhouettes, jutting black against the star-splashed sky. A huge half moon hung just above the edge of the horizon like a half-eaten guava.

His uncle said, ''I lived through your mother's sorrow, Spencer. I saw the love in her eyes for Franklin Bennett and I see that same love in your eyes for his widow. I know what's written on your heart, what is in your mind, better than you.'' Robert put his hand on Spence's sleeve and lowered his voice. Spence knew his uncle's words came from love, but still they were hard to hear. ''Leave, nephew. Leave here before it's too late.''

THREE HOURS LATER, ANA slipped down the road toward the main house, keeping to the shadows near the coffee trees, carefully holding the hem of her turkey-red *holokū* out of the puddles that were scattered along the lane.

Desperation urged her along, desperation fueled by what she had seen when she danced the hula for Spence tonight and recognized it as undisguised desire. Tonight she saw for the first time what Duke had tried to warn her about. Tonight, while she was dancing for Spencer, he was watching Elizabeth. In his eyes Ana saw all the heat, all the burning desire that she had hoped to inspire in him.

While she danced she tried hard to concentrate on him alone, even when she felt her courage falter, but all night long she had been compelled to search out Duke in the crowd. She caught herself watching him laugh and talk and carry on with the men from Oʻahu with the ease of one who never met a stranger. While she found herself tongue-tied and unsure around King Kalakaua, Duke seemed perfectly comfortable, as if he moved in the presence of royalty every day of his life.

No matter how hard she tried not to pay any attention to Duke, she found herself drawn to him again and again. That fact was coupled with the knowledge that if she did not act and act now, Spencer would no doubt do something about his passion for Elizabeth Bennett, and her own chance at winning him would be gone.

She stopped beside a huge old mango tree, hid in the shadow of the trunk, and watched the house. Every window was dark, the house so still after the gaiety and music of the party that the silence seemed to hum. Even Mrs. Randolph was gone. She had left waving a white scarf, laughing and joking with the visitors, as she rode off with them, eager to experience what she called a midnight ride to Hanalei with the most handsome gentlemen in the realm.

Only Mrs. Bennett, the little girl, and Spencer were left in the house, and since she had been inside often enough now, Ana knew exactly where all their rooms were located. She went over her plan in her mind and glanced over her shoulder before she ran to the back of the house. From there, she crept around the lanai to the front, then froze when she hit a loose board that creaked under her bare foot. She held her breath until she was certain no one had heard her, and then she ran on, hugging the side of the house as she went.

Spencer's room was near the front, on the first floor. She felt her way around the corner until she reached his lanai windows. Her heart sank when she discovered that they were closed. She had mended the lace curtains at his windows herself and knew that the lanai door latch made a terrible squeal when it moved. Needing a silent entrance, she continued on to the open parlor doors and stepped inside.

The glass-eyed birds frightened her. She could not understand why anyone would want to keep stuffed dead bird carcasses in her home, but she had given up trying to understand the *haole*—especially since Elizabeth Bennett had ordered the best fabric chosen for her own dresses to be made into cushions and pillows for the parlor instead. Ana knew right then that the woman was not thinking straight.

Her bare feet made a slight *hush hush* sound as she walked on the woven mats on the parlor floor. Excitement slowly replaced her desperation. She was stark naked beneath her *holokū*. She had scented her body with crushed plumeria and pinned more of the blossoms above her ear.

She had rehearsed the coming scene over and over in her mind. Spence would be in bed. She would take off her *holokū* the moment she entered his room, and then she would awaken him and stand poised before the window, turned so he could see her silhouetted in the light of the moon.

She would bask in the adulation of his gaze, tempt and tease, staying just out of his reach until he whispered her name and begged her to come into his bed, into his arms. He would find out that she was more of a woman than Elizabeth Bennett could ever be. That there was more passion in her little toe than in all of that pale, *haole* ghost of a woman.

Once he made love to her, Spencer would discover all that and more, and then her future in this house would be secure.

It would be as simple as trapping *i'a* in a net.

She only hoped that before she walked the last few steps down the hall to Spencer's room she would stop thinking about Duke's flashing smile.

ELIZABETH GAVE UP TRYING to find a comfortable position in bed. Her nightgown was damp with sweat and tangled around her legs, her pillow was as wadded up as an old newspaper. The sheet had come untucked and was creeping up from the corner of the mattress.

She was hot and edgy and miserable, blaming her discomfort on Marion Randolph as much as she did the *kalua* pork, the chicken, the *laulau*, and the marinated squid. She gave up trying to sleep and decided to go down to the kitchen and have some vinegar and water to settle her stomach.

Not that it would do anything for her nerves.

As she went past Hadley's door, she heard the child

breathing undisturbed and envied her ability to sleep through anything. Downstairs, the house was quiet as a tomb except for the sound of the leaves rustled by the trades that seemed to echo off the walls. She made certain that her footsteps were silent as she slipped down the stairs. She had heard Spence tell Uilani that since the party had ended so late he would sleep here tonight, rather than up on the mountain.

Making her way through the dining room, she snagged the hem of her gown on a chair and pulled up short, bent to free it, and then went to the kitchen and searched through the cupboard until she found the vinegar bottle. She pumped herself a glass of water, added a healthy splash of vinegar, and drank it down.

Unable to decide which conversation had upset her more, Robert Laamea's or Marion's, she finally decided that both of them had given her enough cause to lose a ful! month of sleep.

She was bone-tired, so much so that her body ached, but her mind would not rest. Propping her arms on the table, she cradled her head on them for a few minutes and closed her eyes. Two minutes later, she was up again, pacing the room. After another glass of water, she decided to go back upstairs and at least lie down.

Halfway through the dining room, her heart leaped to her throat. She stifled a scream and stood there frozen, watching a tall, slim figure in a dark, flowing gown step out of the parlor and start toward the hall. Her first inclination was to run toward the stairs and head up to protect Hadley. Then, as the ghostly figure walked past a window, she recognized Ana Pualoa.

Dumbstruck, Elizabeth watched the girl creep down the hall toward Spence's door. There, Ana paused long enough to brush her hair back over her shoulders. She put her hand on the doorknob and, as if she were expected, opened the door and stepped inside.

"Aloha, Spencer. Here I am." Ana's throaty whisper

preceded a sultry laugh that easily carried down the hall to where Elizabeth stood watching in shock. All around her, the rustle of the palm fronds and banana leaves sounded like applause.

Elizabeth pressed her fist to her mouth to keep from crying out.

What a fool she had been ever to believe what Marion *thought* she had seen on Spence's face! How could she have ever let herself believe anyone else knew exactly what Spence Laamea was thinking or feeling? Even his uncle had been mistaken.

She had been right all along. He *had* wanted Ana here. Perhaps Duke was in on the plan because he wanted Ana for himself. Maybe the girl was sleeping with both of them.

Spence had never gone so far as to whisper false declarations of love, but he was still no better than Johnny Huffington. His gentle, caring touches, his concern, his kiss—she had taken them at face value, taken them to mean he cared. Was she so hungry for love?

Sick at heart, her fragile trust and stirrings of passion crushed like a tender hibiscus blossom, Elizabeth fled the room, unwilling to chance hearing any more or listening like a voyeur while Spence made love to Ana.

She could not go back upstairs and lie awake while they were together. She had to escape, at least get far enough away to put some distance between herself and what was going on in Spence's room.

She knew Hadley would sleep through the night, and the bluff above the ocean beckoned. She ran through the garden, across the rolling lawn. The sound of the sea grew louder as she neared the jutting edge of land. She stopped to get her breath, doubled over, and put her hands on her knees. She wanted to plunge down the path to the beach, but common sense prevailed. The moon was not bright enough for her to see the dips and roots on the trail. She could not risk falling. She was still close enough to hear if

Hadley should wake up for some reason and call out for her.

She sank to her knees.

Spence was with Ana.

She wrapped her arms around herself and rocked back and forth, too angry to cry. Too empty for tears.

Beside her, the grass rustled. Her eyes flew open and she raised her head. She looked around, saw him standing there on the bluff a few feet away.

"Elizabeth? What's wrong? What are you doing here?"

Sixteen

TOO LATE.

Ana stood in the middle of Spencer's room staring down at the white spread on his empty bed. The top of the chest of drawers was as bare as the standing closet with its door ajar. There were no shoes on the floor, nothing of his anywhere, just the heavy wood furnishings and the undisturbed bed.

She planted her hands on her hips and stood there as her anger simmered, the only sound in the room that of her own ragged, uneven breathing. There was only one place Spence could be—upstairs with his little *haole* widow, who was far more brazen than Ana had given her credit for. To think that all the time Elizabeth was acting so very proper, never so much as touching Spencer's hand or pretending she even *liked* him! Why, the very thought made Ana's blood boil.

It's my own fault, she told herself. Duke had tried to convince her that Spencer had eyes for the widow, but until tonight she had refused to see it. She had half a mind to go up and expose their little charade right now, just to see the looks on their faces when she burst into the room.

She turned toward the door, almost had her hand on the knob, when she remembered Duke and his position as *luna*. If she barged into Elizabeth's room for spite, if she caught Spencer and Elizabeth in bed, Duke might lose his job. He was responsible for bringing her here to Mauna Noe. If she did such a thing, not only would she have to leave but Duke would too.

There was nothing she could do but slip back to her *hale* and be thankful that no one had seen her or witnessed her humiliation.

She was about to leave when the door swung inward and slammed into her shoulder, sending her sprawling onto the bed.

Duke came rushing in. "Don't do it, Ana!"

Tangled in her own long hair and the fabric of her *holokū*, she rolled around on the bed before finally struggling to her feet.

"What's wrong wit' you, Duke? You going *pupule* or somet'ing?"

"Geezus, Ana," he stood there, towering over her, his eyes darting to every dark corner, every shadow in the room. "Where is he?"

"Who?"

"Laamea. Where is he?"

"Not here. Upstairs, I t'ink. Wit' Elizabeth."

He let loose a huge sigh of relief. His voice dropped to a heavy whisper. "Upstairs?"

She nodded, realized that they were standing there in the dark, and said, "What you doing here?"

"I come stop you, that's what." His chest was heaving, his big hands knotted into fists.

"So, what you going do? Kill Spencer, or what?"

After a long pause, he let out another sigh and shook his head. "Maybe. If he touch you."

Suddenly, tears stung the backs of her eyes. A silent sob

caught in her throat, worked its way out, and then cut through the stillness.

Duke heard. "What's wrong?"

"You were right about those two. Now I never get live here in dis house."

She felt his hands on her shoulders, his thumb beneath her chin. The light, lingering scent of Manilla cigars clung to him, mingled with the smell of saddle leather and the sweet *pīkake* woven in his *haku* hatband. He tilted her face up.

"You really t'ink a big house what's important, Ana? You t'ink even if you tie him in bed fo'evah you make Spence Laamea love you like I love you?"

Her heart was hammering in her chest. She felt the heat of his hands where they rested gently but firmly on her shoulders. She had seen the love in his eyes and tried to fight it for so long that she was tired.

"You love me, Duke?" she whispered.

"I t'ink I been loving you since da first day you come running up da river wit' Chuckie."

"But—"

"I know. You want one big house wit' windows and one door. Well, you got one little house wit' windows and one door. Not big like this one, but big enough for you and me, Ana. Big enough for some *keiki,* too."

She felt a hot tear slide down her cheek. It was so hard, this loving, knowing what she thought she wanted and what her heart told her it wanted. She rested both hands against his shirtfront, covered his heart—strong, steady, and sure—with her palms. He slipped his arms around her, enfolded her and drew her up against him.

"You t'ink Spence Laamea ever going love you more than me?" he whispered. "You t'ink he ever could?"

She buried her tearstained face against his chest and felt his arms close around her tight. "You really t'ink you kill Spencer if he touch me, Duke?"

"Mebbe."

"What else you t'inking about?" Ana knew very well what he was thinking about. He was holding her so close there was no denying his arousal.

"I t'ink mebbe we better get out of here before somebody come in."

"And go where?"

"Your *hale*."

"Den what?"

"Mebbe you better wait and see."

SPENCE WAS WALKING UP the last few feet of the beach trail when he glimpsed a flash of white between the trees. He hurried to the top and saw Elizabeth in a long white nightgown, running across the bluff.

He was standing there in shock, camouflaged by the night, when she fell to her knees in the grass, bowed her head, and hid her face in her hands. The moon's light reflected off her silken blond hair. Spence ran barefoot across the bluff until he reached her side.

"Elizabeth, what are you doing here?" He went down on one knee, raised a hand to touch her, then stopped, his palm suspended above her moon-washed hair for a whisper of a second before he dropped his arm to his side. "Is it Hadley? Is she all right?"

Elizabeth's hands came away from her face. She leaned back, drew away from him. "Don't touch me."

"What's wrong? What's the matter?"

"I *saw* her, Spence. You denied bringing Ana here as your mistress, but tonight I *saw* her go into your room. You asked me to trust you, and then you lied to me."

"What the hell are you talking about?"

She forced back a sob.

"Are you telling me that Ana is in my room? In the house?"

"You know very well she is."

"I don't know anything of the kind. I've been down on the beach, Elizabeth. *Alone.*"

He had gone to the beach to think, to walk along the shoreline, to get her out of his mind—but he had failed. All he could think of was his uncle's suggestion and his parting words.

"Leave, nephew. Leave here before it's too late."

If he did go to Kalakaua and promise to become part of the king's inner circle in return for a clear title to Mauna Noe, then he would be free to break Franklin's hold on all of them. Free to deed the place over to Elizabeth and Hadley.

Could he forget this land, this *'āina*? Could he walk away from her?

He lowered his voice. "Elizabeth, look at me. My feet are all sandy. I was walking on the beach, and now I am here with you. How could I have been with Ana?"

Even in the moonlight he read the vestiges of accusation and betrayal on her face. Her cheeks glistened with the silver streaks of tears. Her hands were balled into tight fists at her sides. Beneath her gown, her breasts heaved as she fought back another sob.

He glanced over his shoulder toward the dark shell of the house. There was only one explanation for why she was so upset over Ana's going into his room. He did not dare voice it himself or to hope. He had to hear it from her.

He gave in to the urge to touch her, stroked away her tears, and cupped her face in his hands. Her skin felt as smooth as it looked in the moon's silver glow. Cloaked in the magic of the night, time seemed to be suspended, as if everything that passed between them here on the bluff above the sea was happening in a dream.

"Tell me why you are so upset, Elizabeth. The truth."

She did not fight his touch but looked up at him, her lashes spiked with tears. She took a deep breath. "What do you want me to say? That I was beginning to trust you, to believe in you? That when I saw her go into your room I thought you had lied to me?"

He did not want Ana Pualoa. It was not Ana who fired

his blood with a fierce wanting that he had thought never to experience again. It was not Ana who made him long to risk everything. It was not Ana he wanted, but Elizabeth.

He did not move, did not speak. He was too afraid of what he might do or say.

Elizabeth knelt before him in the soft, wet grass, conscious of the dampness seeping into the fabric of her gown, attuned to his touch, the warm hands that cradled her face, forcing her to look into his eyes. The moon infused her with its seductive magic, gave her an awareness that she might not have possessed in the harsh light of day.

He was poised, waiting for the rest of her truth. She searched his eyes, and her heart stuttered. There was a secret longing hidden in them, something that she could not fathom, but it gave her hope. Somehow she knew that if she did not tell him everything right now, she would never discover that secret.

"Do you want all of it, Spence? Do you want to hear that when I saw Ana go down the hall to your room my heart began to tear itself into tiny pieces? Do you want to hear that when I imagined you taking her in your arms, into your bed—when I thought you were touching her, holding her, kissing her—my very soul shattered? That I was overwhelmed with jealousy and envy? That I wanted to *be* Ana Pualoa?

"Are you asking if I cursed the fact that I am a *haole* and that I was Franklin's widow because that means you will never want me? Is that what you wanted to hear, Spence? For that is my truth. All of it."

Her breath came in ragged bursts.

"It is all I need to hear, Elizabeth."

He pulled her into his arms and clasped her to him, defying the world, daring anyone to stop him, to deny his right to love her.

She wound her arms around his neck, lifted her mouth to his, and urged him to kiss her.

Spence slashed his lips across hers, covered her mouth,

kissed her until she opened to him and his tongue could delve and explore her warm, sweet recesses. She clung to him, moaned low in her throat, and pressed close to the strong heart that echoed the beat of her own.

The kiss deepened, became more than a kiss. It became hands that smoothed and coaxed and explored, lips and tongues that tasted, moistened, teased, until they were filled with a desire for more.

"I want you, Elizabeth," Spence whispered against her ear. "I've wanted you since the day I first laid eyes on you, before I knew you were my father's wife, and even when I thought I hated you because of that, I wanted you. I still do."

He held back, kept himself from taking more than she was willing to give, leashed by the conventions of society and his own sense of honor.

Elizabeth understood his hesitation and the reasons behind it. He would not act, but she could not stop herself. First she put her arms around him, untied the cord that bound his hair, and then ran her fingers through the ebony silk until it fanned out around his shoulders.

Sliding her hands up his shirtfront, she tried to unfasten the button at his throat, but her fingers were shaking so hard that they were useless. Then, overwhelmed by the need to touch him, to run her hands over him, she pulled at the button until the fabric tore.

Spence's hands replaced hers. Slowly, one by one, he unbuttoned his own shirt until it hung open, revealing his dark, smooth skin. Impatient, Elizabeth reached for the striped shirt and slipped it out of his waistband. He shrugged it off and tossed it aside, where it became a creamy puddle under the moon. The edge of his tattoo barely showed above the waistband.

She looked up at him, kneeling there before her, half naked beneath the tropical stars like a warrior of old. The ever-present sounds of palm fronds, of banana leaves and *ti* leaves, of the *hau* and the pandanus, all melded with the beat of her heart and the pounding surf on the rocks below the bluff. She felt wild, and pagan, and as free as the trades.

She lost her frenetic haste and now her touch was hesitant, tentative, the way a child might touch a bright, shining new wonder still full of surprises. Her fingertips kissed the warm smooth skin over his heart before she lay her hand over it and closed her eyes, trying to absorb its beat until hers throbbed to the same rhythm.

When his lips touched hers again, it came as a surprise and her eyes flew open. Gently he forced her back over his arm and lowered her to the ground. The grass was wet and spongy under the fabric of her nightgown. With time suspended like the stars above, she did not care about the damp grass, about the differences in the color of their skin, or about anything that had happened before this night.

Tonight, they were simply a man and a woman with needs and wants too great to deny any longer.

His fingers, unlike hers, were nimble as he unfastened the long row of buttons down the back of her gown. She shivered when she felt his hands on her bare skin. She opened to him like a white ginger bud coaxed into bloom by the sun.

He drew her dress down past her shoulders, exposed her thin white chemise and the rise of her breasts. Her nipples had tightened into hard nubs, her breasts felt heavy, aching with sensation. Before she could contemplate what was happening, he lowered his head and suckled her through the thin fabric of her underclothing. A cry escaped her. She arched higher, pressed her breast against his mouth, let him take more. Wave after wave of sensation pulsed through her, snaked from her nipple to set fire to her loins.

Spence pressed her down onto her back, ran his hands over her, and drew her gown up her leg, caressed her thigh, exposed her damp, heated skin to the cool night breeze. His finely tapered hands and fingers whispered over her skin. She sucked in her breath, trembled when he untied her drawers, bit her lower lip to keep from crying out when his

hand slid beneath the waistband. His fingers moved know-
ingly and unerringly to her mound, opened her swollen,
yearning outer lips and eased inside, stretching her.

There was no pain. Only immeasurable pleasure. She was
hot and wet, throbbing unmercifully when he touched the
nubbin hidden beneath silken folds. As he began stroking
her, she threw her head back and arched her neck, certain
that she was going to shatter. Her fingers dug into the grass.

Spence fought for control when he discovered the warm,
slippery nectar that let him know she truly wanted him. Her
harsh, rapid breathing, the throaty sounds coming from her
inundated his senses and nearly sent him over the edge.
Unconscious of anything but Elizabeth, longing to bring her
pleasure more than anything else, he continued stroking
her, increasing the pace as he tried to shut out the sound
of her desperate cries for release.

Finally she could hold back no longer. She raised her
hips and pressed into his hand, convulsed with wave after
wave of shuddering, intense bliss.

When she finally settled back inside herself, Elizabeth
found she was wrapped in Spencer's arms. He held her
tight, without words. Tears of elation and joy streaked her
face. She tried to hide against his shoulder.

He made her look into his eyes for one long, unsettling
heartbeat. Then he kissed her tears away.

She reached between their bodies, untied his trousers
and, as he had done with her, slipped her hand down and
sought him out. When her fingertips touched his engorged
shaft and traced the velvety softness at its tip, she felt him
quiver, heard him groan low in his throat. She encircled his
heated flesh, ran her hand down the length of him, cupped
him, teased him until he shuddered in her arms.

"Come into me, Spencer," she whispered. "I need
you."

Without hesitation he raised up over her until he was
kneeling between her legs, a deep shadow surrounded by
skin as pale as creamy moonlight. When he shucked his

trousers down around his knees he heard her gasp, felt her fingers tracing the pattern of his tattoo. Her touch scorched his skin as she drew her hand along the evenly set pattern of triangles, over his hip, down his buttock, back around to the outside of his thigh. He slipped his fingers into the waistband of her drawers and drew them off, tracing her skin as he went, evoking chicken skin, shivers, the soft hush of a sigh.

He tossed her drawers aside, drew her chemise down to her waist and tasted her sweet, hard nipples again, drawing on them, laving them until her head was thrashing back and forth in the cool, damp grass. She kept repeating his name in a litany of throaty whispers.

"Open your eyes, Elizabeth," he spoke against her lips, hovering over her, poised at the entrance to her quivering flesh, coercing her with seductive blackmail until she looked into his eyes.

"Say my name," he whispered. He wanted her to remember this night always, just as he vowed he would never forget this woman—pale as ivory, gentle as the mist on the mountain, yet as strong as the singing bamboo that bends and does not break.

"Spencer," she whispered back, the sound on her lips more of a caress than a word. "Spence."

He thrust into her, deep, far enough to feel the entrance to her womb, and then he went perfectly still. Buried inside her, he chanted her name, over and over in his mind, like a sacred *oli*.

Elizabeth. Elizabeth. Elizabeth.

For reasons he could not fathom, his *'aumakua* had sent her to him. She was his, if only under cover of darkness, where all men were alike.

Tonight she belonged to no one else. Tonight she was his.

She began to move with the rhythm of the sea, coaxing him with her body, urging him on until he was consumed with a need so great that when she cried out in satisfaction, he could not hold back. He came with her, crested the wave with her, letting his cry mingle with hers until the sound of their voices was carried away on the trade winds.

When Elizabeth felt Spence pull away, she was as bereft as if he were gone from her forever and not lying just inches away, still touching, still pressed against her. Although her eyes were closed, she could feel him staring down at her. He brushed her hair off her cheek. His fingers drifted across her face, down her neck, across her collarbone.

She felt as if she were floating somewhere outside of herself, as if she were no longer Elizabeth, but something more. A woman lying exposed to the moon and the stars, in the grass beside a man, her lover, and yet something not of the earth, something free and light and unfettered.

Sighing, she shifted so that she lay closer to him. Spence continued to trace his hand over her shoulder, her collarbone, almost as if he were committing every inch of her to memory, slowly, painstakingly, so that he would not forget.

She wanted to ask him what he was thinking, what he was feeling. She wanted to tell him that she had never felt this way, never had a glimmer of what true fulfillment was until now. With Johnny she had been an inexperienced virgin and he little more than an adolescent—an awkward, grasping, selfish young man bent on his own pleasure more than hers.

And Franklin? Except for Hadley, all Franklin had ever given her was pain.

She opened her eyes. The night sky was still clear, the air blessedly cooler. Now and again a ghostly white, translucent cloud would scuttle across the face of the moon and move on. Dressed in night, everything on the land around them had been reduced to gradations of shadow and light that reminded Elizabeth of the way her perception of the world had changed.

When she was younger, her view of life was made up of a rainbow of colors. Later, after her parents died, Aunt Sophie and Uncle Joseph tried to teach her that the world was black or white—right or wrong, truth or lie, virtue or sin. Now, lying beside Spence in the moonlight, she saw everything, including the two of them, in shades of ghostly ivory and dusky shadows that shifted and blended and merged. The palms and pines, the fronds and leaves, the earth and rocks and hills and mountains, black, hulking shapes thrust against the sky—all of nature melded together.

She wondered if he was thinking about tomorrow— about tomorrow and all the tomorrows after that. Very soon she would have to get up and go back to the house, to Hadley and the responsibilities of Mauna Noe. Before she was ready, the sun would rise on a new day. How would she and Spence deal together tomorrow? Would they go on as if tonight never happened?

Would she ever get enough of him?

REGRET SEEPED INTO SPENCE like a slow-moving poison sluicing through his veins, a venom driven by second thoughts and doubts that began to plague him as soon as he spilled his seed inside her. But even regret failed to diminish his desire. He grew hard again, wanting Elizabeth even as he lay there contemplating all the repercussions of what he—what *they*—had just done.

He had not meant to come inside her. He had intended to waste his seed to ensure that there would be no bastard, like himself, no *keiki manuahi*. As a *haole* woman, her life could be ruined if she married a *hapa haole* man.

What they had shared here tonight he would never forget. There had been no woman except Kaala before Elizabeth. There would be no one after her. He knew that for a certainty, just as he had known the first time he saw his *'aumakua*, the owl, and then his pale, moonlight lady, that they were fated to be together.

He had to leave her now, even if it meant leaving Mauna Noe and breaking the terms of the will. He was not strong enough to stay and be tempted again. He could not ruin whatever chances Elizabeth had for happiness.

As sure as the stars hung above them in their groupings, as sure as Na hiku, the Seven; Kamahana, the Twins; and Makali'i, Little Eyes, were up there looking down, he knew that all he could do to put an end to this madness was to get as far away from Elizabeth as fast as he could.

Seventeen

DUKE FOLLOWED ANA INTO the small workers' *hale* and waited while she lit the lamp. Her sleeping mat was spread on the floor. There was a scarred table where she had placed the old rusted Wheeler and Wilson sewing machine that Elizabeth had found in the storeroom. A pallet of fabric scraps lay in a heap beside a bolt of *palaka* plaid. Bare, whitewashed board-and-batten walls surrounded them, bounced the sound of their voices around the spartan room.

Ana turned away from the lamplight. Before she could say anything, Duke wanted her to know the truth.

"Spence not wit' Elizabeth, Ana. I see him go down da beach."

He watched an array of thoughts flow through her mind. His gut clenched, knotted.

"Marry me, Ana."

"Just like dat?"

He nodded, waited for an answer while she stared at him for a long, slow moment, almost as if she were sizing him up, comparing him to Spence Laamea. Then she looked around the room. He knew what she was thinking, saw her scan the little *hale*, weighing its worth the way she had weighed his.

"Get glass windows," she said.

"Yeah. Get glass windows."

"Get one real wood door."

"Yeah, get one door," he agreed.

She smiled up at him. "I get you, too."

He smiled back. "Yeah. You get me, too. Long time ago."

"Mebbe you better kiss me, *hana hou,* again, just make sure."

Duke stepped up to her, took her in his arms. He lowered his head, claimed her, made her his own. He pressed his tongue against her lips. She opened to him, kissed him back, clung to him with arms wound tight around his neck until they were both breathless.

He was the first to break the kiss, to pull back so he could look down into her eyes. "So?"

"All right. We get marry." Her smile lit her eyes in a way that she had never smiled at him before. Then she took his hand, led him to the sleeping mat, knelt in the center of it, and tried to pull him down beside her.

Duke shook his head. "No, Ana."

She dimmed instantly. "What you mean, no? You no want?"

He wanted her in the worst way. He could hardly *think*, he wanted her so bad, but he wanted her forever. He wanted her to be his wife, to have his children.

He wanted her enough to wait.

Duke gently tugged on her hand, drew her to her feet. "You marry me, Ana, and it going be for real."

"I know dat."

He traced the outline of her jaw. "Tonight you go Spence's room. You want sleep wit' him. Now quick like, you say you marry me. I t'ink mebbe you need make sure."

"I plenty sure, Duke." She took his hand in hers, pressed

it against her breast. A hardened nipple teased his palm through the fabric of her gown.

He swallowed a groan.

"No need worry. Spence Laamea not for me anyway. You love me all'a time, since I one little girl. Anyway, I never t'ink about him like I t'ink about you. All'a time dat I try make him notice me, I been try not t'ink about *you*."

"Yeah?"

She nodded yes. "For sure."

"Den not going mattah we wait 'til we marry," he said.

Just to be sure. He wanted her for a lifetime. He wanted her enough to come by at night and sit on the lanai, to watch the stars with her, play his guitar and sing her love songs. He wanted her enough to bring her flower leis, take her for moonlit walks on the beach. He wanted her enough to court her.

When they married he wanted her to love him as deeply, as absolutely as he loved her.

"WHAT DO YOU MEAN, you're *leaving*?"

Elizabeth stared at Spence. He stood in front of the newly washed and glistening store windows, his features unreadable. Fueled by nervous energy, she had been cleaning since sunup, rearranging the leftover stock items, hauling in buckets of soapy water, polishing windows and glass-fronted cabinets. Doing anything and everything to keep her hands busy and her mind off of what happened last night.

After they made love again, Spence had closed himself off from her as he walked her back to the house. He kissed her at the front door, a long, lingering exchange that was more like a bittersweet love song than a kiss.

She had hurried up to Hadley's room, made certain the child was still sleeping peacefully. She stared down at her beautiful daughter, listened to Hadley's slow, even breathing. She vowed, from now on, not to question life but to remind herself that without rain there would be no rainbows.

Then she went to bed alone and slept better than she had in years. Before she drifted off, she decided not to worry about what to say when she saw Spence. She would take her lead from him.

She had awakened to sunshine and the call of a shama thrush outside her window, breakfasted with Hadley, charged Maile with her care, and opened the store. Every time she thought she heard Spence's footfall outside the door, every time she thought she heard his voice, she froze. Her knees went weak and her hands got clammy.

And now here he was. The *haku lei* on his hat, made for Kalakaua's visit, filled the room with the pungent scent of *pīkake* and stephanotis. She had been expecting him all morning, but she had not expected his eyes to look so tired, his face to look so worn.

She never expected to hear him say, "I'm leaving, Elizabeth. I'm going back to O'ahu."

"What do you mean, you're *leaving*?"

Now her hands were shaking. She dropped the wet rag, absently watched a cockroach skitter across the floor and disappear under a corner of the display case.

"I can't stay here now." He said it as easily as if he were telling her it was about to rain. "Not after last night."

"But—" She was stunned. He was leaving *now*? Had that been his intention all along? Was there some vindictive, evil streak in him after all, one that pushed him to sleep with his father's widow to get back at a father who never loved him?

No. This time she would not let herself believe the worst. She would hear him out.

"I can't stay, Elizabeth." His voice faded to a whisper. "I *have* to leave."

Did his voice break? She took a step toward him, but he put out a hand to stop her.

"If this continues, if anyone finds out, *anyone,* word will spread like a disease. You'll be ruined. Your good name—''

"My *name*? My *good name*?" A desperate, chilling laugh escaped her. "*What* good name? I have no reputation at stake, not since I left here half naked, running from my *husband* in the middle of the night." She took a deep breath, braced herself to tell him all of it. "Even before I left Maryland—"

"Elizabeth, this is not Baltimore. This is not Baltimore, where a clandestine love affair might be known only to a small circle of acquaintances. This is an island. You might as well be living in one of those display cases behind you."

"My little indiscretion was more than a love affair. Spence, I was pregnant out of wedlock. I lost a child before I came to Kaua'i." She had refused to say the words aloud for so long that each one reopened a still raw, painful wound. "My *dear* uncle gave me pennyroyal tea, which . . ." She stumbled, unable to finish, unable to say the words even now.

He said them for her, "Caused you to lose the baby." He paused, considering. "That is why you were so adverse to me giving Hadley herbal tea, why you refused it when you cut your hand."

She closed her eyes, remembering the night Hadley's laughter was almost stilled forever. "Yes. Yes, it is."

Elizabeth pulled herself together. She challenged him with a hard stare. "So don't you dare tell me you are leaving to save my good name, Spence."

Outside the window, Hadley and Maile ran past laughing.

"What about her? If you leave, my daughter—your sister—will lose Mauna Noe."

"Elizabeth, listen to me." He stepped into the room, walked up to her, and stopped an arm's length away. "I am leaving to save your reputation. Despite what you say, nothing you have done so far would blacken your name as much as your sleeping with me. I am leaving so that you *can* have Mauna Noe forever. You and Hadley will never have to worry about losing title to this place again.''

''How do you propose to do that?'' She wanted with all her heart to believe it was possible to hold title to the land, but she wanted him, too. Was it too much to ask for both? Did God always measure happiness by thimblefuls?

''You know my uncle is one of Kalakaua's closest friends. The king wants me to be part of his inner circle as well. When I leave here, I'll go straight to Milton Clifford and tell him I am breaking the terms of Franklin's will. He will have to notify the proper authorities and file the appropriate papers. By that time I'll be on O'ahu. I will tell Kalakaua that if he wants me in his court, all he needs to do is deed Mauna Noe to you. No one will ever know what happened between us.''

His argument was well thought out. It would have been entirely convincing if her heart hadn't been shouting no. She could tell that Spence would not be easily dissuaded. He had obviously spent the night working out every detail. There was a distance about him, as if he had made up his mind and had already left her?

She had studied Kalakaua at the *lū'au*. Did the king's dark, soulful eyes hold honesty, integrity, understanding? Did Spencer and his uncle really have that much influence over the man? Enough for her to hope that the king would simply give Mauna Noe back to her?

Spence shifted his stance. The rowels on his spurs jingled.

''I will have the deed sent to you within a few weeks at most. The changes will have to be filed by Clifford and the new title granted by the king.''

''What if Kalakaua says no?'' she wondered aloud. ''How can you be certain he'll agree?'' She could not help but wonder if this was his uncle's idea, a way to get him away from her.

Spence felt her hesitation, the doubt that teetered on the edge of panic. He could not guarantee his plan with any certainty, but he was not about to tell her that. If Kalakaua refused, then he would have no choice but to return. Still, he would not return to her arms. To live here without Elizabeth would truly be like serving a prison sentence.

He could not allow himself to think of failure. He had to convince Elizabeth to gamble on Kalakaua's granting his petition, and then, he hoped, by appealing to the king's romantic nature, he could not help but succeed in freeing them all. He hoped to God he was not wrong.

"I have never asked the king for anything." After last night, he would have asked the king for the moon if she wanted it.

Unable to meet his eyes, she pressed her palms together.

"What if I tell you I don't want you to go?" she asked.

"Then you don't know what's good for you, Elizabeth, or for Hadley." He looked around, envisioned the store as it should be, as it would be again someday. There was so much the place needed—more *paniolo*, gardeners to care for the grounds, farmers to put in more vegetable gardens and fruit orchards. A real blacksmith, a cooper.

Anyone who did not know her as well as he did might have let the vulnerable appeal in her eyes persuade him to stay, but he knew she had a will of iron. She was determined to build something lasting here for Hadley. If anyone could make this place work, with him or without him, it was Elizabeth.

"Stay," she whispered. The word, little more than a kiss of sound, was so very loud in the yawning silence between them.

"Last night was a mistake—"

"No." She shook her head, denying his words. Tears spilled over onto her cheeks.

"Yes it was, and you know it."

"I don't know it. I will never believe that."

She was crying now, standing there with tears streaming down her face without making a sound. He wanted to go to her, hungered to hold her and dry her tears, to tell her he was a fool even to think of leaving, but he wanted to give her more than a few moments' solace. He wanted to give her the one thing she deserved most. He wanted to give her a lifetime of peace.

She tried to dissuade him with words.

"Before you, I never hoped to love again. To live, yes. To succeed here and hold on, yes. But to love . . . no. My heart was dead, Spence. Closed to everyone but Hadley. You made me love again, made me feel something I never thought to feel. You forced me to trust, Spence, so please, don't take that all away. Don't leave us."

She was ripping his heart out and laying it at his feet. She would never know how much he understood, for hadn't he felt the same way when he lost his mother and then Kaala? Hadn't he thought that he would never love anyone again?

"You will find someone else. Someone more suited."

Someone haole.

The words hung unspoken between them.

"Don't you understand? I don't *want* anyone else," she cried.

He could tell that she was on the brink of coming to him. Afraid she would cross the room and touch him, afraid that if he took her in his arms he would never find the strength to let her go, he turned his back on her and headed for the door. When he got there, he paused long enough to look back over his shoulder.

"I'll be gone before noon," he said, knowing that if night fell again and he was still here, he would give in.

Waimea, Kaua'i

WHEN SPENCE REACHED WAIMEA, Milton Clifford greeted him warily. The lawyer was not any more receptive than he had been the day the will was read. The man asked after

Elizabeth but not Hadley, and then grudgingly invited him to sit on the lanai after his wife suggested that Spence might like some refreshment.

The house sat back from a wide stretch of open coastline, surrounded by wind-gnarled trees and bare red earth that stained everything, including the siding on the house. Their conversation was somewhat stilted until Spence stated the reason for his visit.

"I've left Mauna Noe. I'm going back to Honolulu."

Clifford combed his fingers through his long muttonchop whiskers and took a sip of cold tea. He pinned Spence with his stare, as if by doing so he might divine the younger man's thoughts.

"You'll be breaking the terms of Franklin's will," he said finally. "The land will revert to Kalakaua."

Spence nodded.

"Rumor has it the king visited Mauna Noe on his tour of the island. Is that true?"

"It is."

"I did not realize you had any connections." Clifford set his glass on a side table stained with a number of milk-white water spots. "Was it he who convinced you to leave?"

"If you mean, does the king want Mauna Noe back, no." Spence sensed Clifford did not believe him.

"The new constitution of last year stripped him of his power," Clifford said. "I hear the Missionary Party is still very unhappy with Kalakaua. There are even rumors of assassination plots."

"I'm sure the *haole* planters will always be unhappy as long as Hawai'i has a reigning Hawaiian monarch."

"I can see it's best that we avoid discussing politics."

"I have to catch the steamer," Spence said, closing the subject. He was uncomfortable knowing that this man had so few scruples that he had done business with someone as ruthless as Franklin Bennett.

O'ahu lay beyond the horizon, across miles of rough

channel waters. He wondered what Elizabeth was doing just now. He pictured her in the garden, cutting flowers for the tall vases throughout the house.

What of Hadley? When would she ask after him? How long would it be before she even noticed he was gone?

Clifford prodded him out of his thoughts. "I have to follow the letter of the law, even though I'm not going to relish having to tell Mrs. Bennett to move. After I send the proper notification and papers to the government office here and in Honolulu, she will be allowed to stay on the land only until she hears officially."

He looked Spence over and shook his head. "I've got to say I thought that you had more fight in you, Laamea. I never thought you would give up so easily. I guess I was wrong."

Spence did not care what the man thought of him. Elizabeth was all that mattered now. Elizabeth and Hadley.

He picked up his hat and put it on. Then he stood, thanked Clifford for his time, and left the lanai.

At the hitching post, he untied the roan horse he had taken as his own and mounted up, intent upon heading for the landing. It was just past sundown, the sky quickened with rays of orange and tangerine glow. Just as on the day he came to Kaua'i, a *pueo* came swooping out of the trees and crossed the road he intended to take. The owl, his *'aumakua*, was showing him the way again. He should have taken it as a sign that he was on the right path.

Why then, did it feel so wrong?

Mauna Noe
Three weeks later . . .

ANA SAT ON THE edge of her lanai, bare feet on the step below her, her skirt hem hiked up to her knees. She watched the sun fall through a cloudless sky until it finally touched the sea. In that instant, like a sulfur-tipped match, the blazing orange ball sparked an iridescent-green flash that fanned out along the horizon.

Ana caught a glimpse of Duke heading up the lane between the coffee trees. She hugged her knees and hid her smile against them, rocking back and forth. Duke, with his laughing eyes, his teasing smile, and his guitar, walked straight down the road until he reached her house and stopped at the bottom step.

He came to see her every evening when his work was all *pau,* to ask her about her day, to sing to her. Sometimes he brought her fresh fish. Sometimes flowers. Sometimes just his smile.

No matter how hard she tried to seduce him, he stood firm. They would marry. Then and only then would they be together as man and wife.

Duke sat down beside her on the lanai and began to tune his guitar.

"So, Dukie, when we going get married?" She asked him over and over, the same thing, every night.

"When I t'ink you really ready." His answer was always the same.

"An' when is dat?" She put her hand on his sleeve, forced him to stop tuning the guitar and look at her. "I getting plenty tired waiting, you know. I coming *old* waiting."

He leaned over and kissed her. "Pretty soon, Ana. Pretty soon now."

Eighteen

ELIZABETH WAS HEAD AND shoulders inside a glass-front display case, lining the bottom shelf with a piece of muslin, when Hadley burst through the storeroom door and shouted at the top of her lungs, *"O Laka, me ka 'ano'ai aloha e, e ola e!' "*

Rearing up in surprise, Elizabeth hit her head on the case, let out a startled "Ouch!" and then withdrew carefully, rubbing the top of her head as she stared at the apparition in the middle of the room. Over a navy-blue dress with a sailor collar, Hadley was garbed in a skirt made of shining *ti* leaves and matching sandals. Her head was adorned with a lei of *pala'ā* fern, but it had slipped so low it almost covered her eyes. She blinked beneath the bobbing, curled tips of fern fronds. Her long blond hair hung loose around her shoulders.

She looked like a bush in need of pruning.

Elizabeth quickly recognized Hadley's most serious expression and bit the insides of her cheeks to keep from laughing. As she tried to compose herself, Maile stepped into the storeroom, similarly attired, and hovered behind

Hadley. Elizabeth hoped there was at least one *ti* plant left in the garden that had not been stripped of its leaves.

"What have you two been doing?" Elizabeth was almost afraid to hear.

Hadley adjusted her lei, then stood with hands on hips, mirroring her mentor. She did not answer until Maile nodded, granting her permission.

"We are hula dancers, Mama. That was my greeting to Laka, the goddess of hula."

"And what did you say, exactly?"

Hadley shouted again, this time in English. "Oh, Laka! We greet you with love, live on!"

Elizabeth winced. "Is Laka deaf?"

"*Mama.*" Hadley groaned and rolled her eyes. "She's a goddess. She's *very* far away. Ana taught us what to say."

"I see." Elizabeth felt herself age on the spot.

"Don't you want to watch us dance?"

"I will later, when I'm finished. Why don't you run outside and practice for a while first?"

"We can't. Starting to rain," Hadley said.

"You can use the lanai."

"We have to have our steps perfect for Spence when he comes home. We must have another *lū'au* then, Mama. Just like the one for King Kalakaua."

Spence had been gone for a month, and as yet there had been no word from O'ahu. Elizabeth spent her days working and her nights tossing and turning, wrestling with doubt, hoping that her fragile trust in him was not misplaced, that the papers giving her title to Mauna Noe would arrive soon.

Hadley remained convinced that Spence was not gone for good, and nothing Elizabeth said or did could change her mind.

"I've tried to tell you he isn't coming back, honey."

"What if we need him?" Hadley carefully wove a finger through the fern headdress and scratched her head. The lei slipped down over one eye, and the braided strands of *ti* that held her sandals on were coming apart.

"We are going to do just fine." Elizabeth tried to believe it. She walked out from behind the glass counter, reached out and adjusted the lei on Hadley's head, then bent down and kissed her on the cheek.

"What about the magic leaves?" Hadley whispered. She opened her mouth wide like a fish and began to suck in air to test her breathing. Her gasps grew more desperate, her eyes became round as dinner plates. She grabbed her throat with both hands.

"What will I do if we run out of the magic leaves?" she choked out.

Elizabeth knew that if she did not turn the drama quickly, Hadley might very well work herself into a real attack.

"They are not magic. They have medicine inside them."

"Well, isn't that magic?" Hadley was still sucking in deep breaths.

"I suppose it is, sort of." Elizabeth plucked strands of curls caught on Hadley's lashes and looped them behind her ears. "Spence left a huge, huge calabash full of leaves for you with Uilani. You are not to worry." She put her arms around Hadley's shoulders and pulled her close. "Don't make yourself sick, darling. You have nothing to worry about. Do you really think Spence would forget that you need the leaves for tea?"

Hadley's mouth snapped shut tight as a lobster trap. Her bottom lip quivered. She shook her head and mumbled, "No. But why did he leave?"

Elizabeth fought the urge to close her eyes and let her own tears fall. Instead, she smiled, a bright, false smile. "He had business on O'ahu. With the king."

She knew how impressed Hadley had been by Kalakaua and his retinue. Mentioning him changed the mood immediately.

"I hope the king comes back here, don't you, Mama? Maile and me will hula for him with Ana next time."

What would Kalakaua think of a pink-cheeked haole *cherub dancing the hula?*

"Why don't you and Maile run along so I can finish up quickly and then I'll watch you dance?"

"Don't take too long, Mama."

"I won't. I promise." When the girls reached the door, she called, "If you happen to see Duke, would you tell him I need to talk to him?"

The children left, a flurry of whispering, giggling, and rustling *ti* leaves headed for the main house.

"What if we need him?"

I do need him.

Four weeks ago as Elizabeth stood in the second-story window and watched Spence ride away from Mauna Noe, she tried to convince herself that he was right, but she had not succeeded in making herself believe any such thing.

Last night, when she lay awake staring at the ceiling with her nightgown knotted around her thighs and her hair hot and sweaty against the back of her neck, needing his body, needing the reassurance of his touch, she wished she had gone down on her knees and begged him to stay.

She was as frightened as Hadley—but not out of any worry that they would run out of "magic" leaves. She feared losing the magic Spence had worked inside her. She was afraid of losing the heady feeling of finally wanting to embrace life again.

More than that, she was afraid that all too soon she would forget the way he felt beneath her hands, his scent, his smile, his kiss. The longer Spence was gone without word, the more she feared she would start believing that he had double-crossed her.

To keep her doubts at bay, she had thrown herself into the running of Mauna Noe. The monies from the cattle sale afforded her enough to hire on three new men, each at thirty dollars a month. She had turned the stock operations over to Duke, and just yesterday he had reported that the new bull seemed very happy with his harem. Duke was proving to be so capable that she decided not to hire a manager to replace Spence but to promote the *luna*.

By contacting a supplier on the mainland recommended by Marion, she was able to order tobacco, whiskey, and other staples for the workers' store. She did not want to lose her men the way Franklin had, so she marked up the prices only enough to pay for shipping and turn a slight profit.

Everything appeared to be running smoothly, but inside, Elizabeth was in constant turmoil. Milton Clifford had written to let her know that Spencer had seen him and that he had sent paperwork to O'ahu. He advised her to stay on the land until she heard differently. The day the lawyer's letter arrived, she stared at the words, wondering where she would go and what she would do if Spence failed her.

The cold fingers of fear gripped her every time she thought of that letter and what it meant. Spence had gone straight to Milton Clifford before he left for O'ahu.

She massaged her temples. Questions danced through her mind. How long would it take for the king to grant her title? What if Kalakaua could not be swayed or Spence and his uncle fell out of favor? What if the king had already given Mauna Noe to someone else?

At the sound of spurs jingling, her gaze shot to the door. Duke stepped over the threshold, slipped off his woven hat, and held it in his thick, square fingers.

"You need see me?"

"I have something I want you to do for me," she told him. "An errand. It should not take you very long. I'd like you to ride over to Kilauea plantation and take a letter to the manager there. If you don't have time to go today, you can wait until tomorrow."

"Bettah tomorrow." He worried the brim of his hat. "You need Ana tomorrow? I t'ink maybe I take her wit' me."

Since Spence left, Elizabeth had been uneasy whenever she spoke to Ana. She knew it would be a long, long time before she would be able to forget the sight of the girl creeping through the darkened hall and into Spencer's room. No matter how many times she told herself that if it had not been for Ana's bold venture, Spence would not have found her that night on the bluff, she still experienced stabs of jealous irritation upon encountering the girl.

"I don't mind," she told him, sincerely hoping that Ana would not break the heart that the young *luna* wore so prominently on his sleeve. She envied Duke and Ana, tried to imagine herself and Spence being free to ride together across the open pasture, past old fields of waving sugarcane, along the bluff above the sea.

Perhaps Duke and Ana would stop beside a waterfall on their way to Kilauea. Her mind began to wander down a path of its own. She pictured Spence standing naked beside a pool beneath the falls, the bold tattoo emblazoned down his side, his long hair wild and free. In her daydream he reached out for her, beckoned her to step into the pool with him, called her name—

"Mrs. Bennett?"

"Oh, I'm so sorry. What were you saying, Duke?"

"You need anyt'ing else?"

"Nothing. I'll have the letter ready for you tomorrow morning. And I'll tell Uilani to pack a picnic for you and Ana."

Iolani Palace, Honolulu
Island of O'ahu

SPENCE TRIED NOT TO let his impatience show as he leaned back in a velvet upholstered armchair positioned close to the table where King David Kalakaua sat pondering a sheaf of public documents in his library. As Hawai'i's king studied the pages spread out before him, Spence studied Kalakaua, seeing him not as a monarch or a man but as an echo of what the islands themselves had become. The king was an amalgam of old Hawai'i—pristine islands jealously guarded by the sea—and new Hawai'i—a small, isolated kingdom vulnerable to an onslaught of foreign influences from within and without.

In the weeks he had been in Kalakaua's company, Spence found himself continually marveling at this man who was equally at home on a lanai playing a *ukulele* and in a throne room. The king's symbols of power were an odd combination from generations of chiefs—Kamehameha the Great's golden cloak made of 450,000 feathers of the *o'o* bird, the tabu stick Pulo'ulo'u, the sacred torch Iwi-kau-ikaua—as well as a crown, saber, and scepter that he had ordered for himself after an unprecedented trip around the globe.

Reportedly the first monarch of any country ever to travel around the world, he had visited royalty in most of Europe and England, Japan, China, Siam, Singapore, Burma, India, and Egypt. He was welcomed by kings and queens and upon returning to Honolulu began building a palace of which the Hawaiian people could be proud. At a gala coronation he crowned himself and then Queen Kapiolani with crowns he had had fashioned with opals, rubies, emeralds, diamonds, and golden taro leaves.

He lived in a palace that he had designed, an extravagance that took four years to build and cost his people $350,000. He was a scholar who translated many ancient myths and chants into English and wrote them down. He was a poet as well as an accomplished composer, and yet it was widely known that "Taffy," as he was known, could drink five bottles of champagne without noticeable result.

As if he sensed Spence's brooding contemplation focused squarely on him, Kalakaua suddenly looked up.

"So, Spencer. Are you willing to take my advice yet?"

"You'll pardon me if I speak my mind?"

Kalakaua nodded. "Go on."

"I don't agree with what you suggest. I came here to be at your service. I had hoped to see my petition granted."

The king sighed. "I have learned the hard way, Spencer,

that what we are given in this life is not always what we would have chosen."

Spence knew the king would not take offense at debate. "But in this case—"

"*You* feel you have made the right choice."

"It is the only one I can make."

"Sometimes one must think with his head, Spencer, not with his heart. I do the things I do, not because I believe I am right, but because I fear no one else after me will do them." The king pushed two heavy leather-bound books away from his left elbow and leaned forward.

"I know the people who condemn me talk about the great debt I have incurred. My detractors are against the revival of the hula. They speak out against my insistence upon performances of our *mele*, the chants of our ancestors that I have written down and have seen taught once again. But what I have done here," he languidly raised his hand to indicate the opulence surrounding them, "what I continue to do to bring our traditions out into the light, I do for the Hawaiian people—to give them back a sense of pride. I only want to be a king of whom they can be proud. Hawaiians love tradition and form. I have tried to give them their own traditions back as well as the pomp and circumstance I have seen in other kingdoms."

The king spoke often of tradition and form. Closeted alone with Kalakaua, being an audience of one in a meeting he had requested himself, Spence had no choice but to listen. He tried not to look down at the title to Mauna Noe, which lay on the table beneath the king's right arm. Instead, he focused on Kalakaua's dark, troubled eyes.

"I would see you living on this *'āina*, this lovely Mauna Noe with the blue-green mountain wearing her lei of mist, but I would see you living there with a Hawaiian *wahine*, Spencer. I would see you blessed with many *keiki*, many, many Hawaiian children, the way you surely would have been had your wife, Kaala, lived. Our people are still dying out, Spencer, not by the hundreds but by the thousands."

Kalakaua looked out the tall, velvet-draped window, across the wide, manicured lawn that surrounded Iolani Palace. "Sometimes I think they are dying in the same way your mother died, withering away because their hearts and spirits are broken, their *mana* is gone. I would see you strengthen the Hawaiian blood in your line, Spencer and forget the *haole*. In a few generations, all traces of your father's ancestors would be eradicated and the Hawaiian blood would live on."

Spence, too, had hoped that he and Kaala would have many children, but they had been married only a few weeks before she discovered she suffered from *ma'i Pākē*, the Chinese disease, leprosy.

Spence refused to accept defeat. He looked down at his hands, took a deep breath, and wondered, *What is Elizabeth doing today?*

Was she in her garden, on her hands and knees, digging in the rich, moist earth, cupping the tender shoots and roots of her precious ginger in her hands, searching for just the right place to plant it, judging the sunlight and the amount of rain that it would need to thrive? Was she laughing with Hadley? Talking story in the kitchen with Uilani? In the cramped office going over the accounts, her forehead creased, her fine, light brows drawn tightly together while she figured the columns?

Was she thinking of him? Had she given up all hope that he would keep his word? Had this damned delay broken her trust, her spirit?

He had not sent any word to her yet. He could not bring himself to send her a letter, not when Kalakaua's decision kept swinging back and forth like a pendulum. The legislature wanted the king's liabilities taken care of. His opponents were pushing for abdication. That Kalakaua would grant such a huge parcel of land as a gift—simply because Spence requested it—was almost too much to hope for.

He had promised Elizabeth that he would hand her ranch over to her, but right now he had nothing to show for his time here. Hope was the one slim thread he still had to hold on to.

FOUR AND A HALF days of rainfall were three and a half too many. Except for the *paniolo*, who worked in any weather, the rain kept everyone inside. Elizabeth became more and more lethargic and apathetic, wandering from room to room and window to window to watch the rain and wrestle with her doubts and fears. After all her years on Kauaʻi, she was still amazed at the sea of water that could pour from the sky.

She was standing in the parlor, staring out toward the smooth knob of the crater, when a splotch of bobbing yellow on the road caught her eye. She watched a rider adorned in yards of yellow oilskin approaching through the rain. She became curious and excited when the lone traveler turned onto the lane that led to the house.

Uilani, in the kitchen since the downpour had began, was baking as fast as the stove could cook. On rainy days she filled the house and anyone who would oblige her with tempting morsels as well as a few epicurean disasters. Today was chocolate day.

Elizabeth went in and asked her to boil water for tea, then hurried back out to the lanai to await the caller. Mist from the water running off the roof bathed her face and slightly dampened the front of her gown.

The rider reached the garden fence, tied the horse to the rail, and opened the gate that Toshi had mended before the king's visit. Beneath the hood of the yellow oilskin, a vermilion feather, wet with rain, drooped forlornly.

When she saw the red feather, Elizabeth smiled. With her full skirts stuffed beneath the slicker, Marion Randolph looked like a huge yellow hen bobbing up the garden path.

"What a day to come calling, eh?" When she reached the lanai, Marion pushed back the hood and unfastened the slicker, then stripped it off and shook it out before tossing it over a wicker chair. She hugged Elizabeth in greeting. "I suppose you think I'm a bit crazed."

"Stir-crazy is more like it." Elizabeth laughed. "I have a case of it myself. I'm so glad you came. Can you stay the night?"

Marion shook her head. "Got guests at the hotel, so I do need to get back, but I figured Chin Sam can take care of them as well as I for the afternoon. Besides, he's the cook and as long as their bellies are full and the sheets are clean, what do they need me for?"

Marion handed over a book to share, which she had brought tucked deep in the raincoat, and insisted that they ignore formality and sit in the kitchen where she could taste everything the minute Uilani pulled it out of the oven. With two cups of tea and tempting chocolate baked goods arrayed before her, Marion declared she was in heaven.

After she inhaled a second piece of chocolate cake, Marion said to Uilani, "I never get this kind of food at home. Would you come to Hanalei and work for me?"

When the Hawaiian woman paused, pretending to consider the offer, Elizabeth said, "Don't you dare!"

Then Uilani threw back her head and laughed, the boisterous sound filling the room. "Bettah I stay heah."

After discussing the weather, the king's visit to Kaua'i, the dear cost of shipping, Marion leaned close to Elizabeth and dropped her voice to a whisper. "I hope you don't mind my asking, but I'm going to anyway. How are things between you and Spencer coming along?"

Elizabeth blushed. Under the edge of the table, she knotted her fingers together. "I don't know. He left here over a month and a half ago."

"He *left*?" Marion glanced at Uilani, who was absorbed in beating egg whites. "I never heard that he left. What is wrong with my coconut wireless?"

"The king needs as many allies as he can get right now and because of his friendship with Robert Laamea, Kalakaua wanted Spence officially to become part of his trusted inner circle.''

Marion cut yet another piece of cake and forked up a mouthful before she asked, ''What about the ranch? I don't for a minute believe Spence did not care that you will lose everything.''

Elizabeth did not know how to explain Spence's plan without admitting what had happened between them after the *lū'au*.

''Something is going on.'' Marion leaned so far toward Elizabeth that she practically came out of her chair. Then her eyes grew wide as her mouth formed a perfect circle. ''Don't tell me. You took my advice and—''

''Please, Marion.'' Elizabeth swiftly cut her off. ''We—''

''You *did*.''

''Please, stop. You're embarrassing me.''

''Sorry, ducks. I forget you have quite a few of those puritan sensibilities left. I'll just have to use my imagination, won't I? Don't tell me he went back to O'ahu for good, then?''

Elizabeth felt as if a vise had tightened around her throat.

''Oh, no,'' Marion cooed. ''I can see by the look on your face that he did. The *nerve* of that scoundrel.''

''It wasn't like that, Marion. You have it all wrong.''

Hadley and Maile came running into the room, effectively ending the conversation. Hadley's *pala'ā* fern *haku lei* had dried out, but she still wore it anyway. ''The *paniolo* wear them this way, Mama,'' she insisted when Elizabeth started to throw it away.

The crisp curled ends of the lei dangled in her eyes. The girls had replaced their *ti* leaf skirts with a *pa'u* tied over their clothes.

Hadley greeted Marion and leaned across Elizabeth's lap, smiling up at her. ''Mama, may I go over to Maile's for a while? Please.'' She reached for a chocolate drop cookie from a stack piled on a dinner plate and popped half of it in her mouth.

"Take the umbrella and share it with Maile," Elizabeth instructed.

Hadley grabbed three more cookies, stopped beside her friend to carefully count out two, and then, on the way out the back door, tugged on Uilani's skirt. "Good, Auntie."

Hand in hand, Hadley and Maile disappeared outside.

"Was that the same sickly, whey-faced little creature I met in Hanalei a few months ago?" Marion shook her head, her face mirroring her disbelief. "The one you wouldn't let out of your sight?"

"She's gone native." Elizabeth laughed. "I can only imagine what my aunt and uncle in Maryland would say if they saw her dressed like that."

"Or Franklin."

"Unfortunately, I know what he would do. I am sure he is rolling in his grave. Thanks to Spence, though, she is healthier than she has ever been in her life."

"From the glow on your face when you mention his name, I'd say he was good for both of you. It's a bloody shame he isn't coming back. What are you going to do, ducks?"

Elizabeth finished the tepid tea in her cup and then moved to the edge of her chair. Very aware of Uilani at the stove and concerned about keeping the details off the coconut wireless, she suggested they go into the parlor.

A while later, after hearing as much as Elizabeth was comfortable relating, Marion surveyed her with concern. "You still believe he'll send you the deed?"

"I have to believe it, Marion. I have no alternative."

The look on the woman's face threatened to give rise to all the doubt Elizabeth had smothered.

Marion announced it was time for her to don her oilskin slicker again and go back to Hanalei before the river ran too high and full to cross. Intermittent rain was falling, driven sideways whenever the wind blew. Wrapped in her waterproof garb, Marion hesitated on the edge of the lanai, more solemn than Elizabeth had ever seen her.

"I'll send up a prayer for you, ducks. I want to believe Laamea can, and will, come through for you, but from what I've heard visitors from Honolulu report lately, things aren't going well for Kalakaua. The king is spending a lot of time on Pele's Island, on Hawai'i, just to get away from all the opposition. It may not be all that easy for Spencer to persuade him to hand the land over to you when the sale of Mauna Noe would put a pretty penny or two into the government treasury."

Elizabeth bid her friend farewell and watched her ride away, her own spirit as gray as the heavy sky. She reminded herself to hold tight to the memory of the night she and Spence made love beneath the stars. She had played the scene over and over, every touch, every word, every sensation, wrapping the images like treasured keepsakes, storing them in the corners of her mind.

Spence had never admitted to loving her, but she knew he did. He loved her enough to leave her.

She *had* to believe that he would find a way to secure Mauna Noe.

THE AIR WAS HEAVY and close, straining like a spring wound too tight. The sky had lowered until it looked like heavy sheets of iron trailing silver threads of rain. The tension in the air communicated itself to the women in the house as the afternoon shadows lengthened and dampness took up residence in the corners of the rooms.

What Marion had said during her visit had Elizabeth agitated to the point where she found herself jumpy and on edge. She could not concentrate on the novel Marion had left behind, the work of Robert Louis Stevenson, a friend of Kalakaua's. The protagonist in *Dr. Jekyll and Mr. Hyde* reminded her too much of Franklin. She pretended to read as she watched Ana seated cross-legged on the floor, hemming the draperies she had just finished.

When Uilani came marching in, Elizabeth welcomed the diversion until she noticed that the housekeeper's usually serene smile had been replaced by a troubled frown. Ana anchored her needle in the drape and rolled her shoulders.

"What's wrong, Uilani?" Elizabeth avoided looking at a black-and-white-feathered *'ua'u* as she set Marion's book on a side table next to the base of the stuffed bird.

Uilani stood in the center of the room with her hands on her hips. "Bettah get ready."

"For what?" It wasn't anywhere near time for the evening meal.

"I t'ink we get one big *makani pāhili*."

Ana gasped. She quickly reached for the needle and thread, tied off her knot, and then opened her sewing basket.

"What is that?" Elizabeth stood up and looked outside.

"Hurricane." Ana got to her feet, shook out her skirt, and started for the door. "I going home."

"Wait," Elizabeth called, stopping the girl in her tracks. Then she turned to Uilani. "You think a hurricane is coming? How do you know?"

Uilani shook her head. "Feel it." She touched her heart. "Here." She touched her stomach. "An' here."

Elizabeth crossed to the open windows and looked out across the lanai. Whitecaps rode on a sea as ashen as the sky. Rain poured down. She could see knots of cattle huddled beneath the trees. Everything appeared normal to the eye, but there was no denying a strange, oppressive quality in the air.

She put her trust in Uilani.

"Where are the children?"

"We make house ready," Uilani said, immediately moving over to the wall of Bennett ancestors. She started taking the portraits down one by one, setting them on the floor.

"The girls—" Elizabeth started toward the back of the house. Hadley and Maile were still at Uilani's.

"I send dem back when I go pas'," Ana told her. "I going make my house ready, too."

Elizabeth pictured the row of simple board-and-batten

houses with their tin roofs. In terrible winds the little places might blow away like matchsticks.

"You should stay here with us, Ana. Just go get the girls and bring them back."

The stubborn set of Ana's shoulders said more than a refusal in words.

"I tell dem come back here." She tucked her basket beneath her arm and hurried away.

Uilani took charge. She told Elizabeth to go through the house and gather all the lamps and put them in the first-floor hallway, then she found kerosene, matches, sheets and pillows. Any shutters not in disrepair were closed. Breakable items were to be taken down and put in drawers or on the floor, all closet doors closed and locked. They would meet in the kitchen to gather food and water to take into the windowless hall.

Listening for the return of the girls, Elizabeth hurried to complete her assigned tasks, running up and down the stairs, keeping watch on the lowering sky.

She worried about Duke and the other *paniolo*. Did they know? Did they feel the storm coming? Where were they? Would they ride in and take shelter? What of the livestock? Suddenly the overwhelming notion of a hurricane roaring across the vast emptiness that surrounded the island filled her with a numbing calm. Her movements became instinctual as she prepared the house at Mauna Noe for the worst.

Holding her daughter's favorite doll and Alexander the Great in her arms, Elizabeth paused at the window in Hadley's room. Through the tracks of rain pelting the window she saw Duke out in the stable area. The young *paniolo* was shouting orders to one of the new men, who rode to the side corral and opened the gate, releasing the dozen horses inside. The animals ran out of the paddock and headed up the hillside. Toshi was bent over, running into the barn with a wheelbarrow filled with Elizabeth's garden buckets and implements.

She heard the back door open and close and the sound

of Maile's voice. Hurrying down to allay Hadley's fears, she did not realize Hadley was not in the foyer until she reached the bottom step. Maile was there, her eyes red-rimmed. Uilani was holding the girl by the upper arm, shaking her.

"Hadley?" Elizabeth peered into the parlor. Her daughter was not there. Clutching the stuffed horse and the doll, she walked up to Maile. The girl was soaked and trembling.

Stay calm, Elizabeth warned herself. *Stay calm until you know what is going on.* She touched Maile's damp cheek.

"Where is Hadley?"

Maile's lip trembled. Huge tears pooled and spilled over. She hung her head and whispered, "She get missing."

Nineteen

"*GET MISSING?*" ELIZABETH DROPPED Alexander the Great. He hit the floor with a soft thud. "What do you mean she's missing?"

Maile sniffed, buried her head in the crook of her arm and wailed like a hired mourner.

"Maile! Maile, please!" Elizabeth was frantic.

Uilani was far less tactful. She gave her daughter's arm a firm shake. The distraught girl uncovered her face and then broke into a flurry of Hawaiian.

Elizabeth stood by, helpless, trying to understand the exchange. Then Maile abruptly came to a sobbing halt and Uilani looked like a volcano about to erupt.

Elizabeth waited. "What did she say?"

The front door, assaulted by the increasing winds, swung back against the wall with a thunderous crash. All three of them jumped and Maile screamed.

Uilani was glowering at her daughter, her broad features stern and foreboding. The woman was so upset that her pidgin thickened like *poi*, and Elizabeth had a hard time following it.

"She talk story wit' Hadley, tell her 'bout her faddah, how Franklin one *haole pupule,* one crazy *haole.* She tell Hadley her faddah plenty bad man, alla time hollar. Dat he nevah want see Hadley 'cause she sick alla time. He t'ink Hadley too little, sorry she not one boy, dat he got no *aloha* for her."

"*Why,* Maile?" Elizabeth could not fathom it.

"She get me plenty mad. She bust one conch shell belong me."

Elizabeth closed her eyes, tried to imagine Hadley hearing such terrible things from her friend, someone she looked up to and admired so.

"Where did Hadley go?"

Maile hung her head. "Outside."

"She went out in the rain?"

"When it stop for one little while, she run off. Not looking, so I doan' see where."

Outside, the trees were beginning to sway. The sky had darkened so much that the afternoon might well have been mistaken for dusk.

Elizabeth raced to the window. Hadley was out there somewhere, out in the storm, her little heart broken, crying over a father who never cared any more for her than for one of his horses.

A coconut frond went flying past the windowpane.

She turned to Uilani, who sent Maile into the safety of the hallway, ordering her to sit down and not move.

"I have to go find Hadley," Elizabeth cried. "I can't leave my baby out there alone in this storm." She took a step toward the front door.

Uilani put a firm hand on her shoulder. "No."

Elizabeth tried to break free. "Let me go."

"What for you go running off and no can find? Bettah you stay here. Mebbe she come back quick. You need be here."

"I can't just leave her out there! Don't you understand? I can't lose her. She's all I have."

Uilani's face fell. A lone tear dripped down her cheek. She nodded slowly, wiped the tear away with the back of her hand.

"All I got is one girl, too. I send Duke. You stay."

SPENCE HAD BEEN ON Mauna Noe land for an hour, gauging the progress of the storm, riding low over the roan's neck, holding one hand on his hat and the other on the reins as the horse, sensing danger, thundered across the open pastureland.

He was glad he had arrived before the storm peaked, certain that he would reach the house in time not only to take shelter but to make certain Elizabeth and Hadley were safe. He was drained, exhausted from the debate that Kalakaua had insisted on dragging out until one of them broke.

How will Elizabeth accept what I have to tell her?

A white mare, her eyes wild, ran past him, racing a whirlwind of leaves. At least, he thought with some relief, Duke had not tried to shelter the animals in the barn. If the building was destroyed, they stood a better chance by being free and acting on instinct.

One last ravine to cross before he reached the bluff and was in sight of the house. He let the roan pick its way down the slope and through a rushing stream. In no time at all, rain from the mountain would swell all the waterways and make them impassable. As his horse started to plunge up the other side, he heard a noise that raised the hair on the back of his neck. It sounded like the wail of an *'uhane,* a ghost. He looked over his shoulder, back upstream and then down. The horse beneath him wanted to run.

So did Spence—until he heard the high, thready sound again and pulled rein. Over the blowing of his horse and the ever-mounting sound of the wind, he heard someone crying.

He called out a hello and then gave a long, shrill whistle.

His name came floating to him on a gust of wind and he shivered until he recognized the small, reedy voice.

Hadley? He was almost too shocked to call her name. What was the child doing out at a time like this?

"*Hadley!*" he shouted as loud as he could.

When she called his name again, Spence dismounted with a jump. Caught off guard when his horse decided to bolt, he let go of the reins and watched the animal head off in the direction of the house. Threading his way through the dense underbrush, Spence ducked a low limb and was finally forced to crawl through tangled *hau* bush as he followed the sound of Hadley's cries.

He found her huddled in a ball, her knees drawn to her chest, her bare feet and ankles caked with mud. She was wearing what looked like a very sad *pa'u* that was dripping red dye onto a navy dress beneath it. Her blond curls were limp and sopping wet, tangled with bits of twigs and leaves. Beside her on the ground lay a bedraggled brown *pala'ā* lei.

She looked like she had taken part in someone's hula nightmare.

She was backed up to two huge, smooth lava rocks, a small white speck against the black stones. The overgrown hillside provided a perfect place of refuge against the storm. To get to her, he had to hold his hat between his teeth and crawl on his hands and knees.

When he finally reached her, she raised her head and abruptly stopped crying, then dried her tears with mud-stained fingers that left dirt trails down her cheeks. She patted the wet ground beside her, almost as if she had been expecting him.

No sooner had he sat down and put on his hat to shield his face from the rain then she climbed up into his lap and began sniffing and snuffling against his chest.

"I knew you would come," she said. "I just knew it."

Spence put his hand under her chin and made her look up at him. It was like looking into Elizabeth's eyes.

"Are you hurt? I'll get you out of here and back to the house."

Time was of the essence. In a few more minutes the storm would build to such a point that it would not be safe to cross open ground.

"I'm not going back there ever. Never, ever, ever." She pressed the back of her wrist to her forehead and threw her head back. "I'm going to wander the earth like Ulysses."

With a theatrical sigh, she dropped her arm and started to crawl off his lap. "Don't even beg me to go with you, Spence, because I won't."

When she was two feet away he picked her up by the waist, plopped her back down beside him, and anchored her there with his arm around her shoulders.

"Before you leave, why don't you tell me what happened?"

"I ran away."

"Why?"

"Because I'm mad at Maile and I'm mad at Mama, too." She began to blink rapidly but lost her battle with her tears. Leaning against him, she let out a pitiful wail.

"Maile got mad because I broke her stupid conch shell and then she said I was just a silly little *haole* girl and that she didn't like me anymore. She said . . . she said *nobody* really likes me."

"She was just mad because you broke her shell. Maybe you have something you can give her in trade."

"She told me that Papa used to holler at Mama all the time and that he used to hit Mama, too. Toshi told Uilani that he used to hear them fighting through the windows, and Maile heard Toshi tell it."

Spence leaned closer to the rocks and pulled her back with him, trying to shield them both from the ever-increasing wind.

"Maybe I'll still talk to Uilani," Hadley sounded as if she were thinking aloud. "She bakes good cookies and she never lied to me. Maile said that Mama lied to me."

"You sure you didn't misunderstand what she said?" He

knew they were heading into rough seas, and he did not necessarily want to wade through them.

Hadley shook her head emphatically. "I did. Maile said *ho'opunipuni*. I know what that means, I know it means about lying." She pulled back and looked up at him again. "I know lots of Hawaiian words now. Uilani says I'm a fast learner."

"What did Maile say your mama lied about?"

"Mama always told me that my papa loved me, but Maile said he didn't. She said I could ask Toshi or Uilani or any of them if I didn't believe her. She said everybody knew it but me. That's why he never came into my room to talk to me or tuck me in and that's why I wasn't 'lowed to eat in the dining room with him. But Mama told me he was busy all the time."

She picked up his arm at the wrist, shook it so that his hand flopped up and down a few times, and then let go. "Do I look like I just fell off the taro wagon? Do I *really* think someone could be busy *all* the time, Spence?"

Hadley's hurt ran deep. He knew it would fester and spread and in time turn to hatred and anger if he did not try to help.

Elizabeth had done her job too well. She had suffered much to give her daughter a sense of *'ohana*. Any lies she told, she told because she wanted Hadley to grow up believing she was part of a whole and loving family, a little girl with a father who loved her.

He could not fault Elizabeth for perpetuating the lie. But how could he explain that to a five-year-old? What could he say to this child who was his half sister? What words of comfort would help her leave her pain out in the storm and let it blow away?

Just then Hadley said something Spence could not hear. He asked her to repeat it.

"Did he love me?" she shouted.

No, he thought, *he didn't love anyone.*

Spence reached for the edge of her limp, fading *pa'u* and

dried her tears before he pulled her close. He heard her hiccup over a sob and felt the sadness as deeply as if it were his own.

How many tears had he shed over a father who never loved him either? The very fact that her father and his were one and the same infuriated Spence, made him hate Franklin Bennett all the more for hurting this innocent child.

No more, old man.

No more hurt.

Spence refused to lie to Hadley. The wind began to moan and race across the face of the land. He knew this was only the beginning, that compared to what was to come, this would seem no more than a sneeze. The sky darkened, the air was charged with energy.

He hoped that the drama of the storm, the power and might behind what was coming would sear his words onto her heart. He spoke loudly enough for her to hear.

"Hadley, sometimes the people we love don't love us back."

He closed his eyes, pictured his mother, silently longing for Franklin, wasting away little by little. He saw himself, a little brown-skinned boy, a *hapa haole*, looking for a way to fit in, always watching the empty road, feeling like a piece of lost baggage, waiting for a father who never came to claim him.

"You have enough *aloha* in your heart to last you forever, Hadley. You can give it away and keep on giving it away and even though you have to reach way down inside for it, you will always find it there. You will never run out. Sometimes when we are very, very lucky, the people we love give back *aloha*."

He shrugged and added, "Sometimes they don't. But you can't ever let that stop you from loving and trusting."

Because of his father, he had stopped loving until Kaala. And then again, until Elizabeth.

Hadley fell silent, pulling on her lower lip with her fingers, her little brow furrowed in thought. He looked at the tangled growth around them, sensing that it was already too late to leave the protective shelter of the natural nest against the rocks and the hillside. Here they would get wet, but they would be relatively safe from flying debris until the calm in the center of the storm came and they could run for the house.

When he looked down at Hadley again, she was wearing a wavering little smile. Suddenly, without any warning, she threw her arms around his neck. He felt as awkward as hell—but he hugged her back. Despite the storm blowing around them, he could feel himself smiling too.

"You know what, Spence?"

"What, Hadley?"

"I think that it's all right that I don't have a papa now, because I have you."

DUKE SENT TOSHI, MELVIN, and the new *paniolo* to the men's barracks and told them that if the storm proved to be a bad one, they should move to the main house.

Animals were one thing, but he did not care for the burden of responsibility that came with being in charge of men. All of the men in his care had been worried about the storm, yet none of them wanted to be the one to call off the search for the little girl. Duke was *luna*. When trees began to break and topple under the force of the gale, when branches began flying, it was up to him to think of the many and not just the one, to make the decision and call a halt until the storm abated.

Worse than the responsibility for the men and the child, he hated like hell that it was up to him to tell Elizabeth Bennett that they had failed to find Hadley.

He was on the way up the lane to the house, head down, the rain pelting him, when he passed Ana's house and caught a flash of a face in the window, black eyes huge with terror. Then the face was gone. For a heartbeat he thought he was seeing things. He ran up to her lanai and tried to open the door, but it was locked from the inside.

He went to the window and leaned against the glass to peer inside.

"Ana!" he hollered and beat on the door after he saw her crouched in the far corner of the little box house, her arms crossed tight around her knees.

"Open this door or I going bust it." He had to shout to be heard over the racket of the wind.

She crawled across the *lau hala* mat on the floor, scrabbled up and turned the lock. He opened the door and stepped in on a gust of wind and rain, tracked mud across the mat.

Her hair was tangled, her bronze skin sallow and drained of color. Terror etched its mark across her perfect features.

He grabbed her by the elbow. "Come on. You not stay here."

He would take her to the main house for shelter and then rest easy knowing she was safe. Besides, if Hadley had not come home on her own, Elizabeth Bennett would need the women around her today.

"No, Duke!" Ana wrenched out of his grasp and backed away, shaking her head. "I not leaving dis *hale*. Dis da first one I get and I not going leave."

A windowpane on the back wall shattered as a flying coconut smashed through it and hit the floor with the crack of a cannonball. Ana leaped into his arms with a scream.

Duke started dragging her toward the door.

She struggled against him, dug in her heels and refused to budge.

"I still going stay, Duke. I going stay my house."

He lunged for her, intending to scoop her up, toss her on his shoulder, and carry her out, but fast as a mongoose, she scurried back. His shoe caught beneath the bound edge of the mat and he stumbled.

An eerie, grating scream, the sound of tin being torn from nails, filled the wooden house as a rectangular section of the patchwork of corrugated tin on the roof ripped upward, peeled back, and sailed away. From where he landed on the floor, Duke could see a shower of wood, all that was left of a support beam, come raining down.

FROM THE CORNER, ANA watched in horror as the roof of her precious house flew away. A piece of gray-green sky showed in its place. Rain began falling on her upturned face. She backed against the wall and covered her face with her arms.

When the barrage of wood chunks stopped, she looked around and then screamed when she saw Duke lying face-down in the middle of the floor. She ran to him and with much tugging and pulling, finally turned him over.

"Dukie! Wake up, Duke. *Auwē*," she wailed. "Don't be *make*, Duke. Don't be dead!" *All my fault,* she thought. *All my fault.* She smoothed his forehead. A lump was forming to one side.

"Duke, wake up!" She looked up through the hole in the roof and cried to any god who might be listening. "I no want dis house. I trade dis whole t'ing for Duke."

Staring down at him as he lay there helpless, she realized that this house meant nothing without him. The board-and-batten walls, the windows with glass panes, the mats, the flowerpots, the cast-off cooking pans, the battered teaket-tle—they all meant nothing.

She wanted Duke back. She wanted to hear him sing to her again, wanted to see him come walking up the lane with flowers in his hands and a big wide grin on his face. She wanted to swim beneath a waterfall with him one more time, to laugh and tease him, to have a chance to tell him that she really, truly loved him more than anybody.

A sob shuddered through her. Her shoulders bowed with the weight of her grief.

"Duke, no be *make*, please." She took a deep breath and prayed he could hear her.

"*I love you, Duke.*" Ana shouted the words over the wind, crying, tugging at the neck of his shirt, shaking him, banging his shoulders against the floorboards.

One corner of his mouth curved into a smile. He opened his right eye, then his left, and then, as if the world weren't coming down around their heads, he laughed.

"Ha. No can resist, eh?"

She rocked back on her heels, shocked and furious but, above all, overwhelmingly relieved. Duke jumped to his feet, reached for her hand, and pulled her up beside him.

"I going punch you in da face, Duke, for make me scart li' dat." She was still shouting as he dragged her out to the lanai and forced her up against the wall of the house. He gauged the wind, waiting for an opening.

She saw his face get a serious expression on it as he stared up the lane at the big, faded house and remembered the girl.

"You find Hadley?"

He shook his head. "No. Mebbe she up at da house already. I hope so." He grabbed her hand. "You can punch me all you want aftah the storm, Ana," he said. "Right now, we gotta go."

ELIZABETH PACED THE CONFINES of the dark hallway like a sleepwalker, too frightened to cry, too hollow to think beyond each and every step she took. Maile was sniffling at the far end of the hall, her face buried in her arms. Uilani moved up and down, making certain that lamps were out of harm's way, fluffing pillows and blotting up water that seeped in from the other rooms. As if the condition of the wooden floor really mattered anymore.

I should have gone myself. I should be out there now looking for Hadley. I should never have let Uilani keep me here.

Elizabeth hated being locked in the core of the house. It made her feel as if Mauna Noe had finally swallowed her whole. Away from the windows, there was no way to see outside. No way to know what was happening. There was only the awesome, terrible sounds of the wind and the rain and the howling protest of the house itself as nature tugged and pulled it apart.

What if Hadley is out there right now, fighting her way across the lawn? What if she is hiding in the garden? What if she is close enough to see the house and is calling me, wondering why I haven't found her?

Somewhere in a room upstairs, glass shattered. The east side of the structure shuddered.

With a cry she could no longer contain, Elizabeth ran down the hall toward the door that closed them off from the foyer.

Uilani called for her to stop, but she refused to be held here any longer.

She would go insane if she stayed hidden while her baby was outside alone in the storm. She turned the knob and the force of the wind swirling through the house tore it from her grasp, flung the door open, and rocked it back on its hinges. Across the foyer, Duke and Ana emerged from the dining room and ran toward her.

Elizabeth backed into the hall so that they could enter. Duke pulled the door closed behind them, cutting off the light and air again, forcing her back into the hot, humid closeness of the narrow hallway.

She felt Uilani move up close behind her, hovering protectively, and she wanted to scream, to tell the woman to get back, get away. Duke clutched Ana's hand in his. His hat was missing. An ugly welt stood out like an egg on his forehead. The seamstress was out of breath.

Hadley was not with them.

Elizabeth grabbed Duke's shoulders, clutched the soaked fabric of his shirt, searched his eyes, and knew the horrible truth.

The words he did not even have to say tore into her soul. A scream built inside her, threatened to rip her throat apart before a cold, silent darkness smothered that scream. She went numb, dropped her hands to her sides, staggered back against the wall. Her legs would not hold her up any longer.

She slid down the wall to the floor and sat there, rocking back and forth with her arms around herself, ignoring everyone else, shut off from everything but the insufferable, inescapable pain.

THE EYE OF THE storm tinted the sky an eerie yellow. The wind had stopped, but the air was still charged with tension. The birds were silent, as if they knew the hurricane was not over but merely marshaling strength for its next on-slaught.

Spence looked down at the child in his arms. She had cried herself to sleep, but at least he had the satisfaction of knowing she was not crying over Franklin Bennett any longer. She wanted to be home with her mother.

He made his move, cradled her against him as he hunched low and fought his way through the *hau* bush and the smooth, dark-brown guava stems. When he cleared the brush, the hillside was so slick with mud that he slipped and lost his footing. He kept a firm grip on the girl, but the slide backward jarred her awake.

"Mama?" She blinked and looked around, recognized him. "Is the storm over, Spence?"

"Not yet. Just a pause. We're going to run to the house."

"Mama's gonna be so glad to see me."

"Very, very glad."

He wondered how happy Elizabeth would be to see him. By now she must have given up all hope that he would ever send word to her about the land title. The last thing in the world he wanted was to see her look upon him with hate.

"Hang on, Hadley," he told her, doubting that he could break the hold she had on his neck even if he wanted to. He cleared the edge of the ravine and was on the bluff. Across the wide expanse of rolling lawn, the old house still stood, battered but defiant.

He could feel the air shift and the wind begin to rouse

itself. He hurried across the bluff with its huge, close-cropped lawn.

Elizabeth's garden already looked as if it had been flattened by a giant's footsteps when the wind suddenly picked up again. The banana tree trunks, the tall heliconia and torch ginger stalks were all split and broken. What was left of the stalks began to sway in sad imitation of what they had been but a few hours ago.

What had once been blazing with colorful flowers, was now only torn, frayed remains of bushes and bare branches.

"I'm scared, Spence," Hadley moaned.

"I promise I'll get you back."

He had reached the fence. The gate—broken for so long—had refused to fall, even though whole sections of the fence on either side of it were missing. He ran around it, stepped over fallen *ti* and gingers and then an orchid pot that had rolled over and littered the stepping-stones in the path.

He was halfway there, taking in as he went the damage to the front of the house, the missing shutters, gaps in the tin roof. Pieces of the roof that remained had already started flapping in the mounting wind, as if waving him on.

The overhang was sagging where a support post had been blown away from one corner of the lanai. Glass littered the wooden veranda, broken out of the long double doors that opened onto the porch.

He saw Uilani through wicked shards of glass that still hung like jagged shark's teeth in the door frames. She was stepping carefully as she passed through the middle of the parlor. Her face was unreadable from this distance, but he saw her turn and look outside.

Debris was flying again. Pieces of the camp houses, long, rattling hunks of tin roofing windmilled through the air. He hunched his shoulders, wrapped his upper torso around Hadley, and ran on.

The last thing he heard before his world exploded like a string of Chinese firecrackers on New Year's Day in Honolulu was Uilani calling out Elizabeth's name.

Twenty

THE TERRIBLE SOUND OF the storm had abated for a while but then it resumed. Elizabeth was partially aware of comings and goings—Duke said something about leaving for a while, Ana whispered to him, fast words uttered in furious, hushed tones. Uilani was still moving about restlessly. Maile did not make a sound except for an occasional hitch in her breath.

Elizabeth closed herself away from it all, cocooned by a shroud over her soul. She lay huddled on her side on the floor in the hallway, facing the wall. The house could fall down around her for all she cared, this place that had finally sucked away her will, broken her like an eggshell—or a piece of fine china.

When the sound of Uilani frantically calling her name broke through her numbness, Elizabeth moaned at the intrusion—a thin, feeble sound that might or might not have come from her. She could not be certain. She started to draw her arm over her ear so as not to hear, but then the hysterical jubilation in Uilani's voice registered in her mind. Elizabeth bolted up, ran down the hallway and into the foyer.

She could see Uilani through what was left of the front doors. The woman was standing outside on the edge of the lanai, partially blocking her view. Beyond Uilani, someone was running toward the house, bent like an old man. Duke came riding up bareback, charging toward the stranger, galloping the horse through her shattered garden, shouting frantically in Hawaiian over the wind.

The skirt of Uilani's *holokū* shifted and billowed around her, allowing Elizabeth a better view. She stared at the hunched man—recognized his long black hair, the strength in his shoulders, the striped shirt and hat.

Spence.

She knew then exactly what he carried so tenderly in his arms—she saw the muddy bare feet and toes, the little arms locked around his neck. Just then, as if Hadley knew she was near, she lifted her mud-streaked face from his shoulder. Elizabeth could not hear her cry, but knew Hadley said *Mama*.

Elizabeth tore through the foyer and started across the lanai. At the same moment, something large and dark came whirling out of the sky like a bird of prey. As she cleared the lanai and reached the bottom step, Elizabeth recognized the threat as a section of tin roof.

It was headed directly toward the man and the child.

The scream that had lodged somewhere deep inside last night found its way out. In the same, heart-stopping instant, Spence looked back over his shoulder, saw the tin, and ducked to shield Hadley. The tin fell out of the sky as if the wind had decided to let go where it could do the most mischief.

Elizabeth froze, watching in horror as the sheet of metal landed two feet from Spence. Then the force of the fall sent it shooting up again, and when it came down this time, it knocked him to the ground.

Sobbing Hadley's name, Elizabeth ran through the mud and tangle of debris that had once been her beloved garden. She reached for the tin and tried to pull it off of Spence.

She could hear Hadley crying, calling for her. Duke ran to her side and helped her move the tin.

Hadley was pinned beneath him. He was unconscious, the back of his head bleeding, the rain spreading a bright-red stain over his collar.

Duke gently picked Spence up and headed for the house. Elizabeth knelt in the mud and clasped her daughter in her arms, rocking back and forth.

"It's all right, Mama," Hadley said, her arms tight around Elizabeth, patting her mother on the back.

"Ho'i hou!" Uilani shouted from the shelter of the lanai. "Come back! *Ho'i hou!"*

Awareness came rushing back. Elizabeth scooped Hadley up and ran back inside the house, past Uilani, past Ana. The women followed her into the hallway and shut the door. The storm began boiling again, the wind increased until the house shuddered worse than before. Duke already had Spence stretched out and was applying a compress made from a torn sheet to the back of his head.

Elizabeth stood over them, clutching her little girl, unwilling to let her go. Hadley sniffled softly against her neck.

"How is he?" Elizabeth whispered to Duke, trembling, unable to stop.

"Not good." Duke lifted the compress to reveal a jagged, oozing wound.

"Mama," Hadley whispered, "I'm sorry I ran away."

"I know, darling." Elizabeth kissed her muddy cheek. The kerosene lamp flickered, sluggish in the close air.

"Spence needs help more than me," Hadley told her. "And I gotta go sit with Maile and tell her she's still my friend."

Elizabeth turned around and set Hadley on her feet. The child immediately ran over to Maile, who still looked forlorn. Elizabeth flashed a look to Uilani across the shaded hall, a glance that said without words, "Please, watch over my child." Then she knelt on the floor beside Duke.

Spence was shivering, still unconscious, his mind having taken refuge inside itself.

Elizabeth took a deep, calming breath, refusing to give up now, not after he had risked his life to save her child. There was no way she was going to let him die, no way she was going to negotiate with the Almighty about this. She refused to believe she had to exchange Hadley's life for Spence's.

She leaned close, put her lips against his ear. His skin was cold and clammy despite the heat in the close hallway. "Don't you dare die on me now, Spence Laamea. Not now." She leaned back, feeling helpless, wishing she could hold him in her arms all night long and will her strength into him.

"He is soaking wet." Elizabeth spoke aloud, to herself, to Duke and the others. "Help me get him out of these clothes."

There was no time for modesty, no place for social restrictions. Ana came forward, knelt beside Duke, and offered her help. Her eyes met Elizabeth's over Spence's prone form, and in that instant forgiveness was asked and given without a word being exchanged.

Three pairs of hands worked to strip off his leather vest, striped shirt, gaiters, shoes, pants. Elizabeth did not look away, nor did she even blush when Duke worked Spence's trousers down over his thighs.

She marveled silently as she focused on the intricate black tattoo being revealed inch by inch. She clung tight to Spence's hand, speaking softly to him, thanking him for bringing Hadley home to her, smoothing his hair back off his face as Ana took over and worked the pants free from his feet and ankles. Duke covered the lower part of Spence's body with a piece of the torn sheet.

As soon as the wet clothing had been removed and they dried and rubbed his skin all over, Spence finally stopped shivering. Elizabeth parted his hair and cleaned the wound, which did not appear to be as deep as she had thought. The bleeding had stopped.

Duke leaned back on his heel, rubbed his hand over the back of his neck.

"What now?" Ana whispered.

"Nothing." Elizabeth smoothed her hand down Spence's long hair. "We wait."

"Pray," Uilani said softly from her place down the way. "Pray his *'aumakua* give him back his *mana,* make him strong again." She began to chant, the words echoing in the hall, a hypnotic, repetitive sound that raised goose-flesh—chicken skin, as the Hawaiians liked to say—along Elizabeth's arms.

Elizabeth recognized the word, remembered Spence had told Hadley of his *'aumakua* the day he took her into the mountains to collect his saddlebags. She had heard the story often enough. Now she wished she knew about the island gods so that she might appeal to them. The night they had made love, Spence told her that his tattoo was dedicated to his family *'aumakua, pueo,* the owl. She slipped her hand beneath the sheet, pressed her palm against his hip where the pattern stained his skin. She closed her eyes, pictured an owl in flight.

"Help him," she whispered as Uilani's chant reached a crescendo. "Let him live."

When the chant ended and Uilani fell silent, Duke and Ana walked down the hall and, exhausted, sat down side by side.

Elizabeth held Spence's hand in both of hers, unwilling to let go.

Don't leave again, Spence. Not this way. Please, not this way.

There was still so much she did not know about him. She already knew his body well, and she knew he was an honorable man, but what of all the little things? The every-day things. Did he take his coffee black? Was he ill-tempered in the morning? Did he know how to dance? Did he like to stand and watch rainbows until they faded? Had he loved before?

She wanted another chance to persuade him to stay, but if he insisted on leaving again she wanted to stand on the lanai, waving good-bye, calling out *aloha nui*.

She wanted a chance to tell him that no matter how far he went or how long he stayed away—be it months or years—she would be waiting here on the land, here at Mauna Noe with Hadley.

And she would still be loving him.

Everyone settled along the hallway. Uilani's frantic need to keep the lamps lit and safe from being overturned had exhausted itself. Duke and Ana sat with their hands clasped between them, heads back against the wall, eyes closed. Maile and Hadley were stretched out farther down the hall, their differences forgotten, heads together on a shared pillow. Spence had yet to move or make a sound. He lay so still that Elizabeth kept touching his back to make certain he was still breathing.

Sleep was the farthest thing from Elizabeth's mind. Each and every time—too many times to count—that she looked at Hadley, she felt a jubilance that was tempered only by her worry about Spence.

Needing to do something—anything—for him, she reached for his damp pants and folded them, then his shirt. When she picked up his leather vest, a bulky document tucked in an inside pocket fell out.

It bore the distinctive seal of the Hawaiian monarchy. She recognized the coat of arms, the red, white, and blue stripes on the Hawaiian flag, two identical men adorned with capes, an intricate crown above the flag, and an inscription in Hawaiian beneath it. She had no idea of the meaning of the other symbols, she knew only that this letter, marked with the seal, was official.

Everyone around her was either sleeping or resting quietly. Her stomach fluttered with nerves as the weight of the packet in her hand grew heavier. She took a deep breath and gently laid one hand on Spence's shoulder. He did not stir.

She knew with complete certainty that her fate was written on the pages in her hand. Elizabeth looked down at the folded document and knew that she was holding the title to Mauna Noe—that Spence had surely been bringing it home to her.

She pushed herself to her feet. Every muscle in her back and legs ached from sitting on the floor so long. She quietly slipped over to the lamp and knelt beside it, then sat back on her heels. The paper was still slightly damp, so she opened it carefully, unfolding each section very slowly.

Bold black script was penned into blank sections of the printed title. She scanned down it, saw Kalakaua's signature and the seal imprinted on the bottom. Her gaze flew back to the top.

Full title and ownership . . . Mauna Noe . . . granted to Spencer Makamae Laamea . . . said owner must live on the land . . . cannot sell, trade, or sign away rightful ownership until his death.

She held the page closer to the light. Read all the way down again. She searched for her name, for Hadley's name. They were not there. The king's signature and the seal stood out against the white linen page.

Full title and ownership . . . Mauna Noe . . . granted to Spencer Makamae Laamea . . . must live on the land . . . cannot sell, trade, or sign away rightful ownership until his death.

Her hands shook. The page fell into her lap. Elizabeth sat there staring at the opposite wall, watching the lamplight shimmer in the surface of the tarnished gilt *koi* fish that decorated thirty-year-old wallcovering.

After what seemed forever, she finally found the courage to look at Spence again. His skin shone darker in the poorly lit hallway. Stretched out on the floor he looked huge. She remembered the way she had felt in his arms—warm, safe, cherished—remembered it as if she had just left them.

Against all odds, she had fallen in love with this man, and in turn, he had taken everything she had to give—her body, her heart, her trust.

I should hate him.

What a fool she had been to gamble with her daughter's birthright. To think she had sent the man to Honolulu with her blessings. She had begged him to forget any censure they would receive from the *haole* community, begged him to live with her openly.

I should hate him.

At the very least, I should feel nothing for him. The same empty nothingness she felt for Johnny Huffington after all these years. The same nothingness that time was slowly substituting for her hatred of Franklin.

But looking at Spence she could not summon up hatred, or even anger. Not yet. Not while vivid in her mind was the image of him running through the storm with his body wrapped around Hadley, shielding her, bringing her home.

How could she hate a man who had just given her child's life back to her a second time?

She could not. She had to hear him out.

Slowly, carefully, she folded the deed along the same crease lines and took it back to where she had left his other things. She slipped the document back inside his vest.

Weary and confused, she sat down and pressed her back up against the wall, against the once-beautiful *koi* fish condemned to swim the walls of the hallway forever. More than once through the long *makani pāhili* night, she thought she heard Franklin's cruel laughter in the sound of the wind beating against the outside of the house.

ONE BY ONE THEY stirred and came out into the light like inmates on a transport ship who had been locked too long in the dark. Duke was the first to awaken, to venture to the door at the end of the hall and open it. Ana followed him, creeping silently past the sleeping children. Uilani rose, hefted herself off the floor, and stretched. As she walked through the house she stopped to straighten chairs, right overturned tables, shake her head and mutter, "Not so bad. Not so bad."

Elizabeth roused herself. Her neck and back were stiff, her legs numb from sitting on the hard floor all night. The front of her dress was stained with Spence's blood.

She had found no relief when she did sleep, for her mind wandered through a nightmare in which she had searched in vain for her daughter but instead found Spence buried in Franklin's grave.

Since Spence seemed to be resting peacefully now, with no sign of fever, she let him sleep on. Hadley and Maile eventually awoke, and, with the resilience of children, adjusted to the upheaval around them, although Maile, whenever the trades blew a bit harder, wanted to know if they would have to go back into the hallway.

Slowly all of the occupants of Mauna Noe began to piece their lives back together bit by bit. Horses were rounded up and corralled, and the most-needed fences were hastily mended, along with the men's barracks. Toshi worked for hours raking and burning the debris in the garden and around the house, while Melvin climbed up on the roof with hammer and nails and pieces of tin to patch it before the rain came again.

Uilani's kitchen had fared as well as the main house did. Any unfortunate chickens that came running out from the underbrush wound up in a stew pot to feed everyone.

Elizabeth wandered through the rooms, assessing the damage, the water-stained floors and draperies, the shattered windowpanes. She swept and mopped and sorted, wiped and tossed and worked without stopping. She threw herself into the task of making Mauna Noe whole again as if the place were still hers, refusing to think about the document hidden away in Spence's vest, refusing to dwell on the truth of her circumstance.

•   •   •

ANA STOOD OFF TO the side of the lane next to a broken
coffee tree, staring at what was left of the little *hale* she
had so loved even though it was not really hers. There was
not much evidence that the place had ever existed. Nothing
but a few boards left to prove that just the night before last
she had cooked sweet potatoes in the battered pot on the
stove and slept on the mats she had brought with her from
Hanalei.

The back wall, the woodstove, and the floor were still
there. Gone were the windows with panes of glass, gone
was the lopsided lanai. It was the one house on the lane
that had been completely ravaged.

Duke came riding in from the far pasture, where he had
been estimating the number of head of *pipi* that had survived. He found Ana there beside the ruined tree, staring
at what was left of her house, her bright-red *holokū* the
only spot of color left now that the flowers and blossoming
trees had been destroyed.

He dismounted before he reached her and walked toward
her. Seeing her there, with her long black hair rippling in
waves to her hips, her shoulders proud and defiant, he knew
why he would love her forever.

She surprised him by turning to greet him with a smile.
Then she stepped up to him, put her arms around his neck,
and kissed him, long and slow. His hand found her waist,
pulled her to him until their bodies touched from shoulder
to thigh.

She rubbed against him, like a sleek brown cat, then
leaned back and smiled up into his eyes.

"I see you here, I think mebbe you be crying because
house all *pau*," he said.

She surprised him with a shrug, lifted her lips to his,
nipped his lower lip between her teeth.

"No more. I looking at dat place and I t'inking, hey, just
one pile of wood and glass and tin. No mattah."

"Yeah?"

"Yeah. Because I got you, Duke. I trade you for one

haole house anytime.'' Ana kissed him again. "When you gonna marry me?''

She hugged him closer, pressed her breasts and hips and mound against him, made him hot and hard. He felt as if he was going to explode.

"Gotta be soon or I going be all *pau* like you house.''

"Mebbe tonight we get some practice, eh?''

"Practice what?''

Attached to him like an *'opihi* to a rock, she slipped her hand between them so that no one would see her touching him through his clothing.

"You bettah stop, Ana.'' He had a hard time getting the words out as he looked into her eyes. There was no hint of teasing in them now, only the promise of what all their tomorrows would bring.

"I love you, Duke,'' she whispered against his lips.

At long last, he believed her.

Twenty-one

SPENCE OPENED HIS EYES, unaware of where he was or how he came to be there. He knew nothing, except that a headache was blinding him and that he was lying facedown on a mat on the floor. Voices filtered through the pain, floating disembodied from another room. The young, high voices of children.

He struggled to sit up, waited while the walls around him tilted back into their rightful places. Except for a piece of sheet wrapped around his groin, he was naked. His mouth was as dry as rice paper. Slowly the walls came into focus, gilt *koi* stamped on an aquamarine sea.

Mauna Noe.

He sat there with his head pressed between his hands, afraid that if he let go it would explode. Memory came flooding back. The wind, the lashing, horizontal rain. Hadley clinging to him, her little arms stuck around his neck, tight as *he'e* tentacles. Fighting his way through the demolished garden. Uilani's voice shouting Elizabeth's name.

He braced his palms against the wall and raised himself an inch at a time until he stood. The sheet slipped from his hips, started to slide to the floor. When he fashioned a knot at his waist, he lost his balance, rammed his shoulder into the wall. Cursed.

The throbbing in his head gradually subsided. He gained strength with every careful step. He came to a long looking glass propped against the wall. His hair was loose, so tangled and matted that he looked like some wild creature, his complexion sallow, almost yellow. He went on, toward the sound of the voices.

When he opened the hall door and stepped into the foyer, Hadley and Maile looked up from the floor, where they knelt together, winding a bandage around a fat stuffed horse.

Both girls screamed in unison, a shrill, piercing sound that went on and on. Spence put his hands over his ears until Hadley elbowed Maile into silence and the scream stopped abruptly.

"Aloha, Spence!" Hadley jumped up, ran to him, and took his hand. "I thought you were an evil troll."

He saw her eyes grow huge when she noticed the tattoo above and below the sheet.

"Somebody wrote all over your backside, Spence!"

"I need . . . your mother—" He gazed past the children, into the dining room. Chairs. He needed to sit in the worst way. Maybe if he had some water, something to eat . . .

Maile ran out. Spence let his half sister lead him into the dining room. By the time he negotiated a chair, Elizabeth came running into the room.

She stopped in the doorway and looked at him—and through him—in a way that chilled his soul. She seemed to recover herself so quickly that he wondered if he had seen the look at all. She walked up to him and put her hand on his forehead.

"No fever." Her voice was empty of emotion. Perhaps the strain of the storm.

He cleared his throat, rasped out a whisper. "What happened?"

"A piece of roof hit you while you were crossing the garden with Hadley." Elizabeth stared at him a moment more, then left suddenly, walked out without explanation.

Spence looked at Hadley. The child leaned against the table, staring at him with her elbows propped on polished mahogany, her chin cupped in her hands.

"You look terrible, Spence."

"*Mahalo*, Hadley." *Thank you. I feel it.*

"Mama didn't know what to do with you, and Duke didn't think we could all lift you into your room, so they decided to let you sleep on the floor. Isn't that funny?"

"Yeah." *No.* He felt like he had been dragged around Kaua'i behind a horse.

Hadley reached out before he knew what she was about and put her palm against his thigh. "Does it hurt?" she whispered, staring at the tattoo.

"At first."

Elizabeth came bearing a tray with water, tea, and a bowl of something that smelled so delicious his stomach came to life and growled. She set the tray down on the table, walked over to Hadley, and stood behind her. While Spence drained the water glass, Elizabeth simply stood there watching him, her hands planted protectively on her daughter's shoulders. He lifted the spoon off the tray and dipped it into the bowl of steaming chicken stew.

Elizabeth ran her hand over Hadley's hair and then said, "Please go find Uilani, Hadley. Tell her that Spence will be needing his clothes soon."

"Aw, Mama. I wanna watch Spence eat. I never get see one man eat wit' no clothes on already."

Spence choked on a mouthful of soup, coughed it down. Elizabeth did not smile. Her eyes assessed him, measured his worth.

"That is without *any* clothes on *yet*, Hadley, not 'wit' no clothes on already.' Now go, please, and tell Uilani to take his things off the clothesline."

Spence put down his spoon. Waited until Hadley left the

room. He knew what was causing Elizabeth's cool reserve, it was more than Hadley's transgression of speaking pidgin.

They were alone in the same room where it had all begun. Unspoken anger and tension mounted like the energy that had pushed the storm across the island. She was no longer looking at him the way she had the day he told her he was leaving. Other than bringing in the food, she had not even asked how he felt.

She stood there in self-imposed isolation, cool, detached. Waiting for him to make the first move.

She knows, he thought.

"You saw the deed," he said. She did not respond at all.

Suddenly the stew was not setting well on his stomach. He felt like putting his head on his arm and sleeping away what was left of the day, but not with Elizabeth staring him down, insisting without words that he explain.

"Sit down, Elizabeth."

He expected her to argue. She pulled out the chair at the head of the table, sat there as straight as bamboo, folded her hands and waited.

Spence sighed, wishing that this could have been postponed until his head was not throbbing, wishing that he was dressed, at least. Outside, through a hole where glass once lined the window, acres and acres of tree trunks reached toward the sky like fractured bones. He looked at her perfect profile, ached to hold her while he told his story, knew that was even more impossible now.

"I tried, Elizabeth. I waited. I danced attendance on Kalakaua. I tried to be everything my uncle wanted me to be at court—charming, a *hapa* mediator, someone who might be a buffer between the *haole* planters and the king they despise, but I'm not a politician, Elizabeth, I'm a *paniolo*.

"Finally I met alone with the king, told him why I left here and what I wanted. Milton Clifford had sent the proper papers. I carefully explained Franklin's will. I told him I left Mauna Noe so that Hadley could have the land."

He rubbed his hand over his brow, waited until a wave

of dizziness passed. "He flat-out refused—"

"—to give title to Hadley," she finished for him. Her voice wavered, about to break. "But he gave it to *you*, Spence, didn't he? For a lifetime. He gave it all to you. He even ordered you, very conveniently, to stay here, on the land."

He heard her feelings of betrayal in every lifeless word.

"Elizabeth—Kalakaua's back is to the wall. He has tried, since he took the throne, to give some power back to Hawaiians. He is little more than a figurehead now. When I left here and the land reverted to him, he was free to do with it as he wished. He could have sold it out from under us, he could have used it to pay off some of his debt. But he deeded it to me, because of my mother, because of my uncle, and because of the size of Mauna Noe. He wanted to keep this land from being sold to a *haole*."

He touched the back of his head where it ached, felt dried blood in his hair. Dismissed it.

Spence could not—would not—ever tell her that Kalakaua had signed over the title and forced him to live here because the king insisted on clinging to the hope that in time Spence would meet and marry a Hawaiian woman, that they would produce offspring who would perpetuate Hawaiian ownership of the land.

"Our plan backfired," he said softly. "But I think I have found a way—"

"*Your* plan. *You* did not suffer any in this, Spence. You have Mauna Noe now. You have what you wanted all along."

"I don't have the *only* thing in this world I want, Elizabeth—the one thing I can never, ever have," he said softly.

Elizabeth tilted her head, pressed her lips together to still their trembling. He was not simply looking at her, he was caressing her with his eyes. Even though it was breaking, her traitorous heart threatened to respond.

"You are so good at your deception, Spence. You are so very, very good," she whispered.

"I love you, Elizabeth. Nothing will ever change that."

"Stop it. Just stop it." Tears were streaming down her face.

Hadley chose that inopportune moment to reappear. She ran over to Spence, handed him his shirt and pants. They had been washed and although not ironed yet were neatly folded.

"Mama?" Hadley ran to her mother, reached up, and wiped away a tear that was streaking down her cheek. "Mama? What's wrong?"

The child turned to Spence and demanded, "What's the matter with Mama?"

"Nothing, Hadley," she snapped before Spence could answer. "I'm just tired."

"You never cry when you're tired," Hadley persisted.

Elizabeth wiped the tears from her cheeks, raised her chin, refused to let her child see her in defeat. She could not look at her daughter or her will would shatter. She had failed in the one thing she had meant to do, the only thing that mattered before she met Spence Laamea. She had failed to hold this land for her little girl.

"Where is my vest?" Spence had unfolded the shirt, held it in his lap.

Elizabeth sniffed, wiped the corner of her eye again. Her life had fallen apart and he wanted his vest.

"In your room. I put the deed in the pocket and put it on your bed." She took a deep breath. "Hadley, go get Spencer's vest, please."

"I'm so *tired* of going back and forth after everything. You can call me Cinderella if you want to." Hadley sighed, and with a long, slow, theatrical exit, she walked out of the room, dragging each foot as if a *poi* pounder were tied to it.

"You didn't look at the other paper."

Elizabeth stared back at him. "What?"

"There was another paper in my vest pocket. Did you find it?"

"No."

"If you had, you would not be looking at me the way you are now, Elizabeth."

"What do you mean?"

"I found it!" Hadley shouted from Spence's room. She came running, her feet pounding in the hall, across the foyer. She thrust the vest at Spence. He reached into the pocket, took out the deed to the land and laid it on the table. He dug around in the pocket again and pulled out a second paper, this one very thin, folded into a small square.

"Here." He held it out to Elizabeth. His hand was steady, his eyes intense.

"What—"

"Take it." When she did not move, he tossed it to her. The folded page slid across the table.

She opened it. Another formal document, this one witnessed by Milton Clifford here on Kaua'i. *Spencer Makamae Laamea* was signed at the bottom of a simple paragraph.

Last Will and Testament of Spencer Makamae Laamea.
   To Hadley Elyson Bennett, I leave all my worldly possessions, including title to Mauna Noe, land parcel on Kaua'i Granted to Me in this year of our Lord, 1888, by King David Kalakaua. In the event that I am not survived by Hadley Elyson Bennett, or if, upon my death, she has not reached maturity, the above should be given over to Elizabeth Rodrick Bennett to hold in trust for her daughter. If neither party survives me, this holding is to be returned to its rightful owners, the people of Hawai'i nei.

Elizabeth read the will through twice. Struggled to understand. As the meaning of the words came clear to her, she was stunned. She fought to find something, anything, to say to him to make up for what she had already said, but she choked on her humiliation.

When she looked up again, the chair Spence had occupied was empty.

SPENCE REALIZED THAT ELIZABETH assumed he would go back to his room to change, which gave him time to slip out of the dining room and exit along the side lanai. He dressed in the office and was lucky to find Duke not far away, mending a corral fence.

"You don't look bettah," Duke told him, but he was smiling when he said it.

"Mahalo." Spence glanced back at the house. "I need a horse, plenty quick," he told Duke.

Without question, Duke nodded. "I get one good horse for you." He pointed at the animals milling about in the hastily repaired corral.

Spence thought for a moment that his head was worse off than he'd suspected. Across the corral stood Kāhili, head high and proud, sniffing into the wind, as if he had caught Spence's scent. The thoroughbred made his way over to the fence. Spence looked at Duke.

The Hawaiian *luna* smiled. "Mrs. Bennett, she send me and Ana to Kilauea, ask fo' manager over dere sell Kāhili to her. Dat man plenty happy get rid dis one, I tell you straight. Nobody can ride 'um."

Spence realized that Elizabeth must have spent part of her limited funds to buy Kāhili back, even though at the time she had no idea that he would ever return.

He spoke quickly to Duke, gave him cursory instructions. Docile as a kitten, the big black horse followed Spence to what was left of the stables. In the midst of the broken boards and clutter, he found a bit and bridle, slipped it on Kāhili, mounted bareback, and rode up the mountain.

ELIZABETH STOOD IN SPENCE'S empty room, stared at the water-stained drapes, then went to the doors and stepped out on the front lanai. A lazy plume of smoke spiraled above the debris that Toshi had raked into a pile. There was no sign of Spence out front.

She called his name, went back to the dining room. The will and the title to the land lay open on the table near his tray, tickled by the trades that ruffled through broken windows. She felt sick when she looked at the documents, sick at heart, sick of herself for ever doubting him.

She ran around the lanai, crossed to the kitchen.

"Uilani, have you seen Spencer?"

Busy sweeping flour off the floor, Uilani shook her head. Panic mounted as Elizabeth ran to the office, through the store, out to the bunkhouse, and still did not find him.

"Melvin!" She dashed in, found Melvin sound asleep on his bunk, and shook him awake. "Melvin, have you seen Spence?"

Melvin frowned. Scratched his head. Shook it.

"No. I don't see 'um. I t'ink he go Honolulu."

"He came *back*, Melvin."

"Den I no see."

She forced herself to slow down, to breathe, to think. He would not forgive her this time. She knew it. She had seen the hurt on his face, read the condemnation in his eyes. Her distrust had driven a wedge between them as sure and deep as the glass shards that the treacherous storm had driven into tree trunks.

Finally she saw Duke near the stable. She called his name and as he turned, the same shuttered look she had seen on Spence's face was reflected in his eyes.

"Duke, have you seen Spence?"

He took as long to answer as Melvin had. Lifted his hat and rubbed his head. Put it on again. Looked out toward the crater, toward the sea.

Elizabeth's breath caught, shuddered through her.

"He left," Duke said. "Say tell you bettah he go live up *mauka*. Up da mountain."

She put her hands to her eyes. Remembered saying,

"You are so very good at deception, Spence. So very, very good."

She dropped her hands, straightened, took a deep breath.

"I need you to saddle a horse for me, Duke. I have to talk to him."

What was Spence planning? To live on the opposite side of the ranch for the rest of their lives? Ridiculous. He needed time, that was all. Time alone. He would forgive her, he had to. She still loved him.

And although he never told her so, he had loved her enough to petition a king.

Duke balked, refusing to follow her order. "I see his face. I t'ink more bettah you let 'im go."

AND SO SHE DID.

Elizabeth went back in the house, picked up the precious title to the land along with Spencer's will, and locked the documents away in her room, at the bottom of the trunk she had brought with her from Baltimore, in hopes that if she could not see them she would not keep remembering what she had done to him.

She remembered anyway.

Duke wanted to leave too and take Ana with him. Elizabeth begged him to stay, promising he could work shorter days so that he would have time to build a house for Ana, a house of stone with windows and a door.

She gave them leave to go to Hanalei a week after the storm and marry, but she walked the floor until they returned and she could sleep knowing that her young, capable *luna* had not deserted her.

In the weeks and months that followed, Duke was her only tie to Spence.

Somehow the men kept in contact. She sensed that Duke often went to Spence for advice and instruction. It was months after the hurricane before things were moving toward normalcy. The stable was still not rebuilt, but the cattle had been accounted for and moved from one pasture to another. They lost some much-needed horses, so Elizabeth allotted money for more. Wood and nails had to be bought, and precious food to replace what was ruined.

The gardens were replanted, but it would be months before the people of Mauna Noe tasted fruit grown on the land again. They existed on fish and chicken and beef, sweet potatoes, *poi* and rice, coconut.

Spence stayed away. One month turned into two, two into three.

When things on the land seemed to be righting themselves again, Elizabeth made a trip to Hanalei to see Marion. This time she went alone, confident enough to leave Hadley with Uilani and Maile for the day.

The Hanalei Valley appeared to have been trimmed and pruned and hacked back with an overzealous hand. The emerald and jade mountains had been scraped raw by the force of the wind, ancient trees uprooted and tossed about like matchsticks. Patches of red earth showed on the forested mountainsides like scabs. On the valley floor itself, the shimmering silver rice paddies had already been replanted.

Marion Reynolds threw open the door of the bed-and-board before Elizabeth knocked. Her hair stood out in a light-brown nimbus only three inches long. An aquamarine gown highlighted her snapping eyes.

"Marion, what have you done to your hair?" Elizabeth took both the hands she offered.

"Needed a change after the storm. Cut it off and tossed it out with all the damaged goods." She hugged Elizabeth to her and then stepped back, ushering her in. "*E komo mai,* ducks! Come in, come in. I'll brew us a cup of tea. How did the grand Mauna Noe fare?"

They talked story. Each told her version of the storm and its aftermath. Marion cried when Elizabeth told her about Hadley's disappearance and how she spent the first half of the storm thinking her child was lost to her.

"And you say *Spence* saved her?" Marion pushed back

her chair, went to get a floral tin from a high shelf across the room, and then returned. "What about the king, and Honolulu?"

Elizabeth felt the color rush to her face. "Spence came back."

"Aha. And?" Marion began spreading tea biscuits on a tray.

"And nothing. He has been living somewhere up in the mountains ever since."

"In the mountains? On Mauna Noe? Got it that bad for you that he had to move out?"

"I drove him to it."

"I think you have some explaining to do."

Elizabeth told her how Spence had gone to secure the land for her, for Hadley. How when he came back and she read the deed, she had believed he had betrayed her.

"I said terrible things to him, Marion, and all the time he just sat there, letting me go on and on, accusing him of stealing the land." Tears she did not try to hide stung her eyes. "He sat there and he listened and then he handed his will over to me. He is leaving the ranch to Hadley, or to me if she is not old enough to inherit when he . . . when he dies."

"Surely you apologized. It was an honest mistake—"

"I never had the chance. I thought he had duped me, that he had used me—made love to me—just to get me to listen to his plan. I thought he tricked me to get the one thing he really always wanted for himself, Mauna Noe." She pressed her lips together. Marion's image swam behind a film of tears. "I hurt him, Marion. I threw everything he had done back in his face, and before I could say anything to him at all, he was gone."

"Surely you can find him—"

"I could force Duke to tell me where Spence lives, but he doesn't want to see me. He's fulfilling the king's title to the letter of the law by living on Mauna Noe, but he will have nothing to do with me. Duke is the only one in contact with him. A month ago Spence received a letter from the king. I gave it to Duke, who took it to Spence, but he sent it back to me unopened.''

"Kalakaua wants the land back?"

"Not at all. He wanted to make sure Spence has a way to keep the place solvent so he won't lose it to creditors. The king set up a contract for Mauna Noe. We have a standing order to ship cattle over to Honolulu every six months.''

"So you are sitting pretty and Spence is licking his wounds in the hills. That explains a few things,'' Marion said, musing aloud.

"What do you mean?"

"For one thing, that haunted look in your eyes and the way your gown hangs off you.'' She shoved the dish at Elizabeth. "Here, eat. Have a biscuit.''

"I can't,'' Elizabeth whispered. "I don't want any.''

"And it explains the stories going around the valley.''

"Stories?"

"There's been talk of a crazy man living in the mountains. Some say they've seen him at night, prowling through the forest. Others have seen him when they're out hunting or gathering *mokihana* spared by the storm. They wonder if he is a *kahuna,* hiding from the missionaries, or if he is a leper, hiding from the bounty hunters.''

"What am I going to do, Marion?"

"Do you still love him?"

"Of course I do. And I know he loves me. But I've hurt him by distrusting him over and over. Besides, even if he does listen, even if he forgives me, there is no way I'll ever convince him to live near me again. He does not want to ruin me or to create a scandal.''

"Is that the only thing that is keeping you from going to him and laying your heart bare? The threat of scandal?''

Elizabeth shook her head. "I feel the same way you do, Marion. I don't care about what anyone else thinks anymore.''

"What of Hadley? Does the thought of what she might think of you when she gets older keep you from going to him?"

"Perhaps . . . I don't know. I've wrestled with nothing else for months now."

Marion went back to the cupboard and took out a bottle of brandy. When she returned to the table, she had two stemmed glasses in her hand, one taller than the other.

"Sorry they don't match," she said, filling a glass for Elizabeth and setting it in front of her. "The hurricane played havoc with my china and crystal."

At least, Elizabeth thought, *I don't have Franklin's Staffordshire to mourn.*

"Drink up, ducks. I'm going to give you a few pieces of good advice, and then I want you to go home and do some very serious thinking."

Twenty-two

SPENCE LIKED TO THINK that he was running back to himself rather than away from Elizabeth. He stood beside the *hale* he had built on a hill very near the pool below a waterfall. The thunderous sound of falling water helped keep loneliness at bay. Often he thought he heard voices in the falls, but whenever he got close enough to listen, he heard only the roar of the water.

This was his home now, this Kaua'i forest, *wao nahele,* where the vegetation was so dense in places it was impenetrable. The *haole* called it jungle. Although he still could not imagine living out his life here, where the air was cooler and the shadows deeper than on the open land, he told himself that for now he was content.

When he was a boy, just orphaned by his mother and taken in by his grandfather on O'ahu, the wizened old man once told him that if he trained, if he apprenticed himself and worked hard, he would be a *kahuna* one day and might eventually train himself to become a seer of visions.

Here in the forest, Spence had hoped that if he kept to himself, if he lived off the land and the sea, tended *kalo* terraces, hunted, fished, carved what utensils and calabashes he needed, that he would become more attuned to the *'āina*, the land, and that he might nurture and tap the power his grandfather once claimed he possessed.

And so he waited for visions to come. At night he would lie awake, staring up at the grass ceiling in the hut he had made of poles with bundles of *pili* grass lashed to them with coconut fiber. He waited to hear the voice of the gods, perhaps the feet of the ghostly Night Marchers as they traveled across the land collecting souls.

He strained to hear his *'aumakua*, the owl. Although he often heard it call at night, the bird never spoke to him in the words of men nor did it impart anything prophetic.

He never developed the power to see into the future. He blamed it on not being able to think of anything but Elizabeth. He met Duke once a week at various prearranged places on the ranch, sometimes at the cove near the mouth of the stream, sometimes on the high open pastures far from the house. He would ask about Elizabeth and Hadley. Each time Duke would say only that they were getting along well. Not once did Elizabeth send word that she wanted to see him. Not once did she have Duke ask him to come back.

He had been tempted to ride Kāhili down to the ranch proper, to slip across the land under cloak of darkness and enter the unlocked house just to watch her sleep.

But then he would be too close, too tempted.

Some days he wanted her so badly that he thought he would go insane. Some nights as he sat high on the mountainside, he saw Elizabeth in the silver-white moon milk spilled over dark Pacific waters. He saw her in the daylight smiling through a rainbow stretched across the land. He heard her voice in the clear, loud whistle of the *'elepaio* as it darted through the trees.

But during those times he knew better than to think he was having visions. Elizabeth was with him, always in his heart.

One day bounty hunters came, stalked him, burst into his camp shouting and cursing, swearing at him. They knew why he was hiding, they said. They boasted of the money he would bring them—cash money—when they turned him over to the authorities who were rounding up lepers for the one-way trip to Molokai.

They degraded him, these fellow Hawaiians who were terrified of the disease but loved money more than they feared lepers. Prodded him with their long rifles, made him strip off his *malo* and examined him for sores, for lesions, for skin the color of ashes. Poked him with bamboo, looking for numbness in his limbs.

He was clean. He had no *ma'i Pākē*. They left his sanctuary, still swearing, grumbling about the wasted trek through the forest.

The entire experience left him shaken, brought back all the pain he had endured when Kaala discovered she was afflicted with leprosy. They had been so young then, just seventeen, in love and headstrong. The child of a wealthy father who did not want her to marry Spence, she ran away with him anyway. He took her to live on a ranch where he was working at the time. When a neighbor woman noticed a lesion on Kaala's arm and turned her into the *luna*, Spence went with her to Honolulu. He told Kaala he would *kōkua* for her, he would live on Molokai in the leper colony like others who gave up their own freedom to go with loved ones and nurse them through the ravages of the disease.

She refused his offer of *kōkua*, begged him to let her go to the isolated colony on the Molokai peninsula alone. He flew into a rage, shouted at her, told her he would never let her go without him. That night, she escaped the barracks where the diseased were housed and took her own life by drowning in the waters off Honolulu.

After the bounty hunters left his Mauna Noe mountain retreat, Spence suffered through memories of that loss all over again and came out of it convinced that he was doomed never to know lasting love.

Then one day, when he saw Elizabeth walking up the narrow, nearly indistinguishable trail that led to his camp, Spence was convinced he was having a vision. Finally he had broken through the vapor curtain that separates this world from the next.

She was perfect, exquisite. He was amazed at how easy it was to envision every detail—her navy serge skirt, the white blouse with puffed sleeves. Sturdy leather shoes that hugged her ankles, her slim calves exposed as she tucked her skirt up between her legs allowing her to jump from one smooth black lava rock to another along the edge of the streambed.

He began to tremble when it came to him that this image of Elizabeth was much too clear to be a vision. When he heard her cry out and nearly go down on her knees, when she turned her ankle on a stone, he knew she was real.

For the first time in his life, Spence knew panic. He wondered why she had come, if disaster triggered her search for him. From the shaded interior of the *pili* grass shack, he watched her struggle to her feet, test her ankle, and come limping on, while he hid like a woman, frightened of himself, very aware of the blood throbbing like a drumbeat through his veins.

He closed his eyes, forced himself to think of something else, anything else.

"Spence?" She shouted his name. It echoed off the stone wall of falling water, across the ledges, carried to the birds in the trees.

There was a quiet, sure determination in her eyes, and he knew that if he did not show himself she was prepared to wait him out.

When she reached the clearing, she stopped, bewitched by the foaming cascade of water, drawn to the edge of the pond, where she stared down into green water with rainbows sparkling in the mist. Her back was to him now, and when he stepped out of the *hale* and walked toward her, she did not see him, the rushing water masking his footsteps until he was almost directly behind her.

She turned around slowly, a smile on her lips, her blue eyes bright and clear, shining with a peace and inner joy he had never seen there before. His breath caught.

She held out both hands to him, like an old friend offering a welcome. The pain and anger that her distrust had once fueled in him fell away. He stepped up to her, took her hands, looked down into her upturned face. Before he could think, before he could choose any single word out of the infinite galaxies of words, she stepped closer.

There was nothing he could do, nothing else he wanted to do, but enfold her in his embrace. She came into his arms, sunshine and rainbows, gold and ivory, smelling of lavender water and soap and wilted starch.

They stood there in each other's arms, not moving, not speaking, simply rocking slowly back and forth, holding one another close. He would have stood there until the sun fell from the sky, but when he felt her arms slip from around his waist, he let her go.

ELIZABETH HAD EXPECTED TO be terrified, suddenly face-to-face with him after all these many months, knowing her future and Hadley's depended on his acceptance of what she had to say, but she had envisioned this meeting for so long now that the heart-stopping fear failed to materialize.

He looked magnificent, larger than life, a creature of the island. His hair was unbound, so long now that it fell far below his shoulder blades, rippling thick and jet-black. The muscles of his arms and legs were well defined, as were his bronze chest and shoulders. The primitive tribal markings so masterfully imprinted on his skin begged to be touched. She felt dwarfed not only by his size but by the overwhelming animal magnetism he radiated.

"You have created a wonderful place here," she said in all honesty. The gentle slope provided the perfect setting for his terraced *kalo* patches. Water diverted from the stream ran beneath the unruffled surface of the square ponds, preventing them from becoming stagnant. His native-style home was small, but it looked as if it protected him from the elements.

"How did you find me?" He had to turn away, pretend to stare down into the pool beneath the falls so she would not see how she excited him, the power she could wield over him. The *malo* wrapped around his loins left little to the imagination.

"Duke told me where you would be." She did not tell him she had to beg Duke, to threaten to go off alone and not return until she either found Spence or became so hopelessly lost herself that she would surely perish.

"I always met him down the mountain, never told him where this place was," Spence said.

"He confessed that he came upon it one day by accident while chasing down a steer but never told you."

"Humoring me, I guess."

"Duke looks up to you, Spence. He values your advice. Think what you two could accomplish if you worked together full-time."

He turned around then, his face unreadable. "Is that why you came here, Elizabeth? Because you need another hand?"

She had vowed on her way up the hill that she was not going to let him shake her from her purpose.

"I deserve that. I have mistrusted you, continually questioned your honor, your word. You have every right to hate me for what I have said and done to you in the past, Spence. I don't blame you for leaving. But I want you to come home. I want you to come back and live with Hadley and me."

His shock was apparent. He looked as if he had expected that to be the last thing she came to say. As she watched his face, she saw the surprise slide into suspicion.

"Because you feel you owe me?"

She shook her head, again refused to be intimidated.

"No. I'm asking you to forgive me one more time . . . because I love you."

The words echoed loud and clear against the rock wall of the small canyon, sounded over the rush of water. Wrapped themselves around the two figures standing there in a shaft of sunlight.

"Tell me you don't love me," she said.

"I love you too much, Elizabeth, and because I do love you, I can't live with you or anywhere near you. So we are back to the same old argument, the reason I left for Honolulu."

"You *are* ruining my life, don't you see that, Spence? I need you. I want to share my life with you. No argument you can make will ever convince me that it is better for us to be apart. Nothing anyone can say about us, or try to do to us, is as bad as trying to exist without you."

She reached for him again, touched his forearm. "Spence, I'm tired of believing I have to give up someone I love just to save someone else. I have been afraid God would take Hadley from me because I wasn't vigilant and I lost my first baby. I gave up my freedom and stayed with Franklin so that Hadley would have Mauna Noe.

"When you went down right before my eyes during the hurricane, I thought I was going to have to give you up, to trade your life for Hadley's, but that night I refused to bargain with God anymore. I dared Him to take you. I wanted you and Hadley both, and I knew I had every right to happiness. So be warned, Spence Laamea. I did not bargain with God, and I do not intend to stand here and plead with you."

He could not turn away from the weight of the challenge in her eyes, so he shifted the direction of the argument. "What of Hadley? You can't keep her in a cocoon forever. She is going to hear her mother's name slandered. She will be teased and tormented by other *haole* when she goes to school. They will say that her mother lives with a *hapa haole*. She will find out the Hawaiians stand on the lowest rung on the social ladder that the *haole* brought with them to the islands. If we have children, they will be——''

''Mixed blood?'' Her hand tightened on his arm, forced him to turn and look at her. ''Spence, Hadley is such a loving child. She needs brothers and sisters. She will love them because they are ours. If you came back to us, she would finally have a father in her life——''

''I'm her *half brother*, Elizabeth. Have you forgotten that?''

''Of course not. And you could also become the father she has always wanted.''

He looked so stern, so foreboding. A soul that had been through much heartache looked back at her from inside his dark eyes. Her heart dropped to her toes when she realized there was a very real chance he was going to refuse.

''Does your love for me come with qualifications, Spence? If you don't want to be a father to Hadley, say so and I'll stop making a fool of myself.''

''I love Hadley, too.''

She closed her eyes against tears of joy. *''I love Hadley, too.''* He had so very, very easily said the words that Franklin never once uttered.

She was holding tight to emotion with both hands now, desperate to plead her case, hoping that her love would prevail over every argument he could put forth.

''We could be a real family. The family she has never had—that *you* have never had. You can teach her all the things I cannot about this land, this *'āina* that will be hers someday—because of you. You can teach her Hawaiian traditions, how to love the land, to cherish it for her children and their children and any children that we might have together.''

''Why are you so willing to throw common sense to the wind and go against the dictates of your society?''

''Because I love you, Spence. I would put that love above the dictates of any society. Isn't that more important? Love? *Aloha?* Didn't you tell Hadley to always reach down into her heart to find it, that one never runs out of *aloha*?''

"She told you that?"

"She talks about you all the time." She reached up, wound her arms around his neck. "Spence," she whispered, "let me love you. Let me live my life loving you. Give Hadley the father's love she craves. Pass on your knowledge through her. Don't turn us away because we are *haole*. Don't force this terrible loneliness on us because you think you are doing the *honorable* thing. Don't you see that you are letting *them* win if you do?'' She took a deep breath. "I know the road might be a little rocky, but—''

"The road, Elizabeth, will be covered with hot lava."

Although it had not reached his lips, there was a smile in his words and she knew she was winning. His resolve was wavering.

"I don't care. I love you. I would gladly walk through lava to have you with us."

"Will it be enough for you, if our world dwindles to the borders of Mauna Noe?"

"My world once consisted of my garden and the rooms upstairs. Marion Reynolds will accept us. Uilani and others wished me luck when I left to bring you home. Even if we never marry, Spence, it will be enough just to have you home, night and day, for the rest of our lives together.''

She leaned back, looked up into his eyes, waiting for an answer. Her future happiness and Hadley's hung in the balance. He cupped her chin in his hand, traced her lower lip with his thumb.

"Will you please come back, Spence?" She had laid her heart and soul bare. There was nothing more she could say.

"You drive a hard bargain, Elizabeth. I should have taken you to Honolulu with me to talk to Kalakaua."

"We need you. I need you. Say you will forgive me and come home.''

"I have a feeling you are never going to take no for an answer." Spence wrapped both arms around her, held her close.

"I can be very persuasive," she whispered with a smile.

Beside her, the waterfall sang its eternal song. A laugh escaped Elizabeth, a sound of joy bubbling up from inside. She thought of the spoiled, sheltered, naive girl she had been in Maryland, of the woman that time and trials had made of her since then.

She loved this man as she had loved no other, and she intended to demonstrate that love to him, to pleasure him and be pleasured by him. She reached up and pulled out the few pins that remained in her hair after her hike down the trail. She shook out her hair. He ran his fingers through it.

His hands shook when he drew her close, pressed her against his erection. He touched his forehead to hers, closed his eyes and sighed.

"I have wanted you so much," he confessed, now that she had given him permission to say the words, to speak of his love. "You are all I have thought of, dreamt of, for weeks."

She pulled his head down, found his mouth and covered it with hers. She teased him with her tongue until he returned the kiss full measure, exploring her, tasting her.

She braced her hands on his shoulders and looked full into his eyes, let her hands wander to the *malo* tied around his waist.

They were alone, surrounded by the protective forest, by the tall *koa*, pandanus, *wauke*, the paper mulberry, *kukui, hau*, countless other trees she could not name. Nimble and unerring, her fingers loosened his *malo*, and the bark fabric dropped to the ground. He stood naked within the circle of her arms. Propriety and modesty be damned. She wanted to bury them together there in the soft, moist earth of the forest floor.

Elizabeth stepped back, unfastened the buttons that ran down the front of her white blouse, stripped it off, cast it aside. Then she took off her skirt, her petticoat and chemise while, with her eyes on his, she dared Spence to look away.

She drew close to him again, reached between his hard length and her own craving flesh and cupped him, caressed him, massaged him until he moaned and his fingers bit into her shoulders and his eyes filled with lust and desire.

"Taste me, Spence."

She threw her head back, trusted him to support her while he suckled her breasts. She felt wild and free for the first time in her life, like a healthy young animal who had found her mate and he in turn had claimed before the world.

Spence felt her warm, flushed skin, cupped her buttocks and pulled her up to him, drove his shaft against the tight golden curls that covered her inviting womanhood. She cried out, dug her nails into his upper arms. He held her, moved against her until his need was so great he was afraid he would not be able to hold back.

Her tongue flicked out, moistened lips as petal soft and pink as plumeria blossoms. She sighed when he kissed her again, gasped when his fingers found her, gently stretched her, opened her and teased her throbbing flesh until she was crying for release.

"Not yet, *Malamalama o ka mahina*, not yet, moonlight." He whispered love words against her temple, kissed her swollen breasts, tucked her into his arms as he lifted her and carried her across the glen to his grass *hale*. With her sparkling hair and her ivory skin, she would always be as precious to him, as vibrant, as moonlight shining on the Pacific.

He had to bend to accommodate the low door as he stepped into the cool, shaded interior. As he lay her on the mat in the middle of the single room and fanned her hair out, as she lay there staring up at the grass bundles that formed the roof, Elizabeth pressed her palms against the pandanus leaves woven together to become the mat beneath her.

He leaned over her, ran his hand through her hair, over her body lovingly, lingering in all the secret places that made her moan when he touched her, massaging her until she drifted on a sensual sea.

She looked at him through a haze of pleasure, saw him highlighted by the shaft of autumn light that poured through the open door. His hair was long, wild, rippling over his arms and shoulders. His generous mouth and the slight tilt of his rich dark eyes bespoke the heritage from his mother's blood.

Here alone with him in the world he had created, Elizabeth felt transported to a time when the island was raw and new, inhabited by people who had survived long sea voyages from Polynesia in open canoes, who had endured the elements and faced the unknown.

Elizabeth realized that she and Spence were not all that different from those early Hawaiians who had left their world behind, turned their backs on all they knew and loved, committed themselves to each other, to 'ohana, to family, and to the 'āina of this island paradise.

Spence stretched out beside her, pulled her against him. His hands never stilled. She reached for him, needing to touch him too. She longed to move him as he moved her, was eager to feel him inside her again, to enjoy the pleasure without the guilt. Minutes, days, hours could have passed as she lay there beside him in the grass hut. Time stood still.

When she could stand it no longer, when she was weeping with need, dripping for him, crying his name, he took back his hands and lips, rose above her. He chanted her name over and over and then, with a triumphant cry, drove into her.

Sheathed within her, he began to move, to rock with the rhythm of the sea, thrusting until the tension became as strong as the force coiled in the heart of Pele's volcano.

She wrapped her legs around his waist, urged him on. Finally, sweat-sheened, their bodies slapped together hot and frenzied until Elizabeth cried out and Spence came inside her.

THEY STAYED *MAUKA* UNTIL daybreak the next morning. Walking out, they found Elizabeth's horse near Kāhili, both animals grazing in the pasture where the mountain knelt behind the rolling hills. The ride back was slow and leisurely, as if neither of them wanted to end the idyllic time together in the world of touch and taste and gossamer sunlight sifting through trees. He spoke of Kaala, told Elizabeth the story of his first wife, and of her death.

Spence was dressed as a *paniolo* again, the white trousers, gaiters laced to his knees, well-heeled shoes beneath them. On the way back he taught her to fashion a *haku* lei out of fern, young *lehua* leaves with their bright red tips, and *mokihana* berries, found only on Kaua'i. He wore his lei around his hat, she wore hers around her head.

When they reached the ranch proper, Duke saw them first and whistled. Melvin turned to watch in the middle of breaking a horse and hit the ground. Toshi came running around the side of the house on his bowed, bandy legs, with rake in hand. When he saw them, he waved it over his head in salute. Uilani stood on the porch, swinging a huge ladle and flapping a dish towel.

Spence looked over at Elizabeth riding proudly beside him.

Maile and Hadley spilled out of the kitchen door. The older girl waited beside her mother while Hadley kept running, down the steps, across the stable yard. She waited in the middle of the lane until Spence and Elizabeth reined in and dismounted, then she ran to them with arms spread wide.

"You came back, Spence!" Hadley danced an impromptu hula. When Elizabeth leaned down for a hug, Hadley reached up and clamped her arms around her mother's neck and squeezed. Then she let go and stood in front of

Spence, staring up at him with a wide smile. There was a new hole in her bottom row of teeth.

"I missed you, Spence. Did you miss me?" Before he could answer, she went right on talking. "Maile said she bet you were not coming back and that I was *pupule* for thinking that you would. But I told her that you would and you will be so proud of me because I started to punch her in the nose when she said it, but I 'membered what you said and stopped myself and squeezed my eyes shut tight and found some extra a-hola and know what?"

"What?"

"I didn't want to hit her anymore."

"Good for you. But it's *aloha*, Hadley. Not a-hola."

She planted her fists on her hips and rolled her eyes. "I know that, silly. I can say a lot of things in Hawaiian now."

"*Pehea 'oe?*" He tested her with a simple "How are you?"

"*Maika'i no.* I am fine, Spencer. Don't I look fine?"

He still heard the slightest wheeze, but she appeared to be healthier than ever.

"Indeed you do. But you lost something here." He pointed to the space where her tooth used to be.

She shook her head adamantly. "Oh, I just lost it the other day. I hardly ever cough and I still drink my special tea every night." Suddenly her smile dimmed. "Spence, how long are you going to stay this time?"

Elizabeth held her breath and watched Spence go down on one knee on the rich red-brown earth of Kaua'i in front of her little girl. He shoved his hat back to the crown of his head. Then he put his face so close to Hadley's that their noses almost touched.

"How long you want me to stay?"

"How do the Hawaiians say *forever*?" she whispered.

"*Mau loa. I ka wa pau 'ole.*"

"Do you think you can stay that long?" Hadley pressed her nose so close to his that her eyes crossed.

Spence could feel Elizabeth standing at his shoulder. He reached out and her fingers slipped into his hand. He rubbed noses with Hadley, then looked up at Elizabeth and said to them both, ''I'll be here as long as you need me.''

Epilogue

**Mauna Noe Ranch
Kaua'i, Hawai'i, 1902**

A WOMAN STOOD AT the edge of the cliff, staring down at the cove, watching sun-bronzed children digging in the sand, swimming, scrambling across the reef at low tide. The corners of her blue eyes were creased with lines as fine as silk, barely visible—trophies of too many years spent in the sunshine working in acres of extensive gardens.

Behind her, fat cattle grazed on open pastureland that lifted to caress the low hills. Silver ribbons of falling water trailed down the mountainsides. The sky was so clear there was not even a hint of a cloud anywhere.

She hoped no one was watching her from the rambling yellow house behind her on the hill, for she needed a moment of peace and solitude—something very, very rare in her life these days.

Elizabeth Bennett sat on the bluff at the edge of the sea and wondered where the years had gone and how it came to be that she and Spence were thirty-nine years old. She had expected to feel older, but then again, she simply did not have time.

She saw a ship on the horizon, a steamer headed toward Hanalei, and she eyed it with a bittersweet ache, knowing that when it left the bay tomorrow morning it would be carrying a part of her heart away.

A scuffle broke out between two of the children down on the cove, tempers flared and quickly subsided, apologies were grudgingly exchanged. Nothing out of the ordinary, considering there were more than twenty-five children living on the ranch.

Duke and Ana Makakani could account for six of them, three boys and three girls who took after both of their parents, their oldest two boys already accomplished riders. Unlike the other *paniolo* who lived along the lane in the row of camp houses, Duke, as manager, lived on a portion of land close to the cove where he had built his wife a house of fieldstone because—as he explained to Spence years ago when he asked to lease the land—he had promised Ana that he would.

"Mama?"

Elizabeth closed her eyes and sighed. She had dreaded this moment for weeks now, years really, but she forced a bright smile, turned around and watched Hadley come walking up the beach path.

"I didn't see you leave the beach," her daughter said. "Spence is looking for you."

Statuesque, dramatic, with the figure of a woman and the disposition of an angel—most of the time—Hadley was eighteen, and, with her life packed into two steamer trunks, ready to leave for the mainland tomorrow, where she would finish her education.

Elizabeth swallowed the lump in her throat and hoped that she would not embarrass herself by crying, at least not until the ship had left the bay.

"What does he want?"

"The usual. He wants you. Madeline and Eleanor are

fighting over who gets to push Boyd's buggy, and Spence is threatening to take them back to the house and lock them all in the pantry and go fishing.''

"You know he would never do that.'' Elizabeth laughed. She could just picture Spence trying to match wits with their eight- and ten-year-old daughters. Both girls were dark-eyed, dark-haired versions of their father. Boyd, a little over a year old, was blond and blue-eyed with deep honey-colored skin, the male image of Hadley at the same age.

"How did you know where to find me?" Elizabeth asked.

"Mama, I know this is your special place. It always has been. Remember when I had asthma and all those times you brought me out here when I was a little girl?''

Elizabeth remembered all too well. She began to blink furiously, fighting back tears. So that Hadley would not see, she looked out across the blue Pacific waters, watched the white caps play tag and wondered again where the years had gone.

"There is something I've always wanted to ask you about.'' Hadley sat down beside her mother and tucked her skirt under her knees.

Elizabeth never knew where her daughter's conversations were going. She only hoped she could answer the question honestly.

"What is it?"

Hadley reached into the pocket of her skirt and pulled out two very small, very smooth-edged pieces of blue-and-white pottery. They both fit into the palm of her hand. Elizabeth recognized them immediately. Her daughter reached into her pocket again and this time pulled out a curved piece of the same ceramic.

"I know these triangular pieces are from dishes of some sort, but what do you think this one is?" Hadley held up the curved piece.

Elizabeth smiled, looked closely without touching it.

"I'd say offhand that it might be a teacup handle."

"I've been finding these things for years and so has everyone else. I've always wondered where they came from. Do you think they might have washed up after a shipwreck off the coast? Maybe pirate smugglers?"

"This is not the Caribbean, Hadley."

"All right, then, maybe they were in a crate in an outrigger canoe, a present from some Hawaiian *ali'i* to his mistress here on Kaua'i who had to run away from—"

"What will your school friends on the mainland think if they hear you talking about mistresses and Hawaiian kings and runaways?"

"They will think that I am a very interesting person, Mama."

"To say the very least, darling." Elizabeth brushed Hadley's long blond hair back off her face.

"So how do you think all those pieces of dishes came to be on Glass Beach?"

Elizabeth turned and looked at the oblong stone grave marker situated on a spot that overlooked both the gardens and the sea. Toshi had named the cove Glass Beach years before, and more than just the folks living on Mauna Noe called it by that name.

"Maybe," Elizabeth said, leaning close to Hadley as if she were going to share a fabulous secret, "one day, in a fit of temper, a woman who shall remain nameless tossed them over the cliff . . . one by one."

Hadley's eyes widened. She stared at Elizabeth for a few moments as realization dawned, and then she smiled. "Did she feel better after that?"

"She certainly did. She never, ever regretted it."

Hadley put the smooth shards of blue-and-white pottery back into her pocket. "I'm taking them to the mainland with me," she explained. "A little bit of home."

The top of a baby buggy appeared just below the hill on the beach path. It was accompanied by the sound of bickering and a baby's cry. Seconds later the buggy came bouncing across the grassy lawn, the baby crying even louder as two little girls raced along, each trying to shove the other away from the carriage handle.

"Mama! I got here first already."

"Mama! Tell her to get off dis t'ing now!"

Hadley closed her eyes and shook her head. "I'm going to miss them terribly. Maybe not the noise, though."

Madeline and Eleanor argued all the way across the bluff. Finally, exhausted, they parked the howling baby beside Elizabeth and threw themselves down on the grass, where they lay side by side in silence staring up at the sky. The crying stopped as soon as the buggy did and within seconds, Boyd pulled himself up to his knees and peered out with a neglected, bewildered look on his face.

Hadley went to pick him up. Both of her half sisters immediately jumped up and started arguing over which one should hold him.

Elizabeth lay back on the grass, closed her eyes, and basked in the sound of her children's voices.

"Don't tell me you can sleep through this?"

She opened her eyes, shaded them with her hand. Spence stood over her, silhouetted against the sky.

"I'm not sleeping, I'm trying to escape into my own little world."

"Get room for me?"

He sat down heavily beside her, leaned over, put his head in her lap, and closed his eyes. Across the lawn, the two younger girls were walking along, one on each side of Hadley, jumping up and down, trying to persuade her to hand over the toddler.

"I don't know if I can get through this, Spence. I never thought the years would go so fast. I never thought she would be old enough to leave us."

"She's not leaving us, she is going to school. She's coming back, you know."

"What if she finds someone over there? What if she marries and decides she has to live on the mainland?"

"Elizabeth . . ." He could tell she was getting herself worked up over what ifs.

"What if we never see her again? What if—"

Spence rolled over and sat up. "Stop, Elizabeth. Give me your hand."

She did and he held it, tracing her fingers as he spoke. "Hadley will be fine. She is old enough to go to school, and I know she is going to make us proud. Maybe she'll meet someone she wants to marry, and she might even want to live on the mainland."

"But—"

"Elizabeth."

"Oh, all right. I don't have to like any of this, do I?"

"No. Besides, she tries to marry some mainland boy, and I will go over and drag her home myself."

Elizabeth burst out laughing. "You know you are so predictable, Spencer Laamea, for one big, bad *paniolo*."

"Oh, yeah?" He looked up, made certain all the girls were almost to the garden gate and then he pulled his shirt out of his pants, drew it over his head, and tossed it on the ground.

"What are you doing?" Elizabeth sat up. She recognized the gleam in his eye.

Spence started to unlace his gaiters, then stopped and reached for the waistband on his pants instead.

"Spencer Laamea, stop that! What are you *thinking*?" Elizabeth scrambled to her feet and looked over her shoulder toward the house. "Stop doing that. Button up those trousers before one of them comes back or . . . or someone comes up from the beach."

"First, tell me, Elizabeth, you still think I am predictable?"

She tried not to smile. Then she tried not to laugh. Finally she gave up, knelt down beside him and put her arms around his neck.

"I think, Spence Laamea, that I love you too much. What do you think?"

He pretended to be looking at something behind her, then he pointed in that direction. "I think there is a spot over there behind that *hau* bush that might be the only private place on the whole damn ranch. How about we go see?"

Linda Francis Lee

_BLUE WALTZ   0-515-11791-9/$5.99

They say the Widow Braxton wears the gowns of a century past...she
invites servants to parties...they say she is mad. Stephen St. James
has heard rumors about his new neighbor. However, she is no
wizened old woman—but an exquisite young beauty. But before he
can make her his own, he must free the secret that binds her heart...

_EMERALD RAIN   0-515-11979-2/$5.99

"Written with rare power and compassion...a deeply compel-
ling story of love, pain, and forgiveness."—Mary Jo Putney

Ellie and Nicholas were on opposite sides of the battle that threatened
to rob Ellie of her home. However, all that mattered was the powerful
attraction that drew them together. But selling the property would un-
earth a family scandal of twenty years past...and threatens to tear the
young lovers apart.

_CRIMSON LACE   0-515-12187-8/$5.99

High society in New York, 1896—the story of a disgraced woman returning home and discovering a renewed hope for love...